Starhaven

A School of London

CHIP MARTIN was born in Philadelphia, grew up in California and since the early 1970s has lived mainly in London. As Stoddard Martin, he writes and lectures on comparative literature and culture. His previous novellas published by Starhaven include *Proie, South, Liberation in the East* and the sequence *The End of the Road.*

ALYSON SPOONER has provided an image for the cover of this book from her sequence 'Elfin's Room'. Her work is in many distinguished collections; it may be viewed in *Alyson: A Painter's Journey* by Linda Kelly.

A School of London

a trilogy by

Chip Martin

with an afterword by Linda Kelly

STARHAVEN

La Jolla ✶ London

In memory of Alice Thomas Ellis

ISBN 0-936315-32-6

STARHAVEN, 42 Frognal, London NW3 6AG
in U.S., c/o Box 2573, La Jolla, CA 92038, USA
books@starhaven.org.uk
www.starhaven.org

Typeset in Monotype Bembo by John Mallinson

Contents

I

A Journeyman in Bohemia

It was during a Christmas I spent near Munich that I got to know Oliver Murrie. I'd met him five years before, in London. He had been an impecunious artist at the time, living not in a garret but the 1970s equivalent of it, a bed-sit in Hammersmith. The Murries were an old literary clan, Anglo-Irish. Oliver's mother, however, was Cornish, and he had grown up near St Ives where her family had owned an 18th century house. Having gone to Bedales and later Trinity College, Cambridge, he didn't exactly arrive in London with a garret artist's remit. But maybe because of the Celtic strain in his blood, he was taciturn, especially as a young man; this made him unclubbable; he was a loner and, like many loners, an unconscious seer. So he had become an artist.

The journey down was not traumatic. Unlike most of us then, he had little political passion; but he wasn't cut out for the stockbroking classes either, like some conventional public school philistine. On finishing Cambridge, he took a job at a forerunner of English Heritage looking for buildings of architectural merit to put preservation orders on. This at first suited him: he had a native architectural sense: one of his ancestors Murrie had been the designer of some prominent buildings in the West Country, not all of which have been torn down. But Oliver was too creative to be satisfied for ever, or even for long, with a version of civil service. Building reports came to include architectural drawings; drawings came to dominate the reports, and soon he discovered that drawing was all he had time for. Thus his days at his 'proper' job were numbered.

He drew row-houses in Highgate, Islington and Highbury. Arched Georgian doorways particularly appealed to him. Arches led to domes, which he drew as well, first from the outside, then from the in-, working up from the odd Regency turret to interiors of the British Museum, Westminster Cathedral and Chiswick House. An instinctive sensuality appeared in these pictures, many of which his patronesses would later frame. Interiors of domes led to further interests, such as in interior light; and since drawing can only convey light sketchily, Oliver was soon painting in water-colour, which in turn led to gouache and oils – true painting. But this was to come.

I met him through my literary agent of that time, the now-celebrated Margot Wingfield. In those days, Margot lived in an Edwardian row-house 'near Holland Park' – that is, Shepherd's Bush – and was just starting to throw her lunch parties. Not yet quite forty, she had married and begun to produce babies long before she'd come into full bloom. This is possibly why, in that era, she liked to grace her table with promising young men.

'There are two interesting types of people,' she would quote freely from Wilde; 'a woman with a past and a man with a future.'

Margot herself was a negation of this. She had no past anyone spoke of: if she had, she might not have dressed in the present as if in search of a glamorous future. She had emerged into her butterfly state of *grande dame* out of a standard cocoon of fluty-voiced, English public-schoolgirlness. The flute sound had descended to become clarinet-like; the bust had risen by some miracle of nature, despite having supplied nurture to four male offspring in less than a dozen years. The dress had transformed from Laura Ashley to Joan Collins; the heels had become higher, and seams of genuine nylon ran up the back of her legs, bottle-tanned.

It was a remarkable performance, Margot's persona, especially in those militant feminist days. With each cinching in of the waist or patting on of more powder, she seemed to succeed in selling more books. In fact, within a year of quitting her first job as P.A. to the managing director of a now-moribund art publisher, she had a reputation as the most adept packager of new talent around.

Oliver Murrie Margot knew for two reasons. First, she had set up a deal for a biography of his grandfather, the historical novelist Ralph Williams Murrie. Second, she loved painting, particularly water-colours and – as with fiction, which she was just starting to push – particularly work by unknowns.

'I believe in taste,' she announced over the Sunday lunch where I first met him. 'And taste is only memorable when it's new. You learn this by throwing lunch parties. People remark on the food in two ways: behind your back when it's boring, meaning they've had it a thousand times; or to your face when it's intriguing, meaning they're a little surprised, even perhaps alarmed by it and want to find out what the hidden ingredient is. When you tell them it's as simple as coriander sautéed in lemon, dried and ground, they marvel and go home and try it themselves. Of course they don't succeed in creating the same taste, because you haven't told them the truth: it's not coriander at all. So they go around saying nice things about this new dish you've produced that they can't, and people get the idea that you're on to something.'

'Marvellous, Margot,' murmured Simon Lewes, the one guest other than Oliver and me.

Lewes was slim, bespectacled and fastidious. He had been invited, Margot would confide, not for his looks or his wit, which was more in the vein of Quentin Crisp than of Wilde, but for his potential usefulness – he had just opened a gallery in Westbourne Grove.

'Marvellous, darling!' he repeated, as florid with social patter as Margot's husband, Godfrey, was with claret and roast beef.

'Have you beasts left any Yorkshire pud?' Godfrey asked of his eldest, who had excused himself to go skateboarding.

Godfrey Wingfield had a square jaw and two clown-like clumps of red hair above the temples. He wore a buff waistcoat and puce braces and in those days worked for the Hong Kong and Macao Bank.

'Don't overdo it, Simon,' Margot admonished Lewes, perfectly aware that her dandiacal little essay had not quite hit the mark – she was not yet the wordsmith she would be acclaimed as years later, once she had begun writing plays.

Oliver watched. Though twenty-five or six then, he was still shy enough to hide his round features behind a solemn, moon-like expression. Neither callow nor compelled to sallies of wit like the rest of us, he scored no conversational points; but this social tic, so typical of aspirant writers, may be death to fine artists, Margot would contend – they trade in more sensual things. And though Ollie did not rate as a 'fine artist' yet, his way was being staked out.

'But you deserve to be encouraged!' Lewes flattered on.

'Simon! Are you patronizing me?'

'The last thing Margot needs is to be encouraged,' brayed Godfrey, who liked to play put-upon husband. 'Women get too much encouragement these days as it is!'

'But she does!' went on Lewes, who had no experience of marriage, let alone kids, yet was closer to Godfrey's age than Oliver's or mine.

'Why is that, Simon?' – Margot glanced at her protégé, chewing his meat as if a vegetarian: her heart was not completely into chatting up her 'useful' guest.

'The difference between you and other women who ought to be hostesses in London is that you *try*!' the gallery-owner effused. 'They simply wear long dresses and talk like Germaine Greer.'

This was 1976 or '7.

Margot appeared to ignore him. 'What was I on about?' she demanded. 'Taste, wasn't it?'

Lewes nodded. Precious he may have been, inattentive not.

'Take Oliver, for instance' – she got down to the point. 'He has taste. That is to say, he draws things no other artist would but everyone who isn't an artist admires without knowing quite why.'

Oliver dished up the potatoes Godfrey had failed to ingorge and kept his eye on his plate. He knew what she was up to and wanted to keep out of it. And Lewes was right about one thing: she did try. And without trying, as she might have remarked, one hardly deserved to succeed. – It was the dawn of the Thatcher Era.

'I saw Oliver's water-colours first a year ago and bought three on the spot. He wanted nothing for them – peanuts. But as I told him, we in the arts have to support our kind. So I've been tithing one-fifth of my cut of every book I sell. Rather good, don't you think? I've bought thirteen more since the first three, and expect to sell two more new books next week.'

Lewes cocked a brow. For some reason, he declined to look at the object of his hostess's praise. Concentrating on her instead, he repeated 'Marvellous!' as if she had just recited the Bastard's speech on Commodity from *King John*.

Lunch carried on. Tucking into a spoonful of trifle, Godfrey weighed in. Mathematical calculations had been the cue. A man without an apparent artistic bone in his body, Godfrey deployed the ingratiating manner of someone who had done business with numerous Arab or Nigerian men-of-means. Taking off from his wife's figures, he questioned me about exchange rates, which he pretended I should know about, being foreign. Warming to his subject, he refilled our glasses and cut off his wife when she attempted to cut in, suggesting that her talents were only for the frivolous. Scattering allusions to old boys in the City and teasings about 'colonials' and Jews, he pretended his prejudices were too comic to harm.

Oliver watched this performance. Was the artist interested in rates of exchange? I tried to draw him in.

'Don't bore Ollie about money,' Margot snapped. 'Just buy one of his drawings. Better still – you're a lad of experience in these things: help him find some sweet, docile, untiresome heiress so he can quit consulting for the bloody heritage mafia and get on with it!'

Lewes's eyes widened. I did as polite and chuckled at her caricature of me as if I really were some kind of house-broken pimp. Godfrey guffawed; Margot lifted her glass; Oliver alone did not seem to get the joke. He seemed to take her at the exact level of seriousness at which she took herself, which in this case turned out to be quite high; and I went away wondering if I'd been asked to lunch with as much ulterior motive as Lewes – only my job wasn't to get her boy into a gallery so much as to advance the arts by helping him find this mythological creature: a selfless, exploitable heiress to ponce off of.

It was summer in London; I had a revision of my first Rough Guide to finish; my lady-friend of the moment had gone off to France with her children; so I needed companions.

London in summer, a good summer, as this was, is one of the marvels of the civilized world. The wind sighs in the leaves, killing off sounds of traffic. Dappled light wanders across gardens, while the gardens themselves are painted blinding greens mottled with purples, yellows and reds. Evenings extend beyond even Londoners' expectations; children play in the streets; if clouds come, they're gilded coral and pink, not dull and dun-coloured as in winter.

'Gone to France, has she?' Margot said to my sole lament. 'But surely your address-book brings to mind others. I should've thought this was the chance you'd been waiting for.'

One of Margot's tactics, ego-boosting for the shy, was to pretend that all of her young men were Don Juans.

I had dropped by on some pretext, knowing how generous she was with wine and cheese or cups of coffee depending on time of day. We sat in her conservatory, which doubled as office. The doors were open onto a small courtyard. From the bottom of it, a naked torso of Juno or some vestal nymph gazed at us out of a lush fall of clematis.

'That's not my thing, Margot.'

'Love this time, is it?' – She recrossed her legs. 'Don't fall in love, please; it'll ruin your career. You may've published a travel piece or two, but you're not nearly successful enough. I was only warning Oliver about this the other day.'

As she mentioned his name, she looked to the wall behind me where four of his drawings hung: charming if somewhat innocuous studies of the inner space and light of Brompton Oratory.

'What do you think of them?' she added with a keenness which increased my hunch that her interest was not strictly artistic.

'Margot!' I exclaimed.

I don't know why I pretended to be surprised. She was in a marriage identical to my own lady's, so why shouldn't she have been having – or toying with the idea of having – an affair too? Adultery was the done thing among women of the type at that stage, and Oliver was an ideal candidate: young, eccentric yet of 'proper' background; taciturn, so discreet. Maybe I've always had trouble imagining sex with someone I'd never thought of in that way.

'Don't go jumping to conclusions,' she blushed. 'I'm devoted to Godfrey, even though it's in bad taste – being devoted to your husband. But of course I'm devoted to Oliver too, as to you – I simply hate seeing talent threatened with starvation. That's why I'm buying every piece of his I can.'

'You are sweet. But I'm hardly in danger of starving, and I'd be surprised if he was either.'

Having drawn blood, I hesitated. Meanwhile, she uncrossed and recrossed those legs, without obvious purpose this time.

'I'm not trying to make myself out a saint.' she defended. 'I pay him less for them than they're worth, even new; and one day they'll be worth lots. But he asks nothing for them. It's quite unnerving really, these public schoolboys. No sense of money, like you Yanks.'

'Most public schoolboys have money behind them.'

'Not all. His grandfather, being a novelist, made no more than what he spent. The father was a stockbroker; but he and the mother split up when Ollie was two, so there wasn't much in that. They apparently had something, the mother's family – the house in Cornwall. But that got sold in the '60s when the mother moved to Penzance. She died a few years ago in a semi-detached.'

How odd, I reflected. The British gentry, even upper classes, seemed so careless about money from one generation to the next. Children were educated, then expected to make it on their own. This was in stark contrast to what I was used to in New England, where children were not educated, by and large, but were bailed out by Daddy's cash. Maybe it had to do with the bullying in English public schools vs overmothering in American ones. Maybe on the other hand it was simply that America had grown rich since the War, whereas England had become seedily ragged – Mrs Thatcher's despised socialism and all that. Maybe, finally, it was just a matter of bloody-minded pride. At any rate, a more piratical, live-by-your-wits attitude seemed characteristic of the old country. It was one of the reasons that, at that age, I liked London in summer – or any time of year really – better than Boston or New York.

'So that's why you want me to set him up with an heiress?'

'If any such appropriate creature were to be found. But this presents a problem. Artists are no better at relationships than writers, and you know about that. And marriage, especially with children, can be disastrous for them – all that business with nappies, so uninspiring. Besides, men, I've discovered, need a fine balance between expenditure and depletion in order to create.'

I chuckled. Where she had come up with this lore? Godfrey seemed the half-inert, half-slam-bang type of husband and Oliver too young to be worn out by any fugitive snatch of love-in-the-afternoon. Had she had other affairs, or was it just that – given her profession – she'd read all the books?

'That rules out women of his class,' she essayed. 'The English rose can fester her man in a season. Sex is an absolute necessity for her – the climate, I think: wet and fertile, yet so unclarifying otherwise. And then there must be children, the more the better. Unlike your manly American girls, Englishwomen still believe that power and status comes from producing a brood; which means that hubby must become a money-machine. He needs to work at a bank or brokerage in the day, making ruthless, cunning deals, yet come home at night ready to be a serviceable *paterfamilias*. If the régime gets to him, he must tacitly agree to become a cuckold. He mustn't complain and, if it starts causing him difficulties, he should service his secretary or, better still, the wife of another man in the same boat.'

'How cynical you sound!'

'Described your current situation, have I?'

'Or yours?'

My situation of that time has little to do with this story; and since the lady is still married and with her children, it would be wrong to say more than this: one has to wake up from illusions at some stage; nor is it fair to conclude that a woman's a high-class guttersnipe just because you began by idealizing her. Anyhow, guttersnipes can be charming and have their place in the mix too, though the reverse metamorphosis is the more appealing.

'I've hardly been playing the husband,' I said.

'Quite. You're on the other side. You get the woman for lunch, hear her problems, dry her tears, roger her silly and send her to pick up the children from school looking suspiciously radiant in comparison to the rest of us frustrated matrons.'

This was uncomfortably close to the bone. 'That's not quite how it happens,' I lied.

'The problem with adultery,' Margot continued, 'is the same as the advantage – it ends where it began, in sex.'

Did she intend to make me feel as if I were twisting slowly, slowly in the wind? 'There must be better ways to live,' I concluded, to change the subject.

'Exactly my point. Getting back to Ollie, which is where this began: a normal wife's no good for the reason stated: too exhausting. A married mistress on the other hand: too precarious – one's always waiting for some drama to explode. It's a hand-to-mouth existence emotionally; and if things start to go really badly, a promising young man could be tied to an ageing divorcee with five children before he knew what had happened.'

She was determined on warnings. So what was the bottom line?

'Introduce him to somebody else!' she declared with such absoluteness now that it left no room for ambiguity. 'I know I can rely on you not to breathe a word,' she went on, fighting back the only hint of a tear that anyone other than a lover would be likely to see in those elaborately-mascaraed eyes; 'but I'm determined not to destroy three lives, or perhaps seven – though children, I suspect, are more resilient than we so-called adults give them credit for.'

'You mean –'

'I mean that, if you're my friend, you must help me find him somebody else!'

I looked out the doors at the ochres and greens of her plants, fastidious with tending and lush with summer rain. Margot Wingfield was more considerate than her brash exterior let on, I imagined. In fact, she had the same characteristic that had hooked me onto my own lady: a vulnerability – touch of humanity even – under the stucco veneer.

'Give me his number,' I said. 'He must play tennis or chess or something to give me an excuse.'

'I'll owe you.' – She blew her nose.

'You'll owe me nothing. I was only thinking this morning how much I needed a companion or project of some kind to see me through the rest of August. As usual, it's me who'll owe you.'

Naturally, Margot's passion for Ollie made the competitive male curious; but now I realized that, apart from the moony expression when embarrassed, I could hardly remember what he looked like. A relative non-entity at that first meeting, he stood out in mind as little more than an object for her flattery. Godfrey's exchange rate gossip had interested me more, especially now that I'd learned I was about to get a free trip to the Far East.

Oliver had worn a suit, I recalled. Unpressed, tan in colour, evidently old, it had hung oddly around his big-boned shape, a fact which I took to denote authenticity rather than penury. His shoes had been Church boots, old too, but polished over the creases and cracks. About them, there didn't need be much reflection: they were hand-me-downs or a holdover from a time when his family had been footing the bills.

But clothes don't make the man, despite what they say; the body is the truth – at least so my West Coast friends tell me. Is it healthy? Is it fit? Is it well-muscled and durable? Is it beautiful, finally? These are the questions. Men aren't supposed to ask them, at least not in England – at least not the last. Still, we all note more than we let on; and on playing tennis with him, I discovered he scored high in all departments. As a matter of fact, his serve was so strong that he beat the pants off me; and I was cross when he told me over a beer afterwards that he had been a blue at Cambridge for rackets.

Why hadn't Margot forewarned me? Was it part of her teasing to think it a good joke that I should be humiliated?

'She likes you too much not to play little tricks,' he confirmed. 'Besides, she thought you'd be impressed by meeting at Hurlingham – that's why she suggested I agree to tennis, not chess.'

I might insert here that snobbery isn't really my thing, though I don't mind it too much in others. In city life, there are so many people ready to take up your time that you have to make distinctions quickly. I didn't care whether I played tennis at the Hurlingham Club or public courts at Barnes Common; what mattered was the quality of the game. But if Margot liked me better for having slept with a baronet's daughter – if she believed it made me more trustworthy to the people who mattered, or showed that my social aspirations were 'sound' – who was I to object?

'You play chess as well, do you?' is what I answered.

'Not as well as I play tennis, no. But I do play. Fancy a game?'

I said I didn't mind, though I felt unwilling to be bested again. But he was good company, and handsome when you got beyond a Neil Kinnock hang of red hair, and with a charmingly wicked laugh when he got the joke. Anyhow I was curious to see how he lived: as Margot remarked, with young artists one always is, or ought to be. So after a curry in the Fulham Palace Road, I drove him up to Hammersmith – Brook Green, in fact – where he rented a studio.

The area was idyllic then: quiet, green, yet with urban excitement pulsing at a distance. The studio itself sat under a lime tree at the back of a garden by a tidy middle-class house. A self-contained outbuilding, it had only recently been plumbed and fitted with a bare excuse of a kitchen. But amenities were not the point. Though soon to be an up-and-coming yuppy district, Brook Green had long been a venue for artists' studios; and Oliver was in his niche.

His one long window was covered by curtains; a skylight was adjusted half-open by strings on pulleys. Against one wall sat a trinity of earthenware bowls on top of a polished oak table: inverted domes waiting to be explored in still-life. Against another wall the set-up was more dramatic. A carefully painted back-drop was hung of a winter landscape by the sea; next to it stood an easel on which leaned a sketch comprising the back-drop with three figures in front of it, two men dressed and a voluptuous woman nude.

Was it my imagination or did these figures resemble Godfrey, Oliver himself and Margot?

'"Déjeuner sur les rochers", I'm going to call it.' – He'd followed my eyes. 'The landscape is Inveraray. I thought it made a nice contrast: the sensuality of Impressionism against a cold, bleak true north.'

On a table by the easel, alongside his paints, lay a book of photographs, *The Massacre of 1745*. Flipping through it, I got a sense of black-watered streams raging down barren, granite gorges. Extravagant, savage, full of *Stürm-und-Drang,* it called to mind a tension that anyone passingly familiar with Britain might recognize: between an English *ancien régime* unreconstructed from the 18th century, and an older, more romantic, Celtic tradition which had never given up its sense of superior status but – since it had lost long ago in material terms – reverted to poetry and dream. In general, I identified the latter with Ollie and former with Godfrey Wingfield.

Meanwhile, my host swept aside sketch-books, rags, mixing-tins and so on and set up a chessboard on the one non-art-functioning piece of furniture in the place, a padded bench. This I assumed also served for a bed, there being no other. Was it here that Margot had consummated her passion? The idea, unexpected, summoned an image of her body nude, slightly plump, overripe, spread across this space where his bishop threatened my knight: an odalisque out of Ingres with Rubensesque deformations against a rock-scape from, say, Snowdonia. So was that the kind of thing he was destined to create? a kind of summation of the mix of civilisation, sensuality and recklessness that made up this island race? an ironic juxtaposition of dome-like breasts and thighs filled with roseate light against the fierce natural architecture of some Celtic fringe?

I began to see what Margot longed to conjure in him as artist, or thought I did. 'She has great expectations for you,' I let drop after resigning the first game.

He poured a tot from the pint of whisky we'd picked up on the way back from prawn vindaloo. Sensing what I was after, he ignored the remark and pondered a new strategy for isolating my queen.

'Has she seen this big work you're starting?' I continued.

'Hasn't been to the studio,' he murmured.

The moony expression was fixed. From its wariness you could see that he was determined to protect her, and I was touched. But stuck in my Quiet American role, I felt more duty to mission than to their privacy: 'I sometimes think married women of her type are the most vulnerable of all,' I expanded. 'Sexually, that is.'

His eyes looked up quick. At that moment they were violet, a fire behind them. Was Margot's influence making me novelize or was exceptional passion there? Some men you can neither know well or understand. English men in particular, British in this case, seem deliberately to evade self-exposure. Why? Is it true that they're taught at an early age that troubled depths are for Irishmen, Americans, Jews

– anybody other than their own 'ruling class' kind?

As I speculated, the eyes faded back to normal blueness and a perfectly genial mask of concern rolled like a shutter down his wide, slightly freckled face: 'Thanks for breaking the ice,' he said. 'I've been worried about her – I know it can't last. What should I do?'

I can hardly recall the advice I gave him. It was late and, besides, like everyone else, I'm a creature of the moment. In one mood, I might've told him to stick with love, if that was what he felt, whatever the cost; in another (more like what I was feeling myself), I might've said that he was young, the world was at his feet, a variety of women was the best education and, anyhow, the first law of life is to have fun.

There was something wild and promising in his studio, something quite different in mood from the housebroken little water-colours in Margot's office. Maybe this alarmed me: it was fascinating but, to my semi-conscious, not exactly *her*. In the end, I think I came down on the side of marriage (the Wingfields) and adventure (his), by which I meant that he should give her up as a lover and keep her as patroness. – This, after all, is what she might've told him if she hadn't been involved. It was more or less what she told me in so many words about my liaison the next time I saw her:

'You can't just sit around waiting while your woman puts hubby and children first. Ultimately, that will only make her disrespect you.'

This was in fact just what my lady was doing. But what she was doing also, which Margot couldn't have known, was encouraging another lover to hedge her bets with against my impatience over her marriage. However prim the English rose, it has thorns: I was being cut up, then patched up and made up to through lust. Meanwhile, in the midst of the odd half-morning here or afternoon there, there was barely a moment for her to draw breath, let alone conjure disrespect.

'That's what tires me about London,' I answered: 'the games.'

'You just told me last week how much you loved living here.'

'That was before it started to rain.'

'Yes – beastly weather, isn't it?'

We looked to the dripping mélange of her garden, two Londoners doing what Londoners do best: being sullen about the weather.

'When are you going to Bali or wherever?' she mused.

'Phuket. Thailand. Two weeks.'

'Not soon enough, eh? Well, we'll miss you here. Oliver said he enjoyed your game, by the way. Shame this monsoon doesn't let up and allow you to get your pride back in a rematch.'

I knew her well enough now not to interpret this as bitchy so much as a sign of discontent. Her eyebrows were pencilled in especially archly this morning, her lipstick as precise as an architect's sketch. Her hair was waved and coloured with such *ancien régime* artifice that I was sure I'd done the right thing to dampen Oliver's ardour. She wasn't his type. His type would have worn a full skirt and amber beads; been proud, dark, wild, of the spirit – like Eustacia Vye on top of some Wessexian moor: solitary, liable to no compromise, uncivilized yet hardly content with obscurity either.

'I still have your mission in mind,' I retorted.

'My mission? Are you going to start that novel at long last?'

'I'll stick to travel books, thanks: I know my limitations. No, I meant Oliver's heiress.'

Margot's eyes reverted to her garden. 'Yes, work on that. Or, better still, forget the whole thing, at least until you get out of town. I know you're discreet, but talk is such a temptation. Godfrey I don't mind about – a bit of scandal might make him more interesting, at least to himself. The children, on the other hand – it'll be years before they're boring enough that gossip improves them.'

'What age do you think we have to reach to before it does?'

But Margot wasn't into the usual kind of chat then. 'Do you think I'm being beastly?' she asked with engaging self-doubt.

'To who?'

'To him.'

'Oliver?'

'Of course. Godfrey's his own look-out.'

'He can take care of himself,' I shrugged. 'He's still in his twenties.'

'Yes,' she nodded. 'He'll find somebody else no problem.'

But what about *her*, was the subtext.

Poor Margot! A married woman of her type *was* vulnerable, I reflected as I prepared to wash my current liaison out of mind by a dirty holiday on the beach.

Endings are brutal. You have to be a sadist or genuine Don Juan to enjoy them. And woe betide the two or three subsequent lovers you use (there is no other word) to get over the hump. To save the sensibilities of Godfrey and children, Margot would not only have to sacrifice herself and Ollie but any others either of them turned to for consolation. And this is the fallacy of taking the 'right' way out. If she had really been able to make her husband and children happy by giving him up, then her resolution might've been as noble as bourgeois morality would have it. But bourgeois morality is quite unpragmatic. Deprived of the reward of lover at lunch, a woman is likely to be short with her children at tea, peremptory with her husband at supper, offish and more than usually unaffectionate in bed. Meanwhile, the jettisoned lover is as likely as not to go out and pick up some innocent virgin, deflower her with a vengeance and not even remember her name the next day while she sits by the phone sniffing back tears. Are there any right decisions in affairs of the heart? Get the head mixed up with the genitals and demoralisation raises its head. Only abstinence or an even more experienced new lover can prevent this – so it seems to me now. At that time, however, breaking up with someone I had cared for too much, I was too numb, too rash and too heartbroken to think it out clearly.

In the sweaty regions of southeast Asia, I went to bars, watched sex acts, puffed Thai sticks and generally lived that amoral other side of life I had once known in the Philippines, Mexico and such places before recivilizing myself into colder European latitudes. What a relief! I behaved like any jaded, life-long Londoner determined to get off to some sun-spot and go wild for a mo'; draw close even to going native, until the demoralisation and envy of native life begins to hit you and make you see what an existentialist non-entity you might become if you don't finally drag yourself back to a solidifying north.

There were Belgians and Aussies and Americans in these regions, all going aqueous on Planter's Punch, smoking reefers and travelling the same mental landscape as I. Some were running from love, others looking for it, a few just on holiday, one or two trying to find an alternative existence by setting up bars or selling 'substances' themselves. It was a nice compost of northern hemisphere youth, wandering, playing, contemplating its own and others' navels in a remote but safe southern place. I did plenty of such contemplation. And among other navels I took a look into, there was Carine Bleistein's.

Unknown to her, Carine would become the answer to Margot's prayer for a sweet, docile, untiresome heiress for Oliver Murrie to live off of. I had no inkling of this during the week I lost with her. With hindsight she would seem a most improbable candidate to satisfy his needs, with her scatty humour, boyish breasts and loudish rock-and-roll interests. Carine was a 'party animal' in the phrase of the day in Phuket: drink, coke, late night swims, water-skiing, wind-surfing and penis jokes were her stock-and-trade. A Londoner 'as far away from Blighty as poss', she was on holiday because she too had just ended an affair. We exorcised respective beasts with some memorable 'sport fucking'. Then for her it was back to Blighty and job, while for me on to the States and a Rough Guide on the Southwest.

Carine talked about an ex-boyfriend who was a poet in Paris. Apparently there was still much admiration there. Something about her tone, reverent where usually blithe, put me in mind of Margot about Ollie. That and her evident fear of going back to London without a new man to keep her away from 'that shit coke-dealer I used to live with' is what made me think I was doing everyone a favour when I gave her his number.

It was not premeditated. Nor did I have any idea at the time who I was getting him involved with. She just seemed to me a lovable free spirit, good for passing a recreative few days on... But then meddling, when not actually vicious, is almost always naïve.

2.

I said I met Oliver again years later in Munich. This is how it happened: I was back in London, two further Rough Guides behind me. I was sharpening pencils and trying to start the first novel Margot had once said she would like out of me. Margot had by now become too grand for an essential vagabond like myself, I imagined; for my part, I no longer had the taste for the clever classes I'd had in adulterous days. Not that I had become overly moral, yet. Still, I was beginning to settle into becoming my profession, as most people do by their early thirties – in this case, a travel writer for a young audience without a great deal of money.

It suited me well enough. The odd 'dope deal' – a colour mag piece or TV script draft – provided enough extra cash so I could live more or less as I liked. As with everyone else, I sometimes wondered 'Is this all there is?' Maybe that's why, after two false starts and with no particular faith in the effort, I made an attempt on that novel.

It was a *Pitcairn's Island* sort of thing, and some spadework had to be done at the London Library. Coming out of there one brilliant autumn evening, I ran into Carine Bleistein.

'Winkely dinkely doo-dah!' she chimed, never having been one to burden herself with Henry James English. 'Fancy meeting you here!'

We hugged, and I remembered the scent of Opium, Marlboros and vodka-tonic that had formed a nimbus around her in Phuket, making her seem fun and fragile at the same time.

'Must get back to the office,' she said in a voice too deep for her size. 'Just coming in from lunch.' (It was almost five.) 'It's chaos in there. Listen, dwaling, where can I ring you?'

I told her, and after further giggles she dashed off, still a childlike stick-figure in black strides, bomber jacket and ebony curls – though I'd noticed a strand or two of grey. Eager to see her again, I was relieved when she phoned the next week. In the rush I'd neglected to ask her for her number.

'Listen, dwaling, I'm calling from the office and it's chaos in here. Chaos is my life too – just thrown out another two-year-wonder. Need a bod to go round to my aunt and uncle for dinner. Can you manage Thursday? They pour rather good wine.'

Her husky, musky cigarette-and-booze tone sounded wonderfully unaffected compared to the Sloanes I was in danger of falling back in with; so I agreed. There was no chance to ask for details: 'chaos' reigned in her office, which I gathered had something to do with property. – In fact, it was one of the promising new tentacles of the Bleistein-Sloman octopus, and none the less notable for being run by a woman. But I would only learn about that in time.

'We haven't had any novelists in the family,' Uncle Harold observed, puffing at his pipe. 'Difficult to make money at, isn't it?'

We sat in a drawing-room in Serpentine House, one of the last grand terraces in Bayswater not turned into a package hotel. The room looked over the Park and was certainly the largest I'd ever sat in in London, or possibly anywhere. The assumption was that such show-places belonged only to Arabs or executives of multi-national combines; but Harold and Vera Bleistein had lived there since the '60s. Carine's other uncles – Nigel, Rodney and Arnold – lived in equivalent splendour at the three other corners of the Park.

They had London staked out.

'That's not true, is it?' asked Aunt Vera. 'We've had novelists surely.'

'No,' Harold insisted, 'never!' banging his pipe on an onyx ashtray.

'What about Sissy Sloman?' – Vera had blue-white hair which fit as tight to her skull as a bathing-cap.

'Sissy? She writes about fleas and flukes!' Harold coughed.

With his skinny face, huge ears, peppery moustache and coke-bottle glasses, he looked a bit like an insect himself.

Vera laughed self-deprecatingly. 'What am I thinking? of course – fleas and flukes. Types of beetles, aren't they?'

Harold snorted. ''nother whisky?' he asked me.

The room was pear green, the cornice baby's bottom pink, the windows the size of Buckingham Palace's. Flowers false and real sat in bowls all around or in still-lifes on the walls. Mementoes covered polished-topped tables along with silver-framed photos of chaps with wiry hair in tuxedos and white-haired women with smiles. Carine's eyes twinkled as I took all this in. Was I enduring, they asked.

'The second Lord Rothschild studied fleas and flukes too,' Harold went on, handing around refills in thick-bottomed tumblers. 'Never understood the attraction. Butterflies maybe. I go in for standing cigarette-lighters myself. Like to see my collection?'

'Of course he doesn't want to see your silly flame-throwers, Harold. Let the poor man drink in peace.' – Aunt Vera's rebuke was so gentle that her husband made a sound as if he'd been stroked. Satisfied, she turned to her niece-by-marriage: 'What we want to hear how Carine's business is doing, don't we?'

The coaxing, vicarious 'we' was her main party trick, as the pipe and Family vignettes were her husband's. Between the two, we sailed through cocktails and dinner in a dining-room the size of a football pitch. The meal was 'catered by Lord Sieff, I'm afraid,' our hostess confessed. This provoked Harold to describe how the Family had put several British retailers in business in the early days of the century, which in turn led to a description of the Family's own origins in sweet-shops in Shoreditch circa 1880.

I was spellbound. In my WASP preppy way, I'd grown up expecting Jews to be ruthless, neurotic and self-obsessed; but Harold and Vera were solicitous, easy-going, quaint – and Carine appeared in a new light. Though we had little chance to confer, each occupied by host and hostess in turn, she kept her eye on me, ever twinkling and determined that I should find all to taste. What cushier spot could a man hope for, I began to think. In fact, by the time we men had retired for brandy, I was half kicking myself for not having latched onto her in Phuket years before.

The women went off to powder their noses, and Harold took me to see me his cigarette lighters. They were shelved in purpose-built cupboards in his study, which was the size of Margot Wingfield's drawing-room squared. Some had bases of polished granite, others of marble or turquoise. Some were from Tanganyika as it had been called when Harold had run the Family business there, others from Mexico – one even from Catalina, made from the tusk of a boar which Harold claimed to have shot during a day-trip to the island with a famous Hollywood mogul.

'Oh yes? Really! And where did you get this one?' I found myself chorusing, as dozens must have. 'The rich are not like you and me,' I thought Scott Fitzgeraldishly. Uncle Harold's eccentricity was civilized, if curiously devoid of meaning. Too much meaning was what was being escaped, I gathered, recalling another phrase from undergrad Eng Lit: 'He had a mind so fine that it could not be violated by an idea.' From what I could see of Harold and Vera, to say nothing of Carine, this might have made a nice family motto.

He offered a cigar, which I turned down, then settled into his wing-backed chair to pack a new pipe. 'Nobody smokes anymore,' he lamented, 'not one of the men in the Family under thirty – none of the women either, except Carine. But then she defies all the rules.' Coughing again, he struck a match.

Having no response to this leading, if ambiguous remark, I let my eyes travel to the one non-combustive ornament in the room: a painting of a landscape placed rather secretively behind the door.

Harold didn't miss much. 'We did have a painter in the family once,' he observed, returning to an earlier train of thought. 'Lionel's aunt actually. You know Lionel? No? Well, I'm sure you'll meet. Carine's godfather: head of the Family fund, grandson of my father's older sister and my mother's first cousin on – what was it? the paternal side – yes, must be. Lionel's a Sloman, mother a Bleistein. His aunt was the sister of our most famous Sloman, Sir Monty. Heard of him? Friend of Lord Battenburg. Chairman of the National History Museum.'

I said 'uh-huh' with respectful non-commitment.

'The reason she became an artist is that her father refused her permission to marry the young man she was in love with – sculptor, I think. So the next morning she came down to breakfast done up in men's clothing, excused herself, walked out the door, never came back. Her given name was Georgina, so she called herself George and shortened Sloman to Sloam. Heard of her? George Sloam? Rather a cult figure to some.'

I got up and went over to study the painting.

'It's an odd story. She took on the identity of her refused suitor and became a lesbian, in the male role. Dressed in suits and cravats. Ended up seducing the last mistress of that famous Celtic poet – what was he called? Butler? Gates? Can't remember now – something Welsh or Hebridean – anyhow, bottle green.'

The painting close up was more intriguing than halfway across a long room; properly lit, it might have been haunting. The subject was the setting of a red sun across the estuary leading to St Michael's Mount. It wasn't great art, but it had a '30s bohemian sort of attraction: Dora Carrington, Mark Gertler, that type of thing. Given the biog Uncle Harold was retailing, it must have had a certain saleability, I thought, surprising myself by this mercantile response.

'They lived together in a cottage somewhere in the West Country, mostly on her – or his – Family stipend.'

'She wasn't cut off then?'

'Thought you'd ask that. Monty was furious, but it wasn't up to him. Family rule is to take responsibility for the women no matter what they get up to. This was the most extreme rebellion I can remember. Since *she* posed as *he*, we might've been justified in cutting him or her off; but that would've brought up other issues too complicated to go into. Anyhow, he – or she – ended up being quite respectable. Died about ten years ago. Shortly after, there was a retrospective of her work. "Naïve expressionism" they called it. Couldn't make head or tail of it myself. The one I bought is unusually bland.'

A fit of coughing cut short this narration. Meanwhile, as if on cue, the door opened, obscuring George Sloam's *opus blandum*, and Vera's head popped in. She chided her husband not to bore the young man with stories about people he could not have known or cared about.

'No, no, no,' I protested. 'It's intriguing.'

'Join you in a minute, dear,' Harold spluttered sharply to his wife; and once she'd shut the door again, his tone changed.

He had told about George Sloam with the same light deprecation he had used when relating a joke on his tribe, but now he said solemnly: 'We do hope Carine is getting on better these days. I don't know how well you know her, but it seems to us the more successful she gets, the less able she is to maintain a relationship.'

This was awkward. 'I don't know her well,' I answered with care, 'but I couldn't imagine a girl of her sweetness having much trouble.'

'Oh, she's had men buzzing around her like flies,' he said swatting the air with his pipe as if they were present. 'Too many of 'em after her for the wrong reasons, tho'. Even the good ones can be turned bad by the prospect of so much more money than they're used to.'

'Harold Bleistein, are you being indiscreet?' demanded Aunt Vera, popping her bathing-cap around the door again.

'With you in a minute, dear.'

The door uncracked. 'Men!' she trailed off down the hall.

'It all started a few years ago,' Harold confided. 'She did the ill-advised thing and fell in love. Man was an artist too; nice chap at first – well-educated, connected, all that. Too bohemian finally, I gather. Carine's bourgeois, for all her love of fun. You might ask her about it if you get to know her better. Fellow's name was Oliver Murrie.'

I didn't follow up on this after we left, though naturally I was surprised and – considering what Harold had said – not only curious but slightly guilty-feeling. What had I set loose? Events came back as I turned to Carine in the cab; but she didn't want talk then – certainly not traumatic probing – nor did I wish to add present insult to past injury by being ungracious. So I went back with her to her flat in Montague Square and spent the rest of the evening smoking hashish, trading jokes and 'playing' in her most recent ex's water-bed.

'He left it here when I threw him out,' she explained. 'They all leave half of their lives with me when they go. I've got a closet full of Andy's old clothes. What size are you, by the way?'

Such was her generous nature.

It was a night full of fairly innocent delights, yet as sleepless as the thousand and one that Scheherazade spent with the sultan. Carine took all in stride. In the morning when the alarm went, she got up, rough as she felt (I certainly did). 'Play hard, you must work hard, is my motto,' she gurgled, rummaging through clothes piled on the floor. Half she kicked toward the laundry bin, the other half threw onto her body. 'Sorry about this mess – I don't think I ever learned to tidy up properly.' No. She'd grown up in a palace where all practical needs had been supplied by a cook, a butler, a chauffeur, a nanny and two maids. 'Have a lie-in for as long as you like,' she concluded. 'They're croissants and fresh orange in the kitchen – must dash now, late already. Will phone from the office. Bye-eee.'

Her blithe trustingness was disarming. She hardly knew me, and that had been years before. But Carine seemed to have natural faith, extending to all. It was as if, having come out of a gilded cage, she couldn't bear the outer world to contain anything but niceness. So she was complaisant, chuckling and cooing, making love as you wanted – doing whatever you wanted, unless and until you misused her. 'I have one requirement,' she announced from the start. 'Faithfulness in a lover. I know it's silly – everyone violates it – I'm a romantic, I guess. When I lose trust, it all goes; then they have to go too.'

It was heartbreaking potentially. And as the morning picture grew clear, I realized I could not allow myself that luxurious lie-in. It would have to be up, pull socks on and be off.

This wasn't so easy either. I'd lived a wild life from time to time, but nothing had quite prepared me for Carine's brand of it. A weighty fog engulfed me in her front hall, and I had to retreat to the drawing-room and sit on the sofa – lie, in fact – and spend another half-hour dozing off the effects of brandy, Lebanese and seminal depletion.

Waking later into a trance, I gazed at the odd assortment of objects around. Besides the chesterfield I lay on, these included a mirrored sideboard that looked like it belonged in a Edwardian hotel, more mirrors, several palm plants, a mahogany dining-table, two oversized stereo speakers, the latest in TV-video paraphernalia, two life-sized porcelain statues of Dalmatians and a pair of jokey Ralph Steadman cartoons – the solid and ephemeral jumbled with an insouciance that would never've done in any proper WASP living-room.

The phone rang. 'Did I wake you? No? Good, Found brekkie? Well, you must: croissies'll be stale by tomorrow; besides, I don't know when I'll be home tonight. Fancy dinner in a day or two?'

It was all I could do to pretend I hadn't fallen back to sleep and dawdled away the morning. Having no excuse handy, I arranged to see her the next evening against better judgement. Carine was the type of girl you were meant to fall in love with: the kind of damsel a decent, unsnobbish chap with an eye for happiness should have tied himself up with *sans* ado. If he wasn't prepared to do that, leading her on for one minute could only be despicable.

So what about her and Oliver Murrie? I began to wonder as my hangover receded and facts percolated through.

'Ho-hum, tiddly-pum,' is what she answered the following night, when I put it to her.

We were sitting on the chesterfield again, having consumed Chateaubriand and a flask of Margaux – that is, I consumed, she drank.

'By the way,' she went on, skirting the question, 'I owe you one, putting me on to him.'

The turn of phrase seemed too louche. 'You don't owe me a thing. Anyway, if this meal is payback, he must've been stupendous.'

'You're nicsch,' she gurgled, and sipped.

I wasn't sure whether the word was mock-Yiddish or inebriate. Still, it cut off my line of chat; and any hope I had of returning to it dissolved the next instant when she added:

'Sorry if I'm a bit boring tonight. I'm utterly shattered.'

With that, she fell back into the cushions and passed out.

Her arms folded over her little breasts; her jaw sagged onto her collarbone. Breath trying to get through her nose hit on an obstruction, making a sound between baby's gurgle and death-rattle. I gazed at her for a spell and saw both an infant and elderly lady lying there, a *bonne vivante* and naïf behind the salt-and-pepper curls. Then I looked to the TV, which had been blaring unwatched through dinner and now waxed deadly serious with the Nine o'Clock News.

Menachem Begin had sent Israeli troops into Beirut; members of the old guard at the Foreign Office were protesting to save Britain's face with the Arabs – that sort of thing. What would Carine have thought, being Jewish, I wondered. Relieved she was asleep, I switched the set off before trying to wake her to get her to bed.

The erstwhile bundle of energy had become dead to the world, so I had to carry her to the bedroom finally, grumbles and protests issuing out of dream-babble. Her subconscious consented to have her sandals taken off, but a hand whisked up the duvet before I could tug down her clothes; and when I tried to peel it back so she wouldn't be too hot, a swift kick to the groin – accidental, I'm sure – made me think better of it.

It would be completely wrong to get into the habit of spending the night with her, I thought, going back to the drawing-room. On the other hand, to run out without a credible excuse would be cruel. I could tell her I was married or seeing some other woman; but that might be a blow to her self-esteem, and it seemed she'd taken one or two of them lately. I could tell her I had to go to Spain to update a Rough Guide, but lying wasn't my stock-in-trade; besides, what if she saw me coming out of the London Library the next week? Truth was best, I concluded, flipping through her records (this was before the era of CDs). And if I had to get out of town to make untruth true, what about going early to friends near Munich who'd asked me to come meet my new godson at Christmas?

Blissfully familyless, I had always jumped at this sort of invitation. Couples oppressed by establishments love to think they can comfort the rest of us sad mortals so unlucky as to not have proper homes. I would be pampered. In fact, since my friends had a flat in a castle, they could afford to give me a room of my own to write in – possibly the whole place if they had to go back to the States at the last minute to pay Xmas obeisance to their own families.

I put on a Mozart piano concerto – the 21st, I think. Listening to it right through, I firmed up this utilitarian plan. When it was over, I went to Carine's spare bedroom, a sleeping-spot which – out of politeness or modesty – she had offered me the first night when we had rolled in from Harold and Vera's. 'I don't know if anyone could sleep in there,' she had warned: 'haven't opened the door on it in yonks. I should think Andy [her most recent ex, Ollie's successor] left it like Hurricane Hilda hit.'

Truer words could not have been spoken. The room looked as crazy as zig-zags of her curls when her head shot up in the morning to the sound of the alarm. Actually, I might've given up trying to shove the door open if I hadn't caught sight of something familiar under débris. This was a painting in oil, enormous, rich, evocative: a grey, black and white background of sea, cliff and cloud with three figures against it, one a stout man in dandiacal dress, another rake-thin pouring a glass of champagne, the third a woman naked and stretched out on rain-slicked stones. – Their faces, unmistakably, were Margot's, Carine's and Oliver Murrie's.

'Munich?!' she exclaimed when I told her what I'd planned.

She seemed taken aback, though not exactly by me.

'Why does everyone skive off to that old Nazi place?'

'It's not Munich exactly. My friends live in a castle by the Starnbergersee – a flat in a castle actually, a conversion. It's about forty minutes outside of town.'

Her annoyance, if annoyance it was, appeared to vanish as quickly as it had come up. To cover, she offered polite conversation about the idea of turning castles into flats. 'Sell 'em for a bloody fortune,' she mused. 'Your friends must be sitting pretty.'

I made explanations: American prep-school buddy, German *Wandervögel* wife... We were in Carine's office, secretaries and other factotums buzzing around. Her desk existed only notionally under an avalanche of paper. She herself was perched dwarf-like on a swivel-chair which backed onto a great Deco window looking over the hubbub of Victoria Street. The window might have been cracked, I thought: fresh or not, air might have stirred up the fug made by her half-dozen cigarettes an hour. But Carine, bless her, seemed blissfully unconscious of the aromatic nimbus she dwelt in.

'Does the marriage work?' she inquired.

It only struck me then that she might be worried I was 'skiving off' to Munich for illicit romance. She knew something about the adultery in my background; and though she would never have moralized, it's possible that she wanted to send a message that a return to old ways could not be on the menu if I planned to see her again.

'Don't know really,' I answered. 'I've only seen them once since they tied the knot. They looked terrific – blonde and rugged with Alpine sun.' Regretting this image as soon as I'd evoked it, I added: 'She did complain of a migraine.'

Lighting a ciggie, Carine smiled twinkly-eyed. I hadn't the slightest idea what was going on beyond those brown lashes.

'Bloody chaos in the office today,' is all she said.

I felt like a heel. After listening to more complaints about office-life than I'd ever heard from her, I finally suggested:

'You could come too if you wanted.'

'What? to Munich?'

'Sure. My friends have to go to the States on Christmas Eve. [I'd called them by then and ascertained plans.] I'll have all that empty space to write in. Might get kinda lonesome.'

'Aw,' she pouted, genuinely caring. 'It's nicsch of you to ask. But I'm afraid Christmas here's one endless party, what with the business and Family.'

I nodded. There didn't seem to be much more to say.

'Don't you know anyone there?' she asked after a puff.

'Not a soul. But sometimes I like it like that. I'll manage.'

'Yes. Sometimes I like being on my own too. But not often.'

Touché. – Were we both thinking of Phuket?

'I do know one person down there,' she added after another inhalation. 'You do too as it happens. It's part of the reason I don't think I should come.'

The landscape in my mind's eye might have changed then, so that the three figures became him, me and her.

'You know who I mean, don't you?'

'Oliver Murrie?'

'Got it on one.' – She stubbed her cigarette out and lit the next.

'How did he get there?' I wondered.

'Better ask him,' she exhaled.

Which was exactly what I would do.

3.

It was during his period with Carine that Oliver had begun to come into his own as a painter – that is, to work seriously in oils. This I knew from another, much more extensive look through the contents of her spare bedroom. There were a dozen or more canvases, all dated on back, so that you could piece together his development. Carine herself wouldn't, or couldn't, explain this; knowing it instinctively, I didn't bother her with more questions. Nor did there seem any reason to let her know that I had rummaged through his, and Andy's, and no doubt other predecessors' left-behind goods.

Shortly after they'd met, Oliver's taste had changed from domes to steeples. He painted one or two London parish churches, including St Paul's Hammersmith. A pious note entered his vision: the most extensive work of that phase showed a figure like himself dressed in a fringed leather jacket contemplating the effigy of an ancestor buried in Wells Cathedral, light refracting down through stained-glass windows. This picture had an innocence, sweetness even, which showed the influence of Carine at its best. Eros was another matter. At first glance, the sex-interest seemed invisible: tucked away back in the period of Margot Wingfield and his first sketches for 'Déjeuner sur les rochers'. Gradually, however, in the era of Carine it began to seep out in less declarative ways.

First there were landscapes – a couple of evocations of trees: complex studies in form where branches seemed to twist and couple acrobatically, in balletic contortions. Then came studio work: paintings using models. The earliest of these was a darkly-lit scene with a fully-clothed man sitting on a bed while in front of him a naked woman played cello, one of her sides illuminated by lamplight. The woman's body was odd: not beautiful in a glossy magazine sort of way but vivid in reality and immediately recognizable as the truth of many female bodies of the time – slightly flaccid in thigh, pear-shaped in breast, bony at shoulders. I wondered why Oliver had chosen this type and what it meant that the man in the picture (it looked like Godfrey Wingfield, fully bald) should have been covering his eyes. Vaguely, I was put in mind of Flemish nudes of the post-Renaissance – a more modern, realistic version of Van Eyck's women, stripped.

A few single-figure studies of similarly unusual nudes followed, each posed against variously coloured backdrops and measured implicitly against the other principal form in the painting, an earthenware bowl on a table. In this manner, there was a thin, short-haired model against a yellow background with a shallow blue bowl beside her and a plump, long-haired model against chartreuse with a deep, grain-coloured bowl beside her. This kind of study built up towards a large canvas in which a naked man sat by a table with a tall, striated bowl, almost a vase, beside him and watched as three nude models revolved around the room, a thin one, a plump one and one with a fine head but unfortunately stubby legs.

In all of these there was atmosphere: brooding, melancholy, slightly sardonic, musical. Beauty stayed somewhere to the side of consciousness; in its shadow, an analytical eye seemed to want to explore the grotesque. The result, beyond the extraordinary, autobiographical reprise of 'Déjeuner sur les rochers', was two paintings of a menacingly romantic flavour, both composed with painstaking care in the knife-stroke, blade-thickened *pointilliste* manner he had been working up to.

The first was a version of a 17th century etching in which a man with demonic features and a hat over one eye led a troupe of youths through a wood towards an Egyptian shrine. The second, much larger and even more striking, showed a blonde-haired nude of androgynous aspect sitting on a chair against a brilliant azure wall on which the first painting, version of the etching, was hung. The body of this fleshly creature was tilted, so that the head seemed to strain semi-consciously towards the painting. The form was intrinsically phallic despite the model being female, so that the painting towards which it was bent could be interpreted as an extension or expression or perhaps perverse explosion of erotic energy.

In spirit, or negation of it, this seemed a wilful opposite to the delicate steeples of his first months with Carine. So: had life imitated art then by his transposition to Munich?

He had settled in Schwabing with his new woman, Gisela. Schwabing was no longer the Suburb of a New World as it had been called in the '20s when its inhabitants included Klee, Kandinsky, Stefan George and the Society for Modern Life, as well as various mystics, political extremists, avantgardists and reactionaries. Now it was the *haut bourgeois* residential sector of a city whose main works of art were housed in rococo or Nazi mausoleums and whose mania for order was only occasionally subverted by longing for ructions of Weimar days. – Oliver would tell me of his leather jacket being slashed in the Lola Montez nightclub because he was a foreigner. 'The irony was good for me,' he added.

I only understood what he meant once I'd heard the story of his demise with Carine. But that didn't come out easily, or at first. He turned out to be difficult to get a hold of and almost impossible to talk to on his own. Having taken him off a woman who was nearly his wife, Gisela was determined not to let him out with an acquaintance likely to stir nostalgia for London. It became clear after a couple of phonecalls that it was up to me to seduce her, as it were.

This became easier once she learned that I was staying in a Schloss near Starnberg. 'That is where all Germany wishes to live,' she observed. 'You must be rather wealthy.'

The Schloss was lovely enough, though conversion had made it seem oddly American – more than American even, with (for instance) heated tiles on the bathroom floor. But its situation was wonderful. Five large windows in three generous rooms gave views of the lake and the Alps. Two of the five were full-length and opened onto a balcony, so that you could sit sheltered from wind but open to a sun which seemed almost Mediterranean, reflected off snow. The air was brilliant and made beloved London recede in the mind as a hazard to one's health. All day long the radio played Beethoven and Schubert, live; and contrary to received opinion, the German language – allied to music, at any rate – seemed euphonious to me, or at least stimulating to the ear.

'It's the consonants,' Oliver observed when I voiced this opinion. 'They pierce through like little spikes, nailing it into place. Otherwise it might be as fluid and un-rational sounding as Italian.'

'Un-rational sounding' sounded like German English to me.

He and Gisela had come out on the S-bahn on my first Sunday there. They didn't stay long. From the first, they seemed to be at odds:

'You don't know what you're talking about,' she chided. 'There are many different kinds of German. *Plattdeutsch*, for example, has a frightful sound. It is nothing like what we speak here.'

She proceeded with a lecture on the subdivisions of her nation, this as much for his benefit as mine, though he could hardly have been ignorant of fundamental geography by this stage. The lecture expanded into an essay on the true affinities of Bavaria, which were to German Switzerland, Austria and northern Italy, according to her. A vision of a new Holy Roman Empire began to take shape, only without the Holy or the Roman, just an ideal of a cohesive European heart-land, with Munich at its centre.

'Gisela is a regionalist-nationalist,' Oliver explained, careful not to let irony taint his tone.

She looked the part, being big-boned, wide-faced, blue-eyed and blondish. Her hair she wore – somewhat incongruously, I thought – in a style of modified punk spikes; otherwise, she was *weiblich* in a New Age sort of way – attractive physically and only subliminally similar to the androgynous nude of that last painting I had found at Carine's. She had been the model for it, though. I was also informed that Oliver's models in London had become a kind of harem by the time he had met her; nor was Gisela about to let him develop any such retinue here. This she emphasized with a look, which he didn't acknowledge. When I asked how was he going to be able to paint without models, she shifted topic to repeat:

'Lovely place you are living in.'

She showed herself nearly as impressed with my Schloss-flat in person as on the phone. Expostulating about prices and how rich Germans from the north were coming south to buy everything up, she gave off a material avidity that made me feel like a *poseur*, considering that the flat wasn't mine. Oliver, I noted, declined to join in in the 'oohs' and 'aahs' which she lavished over my friends' deep, upholstered sofas and porcelain Indian-elephant lampstands. Bohemia still dominated the bourgeois in his aspect, though his focus now seemed to be floating, like a bird-of-prey not ready to perch. As a matter of fact, the bird-of-prey image is only partly apt: he looked sharp now but not well, alert but not aquilinely superior. He was the artist in journeyman phase still, hardly settled master. Munich for him was *reculer pour mieux sauter* – at least so I hoped.

Carine phoned from London the day after their visit.

'What about Ingeborg or Hildebrand or whatever her name is?' she joked, disguising vulnerability, not malice.

'Very *mittel*-European.'

'Mrs Hitler?'

'Mrs Kapitalist Bundesrepublik anyway.'

'Are they happy?'

'Well...'

She inhaled audibly. 'You must tell all after you've had a recce. What's their place like?'

'Haven't been yet.'

'Then you haven't met the daughter?'

'Oliver has a daughter already?' – That would have been novel: Gisela showed no signs of being pregnant, and they'd only been together for eight or ten months.

'It would be rather quick, wouldn't it? No, I meant *her* daughter – it is a daughter, I think. Previous marriage, or relationship.'

'Ah. I didn't know.'

'Everybody has 'em.'

'Has what?'

'Many ex's.'

'...I guess.'

She asked what I'd been doing and I said I'd been listening to Mozart and thinking about her, which was mostly true. It was lovely to hear from her, chirpy as her tone was (and tone, as Margot Wingfield might say, is three-fifths of all.) Besides, her interest gave me a purpose at least as compelling as my own curiosity. So a few days after Christmas, I tried to get through to Oliver on his own; but Gisela again was all I could reach.

'I'm having some people in at New Year,' she said. 'Would you like to come then also?'

The *I* rather than *we* added to my impression that this was an individualistic female. For a moment I wondered if she could really love him, or was capable of loving anyone outside of herself. Was that unkind? I reminded myself that I didn't know anything about her in fact, or Germany and the Germans.

'Thanks,' is what I answered; after more details – 'Is Oliver there?'

'Oh no, not now. He is not here in daytime, you know.'

'No? Does he work somewhere else?'

'Of course. As I work here, it would be too much.'

'I see,' I said though I didn't quite. 'You couldn't possibly tell me his daytime number, could you? What is it, a studio?'

'This is the studio,' she corrected. 'He works in the street. There is no phone there. What a funny idea!'

She gave a perfunctory laugh, and I reflected that the course of his life must've changed a good deal more than I'd realized. Was he a street-artist now? in this frigid weather? If so, no wonder he'd looked pinched. What was he doing? sketches of well-heeled *Wandervögel* at an U-bahn stop?

The idea sent me into Schwabing with some vigour at New Year. No doubt isolation at Starnberg, in whatever splendour, contributed to it, making me concentrate more than I might have on one proximate human contact. There was a woman behind the bar at Schindler's café and a girl who eyed me as she drew in a notebook waiting for a train at Possenhofen S-bahn stop; there were lots of other contacts to be made, as there always are when you travel. But making them is an art, and most of us long for the familiar, whatever talent we have for being on our own. I wanted to drink a beer with an old friend or acquaintance and hear about his progress, maybe have a game of chess or two. Besides, my novel had frozen up; and continental winter was making me feel like I might do so myself.

In the event, Gisela's New Year failed to thaw me. I got there early, chilled to the marrow, and climbed numberless stairs to the top of a Wilhelmine building undestroyed by the War. A dialogue was going on in several tongues: German, English and something I couldn't quite place. Oliver was not in evidence, nor any other non-family guest; so I stood in front of a tall, porcelain stove trying to shiver myself back into warmth while Gisela inveighed against a huge, ursine man dressed in motorcycle leathers.

This was her ex-husband, Oskar. Greeting me with a Mephistophelean smirk, he cut off his onetime spouse to continue with the speech my entrance had interrupted.

'You must get these terms right,' he was saying to a young Venus in Carmen-style shawl. 'What, for instance, do we mean by "modern"?' – The speech had been about art and might've come straight out of a *fin-de-siècle* novel-of-ideas.

'In music, Schönberg and Stravinsky. In painting, Picasso, Braque, Léger. In literature, James Joyce, Jack Kerouac –'

'Exactly!' he motioned, splayed out on a sofa next to this gorgeous girl of sixteen. 'But Postmodernism, which is what I was talking about, is *post* all that, don't you see? It rejects the Rejectors and is not hung up on breaking new ground. It recalls the Past fondly and yearns to produce the well-made piece of writing, or painting that doesn't look like schrapnel on a wall or music that doesn't sound like a war of ping-pong balls. It's humanist art,' he summed up.

Heavy in face as well as body, Oskar's eyes were black marbles, glittering, circumambient, while his hands were small wildcats at play. At irregular intervals, one of them would jump up to swat at a mane of black hair which fell down his temples from a fine widow's peak. This hair had the same oily texture as that of Magdalena, which was the girl's name. Gisela asked her to go to the kitchen and check on the oven. Magdalena looked to her father, who winked, and did not budge. 'Does that mean I could understand it?' she asked.

'Of course, my Beauty. You're the Audience-of-the-Future, aren't you?' – He smiled irresistibly; she nestled closer.

'Well I don't understand,' mama trilled, rearranging furniture, which was a cross between '50s functional and '60s eclectic. 'First you criticize Magdalena as mindless – a self-indulgent teenager brought up to be bourgeois like *Mutti* – then you say she is the perfect audience for the most avantgarde developments in arts. You contradict yourself, Oskar. You always have. You will be the reason she turns out badly, the way you spout idea after idea which only confuse.'

Still huddled in the embrace of the stove, I began to glean a subtext.

'Magdalena,' explained papa, 'may be self-indulgent and perfect New Audience both. Why must all things contradict?' – Turning to his daughter, wide-eyed, he resumed: 'In the past, we had High Art and low. The High was for intellectuals and rich socialites like your *Mutti*'s people, the low for normal working-class blokes like me Dad. While the High filled suburban villas with abstraction, the low produced heroic bodies for Socialist Realism. But today all is middle. Your mother is not High; I am not low. We are brought together by the TV, etc. We want the same things in general: neo-humanist art: figurative, representational, above all accessible, but cut with ornamentation, idiosyncrasy, irony.' – Turning to me, with false grace he added: 'Is this not what you find in England? Or is it the States you come from?'

Oskar, it emerged, was a part-time university lecturer. Both women were clearly under his spell, if in opposite ways. Neither seemed to notice Oliver when he stepped into the room.

'I think I follow,' Magdalena nodded, eager not to be upstaged. 'You mean that people didn't understand Modernism because it was too abstract and didn't enjoy it because it was too ideological?'

Peeling off his parka, Ollie eyed the girl. Gisela bumped past him to go for the bell: other guests were arriving.

'Yah, and inhuman,' Oskar gestured. 'Messianic; trying for the Universal, Beyond. Man trying to play God, eh artist?'

This was by way of salutation to Ollie. Gisela, however, was not having her new man and her ex establish rapport:

'Well I'm for the human,' she interposed; 'also the natural, which is why I'm a Green. I hate nuclear power; and if I believed in a god, it would be of the pagan type – Frau Erda. Perhaps then you'll consent to recognize me as this kind of "postmodernist" too? Or is it just an exclusive club for pretentious males?'

Oskar winked at Oliver as if they shared some secret in common, which in a way I guess they did. 'Ach, you Germans loved the humanist Neo-Classicism even in the Nazi times,' he shrugged. (I gathered from this what was later confirmed: Oskar was not German but from further east, which may explain why he had such ebullient need to see the world in definable isms.) 'Hitler could not understand Modernism either. Arrogant, obscure, subversive, created by a conspiracy of Jewish-capitalist critics who couldn't praise anything unless no one but them understood it – that's how he saw it.'

He put this in English so I could follow – maybe so Ollie could too. Oskar was clearly the kind of charismatic who lived for whatever new face might chance through the door.

'Are you calling me fascist?' Gisela demanded; but now the bell buzzed again, absolving him from an answer which may have been a *casus belli* between them for years.

'Of course,' he went on for the rest of us, 'postmodernism has some element of longing for fascist order. Our *ragazza* here needs that too, if she is going to be Woman of the New Age – eh, *bella*?'

Like everything else, he put this in capital letters. Magdalena, looking down, blushed till her ivory skin was puce.

Seeing Oliver's eye on her, papa continued: 'But there's more to our era than fascist attitudes. Now we incorporate Modernist dissonance into traditional forms. We are against cacophony no more than harmony. We are too pluralistic to accept Classicism just like that. We take from the old schools and invent new ones. We live in the Present, in the city, not in the Future or dreams of Outer Space. We are not alienated from our time as they were in those decades: Man is our centre of attention again, not inexplicable cosmic forces. But Man is *kitsch* now, and nostalgic. What he does recalls the '60s or '50s or '20s or Secessionist period. He is at home in the Empire or ancient Greece. His work is about content as well as form, which was all the Modernists cared for. Minimalism is too spartan; absolutism too restrictive. A sense that we are swarming into a world which is not bound by a single answer has become a happy, at least tolerable, condition; whereas sixty years go, it was cause of massive neurosis.'

'You may stop lecturing now,' Gisela commanded, leading in a fur-coated troupe. 'Or, if you must, the university is down the road.'

Oskar winked at these new arrivals. Would they become disciples in his jovial game? Oliver gave no clue as I tried to catch his eye. What a school he'd been going to here!

'I met the daughter,' I reported to Carine. 'She's sixteen, six-foot, eleven stone, sullen, beautiful and dressed in black. I also met her father, Gisela's ex, who's an "alternative postmodernist design-professor" or something. My handbook German was not up to it.'

'You mean *Schicksal in der Schwiebelkuchen mit Kartofelln in diese Samstag abend jetzt*?' – This in the same telephonic fuzz-buzz as 'Ho-hum-tiddly-pum' and her other endearments.

'Something like that. I thought I was kind of an intellectual before I came here. But to hear these people argue about postmodernist neo-classicist narratology driving out the pretensions of modernist eclectic pseudo-allegory makes me feel like I've spent my life selling baskets on a Mexican beach.'

'Winkely-dinkely gobbledy-gook,' she laughed. 'Poor thing. What about Ollie? Is he really into that now?'

'I'm bewildered. His face is as non-committal as the moon. I think he's studying them: learning, I guess – it's the best gloss I can put on it. But at one point it occurred to me that they might be learning from him. He seems above it somehow, or maybe below it – removed anyway. Sometimes I wondered if he was listening at all: his eyes are pretty vacant. He looked at Gisela a lot, or beyond her. The strange thing is she didn't look at him ever, except when she wanted something like a bottle of wine opened.'

'She treats him like a doormat?'

'I wouldn't say that exactly, but... I invited him out here, just him, on the quiet; but all the way on the other side of the room she heard me and interrupted one of the Kultural machine-gun battles to say they were busy on whatever day it was I suggested. And when he said they could take a break from the schedule, or at least he could, she shot something at him in German which sounded a bit like "Shut up, kid, or I'll send you to a concentration camp".'

Carine went silent. If I was relying on clichés, it was only because I wanted to sound clever, not tactless.

'I nodded a lot,' I went on, 'and grinned. There were twelve or fifteen others there in the end, mostly friends of the ex-husband I gathered. Gisela was eager to impress them. The daughter spent the whole time sitting next to Dad, who was dressed like The Wild One from head to toe. She idolizes him. There's a nasty bit of competition there, I suss. The daughter ignores Gisela and speaks to her when she does just as rudely as Gisela does to Ollie.'

'Bloody hell,' came a sigh from the other end of the line. 'Families!'

'Anyhow, that's how it looked. But this is all without any real chance to talk to him. The apartment's a "penthouse" by the way. That means it's top flat in an old block in an unrenovated, never-bombed section. The're eighty-seven steps to get to it, I was told. Everyone here smokes, so no one made an entrance without looking like he needed an oxygen fix.'

'I'd have bloody heart failure!Listen, dwaling, thanks a mill for phoning – have to fly. It's chaos in here, and I'm off to dinn-dinns with Chunnel Properties and Nagyasagawy Land Development, Ltd.'

'Naggy what?'

'Jappy-dappy-doosits,' she explained. 'Can never pronounce 'em, but they certainly know how to eat.'

'You mean you actually *eat* on your business outings nowdays?'

'Mostly I drink saké when I go Japanese. But I do love the sushi as well – it's so clean, a bod could get healthy off it. Anyway, let me call you at the weekend. You think you'll have seen him by then?'

'Hope so. I found out where he works in the day, surreptitiously from the daughter. She's too lazy and eager to upset her mom to keep a state secret.'

'You'd make a good spy.'

'On Her Majesty's service.'

'Whose majesty's's that?'

'Who am I informing?'

She laughed once again, half-embarrassed; and I reflected how difficult it was not to be more 'nicsch' with her than anyone else.

I tried to apply myself in earnest to my idea for a novel but spent most of the next days listening to music and walking by the lake. When that failed to focus me, I took my friends' car out for a drive towards the Alps and Neuschwanstein, the mad King Ludwig's fantasy Schloss. It turned out to be overrun by tourists, mostly American military and dependents, which ruined the atmosphere of free, purposeful wandering I wanted to wrap myself up in. So I went back to my lair, sharpened pencils and listened to Beethoven's symphonies right through. Wonderful! Still, you can only live in Caspar David Friedrich solitude for so long. Fresh air, nature and silence are very well; but I'm a city-boy finally (I was just beginning to admit this). So a week after Gisela's party, I drove back into Munich to find Oliver.

He was in Heidhausen, a district where ageing dropouts in various stages of removal from the '60s sold crafts, handmade clothes and other wares to Bavarian equivalents of patrons of Portobello Road. I'd hung around such places enough to know the attraction. Buskers played your favourite old rock-song; smells of incense hung counter-culturally in the air; girls wore t-shirts and tight sweaters without bras. In the actual '60s and after, such a bazaar would've been at least half-sustained by sales of pot and paraphernalia; but the rise of the yuppy had put paid to an older, anti-materialistic sort of ideal; and now amid legitimately hand-painted scarves and sand-candles, you could find stalls of furniture produced in Romania last year posing as antiques and dresses made in sweatshops in Bombay posing as hand-sewn by braided Frauleins atop an Alp.

Commerce, in short, was abroad. Maybe this has always been the case and I'd just worn rose-coloured spectacles through my teens. Still, it seemed to me that in the Reagan/Thatcher/Helmut Kohl era, an Edenic atmosphere was being lost. Ibiza had become for package-tourists, not just paradise-seekers as in 1969; and what Oliver was peddling on that cold Saturday in Heidhausen was enough to turn your hippy soul to dry ice.

On his stall sat placemats, posters, framed reproductions: images mass-produced in plastic to sell to downmarket, unaesthetic hordes – the despised *Gastarbeiter* mostly, Turkish and Greek. The images were literally tarted up, airbrushed and made vulgarly romantic: sci-fi fantastic, musclebound, soft-core porny scenes taken directly (though who would've known?) and carefully degraded from his oil paintings.

Was this some perverse application of Oskar's theorizing?

Here church steeples turned into spires of space-stations. The seeker studying his ancestor's effigy became Luke Skywalker sniggering over a time-frozen Darth Vader. Twisted tree branches became the Medusa-like hair of a Queen of the Night. The dressed man and nude woman with cello became a semi-Martian lusting after a naked maja who toyed with a snake. Figure studies of female nudes next to bowls became come-on poses of space maidens next to helmets shaped suggestively, just removed to loosen glossy-magazine hair. There was a Cro-Magnon spaceman in loin-cloth deciding between three of these beauties; Darth Vader leading aspirant evil types towards a space-age Masonic temple; and Gisela beatified as a space-*Mädchen* herself dreaming toward the Darth Vader picture.

It all seemed as if someone were blowing a giant raspberry at *Heilige Kunst.* The images were set against backgrounds of black, salted with tiny stars, which turned out to be heads of pins. At a position of honour at the back of the stall hung a day-glo version of 'Déjeuner sur les rochers' with Scotland turned into a moonscape of Vulcan and all figures nude or teasingly close to it, though helmeted and bound with *de rigueur* capes. The trinity this time wore faces of Gisela, Ollie and Gisela's ex, if 'ex' he was, which by now I'd begun to doubt. Oskar was tall, dark, heroic-looking and sinister all at once, making Oliver seem a precious wimp… I was non-plussed.

In the flesh, Ollie's face was only half-visible behind the fur collar of his parka. 'I'm thunderstruck,' is how I greeted him.

His cheeks were red, as was his nose, whether from fresh air or fever wasn't clear. A certain maturing gauntness had added contour to the moony features. He shrugged in the same way as he had when Gisela had snapped at him at her party.

'It's necessary to eat, isn't it?'

'For godsake, you're hardly starving.' – Margot for some reason came to my mind. How impatient she would've been!

'Settle down, mate. We're not living in the Art-as-religion era anymore. This is fun. And may be good for me too.'

'Good for you?! Come on, I'll take you to lunch. Apparently I'm more ignorant than I imagined. You'll have to explain.'

Of course he wasn't required to explain a thing. Nobody owed anybody any explanations: it was Fate that ruled all, and Desire – and Economics. If he wanted to degrade his art, that was his business, *nicht wahr*? Besides, not only was it necessary to eat (we masticated large salads as he held forth), it was imperative to question.

'Question what?'

'Everything!' he exclaimed; 'not least oneself, with one's precious self-image and vanity.'

Nothing meant anything in a vacuum. He had not sold his paintings, so whatever progress he'd made was not good enough.

I wanted to say that this was a rash judgement but he didn't seem bothered. What was time, after all? And where was the fire?

'Margot thought you were good enough years ago,' I objected, failing to add that his rhetoric sounded like slogans sprayed on a wall.

'Margot cosseted me,' he shrugged, as if such treatment were an example of prejudice, or misapprehension.

We were sitting in a bistro, drinking chai now. It was a trendy, wooden-boothed place a grade too tasteful for plastic placemats.

'Carine would've supported you,' I continued.

'Carine did support me! So what?'

'So why don't you let her do it again? It's gotta be better than perverting your talents in a Second World caricature of gringo great art.'

Those violet, slightly thyroidic eyes drilled into me. The moony expression was alert and more genial than you might've expected, given the line I was taking.

'You're quite a romantic, aren't you?'

'Yeah, Americans and their sentimental streak – I know that one.'

'That's why you want me to go back to Carine suddenly, is it?'

'I didn't say I wanted that.'

'You didn't have to. I wonder why.'

We sat there in mutual challenge, each pondering what the other might say next. At last, he made what was possibly the most effective remark he could have to stop me in my urge to save or reform him:

'You can give a man any amount of advice on his profession, mate. But don't try to tell him what to do with his cock.'

We traded some niceties and finished our cups. I paid, and he went back to work. Driving my friends' BMW home to Starnberg, I told myself crossly that that was the end of it. But it wasn't. When I got up to the door of my friends' luxury flat, Gisela was waiting for me.

'What you don't understand,' she began, 'is that I saved Oliver.'

There were too many attempts at salvation going on, I might've said if this had been London or her native language English. Across tongues, it's more of a chore to be witty – which may be one reason our mixed-up century had gone in for such violence and crudity.

'Sit down.' I motioned to the sofa. 'Would you like coffee? tea?'

I switched on the radio. *Hammerklavier.*

Gisela brushed up her blonde spikes – the roots seemed black today; I guessed they needed redyeing – then launched into her version of events:

Oliver had found himself ensnared in a 1970s version of a turn-of-the-century Jewish family: a bourgeois nightmare that offered success but threatened smothering. Gisela was sure of this: she'd made a study of it. With the Holocaust haunting her, like many postwar Germans, she was obsessed; and Oliver and Carine had provided a golden chance to analyze the syndrome down to its bones:

'Such kind of family makes its way through business,' she explained, as if I'd been born in Dar-es-Salaam. 'Maybe one or two daughters dabble in the arts; one or two sons go to university; for the rest, sons go to learn the money-making and daughters become wives like their mothers. The daughters get some cash – one-thousandth of the family fortune, perhaps – but the family is worried of husbands or boyfriends who use them, so the money is governed by what they call a Trust. This means the daughters do not become adult, which means that they wish to be rebels but at the same time cannot be. Yet of course rebellious instincts have to come out. In America, the Princess of the type develops into what they call a "serial polygamist" or careerist; both seem to present ways to compete with the males, who retain money and power. Both also keep females from successful relationships; and in the end women must remain women, even when trying to be men. I mean by this simply that they retain the yearning to raise children and furnish houses like their *Muttis*. So one gets this mixed-up type with a man's ambitions yet a woman's desires: neither one thing nor the other – a unisex, postmodern rebel child who does not rebel; who holds the potential for neurosis and maybe the reality, but in any case the unhappy energy which rises from it.'

This didn't sound like the Carine I knew. It sounded like more theorizing of the Oskar type, and I was weary of it.

'Can't that energy be happy?' I asked, thinking how in real life Carine might've responded with a twinkle in the eye and a 'gobbledy-dobbledy-gook'.

'This is a question they must take to the psychoanalyst.'

'But Carine doesn't go to a psychoanalyst. She wouldn't have time.'

'It is what they call the "displacement activity".'

'What?'

'She goes on ski-trips and sun-trips and drives the GTI convertible. There is cocaine and nightclubs for fun of a kind which might drive a normal bourgeois to drink, as it has done one or two of her cousins. This was not right for an artist like Oliver.'

I got up and poured myself whisky from a decanter by the stereo. I offered her one too *pro forma*. At first she demurred. Then, seeming to take a new tack, she asked for a glass of wine.

'How did you meet Ollie?' I put to her, coming back from the kitchen with a bottle and corkscrew.

'We lived two years in London.'

'We?'

'Oskar and I, Magdalena. Oskar lectured at St Martin's College; I worked as a model, when I was not busy with the airbrushing.'

I hadn't known until then that Oskar had lectured in England, but somehow it didn't surprise me. At the moment, however, another thing was starting to attract my attention. Oliver's comment about his cock resurfaced as she rattled on: the black trousers and turtleneck were tight enough to suggest a body that had not yet felt the full gravity of middle-age – but it was a close-run thing, and there would only be one way to find out.

'Sounds to me like you disliked Carine because she was Jewish,' I observed, trying to turn curiosity from where I didn't want it to stray.

'You are somewhat cruel,' she replied, as if hurt.

'It must be the air.'

I tossed back my whisky. Outside it was clear, frigid, dry.

'I am not an anti-Semite,' she defended. 'We Germans have learned. Anyhow, Carine is not Jewish. Her mother was Irish; that's why she drinks. Oliver was the anti-Semite.'

'Oliver? But Oliver's British.'

'And so? I told you I saved him.'

We see in people what we look for. At any given time, you can find just about any projected evil in someone else.

'How do you mean "saved him"?'

'Did you know that the Bleistein-Sloman family crest was a *fasces*? Oliver and I discussed this. It represents a symbol of their success. They only invest in a group, the strong binding the weak in a fist. That's how they became rich. Of course Carine is no intellectual; and when Oliver asked whether she thought this procedure was moral, she answered what every Bleistein-Sloman child is told to from birth: "It's a highly elevated form of communism, really".'

Gisela's attempt at Carine's accent did not make me smile. 'Are you implying that the Krupps and the Thyssens never "invested in a fist"? And what about the Rockefeller Cousins or the Crown Agents?'

Her ancient, Central European animosity against the making of money was at least as boring as the making of it itself. An American version of this was one of the reasons I'd become a traveller from my own country, I recalled and went to pour another drink.

'You are one part of the *Zeitgeist*,' she countered; 'Oliver with Carine became another. When she complained that she could not get ten pence from her Trust, he said it was sexist and that the male *bund* of the Family should be taken to court. He was on her side, but it was complicated. It is one thing to complain about your own family and another for someone to do it for you.'

'Ah.' – For the first time, I spied a glimmer of sense in her.

'Oliver complained about the men. There was one who controlled apartments in some sector of London. "What did he ever do but collect cigarette-lighters?" he said. The sons were given million-pound houses even when they could not get through university. "What does an 'elevated form of communism' do but keep them as morons forever?" With no struggle, there was no will-to-succeed;

that's why the Family was "going to the dogs". This is what he would say when she complained; then he would wipe his brush and turn to his easel, and it was all right for some time… She encouraged his art. She paid for everything. She took him on holidays, and he was happy – so happy, he told me, that he even thought about giving up painting and becoming a journalist, to make a life more suited to hers. This would have been one solution: for him to adapt to the situation – become, as he said, a kept man. (We have those in Germany too in these days of low employment.) But Oliver did the other thing – men are so vain. He let her good treatment of him seduce him into becoming a Force of Nature and doing just as he pleased.'

Gisela had set her glass down, half drunk. She was sitting upright, winter light reflecting in her eyes across snow out the windows. Subtly unsullen, half-illuminated, she was transforming into a startling beauty of white, blue and gold: the sort of ice-and-fire, earth-mother cum androgynous New Age type that German women can be at their most glamorous.

'But no one is given such licence,' she went on. 'He offends. He asks for too much. He becomes petulant and destructive of perfectly innocent conventions that do no harm in bourgeois lives. He rebels against her. What does a bit of cocaine have to do with the career of an artist, he asks. So what if he wants to make love with one of his models? What if he wants to go for a month on his own to paint in the Alps? Why should he have to be polite to her family, or follow their sexual ethics, or make fortnightly visits to this uncle or that?… He found himself flying into a kind of mad, neo-romantic rage. He could not be domesticated anymore, she realized. But the more she worried, the more his demon took over.'

I was sitting in my chair like I'd been pinned to it. Whether she was telling the truth or just a hackneyed fantasy, her energy had become a blue flame. Nor was it possible for me to keep from stripping her down in mind to bare nipples and sensual gyrations. Her skin I saw tanned, glistening, tinsled in golden cilia, like some blonde-bestial, northern European goddess on a Mediterranean beach.

'He lived on her now. What had at first been subconscious became deliberate. He exploited her. He let his words against convention and the power of her family fly loose whenever he wished and not just in defence of her position. It is an old story: the artist always revolts against his patron in the end; meanwhile, the patron loves the artist most when he's poor and weak. This combination in love makes a sado-masochistic possession. Carine became unhappy; Oliver accused the Family of being at cause, even though he knew it was he who would have to go. So he transformed from her knight-in-shining-armour into a kind of dragon bringing sorrow and gloom.

'She'd had previous boyfriends, and something similar had happened with one. Using this as an example, Oliver suggested that she "seek help", even though he did not believe in analysis. She said she thought she was going mad; he in his heart knew the crisis was near. All they wanted – all she had wanted – was for him to drink their good wine, eat their food, practice reasonably good manners and be nice to the Family; otherwise he could carry on as he liked. They did not want him to rave about miners in Yorkshire, or Mrs Thatcher or poverty in the Third World, which was the other face of their system, he said; but they had allowed him enough privilege that he believed that he could really become a free man entirely; so he forgot to be careful and learn what we Germans know too well – that we must realize our limitations and never try to overreach in the old, bad *romantische* way.'

I was reminded at this point that, to the English, the Germans are intellectuals but not wits; that humour, if it exists, has a cruel or self-deprecating streak and that illuminism is their life-flame, not sparkling repartee. The music of Mozart or Schubert was Viennese, which was different, Gisela's regionalism notwithstanding. Bavaria, musically, had produced the later Richard Strauss; and now from Garmisch where Strauss had spent his last years, came one of those bitter, sudden Alpine storms that make Germany in winter so much more hard and absolute than damp, fairly temperate England can be.

It hurtled down on us without warning, eclipsing the sun which had lit up her face. She cut off her monologue abruptly, as if worried that she'd over-stepped, and began making awkward small-talk.

'This wine is nice.'

'Is it?'

'It is German?'

'I don't know. It's just what my friends happened to have. Would you like me to check the bottle?'

'Please don't bother.'

'No trouble.'

'German wine is improving. They say now that we have become

well-off again, we may at last learn to eat and drink like the French.'

'Yes? Would you like another glass?'

For several reasons, I was hoping she'd say no. Among other things, I had a sudden urge to phone Carine, to say what I'm not sure. But now Gisela seemed determined for me to find her attractive.

'Yes, I think I will,' she replied.

I went for the bottle. 'It's snowing,' I observed, topping her up.

She glanced towards the windows.

'Would you like me to drive you to the station?'

'No, it is an easy walk. I shouldn't want you to bother."

'No bother. I have my friends' BMW. But we'll have to go before it gets too deep. After you've finished your wine.'

'Prosit!'

'Prosit.'

She seemed in no hurry, so I poured myself a last whisky – at least what I thought would be a last one. The radio was now onto 'Death and the Maiden'; my nerves were on edge; the Schloss felt like a tomb. Germany without sun seemed all of a sudden as dreary as an unending Dostoyevsky novel.

'You don't say much,' she spoke up.

'No?'

'That's very English,' she added.

'What's "very English"?'

'Asking a question to avoid giving an answer.'

'What answer were you looking for?' – I didn't bother to point out that I was not English, only American.

She tried another tack. 'Why do you not like me? Is it because I took him away? But you aren't in love with him too, are you?'

Why is it that some women when insecure have to hit below the belt? 'Come on,' I said. 'I have to take you now or we'll be snowed in.'

'Does this frighten you?'

I stared at the spikes of punk hair that made a thirty-five year old look slightly ridiculous. 'What I can't abide,' I answered, 'is that he's given up his art. Sold out for ruddy crass, commercial airbrushing.'

Now she was offended. 'I do the airbrushing,' she corrected.

'I gathered.'

'And it happens' (she threw her wine back) 'that what we have is two artists, not one. A collaboration, not the old, dangerous individualism that led to arrogance and fascism. This is art for the people:

popular art. Oliver and I are like Paul and Linda McCartney.'

If I'd had as much psychological insight as she pretended to with Carine, or at least the bad taste to express my prejudices openly, I might've challenged her then. There was something as inevitable as waste passing through the body in the way she evoked a mild sadism in me. Was that what had been in Oliver's mind when he'd made that comment about his cock? not just her handsomeness or some secret about her sex, but a sadistic possession? It would fit in: the lurid, dark, porny paintings; the half penitent way he was violating his potential. So having played sadist with Carine, if Gisela's tale were true, was he now playing masochist to her successor? Was that why he could say 'It was good for me' when his jacket had been slashed and she could comment 'I saved Oliver' when all she had done was to become an instrument of his self-exploitation?

'Come on,' I said standing, flipping out car-keys.

'You are not a nice host,' she commented, fairly enough.

'I'm sorry. What I'm trying to do,' I added insincerely, 'is to get you home safely before it's too late.'

'Why should you worry? You don't like me.'

'I like Ollie.'

'All the more reason, since you think I'm bad for him.'

She had me there. 'You win,' I concluded, giving her a smile – at least making a stab at it.

She looked me down with the cool, ice-blue eyes of a beautiful woman who knows how to use the ultimate weapon of sex once her limited resources of charm, wit and kindness have failed.

The BMW could not get up the driveway. It had no snow-tires or chains, being too new to have lived through a Bavarian winter, and had to make it up a 25% slope and do a 90° turn to get onto the one-lane road which led to the highway. This proved impossible: the drive could be mastered with a rolling start from the garage, the turn could not. Ice had formed under fast-gathering snow, and a sudden spin sent the rear-end careering into a drift.

'These cars are notorious,' Gisela remarked. 'They cost 75,000 marks and cannot manage. You should have bought a Mercedes.'

I didn't point out that I had bought nothing, nor that as a regionalist-nationalist she was being disloyal to one of her region's most successful products. I just go out of the car and discovered that my friends' left rear tail-light was cracked, the fender-finish scratched and license-plate knocked off. Cursing under my breath, I tried to drive free of the drift, the Prelude to *Parsifal* playing solemnly on a cassette as wheels spun. But it was no use. We just dug in deeper as snow blanketed down, heavily, blindingly.

'It's hopeless,' I said. 'We'll have to walk.'

This sounded elementary: Possenhofen S-bahn station was only a quarter-mile away, out the one-lane road and up hill. My chief worry was about leaving the BMW blocking the drive and not finding our way to the station or, worse, getting lost. But this was naïve, and Gisela knew it: 'You are quite brave,' she mused. 'Perhaps we can get there, but if this keeps up, I pity you trying to find your way back.'

Ridiculous, I thought. City-boy that I was, the idea of being under the will of the elements seemed the stuff of old movies. I had taken shelter from monsoons and tropical rainstorms, 120° heat and even once a flash flood; but despite travels, I'd never encountered disaster and no longer really believed in a world that our ancestors wrote about – great white whales, avalanches in the Klondike and so on. That sort of thing belonged to the evening news: apparent fictions like the memory of World War II, or Israeli invasion of Beirut.

Gisela, however, being native, knew whereof she spoke. It took us an hour to find the station. Crossing the highway, we had to step out of the way of a car driving backwards, slowly inscribing circles as it found it impossible to brake, even going at five miles an hour. No sound came from anywhere except a whisper of snow as it blanketed, blanketed, blanketed a freezing world. The station was deserted; train tracks, though heated against this sort of weather, were covered in drifts. Would there be more trains? Gisela doubted it. I insisted on calling the head-stop, Tutzing, to find out. But as you might have predicted, the phone in the call-box was dead.

'I shan't be able to ring Magdalena,' she fretted, making no mention of Ollie, although by this stage I wasn't surprised by that.

'We should wait a while at least – a train may come.'

'To take one only as far as Starnberg or a few stops down the line? And then what? neither here not there. I should think there is a more obvious solution.'

Of course she was right. Not a soul animated Possenhofen station. Not another soul inhabited this world, so far as you could see. Snow came down calmly, relentless, unaggressive. It didn't seem like death, more like comfort – maternal comfort, Nature laying on its duvet – except that it was cold, deadly cold to the bone.

I felt my skeleton freezing. 'All right,' I conceded.

'We start back?'

'Yes.'

The drifts, even on the main road, were now up to our knees. 'Do you mind if I hold onto your arm?' one of us said to the other. There was no choice: we needed mutual aid. And once we had fought our way back to the warmth of the Schloss, drenched, frozen, scared and shivering, there was little ceremony in how we stripped off sopping clothes; embraced; hung on one another pathetically like animals, making love; slept and dragged ourselves into a hot tub over the mercifully civilized heated tiles of that oddly American bathroom floor.

'What about Oliver?' she asked.

'Well,' I began…

My friends' enormous double-bed was covered in white duvets and bolsters; it looked towards a wall of sliding mirrored doors, behind which were shelves and hanging closets. The shades on the bed-lamps were peach; the mirrors gave back a golden glow in which her body (mine too for that matter) looked more blessed than seemed possible in the flesh. This, I recall, is an important part of the unreality of what happened. In due course she must have described it to Ollie, because there exists a painting, stuffed away in Margot Wingfield's attic, which seems to depict just what we seemed to become on those two, hermetically-sealed-in days.

'Does he have to know?' – I felt surprisingly guilty, a response having more to do with Carine and the fact that I didn't like Gisela really than any sense of having violated him.

'That's not what I meant.' – Her body was warm and pliable under my arm, her hand not content to stop stroking. 'Of course he must know. Magdalena will tell him. I had to stay somewhere, and I don't lie to my daughter. What I meant was, what shall I do with him?'

The painting would come from his renaissance: a phase which, ironically, our betrayal of him may have helped provoke. Clean, clear, Hopperish lines would characterize it. In the left foreground of a large rectangular canvas, he would place himself, arms over chest: a much franker, more realistic version of his persona than ever, wearing a fur jacket with snow behind him leading to a series of mirrored images of her and me fanning out from centre to right of the frame. We looked like modern bourgeois gods as we sat upright in bed admiring ourselves in a mirror, the mirror in turn reflecting us back kissing, the mirror within that reflecting us back grappling, the mirror within that reflecting an image of bodies in intercourse, the mirror within that reflecting a ball of sexual energy of a Francis Bacon type, the mirror within that showing this ball becoming abstractly swan-shaped. This shape, at last, would attach to a hyper-realist emblem of a swan on Starnberg waters appended to the upper right-hand corner of the canvas like a stamp. 'Postcard to Carine', he would call it, more out of self-chastisement than bitterness, irony than cruelty. But these qualities had become mixed in him by then, I would realize from my time with his German mistress.

'What do you mean, what'll you do with him?'

'You are right, I don't love him,' she admitted, climbing back on me. 'He would never have wanted me if I had.'

'I don't get it.' – Her body out of clothes, it emerged, was as firm as a statue of Juno, though not so cold.

'I have been a phase he was going through. If he stays, I exploit him, as I know he's been using me. This is not right. I must help him on to the next phase. It is only a question of how.'

'I'm getting a little bored with worrying about his career,' I concluded. '*Ist klar?*"

She was extraordinary sexually. There was no longer any question about what he had meant about a man and his cock, nor any doubt about where those *Star Wars* bastardizations of his early work had come from. The imagery seemed to flash from her – body, hair, motion – especially in the mirrored light. It was not Scotland, Chiswick House or an ascetic bed-sit in Hammersmith here; it was Vulcan, or Castalia.

'You mean you enjoy making sex with his girlfriend?' she teased.

I didn't answer. Body and fate were doing that for me. Spirit was elsewhere. And by the time I got back to London the next week, I'd decided that my life as a wandering writer was over and I had to marry Carine.

4.

Oliver went to Italy. Gisela took him. Magdalena went with them, though she protested that she would've preferred to stay in Munich with her Dad. Maybe the girl sensed that she was going to be rushed into adulthood and wanted to prolong an age of innocence a bit longer, snuggling up a last time to a man she'd never had enough of, as she complained. But Gisela was not about to leave the only person on earth who *had* to love her in the hands of someone that person could love better. Gisela may also have come to a subconscious conclusion that there was an advantage in letting her lover be the one to take her daughter's virginity.

This and other aspects of the case you could only speculate on. Later I would hear Gisela's version of it, then Ollie's, the one florid, the other wry. Meanwhile, it was spring; snows were thawing as they came down the south slope of the Alps, and a splendour such as has touched the European soul at least since Byron wrote *Childe Harold* captivated them. Magdalena, contrary, claimed that the valleys looked like bad paintings; Oliver chuckled, Gisela chastised. Bad or breathtaking, they looked like paintings; and it was from this time that he started to harbour his passion to find the perfect earthly landscape in which to make love and art.

'I had this dream,' he would tell me later, 'of a town on a promontory overlooking a river. The town is built up just where the river turns; in the hollow of its bend is a shingle beach, on the bank opposite bank a profusion of trees. Several villas are tucked away looking back at the town but completely off on their own. In my dream, it is lateish: a summer afternoon, quite hot. Most of the town has gone down to the beach to enjoy a last hour of sun. Light breeze comes round the bend over the trees on the far bank… This is the paradise I've gone looking for: town, happy people, river, trees, sun. One of the villas I make over into a studio: an uninterrupted space of gallery with plate-glass windows overlooking the scene, catching each alteration of light under the sound of the leaves.'

Gisela, not illogically, had retorted: 'You're going to have to have some great success to afford that.' To which Oliver had apparently shrugged, before urging them on past Lago di Garda and into the upper Veneto, searching.

What Magdalena thought is not reported, though clearly she

was essential to his renaissance in this phase: his most vivid, straightforward portraits of her date from then. Gisela might take credit for it too: she allowed, even encouraged, what happened between them, restraining herself – that is, her inevitable jealousy at watching her daughter supplant her as his object of beauty. (It was not just of sex, Ollie would maintain). Gisela may also have been jealous of his real ability to compose a picture, which showed up her own pretensions via airbrushing, though Gisela herself was relaxing into a sort of wisdom by this stage.

I too might take some credit for Ollie's renaissance. Hadn't I been the one who had prompted her to release him from the thraldom to semi-porn she had led him into?

I comforted myself with this thought. Marriage, meanwhile, was changing my life. I don't want to say anything against Carine or the Bleisteins and Slomans: never have I been treated with more sweetness, nor do I expect to be again. But something in Gisela's account of Ollie's fate with the Family must have had a metaphoric accuracy. A certain muffling lurked, and neurosis, and problematic relations to great fortune and hard politics.

These I don't, and didn't, want to go into. I myself had determined to become a 'mind so fine that it could not be violated by an idea'. But though I loved Carine as a person, I was not, finally, in lust with her. Nor did dwelling in the bosom of the Family come without its avocational cost.

'I'm disappointed in you,' Margot Wingfield said when I told her I'd started that novel only to give it up. 'But I'm hardly surprised. Men of your type are too free of ambition to be a success. That's part of what makes you attractive.'

Margot hadn't changed as much as her reputation might have led you to think. Neither too stout yet nor otherwise marked as a middle-aged matron with six offspring, she still looked about forty – in fact, anywhere between thirty-five and fifty: you could hardly tell through the carefully-calculated frosting of hair, make-up and bodices which in another era might've been corsets and stays. What was her secret? Surely not Godfrey, who barked, ignored and appeared to carry on in the clubbable Englishman's productive ignorance. Did she have a new young man? There were rumours. But confronted with them, she would not illogically say:

'My agency's done it. I've had amazing success; it sustains me. I can't think how I deserve it, but there we are. Artists go starving while philistines like me go to all the parties and are interviewed for Breakfast TV.'

We were sitting in her new office. Fresh from my honeymoon in the Maldives, I felt tanned and cosseted and not too much of a middle-class hippy anymore for her grandeur, such as it was. Her new office was in their new house in Ladbroke Grove, the posh part. In addition to her success, Godfrey had 'gone from strength to strength at the bank'; so they could afford what she had long aspired to, a move up from 'tatty' Shepherd's Bush.

'I always found it downmarket though it wouldn't've done to have said so. Of course nowadays a lot of impecunious aristos have moved in; but there're still all those unhappy black men and refugees of the '60s wandering about, wishing they could rise to the level of selling knick-knacks down Portobello Road.'

I thought of Oliver in Heidhausen. His water-colours still hung in a position of state on her walls, despite the walls belonging to this imposing new venue.

'It would never've done for the children to've stayed there. Did you know I had two more? The youngest is just three. Him I could not have toddling about in the street picking up dirty needles and God-knows. Other women with fewer may have more time to look after them, but I have a business to run.'

One of her authors had just been nominated for the Righter Prize, she told me. Another had been short-listed for the Compton Mackenzie Award.

'I'm thinking of writing a novel myself,' she added, 'under pseudonym, of course. What are you going to do now that you've put away the pen?'

'Well,' I began –

'You aren't going to just live off wifey, are you? A good-looking man might seem to have that option, but she'll get bored and make life miserable for you if you try.'

'Don't you think married life can turn out happily for anyone?'

'Marriage or no marriage, relationships are tortuous long-term. I don't know anyone who's worked it out, no. If you tell me you have, you're either lying or young and naïve. If it's not sex that's the problem, it's economics. Fortune has blessed Godfrey and me in that respect. Otherwise…'

This was left dangling, not to be talked about, at least not overtly. The implication was that Godfrey was jealous of his wife's success and cross about having so many mouths to feed.

'It could be worse,' she defended against this phantom barb. 'There are women in my position who demand a house in the country as well as in town and private schools for all the children. I only send the little ones privately, to church schools, which cost peanuts. I use just one nanny and don't drive, so I'm hardly uneconomical to run. When one thinks of some of the debs dear God might've got stuck with…'

There was a subtext here, but the Wingfield marriage was not my business nor the point of my story, at least not then. Plenty of women writers were novelizing about such things. Besides, my principal reaction was to thank the stars that I'd come to grief with my married Sloane years before and ended up with someone as sweet as Carine.

''nother cup?' Margot asked; then – 'What about Oliver?'

'I was waiting for you to get around to that.'

'Of course you were, but you didn't want me to just rush into it without letting you imagine I was interested in you. Thingie – Carine – your wife, for godsake – lived with him two years, didn't she?'

'He with her.'

'Point taken. What happened?'

I told her one or two things – certainly no saga like Gisela's.

'Does she still love him?' Margot mused, cutting as close to the bone as she could. 'Sorry,' she added as if just realizing.

'No bother. Do you?'

'Do I what?'

'Still love him.'

Now she looked to her garden, which was three times as large as the one in Shepherd's Bush, though not as lush, it being April. 'You can't afford to be indiscreet,' she chided. 'I know something about your past too, remember.'

'But a man with a past isn't the same as a woman with one,' I quipped, recycling one of her old purloined lines.

'Men are expected to have pasts and forget about them; women are meant to remember and pretend they do not.'

I chuckled. 'If we're not careful, Margot, we're going to end up sounding dated.'

'But darling, we're stalling – at least I am.'

'He was in Italy the last I heard.'

'Making the Grand Tour, eh? Rather extravagant for someone who can't have a bean.'

I told her about Gisela, though not Magdalena, whom I didn't know about – or all about – then.

'Sounds perfectly hideous. What's the attraction? Sex? Or is he really just desperately low.'

That was difficult to say. In some ways, I felt Oliver was higher than the rest of us even then, on account of his footlooseness. At any rate, his potential was still all before him.

'I don't think he's low as such; only turning.'

'Turning?' she queried.

'Into himself.'

'Ah. So you are in contact with him, are you?'

'Could be.'

'Well do us a favour and find out a bit more. After all, you need something to occupy you now you've taken this Machiavellian turn.'

'Machiavellian turn?'

'Deciding to be a kept man.'

I could endure her light chidings. There was a touch of gall behind the bright veneer, the source of which is facile to speculate on – a traditional upper-middle class English wife's complaint against a husband who gives status, money and babies but precious little interest otherwise? Godfrey was frequently off on business, you heard; and if not cheating on him, Margot was surely asking herself why she was sitting on the sidelines while Time cantered on. Is this all there is, she must've wondered, like all of us do. Now that I'd planted the seed, she may've even started dreaming up an image of Ollie out on some Apennine slope, standing in front of an easel with a naked young female beside and bottle of Chianti in hand.

Carine and I, meanwhile, gave dinner parties. My sweetheart gurgled and drank and produced lovely meals, of which she ate hardly a bite. Guests stayed late, seeming to enjoy our coffee and brandy, which were the best, even if conversation sometimes seemed a bit stale. This was married life from the inside. Carine worked hard at it, and I tried. We went to bed in the wee hours, forgot about making babies and staggered up in the mornings to separate lives.

It was not an intolerable condition. Compared with Margot and

Godfrey, Gisela, Oskar and the rest, I think we had it quite good. What was not there in passion was made up for in affection, which is more durable, they say. I'd had beastly passion and knew it was often allied to doctrinaire bolshiness on the part of one party, so that cohabitation wasn't so much a sharing of duties as one person performing all. This was not the problem with Carine: she was an entirely traditional wife; I can't count the items she bought to make the flat as I liked, satisfy my permanent hunger or irrepressible dyspepsia and entertain us of an evening. So why dwell on little incompatibilities?

Daytimes she devoted to the perpetual 'chaos' in her office. Meanwhile, from home I talked to Uncle Harold on the phone about a quiet property deal he wanted me to help with.

Not a Bleistein or Sloman, I didn't qualify as a member of the Family *bund*; but Harold liked Carine so much that he took a shine to me; and since his own son was under suspicion of Jewish fireworks to some warehouses in the East End, which the Family had bought to sell to a Docklands development group, he needed a surrogate. Harold knew that I wanted to feel flush in my own right and that, besides, it was always useful for the Family to have an ally or two who could seem to be out of the loop.

If this hints at a side-plot, I will go into it no further than to say that it offered me a status somewhat superior to the 'kept' one apparent to Margot and Co. It also provided an opportunity to slip into art-dealing by the back door – a profession which, despite my interest in Oliver's painting, I'd never thought of for myself. But then a Dover Street gallery approached Harold to see if it could buy his George Sloam: a biography was shortly to come out about her/him, and nostalgia for gay life in the interwar period was likely to produce a revival of interest.

'Why don't you deal with this,' Harold suggested. 'On no account let 'em know we have three more hanging in the Members' Room in Montague Square. Get 'em to make an offer.'

This was the first I'd heard of the three further Sloams. It was typical of the Family only to let the other shoe drop gradually; it kept you intrigued and reminded me of certain negotiating techniques of Margot's which she contended were 'the secret to all success'. So I played along with the gallery, whose new owner turned out to be a wizened Simon Lewes, that ageing public schoolboy I'd met at the Wingfield's on the same Sunday I'd met Oliver for the first time. He and Ollie had hardly got on then, I recalled, despite Margot's little plot, and now I realized why: they had about as much in common as the acting methods of Stanislavsky and Coquelin.

Nothing of the kind inhibited me. Realizing what was called for, I fielded Lewes's first offer with dithering and *double-entendre*, which frustrated him enough to make a second, which I met with more of the same. This annoyed him so much that we arrived at a price Uncle Harold was pleased with and closed a deal, providing me with a nice fee. After that, Harold and I began plotting how and when we might slip the other Sloams onto the market.

I rather liked this sort of thing, I discovered – not least the money. I even began to wonder how I'd managed to live up till then in such relative straightness. Meanwhile, the Sloam gambit got me thinking about those paintings of Ollie's stuffed in Carine's spare room.

'You think he'd appreciate me trying to sell them?' I asked her one rainy Sunday afternoon as we were immersed in a marathon of black-and-white films on TV.

'Who?'

'Oliver, of course?'

'Sell what?'

'His paintings.'

The film of the moment was a version of Somerset Maugham's fantasia on the life of Gauguin. My darling was fixed on it and not eager to let conversation break through a gentle haze of hashish.

'You can't do that without asking him,' she coughed.

'He's not exactly easy to get a hold of in Sicily or wherever he's got to by now. Though I suppose I could call Munich.'

She showed no resentment of the German allusion, as she might have in the past. We'd reached a stage in relations when grounds for suspicion seem almost too remote. Carine was too trustworthy not to trust me, just as I was too promiscuous not to wonder if her lack of concern masked something I should worry about.

'Why should anyone in Munich still know where he was?'

'Gisela's ex must.'

'I didn't know you knew him really.'

'Who?'

'Her ex, of course.'

'I don't really. And I'd rather not call.'

I failed to mention that this was because I already knew, having received a postcard, that Gisela herself was back in Munich. There had been dramas in Italy, and she would not be uneager to see me.

'The paintings are technically yours, aren't they?' I pursued.

My darling was hunkered down in a duckling-yellow jumpsuit, smoking ciggies and sipping port. Engrossed in a vicarious sea-voyage to Tahiti, she was the portrait of a lady on furlough from unnecessary effort to impress her man.

'Sorry?' she murmured.

We were devoted to each other, of course. But since we were married, devotion had become just a new pretext for being laid-back.

'His paintings. Technically they're yours, aren't they?'

'Technically,' she confirmed. 'Morally's another question.'

Carine was too 'nicsch' to consider capitalising on an ex-lover, even if he'd lived off of her, cheated on her and ultimately gone his way; and knowing she'd be appalled to discover how my mind was tending, I dropped the subject and simply lay there watching her watch Hollywood give its version of *la vie bohème.* I did adore her, I realized, worrying about her cough. But the irony of love – at least of the kind that I had for Carine – is that the more you say to yourself 'My God, I love her!', the more another part of your psyche seems to answer, 'Yes, but…'; and the 'but' in this instance, mixing with Polynesian maidens and easels under palm fronds, had to do with flying loose from a trap – from rain-sodden London and hunkered-down domesticity. It had to do with an image of him greeting the dawn on some Mediterranean beach, poor but happy, painting Magdalena in bed: Magdalena the lovely, now pregnant as if by a god. It had to do with bursting out with the full vitality of Pan; ripping clothes off and, like Tyrone Power or whoever that actor was in the film, taking a plunge in a crystalline sea…

'Have you ever thought of selling Ollie's water-colours?' I asked Margot the next chance that took me to Ladbroke Grove.

The most efficient literary agent in town (her description) was done up in high heels and a puff-sleeved blouse with a Thatcher bow despite the fact that she had no earthly reason that morning to get closer to any non-family member than the end of a phone.

'You must be joking. It's all that's left of him here, unless your wife has something we don't know about. When're you going to invite me to dinner?… No, I wouldn't sell them. Who'd buy them anyhow?"

'I might.'

I supposed she was dressed up on the off-chance that someone like me might drop by. Or was it someone in specific?

'You? That just confirms my suspicion. They'll be worth a bundle one day.'

'You think I'm so prescient?'

'I think you're showing distinct signs of becoming a shark. And that means something, coming from me.'

'Takes one to know one?'

'It would take,' Margot opined, 'a great deal of push to make Oliver a name sufficient for me to even recoup my investment on these.' She gazed at her water-colours. 'But I suppose it could be done.'

I didn't let on that that was exactly what I was hoping she'd say.

'Promotion's dead easy if you've got the goods. And Oliver's got 'em. Always has had.'

'Isn't that why you were interested in him in the first place?'

'One's motives alter with one's experience. Whatever I saw in him then, if he became successful, the world would imagine I'd been after his star-quality all along.'

'That wouldn't be bad for your reputation, would it?'

She looked to her garden. 'You've grown rather hard. It's attractive, up to a point. But I don't let it get out of hand.'

Margot ever liked playing guru. Her profession was to be a mentor, after all. A subtle mix of self-interest with genuine fellow-feeling was what this entailed. Civilization *chez elle* appeared a product of success over ease, maintenance over being, form over content. Ironically, the appearance is part of what made her compelling: because concentration on superficials seemed to have forced her to neglect the essentials inside. A whiff of pathos hid some private sorrow that she'd be damned if she were going to show.

'Comes of good family, went to a good school, did a romantic apprenticeship…' She made the pitch. 'Career abroad's promising so far as we know: kinkiness in Germany, which everyone expects to be kinky, if it's not a bore; love and struggle in Italy. It's positively Byronic or Shelleyan, or something. Biographers will have a romp.'

'Would you handle him?' I asked, trying to disguise my real interest, 'if I could find him, or at least put a hand on some of his work?'

She studied me now, too subtle to miss a beat. 'Wifey *does* have something you aren't telling me about. What is it? that oil-painting of me he started at Brook Green? You can't possibly make that public.'

'It won't,' I assured her.

She looked to her garden again without betraying emotion. 'I'm a literary agent. But I suppose PR about an artist's not beyond me. Much easier if you'd just write a book about his career – I could push it no problem – possibly even get you a grant.'

'I don't need a grant, thanks. Anyhow I was serious about giving up writing. I don't have the sense of the ridiculous for it in this country; besides, it's too much like hard work. No, Margot, my idea was maybe to open a gallery; become an agent like you, only a painters' one.'

She smiled as if with genuine satisfaction. 'It's one of the things I love about London: the endless ways people change. Yes, do it: why not? Rather like me going from agent to novelist, which I'm bound to do; it just needs a jolt, like walking out the door and letting Godfrey worry about his own bacon-and-eggs. Of course I'd help. I've always been willing to promote your career. As for Ollie – when are you going to get a move on and find out what's up with him? He must have new work: I'm dying to see it. You and I might even be able to buy one or two to keep him going – isn't that the idea?'

I couldn't make out if she'd fallen in with me or was just playing along to see how far I might go to exploit the efforts of someone she'd loved, or appeared to. The answer lay in this last proposition: had she loved him really, or had it been just sex, interest in youth and dalliance in fantasies of his potential? Maybe she herself didn't know. Maybe she never had known. Either way, I was willing to take a risk on her motives. For her part, she had every reason to keep me sweet, I concluded, so long as she wanted him back in her life – even if only to profit on.

That was the prelude to our little plot. Gisela fell in with it unwittingly. It's amazing the mixture of love, jealousy and self-interest that goes into the making of a career.

I went to Munich, ostensibly on business – 60%, if truth were told. Gisela met me at the airport, and we rode the U-bahn to town. 'Why waste money on that?' she said when I suggested renting a car. – She did not know of my marriage, and I saw no point in flaunting it. She'd had a bitter few months, it seemed.

'We'll go to the Englische Gardens if it's sunny,' she announced. 'They all lie around without clothes. You'll like that.'

She was trying to be sexy. Before, in our snowstorm, she hadn't had to try; but half a year can be half a life at a critical age, and Gisela had reached it. She'd turned from thirty-five-looking-thirty to thirty-five-looking-forty in one-sixth of the time it had taken Margot to stand still. Lines I'd never noticed ran down the edges of her mouth; the mouth itself seemed tightened, with little cracks of suppression around it. The eyes seemed smaller, less blue, less potent and insightful. The body beyond clothes might not've altered; but now she wore shorts (it was meant to be high summer, though you couldn't tell through the rain) and these showed something I hadn't remembered from winter or bed – her ankles were beginning to expand and lose shape in the way of a peasant matron's.

Oddly, it made me feel for her. Like Carine with her tiny chest and alarming cough, Gisela with imperfections was more moving than any paragon of success and beauty. But for this kind of feeling to be sustained, loss of physical attraction has to be matched by a rise in spiritual sympathy; that's what had happened with Carine, though no doubt my darling had always been less than a paragon physically. Gisela, once handsome, suffered more with her loss; but she hadn't suffered enough to come through to the other side, as it were – which may be part of the reason she couldn't resist laying blame:

'He has turned into a demon,' she declared of Oliver once we'd arrived at her flat, got down to the business of making sex and – that finished – began to talk.

'Sounds lurid,' I mused.

The sex, which had been animal in Starnberg, was manic now: sour with compensatory need. I disliked it and disliked the 40% of myself which had come to Munich for it. I was cheating on Carine; Carine doubtless knew, at least subconsciously; and except as a confirmation of the good sense of our marriage, it hadn't been worth the price of a ticket.

'He has bewitched my daughter,' Gisela went on.

The turn-of-phrase made me smirk. 'Has living in Italy made him to take up sorcery?'

'He doesn't need to.' – She shifted from me and gazed at the sky of a dull afternoon. 'I made the first mistake; I must blame myself. But he has taken it too far.'

Rolling onto my side, I put an arm around her – must be sympathetic even if you don't fancy her anymore. Besides, what she was relating was the practical part of what I had come for...

It was in the Mugello where she had consented to let him start painting Magdalena in the nude. The girl had wanted this, knowing it would annoy *Mutti*; Magdalena of course also wanted Oliver to prefer her sexually. At first he showed no sign of being interested in anything but painting. A nude by a farmhouse in European Wyeth style was the first large composition he'd started since London, and it was crucial for him to succeed. Gisela, sensing this and borne down by the blame I'd laid on her for having vulgarized his talent, took up the role of wife-mistress as servant.

She paid; bought their food; went to Bologna to get paint, canvases, sketchbooks, brushes – all he could need. She cosseted Magdalena to make her sit still for hours, under which régime the work progressed. They went on to Ravenna, and she did not make a fuss when Oliver stopped paying attention to her in bed. Putting it down to concentration on his painting, she reminded herself that, since money was low, success had become a necessity as well as hope.

In the room they had taken, he placed Magdalena by a window as per the myth of the Danaë. Afternoon light streamed through open curtains to fall on her body from the thigh up where she lay, sheet peeled back. During these sittings, Gisela must have realized that something was going to happen. Under the gaze of the artist at work, the girl visibly softened: she stopped complaining about being bored and dismissing ancient buildings as 'a bad film set'; she gave up talking about living with her father and even refrained from treating *Mutti* with alternate curses and narcoleptic stares.

In short, Magdalena grew content. Ollie did too; and Gisela, controlling the practical side of arrangements, had, in a sense, all she wanted – child, lover, power, creation (at least vicariously) and respect. So she rationalized, though in fact what she had was reality, not an inner core: a superficial relation to a situation she had created but had a diminishing place in. Ollie gazed at Magdalena. Magdalena stared back. In the trance-like connection between artist and model, the outer world vanished, and Gisela with it. That is why daughter became polite to mother: the girl had ceased to register *Mutti* at all. Oliver likewise seemed to have gone elsewhere. It was only a matter of time before the predictable occurred.

Gisela went out afternoons during sittings. She wandered the markets to buy evening meals; sat in a café, read a book. She too might write a novel one day, she fantasized, recalling my 'sense of purpose' in Starnberg. Then worry about money hustled her back to check on the progress of painting… and there she found the two of them as she'd half anticipated, though not hoped.

'All right, this is enough! I shall go back to Munich with these.' – She snatched the Danaë down from the easel though, as Ollie objected, it was only half-done. 'Magdalena, you're coming.'

'No I'm not.'

'Don't give me your cheek, girl.'

'I'm staying here.'

'No you're not. Don't be silly.'

'Yes I am. Oliver and I are in love.'

'In love?!' mother mocked.

Yes, daughter insisted. But Oliver was not capable of love, Gisela scoffed. Magdalena, in tears, asked him to confirm that he was. Oliver, who had whispered more than a few sweet-nothings into a pretty ear, murmured that the girl be allowed to do as she liked.

'You are absurd,' mama retorted in high dudgeon. 'She's below age, and you don't have any money. What do you propose? To send her out in the streets while you paint? Wait till Oskar hears!'

Words became heated. Gisela slapped Magdalena; Oliver slapped Gisela. Tears exploded.

'At least let me finish this canvas,' he concluded that night after the weeping teenager had gone to bed and mama and he got drunk on a gallon of *vin ordinaire*.

That made some sense. 'For a week we stay on,' she relented. 'In the meantime, I stay in the apartment while you paint.'

This formula proved both practical and naïve. The painting was completed, but every night there were rows. In order to make sure that Ollie didn't stray from his sofa into the girl's bed, Gisela had to stay up till dawn. By the third morning when she dozed off, they were at it again. Whatever her real attraction to Ollie, Magdalena could not resist the chance to outwit her suppressive *Mutti*; and Oliver himself was by now if not 'in love', at least irrevocably in lust.

'What is it with you?' she demanded, once this saga was finished. 'Have I become so old and unattractive in six months?' (We were in bed still.) 'You fancied me then. You liked it when I did this, and this. You even begged me to allow you to do this to me.'

It was true. She had had me screaming at the moon in Starnberg. But as is often the case with people you go mad about sexually but don't love, her effect now was at best neutralizing. What had looked marvellous, tasted delicious, smelled like – well, never mind. What had once been so overpowering had become unnerving; and a sad sympathy was all that made me go on, disliking myself for it and pledging myself to be true to Carine forevermore.

'Ach!' the sex-goddess muttered, 'forget it!' And throwing on an oversized man's shirt (Oskar's, I assumed), she got out of bed, crossed the room, lit a cigarette, put on a Bessie Smith tape and sat looking out the window at the onion-domes of the Frauenkirche. 'Men,' she concluded, 'are demons.'

There was little point in trying to contradict this: I had done my best. Life was simply dealing her a dud hand, as it does all of us at its promiscuous whim.

'I called Oskar when I arrived back,' she went on after a time. 'Do you know what he said? Oskar may be an intellectual, but he's a fool. He said, "Perhaps this kind of relationship is the best way to begin for a young girl." Men!' she repeated. 'He is chasing a twenty-year-old himself. And Oskar is fifty!'

I refrained from pointing out that that would make Oskar exactly the age in relation to her that Oliver was to Magdalena. Nor as Gisela went on about fears of the girl getting pregnant, did I note that a child born of their liaison would be born to parents almost exactly the age that Gisela and Oskar had been when Magdalena had arrived.

Maybe she was thinking along similar lines. 'Oskar and I ran off in the '60s,' she mused. 'But we were in love then. My parents were beastly. He was a wild, handsome man whom everyone admired: radical, idealistic, full of appetite – a hero who squandered his talents, as he still does. But Oliver – this is different. He has no views; he just listens, and takes. Mankind is not his problem; he thinks only of himself, and sex and art. And Magdalena – she goes with him only to get at me. She is too young besides. She will be ruined! He'll leave her for some rich woman, I've warned her. So what, she tells me. Ach, teenagers these days! they are so without respect. It is all your American influence – movies made by Jews.'

A mother's lament can be forgiven, I guess. Whether or not, she now burst into tears. So I went over and sat beside her.

'Put some clothes on!' she chided, pushing me away. 'You can't be by the window like that. The people in those offices in those skyscrapers might see you.'

They would've needed binoculars. Nor were what she referred to as skyscrapers more than six storeys tall. Besides, who in German cities in summer has ever been abashed by little nudity?

'In that cupboard – yes, over there. You'll find one of Oliver's dressing-gowns. It should fit.'

I did as told. And in the cupboard in question, sealed in a tall, thin cardboard pack, were his new paintings.

I realized this on the instant. 'May I?' I asked.

Wiping her eyes, she let out a sigh, perhaps in admission that she had little illusion about what 60% of me had come to Munich for. 'You may as well. I have shown them to Oskar who says they are very good. His best yet.'

The package was slit at the top. There were three canvases in it. Pulling them out one by one, I studied each.

'Oskar says these are Fantastic Realism,' she sniffed. 'He says they satisfy all the rules that high thinkers have been laying down for a Neo-Classical Renaissance. There is no accidental abstraction here; it is an orderly world; distraction only exists in Magdalena's eye. There we see nothing, mixed with anger and indifference. God is absent; a vacant space in the centre. Oskar has quoted a great Irish poet of your land: "Things fall apart; the centre cannot hold." That was the motto of Modernism, he says; but in Oliver's work, it is not that discredited era anymore. "Things fall together; there is no centre, only connections" is how Oskar explains it.'

Wasn't she wonderful? Though tearful and bitter, she hadn't lost a jot of admiration for her ex-lover/betrayer. As a matter of fact, where she'd once been willing to exploit his art, she now felt chastened by it; so that in support for the work, if fury at the man, she performed a volte-face – a form of penance, I thought, and was for her again.

The first painting showed Magdalena in the nude but covered in part by a shawl, looking directly ahead from the right quarter of the canvas, leaning against a barn under cloud-scudded sky. Here were Balthus, Wyeth and recollections of recent figurative tradition; but in treatment, the girl – her virginal roundness – had a resonance of Italian masters as well. The title might have been 'Madonna Waiting for an Annunciation'.

The second painting, the Danaë, was more frankly sexual. The figure spread back on bed took up half the space, not a quarter, her gaze now partly inward, more satisfied, less manically searching beyond for some force to approach her. The force was immanent now; the model could seize it in motes of light streaming through the window. No shawl obscured her: the young female shape was all visible, its sex tidy, unbroken, waiting softly between her thighs.

In the third painting – startling, coy yet exuberant in its frankness – the girl sat on a chair illuminated from above by a triangular spread of lamplight. Her hair was down, her eyes half-lidded, her lips parted in a sensual smile, full of calm enticement yet without pornography. She was gazing at you, the viewer, as if lover. Her nipples were erect, her breasts small, symmetrical domes. Her legs were parted and sex opened slightly, the petals ever so gently peeled back as it were. On the table beside her a slim, white vase held a violet snapdragon.

'You must sell them,' I murmured.

'Of course. But I only know a vulgar market here, as you know. And I don't have the heart to airbrush these.'

Thank God for that, I thought. 'I'll arrange it,' I said.

'You?!' she derided.

'Yes. I know people. How much do you want?'

I called Margot from Heathrow and went straight to Holland Park in a cab. Her tone was sharp, as if I were a lover turning up at an awkward moment. What triggered this? the aura of adultery on me? all-too-clever chirpiness? Trying to suppress myself, I speculated that she must've been suffering from pre-menstrual tension or some inordinate snappiness from Godfrey.

'I'm rushed off my feet today. We must be quick. What've you got?'

'Something that might make you slow down a bit.'

'When one has six boys and a business to run, there's no slowing down. You should try it.'

'I wouldn't look good pregnant.'

'I guess not.'

I slipped the three canvases out of their package and set them against the bookcase facing her garden.

Margot was wearing a cardigan-dress: it was November in August. Squeezing forearms across her bust, she stared.

'This is first one; then this; then…' I led her through them.

She continued to stare. What on earth was going on beyond

the mascara? I glanced to his water-colours. The distance between them and this new stuff was even greater than between a bed-sit in Hammersmith and row-house in Ladbroke Grove.

'Did you buy them?' she asked.

'Of course.'

'You shouldn't have.'

'Why not?'

'They're worth their weight in gold, or some precious substance.'

This seemed obscure. 'That's why I did it. We'll make a killing. I gave his ex-mistress twenty-five hundred for the lot.'

Margot's face darkened. The last of the three canvases particularly held her. I was reminded of the day years before when she'd asked me to help get him free of her.

'What is it?' I asked.

'The snapdragon,' she murmured and walked out of the room, leaving me to ponder, non-plussed.

Dimly, the morphology of a snapdragon merged into shadowy images of lover and beloved in his Brook Green studio. The passion and angst of my old adulterous liaison came over me: fugitive scenes of love in the afternoon... Before I'd got back to the present with everything in place, Margot had reappeared.

'This beastly weather,' she said, dabbing her nose. 'Summer colds are the worst.' – Heavily, she sat.

Now I stared. She wouldn't look at me. So I sat in one of the chintz-cushioned chairs by her door.

'Why did you bring them?' she asked. 'To annoy me?'

For someone trying to be stoical, she hardly obscured the subtext. I understood all now, I thought, though naturally I acted surprised.

'Didn't we have an arrangement?'

'If you think I'm going to be a party to ripping him off for the value of his work, then you'd better think again.'

Why was she snipping at me, for Christ's sake? *I* hadn't intruded on their affair or caused whatever lack of romance was gnawing at her. 'Maybe I don't appear the most ethical person alive,' I threw back, 'but this is a bit much. Gisela can't sell the things in Munich, and Ollie – you know what he's like: *dolce far niente* in Italy and all that. He couldn't market them to save his life.'

'That's not my point.'

'What is then?'

'How you and I justify "making a killing" off them. You're probably right that we could; but I'm not bloody starving, and you… even if your wife's run through half her money and you don't have tuppence to your name, which I doubt, you're still rolling in it, relatively-speaking. Meanwhile, the artist sits there on some beach with an underage girl, penniless, painting-less. It doesn't wash.'

There was enough here to make me twitch. There was also a fair dollop of projection in it, as in most self-righteousness. Poor Margot. Not only had she lost her lover, but in a few years she'd be entering menopause, which must have seemed like an end for a woman like her. Life, as she might've quipped, loves to be cruel.

'I didn't know you had such a socialist urge,' is what I answered.

'It's not bloody socialist! But I do sit here every day trying to promote the cause of driven young men and women (some not so young) who've quit good jobs and mortgaged their lives to try to say something they're burning to say – to find out something of the spirit for mankind, if you must; or if you hate the Pseud's Corner truth, to get a laugh out of the essential despair we all have to confront. Given as much, I see my role as something other than just Mrs T's form of arrant capitalism. So unless you're prepared to view this in some other way than making a killing, I want nothing to do with it.'

In another mood I might've made the same speech myself, or something like it – which just goes to show how much the things we blurt out depend on our mood of the moment, about both ourselves and who we're talking to.

'Do you mean you expect me to take them back to Gisela for her to airbrush and massproduce as plastic table-mats?'

'Why don't you just take them home?' she concluded as if weary.

Touché. I could hardly say how reluctant I was to expose the paintings to Carine. She would have similar questions about exploiting Ollie and might even've wondered what I'd done to get them.

'I thought we had a deal,' I repeated. 'Weren't we going to team up to promote him?'

'Promotion is one thing, exploitation another.'

Again I was non-plussed. 'All right, Margot. I'll give them to you for cost and you can do with them what you like.'

This appeared generous. I didn't add that there were ten other canvases back at Carine's, not so marvellous but with the right promotion also quite marketable. Anyhow, she turned from the paintings.

'I hate them!' she hissed. – There could only've been one reason for this. 'And love them,' she added, 'once I'm able to swallow regret and jealousy. Lord, why have I allowed you such power over me?'

'*Me* power over *you*?'

'Yes. You and you alone know what this is about.'

Did I? Not really. In that moment, her motives became obscure.

'I'm not omniscient,' I argued.

'Maybe not. But you know what I mean.'

Well, maybe I did. And maybe what she meant was that we could read one another too well and that had become unacceptable.

'You don't think I'd expose you?'

'I do not know.'

'Why shouldn't you trust me?'

'Do you trust yourself entirely? Besides, what do you have to lose, being single – without children anyway. If Carine left you, you'd still be standing, if you see what I mean. I have six children: it's different. Of course I want the paintings! What would Godfrey say, though? He found out about us back then; that's why I was so keen to get rid of Ollie, the only reason. It was that or divorce – a divorce in which I, being the guilty party, stood to lose everything.'

Now my sympathies began to be engaged. 'I didn't realize.'

'Of course you didn't. No one bloody did. Do you think I wear my heart on my sleeve like some wretched girl? But Oliver knew: he was the one person. It nearly killed me to lose him. When he lived with Carine, I imagined it would be all right: at least she had money and was his own age. But the phonecalls – he was wretched: hated himself for exploiting her. He still loved me. I know it sounds preposterous, a painted old tart like I am. But love is blind, as they say; also bloody destructive. I think I've come to detest it.'

She was in a whirl now. Nor was I exactly cool myself. Neurosis is contagious – avoid at all costs. What about Carine, I was thinking: what set-up was I going to subject her to again?… I filled up with remorse. Everything turned grey.

'You keep 'em now,' I said of the paintings. 'Hide 'em from Godfrey if you have to; there must be somewhere in this house to do that. When you've decided what to do with them, tell me. I'll be governed completely by what you decide.'

With that, I went out, saying under my breath, to hell with Margot Wingfield, and longing to get back to the unprickliness of Carine.

In Holland Park Avenue, I hailed a cab, my mind full of glimmers, the kind you get on the morning after a night of too many guests, drink, smoke: a mélange of petty paranoias, hopes, crossed metaphors, realities, all overlaying instinctive trepidation and (as often as not) sexual angst. In this condition, I watched another cab turn the corner and veer into the street I'd just come out of. I thought I saw Oliver Murrie in it, hurtling purposively toward Ladbroke Grove, a large packet obscuring his moon face and rusty hair.

A delusion, I told myself as we sped on through drizzle. Shoving it and him out of mind, I concentrated on the fact that I was tired – jet-lag or something – and what I was going to say to Carine when I got home. But *what if* kept intruding: what if Margot had put on her performance to con me? what if the pictures even then were being whisked off by Ollie, into hiding not only from Godfrey but from me, and without even my outlay to Gisela being reimbursed?

No, I assured myself. Whatever the twists of Margot Wingfield's psyche, this kind of duplicity was not her. Or was it?

In Montague Square, I went straight to the spare bedroom to check on his paintings. Carine wasn't home yet and the place had descended into the kind of untidiness that had reigned before I'd moved in – glasses, full ashtrays, records strewn around as if to show that she had hardly denied herself life while I'd been on my 'business trip'. So what had she been doing, and with whom?

From the spare bedroom all his paintings were gone: all except 'Déjeuner sur les rochers'. Blood pressure rose up my neck. Going to the phone, I rewound the answer-machine. One message for me: 'Call Harold when you get in.' Another for Carine, male voice, accent mixed. The single word it uttered was, 'Thanks'.

5.

Uncle Harold said he wanted me as a fourth for bridge; but when I arrived at Serpentine House, there were already four there – two of Carine's other uncles, Nigel and Arnold, and her godfather, head of the Family fund, Lionel Sloman. This collection of late middle-aged men wore dark suits and thin-soled leather shoes without laces. There was no longer a thick head of hair between them; what remained was slicked to the skull in the manner of T.

S. Eliot. This marked them out as a generation which had come of age in the era of *The Cocktail Party*, *The Elder Statesman* and *The Confidential Clerk*. The words they spoke had a clipped, Eliotic air to them: impeccably considered, clandestine, genial.

'Delighted to see you,' purred Arnold, the eldest, smiling through new false teeth. Having had a coronary the previous winter, he did not get up from his chair.

'We've been very pleased Carine made such a good marriage,' added Lionel, who was thinner and taller, as well as younger, than his cousins. He shook my hand as if merely a friend, not the single most powerful determiner of the fate of hundreds of millions.

'When are you and Carine going to come with us to Glyndebourne?' asked Uncle Nigel, who had given a world-famous political leader her first job as a researcher into ways of making synthetic ice cream. Nigel was short, energetic and tough, I had gathered: he was the one who'd put thumbs down to Oliver after an argument about the 1984 miners' strike.

'Glyndebourne's over this year,' grumped Uncle Harold, who sat at the card table shuffling. 'Besides, why would a young man want to go hear some fat dame trying to clear her tonsils?'

'Harold's always been a philistine,' purred Arnold in faint praise.

'Do you actually enjoy opera?' Lionel asked, as if it were pertinent.

'There's a marvellous new *Faust* at the ENO,' said Nigel. 'Carine might stay awake through it. Let me know if you want tickets.'

So it went. The sound of their voices was the sound of four accomplished old actors reading a Harold Pinter play: a kind of syncopation of pause and surge, each careful not to dominate, so that after a while you felt subliminally that all were part of one whole. Of course, this being the 20th century, it would've been impossible for the quartet not to have had dissonance. Nigel and Lionel were not mates, it was clear: the one had run the largest of Family businesses and resented the fact that the other was now head of the Family fund, while the other had made the fund double in value due to the Prime Minister's help-the-rich schemes and resented his cousin for trying to catch him out on every detail of investment, however shrewd.

I knew this subtext from Harold, who had the reputation of being the most indiscreet of the lot. Arnold, who sat on a dozen charitable boards and had an OBE, was known as the most sympathetic, a quality of use in the aggregate too.

'You play with Nigel,' Harold put to me. 'Lionel can be my partner. He's still a novice.'

I looked to Arnold. 'Don't worry about me,' he smiled. 'I dislike Harold's games almost as much as Nigel's cultural beanos.' – This was delivered with such luxuriance that it might've been taken as flattery.

We sat down and played a rubber.

Harold and Nigel played as if they were negotiating the future of the West Bank. Lionel, though fifty, looked a confused boy. I became dummy twice, in which intervals Arnold winked and mimicked the expressions of others for my amusement. Suppressed hilarity lurked at some deeper level of the proceedings, though a dominant sense of purpose kept anyone from jumping up and gibbering like a monkey. What they represented seemed a cross between the Marx Brothers and the four eldest Bonaparte males: whimsy allied with steel. Beyond either radiated an aura of comfort, which must have come from the fact that they had never been plagued by material need.

'We've decided to start a small private bank,' Lionel announced, once he and Harold had lost a second rubber.

Harold vanished to get drinks.

'We don't want this to be known widely,' warned Nigel.

'Of course he understands,' Arnold smiled.

I felt as if I were being hazed into a fraternity.

'We thought,' Lionel went on, 'that, since you're part of the Family yet not, if you see what I mean, you might enjoy taking a role.'

'Not a day-to-day role,' Nigel clarified. 'That can be done by accountants.'

'You wouldn't have to do anything but what you wanted to,' Arnold said.

'That's right,' assured Lionel. 'Go to board meetings. Anything else as you chose.'

Harold came back with a decanter and glasses.

'One thing he might take an interest in is the arts,' suggested Nigel.

'What Nigel means,' Arnold explained, 'is that he doesn't want you to muck up the works. He just wants a sympathetic eye on the board.'

Harold poured whisky. Nigel looked somewhat crossly at Arnold, who smiled. Lionel said, 'Just water for me,' to Harold. 'What Arnold means, is that, to put it crudely –'

'For Heaven sake,' Harold scoffed, 'just tell the boy the facts. We can't take too high a profile in the operation ourselves for tax reasons.

We don't want you to do anything; just sit on the board and if something comes to your attention that we haven't seen, let us know.'

Eight eyes peered at me. I raised a brow. 'You'd be paid a standard, quite generous director's fee,' Lionel resumed.

'Not too generous, I trust,' Nigel qualified.

Lionel failed to second this amendment. 'But maybe the dear boy doesn't want to sit on a board,' observed Arnold.

'Course he does!' – Harold banged his pipe. 'Been invaluable to me already. Sold my George Sloam for three times its worth. Have half a mind to ask him to get me an offer on my cigarette-lighters next.'

'You'll never sell those,' Arnold purred.

'Have to do something with them when I turn up my toes.'

Clicking one of the lighters, Harold sucked at his tobacco. Lionel continued to look at me for response. Nigel gulped whisky from one hand and a mouthful of cashews from the other.

'Go on, tell 'em,' Arnold smiled on: 'you're not interested in their daft scheme, are you?'

'O but I am!,' I spoke up. 'And flattered.'

Their faces were bright and satisfied but no more surprised than those of the hazing committee when telling a pledge he can join.

'May I just ask one question?' I added.

'Please do,' assured Lionel.

'Could there be any effective role in it at all? I mean, for instance, what Nigel says about the arts – what would you think if, for example, I wanted to organise an exhibition from time to time, under the bank's sponsorship?'

This inspiration emerged out of sheer need to have something to say. No doubt Harold's remark about the Sloams prompted it. Anyhow, it made Nigel leave off his nuts and glance up, apparently pleased.

'What a capital idea!' breathed Lionel. 'Really top-drawer!'

Arnold looked to Harold. 'Since when've you become such a good judge of character?'

Harold stared at me with mixed satisfaction. 'Told you Carine had made a good choice.'

'I'd like to hear what you have in mind,' Nigel put in, adding a note of realism. 'And of course, how much it would cost.'

'Cost?' Harold snapped. 'He made a pack on the Sloams. No reason on earth why showing a few paintings shouldn't make us a bob.'

Lionel smiled. Arnold had been smiling for the whole hour, it seemed. They were all wreathed in smiles now, so that it would have been impossible not to have felt a touch self-satisfied. On the inside, however, I felt as much of an imposter as when Gisela had praised me for my borrowed Schloss. But seeing that self-doubt was not what the moment called for, I waffled on about how an exhibition or two might fit in with their scheme.

Before I'd dug too deep a hole, Harold cut in: 'We just have time for a deciding rubber. Give 'im the name of that new MD we've hired. They can get together and work this out on the phone.'

'The first board meeting's scheduled for October,' Lionel mentioned, slipping me a card on which was written the name and number of the MD-designate. 'We understand you know the man vaguely, or his wife. Done a splendid job at the Hong Kong and Macao, we've been told. Really a top-flight type to have as one's front-man, don't you agree?'

'What do you think of him?' Arnold purred as my eyes widened.

'Is he as smart as they say, or is his wife the real power?' added Nigel, engorging the last salty nut fragments.

Their motives, as ever, were more complex than they'd let on. The name on the card was Godfrey Wingfield's.

Carine was in the kitchen when I got back to Montague Square. There were three bags of shopping on the counter and a large vodka-tonic in her hand. She looked slim and serious as she went about trimming cress to make soup. Watercress soup was my favourite. There was also filet steak and a bottle of Haut Médoc in the bag. She was trying to please me, or at least be noble. My own emotions were a mix of enthusiasm, guilt and accusation.

'How was Starnberg?' she began.

There are ways and ways of saying things. The way she put this told me she knew I had not gone to Starnberg to visit my friends in the Schloss. How? She hadn't acted suspicious before I left; when I'd asked if she wanted to come, she'd said she had too much work on but thanks for the offer. Maybe I'd been too ready to take that for an answer. Or maybe I was just now exuding guilt.

'Fine,' I lied, breaking open a package of carrots and crunching into one. 'Guess what Harold wanted.'

Carine's chin, which was a bit weak in the best of times, was pulled back more than normal – a sure sign that something was up and that

that something was not very 'nicsch'.

'To ask you if you want to sit on a board.' – She sipped her drink. 'Nigel called yesterday to feel me out about it. I didn't blow your cover and tell him whether I thought it would be enough to keep the marriage together.'

She put the cress on to boil and, lighting a ciggie, started unwrapping steaks. She wouldn't look at me. Her chin drew back a few inches more. A storm was about to burst; and I loved her.

'I bought some paintings in Munich,' I said.

'So I heard. Where are they?'

'Oliver was here, was he?'

This conclusion was both paranoid and logical. But then most paranoia is too sensitive not to have a helping of logic in it. And guilty people when challenged often find it natural to attack.

'Possibly,' she answered, inhaling.

'And you gave him his paintings back, did you?'

'I thought it was the least I could do under the circs. He left me one for old time's sake. And then we have the three you bought from his ex. Are you planning to live with her, by the way?'

So: she knew everything. Damn Gisela anyhow! Was she really so egotistical and wounded sexually that she had to blab about her return bout with me? and to Ollie of all people? Or was it Magdalena that she'd been indiscreet with?

'What kind of remark is that?' I countered.

'I guess I must be naïve,' Carine said, 'but in my book when you go to bed with a person it means something.'

She put potatoes on to parboil.

'Did you go to bed with him?' I asked.

If the typical method in this kind of scene is attack, the attack in this case was not only aggressive/defensive but also self-lacerating; because if there was anything I had no wish to hear, it was that my wife had slept with a man she had once been in love with and who, in a general existential sense, was a rival to me.

'I don't think I need to answer that,' she said.

'What's good for the goose is sauce for the gander?'

Carine was not adept enough at word-games to retort that I'd got my cliché back to front. In any case, the real text here had to do with the way she clacked her glass on the counter and yanked the saucepan off the hob. 'Watch out or you'll get burnt,' she warned, bustling past me to the sink, efficient housewife as martyr.

'Why did you do it?' I asked.

'Do what?'

'Give him the paintings.'

'I didn't give them to him. I don't own them. They are now and always have been his.'

I detected a change here. 'I thought you once said you'd only give them back once he'd paid off the debts he ran up living with you.'

For a time she kept tight-lipped, puree-ing cress. 'I don't think there's much point in being self-righteous with me,' she went on. 'Giving Hildegard or Irmaborg money for his paintings when you know he's starving in Italy is pretty low. I guess she told you she was going to send him the money.'

'Part of it, she'll have to.'

'Why?' my darling asked.

'How else is she going to get her daughter back? Or didn't she tell you about her? I suppose it wouldn't make very seductive pillow-talk, going on about a sixteen-year-old he's been bonking.'

Carine's chin had now virtually disappeared under an inordinately tight mouth. She wouldn't yell at me, which made me feel guiltier. I half-wished she'd slap me or start throwing pots. I wanted to grab her, shake her, growl at her and make passionate love; but she was too sweet-souled to be handled like that. I'd violated her, of course; and though at that moment I could hardly admit it, I ached for some way to prevent our innocence from being lost.

'She's not going back,' Carine let drop.

This bemused me. 'Who isn't?'

'Magdalena.'

'So you know about her too.'

'Of course I know about her. Ollie has no reason to lie to me nowadays: he doesn't live with me anymore, I have no rights over him. And being married myself, there wouldn't have been any question of me sleeping with him, even if he had wanted to, which there was no indication of.'

An element of masochism drove the message home. And it would have been malicious of me to continue to pretend I could doubt her.

'What did he come to London for then?' I asked, sitting.

'What do you think?'

'I'm not as smart as I make out sometimes. Why don't you tell me?'

'You mean, if it isn't sex, you don't have the nous to get it?'

'There's no need to go over-the-top, Carine. You're sufficiently in the right that you can afford to be generous.'

'That's what I thought.'

'Meaning?'

'Meaning that, especially since you plan to make a steal by buying his only new work from Gisela, the least I could do is help support him and his pregnant new lady by buying a painting off him. He wanted to give it to me: he may've lived off me for two years, but he's not really mercenary – otherwise he wouldn't have felt so guilty that he almost ruined his career when we busted up. I think he's been through enough. Anyhow, I don't consider he owes me much now that three years've passed and it's obvious I'm even more prosperous. I gave him twenty-five hundred for the big painting with me, or me-ish, in it. He took the rest away. Under the circs, I could see where he might not feel that this was the safest place for them.'

Now I was fuming. Why did everyone suddenly – Margot, Carine and Oliver too, I guess – want to depict me as this rapacious exploiter whose sole motive in life was to make a buck off a struggling young artist? My only idea had been to promote him; to guarantee him the freedom to do the really valuable work his apprenticeship promised and pull himself out of the slough he had fallen into in Munich – and, yes, live the charmed existence of *dolce far niente* that we all dream about and are envious of when someone else achieves it, yet absolutely need someone we're attached to to live out for us.

'He took them to Margot's, did he?'

'What makes you assume that?'

A residue of jealousy for the first Other Woman lingered, making me think that – even if she hadn't slept with him, which I believed – Carine did still love him at some level.

'Well, it's logical, isn't it?'

I didn't want to tell her I'd been to Margot's: it could only gum up the works more. In fact, I realized, I would have to think how I was going to explain why I hadn't brought his new paintings home – she knew about Gisela and me from him already, so what reason was there for further concealment? Everything I did now would have to be tailored to restore my sweetheart's faith in me. Meanwhile, Margot sat on both lots of paintings; and if Oliver had had words with her about me, as with Carine, there was no telling what she might do.

I made a mental note to phone her in the morning. In the event, I got her machine. Waiting for her to call back, I lay on the chesterfield where I'd made my bed and rued exile from the marital nook but thanked gods for my one bit of luck: being in cahoots with the uncles. It would help me make up with Carine eventually. It would also give me leverage over Margot should she try to keep the paintings locked away: they held the whip hand over her husband.

What a petty machiavel I had become, and how fatuous! Margot did not ring back, not that day or the next; and Carine stayed out late after work – she needed space, she said – and came home most nights around two in the morning. Enter that stage in a relationship when love begins to resemble trepidation.

I moved back from the chesterfield into the bed (it was not Andy's water-bed any more: we'd punctured that in the first month of nuptial bliss). But with my darling in late, squiffed, and up early, we never made love – in fact, we hardly spoke to one another for six weeks. Over the phone from her office, Carine was as bright and brusque as with any business client; meanwhile, agonizing over what had died, I set about repainting every room in the flat.

She voiced appreciation but stayed remote.

In July, through Nigel, I got us tickets for *Madama Butterfly* at Glyndebourne, thinking it might be a special treat: Carine would love putting on the Ritz with friends of the Family during the intervals. But the story of Cio-Cio San's thraldom to an American con-man was perhaps not the best choice for restoring her confidence in me. Her reaction was to snore through the second act and, once home, phone an old friend in Paris to report on the outing as an example of her uncles' generosity, nothing more.

I ate a cheese sandwich as I did most nights, her cooking being off the menu. Drinking two glasses of port, she passed out on the sofa; and I had to cart her to bed. For an hour or three, I lay in the tub meditating on God knows what... So went the summer.

Time, that lugubrious actor in Shakespeare, stepped in to play his role. London went hot, London went frigid; there were torrential rainstorms; August burned to an end. Failing to get through to Margot, I at last talked to Godfrey: he thought it daft to try to plan a one-man art-show before the bank had even been set up; but unlike the women, he was in no position to ignore my calls. So I went on with this displacement activity, failing to tell him the name of the artist in question or to ask him to intervene with his wife re the paintings. Such things could be dealt with in time.

I phoned Simon Lewes. Other galleries I approached. More time passed, and now a thing happened which happens even to people who live in great cities, even jolly London town. I went glum. Dejected. I had cashed in my chips as a free-wheeling spirit and what did I have to show? I sat around watching soaps on day-time TV!

One afternoon I ambled into Hyde Park and sat by the Serpentine with the first two chapters of that novel I'd put in a drawer after Starnberg. A mere eight months before, Life had still held such promise. I had been young; a top agent had been charmed enough to read anything I wrote; a sweet-as-pie heiress had been ready to marry me; the sexiest woman I'd ever met was snow-bound and fucking me blind. What more could a chap have asked for?

Pish-posh and golly-gosh, as Carine might've said in her former oodly-poodly mood. It's in the nature of imaginative souls to want more than they can get, Margot might've added, cf. Wilde. *Amour de l'impossible* is what was I was ill with: an affliction common to many and, if you're so bent, prelude to philosophy or religion.

I gazed at the sky. I read books – poetry, for Christ's sake! I grew mad in a mundane sense, and at the root of this madness lurked one obsession, one envy... Another man's life is what I wanted.

Of course this was absurd. No other man's life is what we fantasize it to be: not Beethoven's or Picasso's; not Bonaparte's, Maugham's, Onassis's or J. Paul Getty's. Every one of them fell ill; every one raged; every one lost in love and was consumed by hate at some time and devotion at others; every one was impelled in part by this envy, this madness, this longing for something – this *amour de l'impossible.* That's part of what greatness was maybe, I concluded in my new, self-consoling mode. But if so, a jealous voice inside me added, it did not afflict Oliver Murrie.

So he was poor – so what? He was happy for all you could tell. He seemed to be living the life I'd travelled the world to find; only some factor of talent or genes had allowed him to get it, whereas I'd spent my time dawdling, entertaining self-doubt. I disgusted myself finally. No, disgust's the wrong word: I'd disappointed myself and lost the one sure remedy for this shallow disease, the love of a sensible woman. Now I had to pull socks up...

What *had* happened to him?

He had heard from Gisela that she'd sold his paintings to me. He had also been told that he would only get his cut if he sent Magdalena back to her. Magdalena had become pregnant by then; wildly in love as she imagined she was, she wasn't about to give up child or father. Ollie for his part didn't want to give her up now either – so he'd explained to Carine on the phone. Carine had prepaid a ticket to London so he could collect his other paintings and sell one or two. The twenty-five hundred she'd given for the one she kept was enough for him to get on with; this was topped up by Margot's advance for the pair he had left at her place.

So there he was now, back in Ravenna, with enough cash to treat his *ragazza* like Countess Guiccioli – to take her to the summer festival and hear singing that went over her head; to buy a beaten-up Fiat and continue the grand tour through Ferrara and Parma, Florence, Siena and Rome. He could compare her to the Venus of Botticelli and paint her under extraordinary domes. Every instinct for inner light and space he had could be brought into focus: the great buildings; her body. His brush, I imagined, swept over pristine tableaux with love. My own arm ached to be his, inscribing epics, filling studios of the mind where – in the centre, as if spirits invoked – he splayed huge, gorgeous arches of colour, of joy, of *amour de l'impossible* in the only form that can hold it: imaginative art.

That's what I envied.

Of course, the young girl, the passion, the travel and prospect of child and success all appealed to me too – who can resist Life's little perks, as Margot might say. But there was more finally: some dream or glimmer of transcendence behind it. I felt rash and malcontent. He could grasp things; I could not. My God, I cried out (this is fantasy, of course: no one at our end of the 20th century did anything of the kind, or admitted it), what could I do, wretched urban conniver that I'd become? Personal gain in the end meant nothing: Margot and Carine were right about that. Measured against what he was after, the profit-motive was petty, absurd. I wanted to promote him because I wanted a piece of eternity; that was all. And if pounds and pence were part of it, it was only because – the way our wicked world works – they're part of what you had to have to achieve it.

*

In the dead of winter the exhibition came off, and it would be a signal success. The process was an education, however. Art is long and Life is short, Margot would quote. Suffering is part of knowledge; both stand in relation to the quality of production; and if the artist doesn't suffer and grow wise in Time, then by some necessary alchemy of the creative act, those who make his career must.

Pseud's Corner truths passed between us like a hash-pipe between hippies, as preparations unrolled. If I'd been trading them with the old Margot, they might've lost their bathos and turned into jests. But the old Margot seemed lost to me now: mislaid at any rate, like the old Carine. Why? It would have been paranoid to ascribe powers of witchcraft to Ollie. But whatever had transformed these ex's of his dated from that flying visit to London.

It was certainly apparent on the evening around Halloween when Carine and I went for dinner in Ladbroke Grove.

'Dad, they're here!' a child's voice cried at the door.

We were ushered in by a trample of small boys, half in pyjamas, half still in school uniforms.

Godfrey appeared at the foot of the hall: 'To bed, you beasts!'

A hail and susurrus of objection. The eldest, Augustus, wanted to watch a play on TV; third-born Matthew complained that he couldn't finish his maths if Augustus kept the TV on. Christian, the second, looked at us with a seraphic gaze; while Marcus, the fourth, attempted to navigate stairs on a skateboard. Half a flight up, baby Johann was crying: the next youngest, Lucius, had just slammed a toy-box lid on his head. All gurgled and argued, poked, ran away, came back, smiled up under lashes, ignored and went through the repertory of a well-bred yet well-indulged brood, ages two to fourteen. Finally, at *paterfamilias*'s command, they vanished heavenwards to their nanny and respective ends of the evening.

'Sorry about that,' he apologized, leading us down to the kitchen. 'If one had only stopped at a conventional two-point-two, entering this house might be less like being mobbed in Cairo for baksheesh.'

Margot was manipulating pots on an Aga. 'Is Godfrey complaining about my productivity again?'

'They're lovely!' Carine remarked of the brood.

This was the first time the two women had met, and it was a study in contrasts: the one robust, the other frail; the one dressed to the nines in spite of the venue, the other rag-tag in spite of the cost of her clothes. Margot was confident, self-effacing, quick; Carine eager, unself-interested, apparently un-clever. What had their mutual ex seen in the other, each wondered as both stole a glance. Neither dared to look too closely.

The process was stilted. We had come to see Ollie's paintings: Margot had been persuaded by my leverage over Godfrey to stop trying to hide them, but she was hardly thrilled by it and greeted me with the teeth-gritting politeness of old friends who've known one another too long. Godfrey still thought the idea of an exhibition cock-eyed but could not insist. Carine was only just back on terms with me; and meeting her ex's grand passion was, in her words, 'a once in a lifetime experience, I hope'.

We went through the paces. Margot served a chicken-liver salad. Carine commented on the 'lovely, homely' feel to the kitchen. Godfrey suppressed a burp. It was daft that Margot should've taken to serving meals here when they had a perfectly good dining-room upstairs, he remarked. Eyeing her pearls and lipstick, I said that I'd had no idea our hostess could be so down-to-earth.

'The more I see of London life,' Margot pronounced, 'the more I realize how little any of us knows about anyone else.'

This might've been pursued in a *tête-à-tête*. Under the circumstances, you could only guess the subtext. Margot seemed more discontent than I'd seen her; and since her agency was going from success to success, there could only be some personal reason.

'Lamb choppies, my favourite!' Carine enthused, though both of us were surprised that a hostess who prided herself on cuisine should've served a main course so mundane.

Godfrey poured a decent but unexceptional bottle of Fleurie. He and Carine chatted about property values and where the residential market was likely to flatten out first. Margot sipped, served and sought to ignore them.

She looked penitent, I thought; but if penitence it was, it was hardly over having snubbed me. She seemed to harbour a grudge against everything now: having to cook, having to talk, Godfrey whom she was sharp with, the weather which in *de rigueur* London fashion we reverted to. The weather?! Imagine Margot and I being reduced to that. What was going on here? At one odd moment, she put a hand to her side as if feeling a pain; at another she apologised for 'being a bore'

– 'One of my authors just missed winning the Righter Prize for the second year,' she explained; 'he's depressed and I'm annoyed.' – but I was sure it was not just that.

Over cheese, we got down to the subject of Oliver's work.

'He's bloody good,' Godfrey opined, offering a cigar. 'I just wish he wasn't so indiscreet about using friends' faces. If he was a novelist, he'd be sued for libel, wouldn't he, dear?'

'People only recognize themselves in novels if the portrait's favourable. If it's not, they can't believe it could be them, even if everyone knows. People,' Margot summed up, 'are vain.'

Godfrey fielded this with another burp; and when we went up to the drawing-room to look at the canvases, there seemed little reason for him to worry. 'Déjeuner sur les rochers' belonged to Carine now, and its final version did not include him; meanwhile, the ten smaller pieces of Ollie's time with my darling had no visible relation to anyone but the models he'd hired, unless in a morphological sense to her. The three Magdalena paintings referred only to Magdalena; Margot was the sole viewer likely to catch any cryptic message in a snapdragon. Three 'Childe Harold' canvases were new: Italian vistas with self-portraits near the left-hand margin and stanzas from Byron's Fourth Canto in calligraphy in the upper right – Magdalena's artsy touch, Margot surmised.

We studied these. I mentioned that they were a result of Carine's money, which Carine pooh-poohed and Margot pretended not to hear, letting drop that she'd had them framed at her expense. The frames were wide, white, flat and designed to Oliver's specifications, letting images float into a universe of their own: a narrative space beyond the predictable reality of the Wingfield's book-lined drawing-room. So as we gazed at a punk-clad, red-haired Childe Harold, we were looking at someone we knew less than an imaginary being of our time as he might be viewed by others two hundred years from now, as Byron had been by him. And so time would move on, leaving us in its wake, propelling him toward posterity with his subject matter, no death intervening. Nor would there be any indication of the winces of longing and pain the images had evoked in too-knowing spectators as they'd come into the world.

Margot put a hand to her belly again. Carine lit a fag.

'It's rather eccentric,' Godfrey observed, 'for a new bank to sponsor an exhibition by an unknown. Of course I don't know anything about the quality of the work myself. But –'

'Then why comment on it?' Margot cut in, coiling onto a chair.

It was the most involved remark she had made all evening, and Carine and I both looked at her.

'I'd like a word with you sometime,' she went on vaguely to me, 'about arrangements, financial and otherwise.'

'Of course. Whatever you'd like.'

'I can guarantee costs,' Carine offered, embarrassed, shooting a look at me. 'Is that all there is?' she added, turning back to the paintings.

Margot glanced at Godfrey. He shook his head *no*. 'What's the matter, Carine?' I asked. 'Don't you find anything here you like?'

'Don't be stupid. I'm not expert on these things either, but isn't – what is it? – sixteen canvases awfully little for a show?'

Margot still looked to her husband. 'I could throw in my watercolours,' she said.

'Yes and I could throw in the big one I've got,' Carine added. 'Personally, I don't mind my face in it.'

Did Godfrey realize that the other face in that picture besides Ollie's belonged to his wife? On a slight nod from her, he weighed in:

'Are you sure that isn't overly generous?'

'Why not?' Carine shrugged, perhaps being more clever than I gave her credit for. 'My pride isn't so precious. Besides, it's not cartoon slander or anything like that: it's serious art.'

'That's right,' I chimed up. 'We'll all be dead in forty years, and what will this *roman à clef* business matter?'

'Shakespeare's sonnets,' Margot murmured. 'Eternizing, etc. Go on then,' she told Godfrey; 'show them.'

As if reluctant, he went round to the other part of the L-shaped sitting-room and from behind the piano drew out a last canvas, a large one which had been facing the wall. Turning it forward, he exposed an image I've already described: the one entitled 'Postcard to Carine', which depicts Ollie on the left margin watching Gisela and me in the mirrors fucking ourselves into a swan-image against Starnberg snow. If there was malice in this, there was something formidable as well, maybe even great. Yet it stabbed at my guts to see how Carine's chin retracted until it almost disappeared.

Her lip trembled; Margot's eyes watched, sphinx-like; controlling a stammer, my brave darling breathed, 'It's lovely!'

You're wonderful, I thought. But kissing her in the cab on the way home, I had to fight down suspicion that some perverse joy in rescuing her from social sadism was part of my love, tainting it. And an hour later as we had sex in the stripes of the new blinds I had hung in her bedroom, I had a sensation of embracing a wraith in a death-camp. So: what was the matter with me?

The private view was in The Mall Galleries on December 15th. Christmas was close enough that midwinter spirits approached something like genuine gaiety. The doldrums of October/November had passed; deadly February wouldn't have to be endured for two months. All London thought parties. I recalled a Christmas years before when I'd put on a tuxedo, filled a carrier-bag with presents and hadn't come home for a week; at three o'clock in the morning on Boxing Day, I'd had a mural grafittied onto my chest at the house of one of Margot's bestselling authors, whose teenaged children were busy inscribing nude bodies and pop mottoes on the walls.

Most of London recalled some such antic; '60s children tried ardently to yank back a receding youth with parties, parties and copious champagne. It was high noon of the Thatcher era: money was sloshing to and fro through the town; eat, drink and be merry was the phrase of the day.

Carine wore a new grey-and-black leather suit I'd bought her at Harrods: to make my sweetheart smile again was a *leitmotif* of my régime. Margot appeared in voluptuous green satin, hair freshly frosted and make-up looking like a throwback to the 18th century. Godfrey chatted with Lionel Sloman and Arnold and Nigel Bleistein, all of whom were in dark business suits and attended by identikit Bleistein-Sloman wives. The doyenne of these, Aunt Vera, bustled among members of the clan, hair so white that it hurt your eyes and manner so sweet, trivial and self-effacing that you could have told her Dr Goebbels was your father and she would've answered, what a lovely party! and wouldn't you like to meet nice Mr Wasserstein, the film-maker, just in from L.A.?

That was one set. Intermingled with them were besuited men and hairdoed dames who had to do with various Family businesses: the suburban types who really run life as we know it and we're meant to grow into but never do. They suffered at edges from unconfessed worry that Time was passing them by and came to such openings, imagining them glamorous, to recall for years after how the women got tipsy and flirtatious while the men were dared into buying works-of-art they could just afford but just could not understand.

Bleistein-Sloman, a canny bunch, had these villeins staked out.

'Come look at these paintings by my niece's ex-boyfriend,' enthused Vera. 'Her husband's his agent – all very incestuous. No, don't look at that one: it's naughty. But this one – the bowl or soup-tureen or whatever – don't you think it would look lovely in your new kitchen?'

Uncle Nigel had a colleague from the Takeover Commission deep in contemplation of the Danaë nude. 'In a hundred years, his reputation could be what Monet's is today. I was having a chat with one of my cousins's daughters who writes for the arts page of *The Times*. She says she's going to do four pages on him in next week's colour supplement. This is the time to get in on the ground floor.'

They were remarkable. Through their efforts, six red discs went up in the first hour, for a total of nearly £12,000. Oliver was being made. Nor was this entirely owing to Bleistein-Sloman self-interest with the bank. That scheme had been put on hold all of a sudden; Godfrey was being paid, but the Family had gone cagey. I hadn't been told details yet by Harold – he'd felt a chest cold coming on so had stayed home. But Godfather Lionel had phoned me to say that everything already in motion should go forth; by which I had assumed he meant the exhibition and so continued to push.

The Family had pledged up to £5,000 for venue, publicity and risk, and agreed to buy at least three paintings themselves if more than half weren't sold. This was the deal I'd cut with Simon Lewes of his St James's gallery. For the world it would seem as if the brainchild were his, or his and Margot Wingfield's; but Lewes had been brought in principally as a front. It hadn't even been his wheeze to use an old trick to attract greater numbers, combining Ollie's show with a retrospective of famous abstract modernists of the '30s.

That had been Margot's inspiration too, also the pre-publicity. The result on the night was that the Bleistein-Sloman crowd was matched in number, and far exceeded in colour, if not cash, by the liggers and demi-artists of Bohemia. There was gorgeous Jim Jolly in his famous black shirt, white tie and checker-board suit, topped with trademark homburg; the sculptor Grip Nattye in his Archie Rice outfit, the most strikingly ugly man in the place but attended as ever by a Marilyn blonde; the hirsute Lord Frome kitted out like a Nigerian sultan, hair, beard and earring unchanged since 1969; the Kentuckian heiress Booby Vaander, who looked the drawing-room curtains had dropped on her and whose Picasso-like features did for womankind what Nattye's did for men; Flordiligi Dorabell, the Tobagan enchantress, in epaulets and hair done to match her pet Pekinese, which fluttered under her arm; the Belgian marketing twins, Tito and Rolly van Kahnmann, always game for free drink, slipping in at the sides of Soraya Fawn, the Page-Three model agent, who asked if I wanted to feel one of her silicon tits.

Most of this lot could not have afforded a painting between them. Some had come on the strength of the British abstract lark – Jolly had been an ersatz painter in the '50s, just as he had been an ersatz jazz oboeist in the '60s and was an all-purpose media personality now. Others got in because one way or the other they had wangled themselves onto Lewes's list: galleries and event-makers always need interesting faces to swell an audience or fill a crowd.

'Do you know these demons?' I asked Margot in passing.

'In London one knows everyone except those one doesn't, and in that case one claims to. If you say you met them at Lord Minchin-hampton's drinks party for Lady Pamela Brindlemass, they'll never admit that they weren't there.'

She was right. They all faked. We all faked and connived, until sometime in the second hour I took inventory. Now twelve of Ollie's fifteen canvases had red dots on them: £20,000 – 10,000 short of the max. 'Déjeuner sur les rochers' in deference to the Wingfields Carine had held back; but 'Postcard to Carine' without title hung in stately prominence, the one of its kind – and no one recognized me in it without clothes.

No one, by eight o'clock, paid attention to his paintings at all, except to remark how in colour, figure and composition they contrasted with the '30s abstracts.

An old Etonian with cigarillo inflected: 'But don't you find them just a wee boring?'

'Not boring, expensive,' Booby Vaander said. She was worth $20 million on a generation-skipping trust yet went around dressed like Madame Blavatsky.

'Somebody was saying they represent a new wave: post-classical modernism,' Flordiligi put in. Always afraid of appearing a bimbo, she never tired of trying to sound 'inty'.

'Postmodernist classicism, dear,' Grip Nattye corrected. He was not quite the yobbo his outfit proposed.

'That's all rubbish,' opined Jolly. 'Let a thousand flowers blossom!' He added that he would as soon trade five of Oliver's oils for one drawing by Magritte, from which they 'obviously' derived.

Somebody muttered, 'Jolly's over-the-hill. That old surrealist crap.'

'Jealous, isn't he?' murmured another. 'This kind of painting proves what a wasteland his part of the century was.'

'Had to go through there to get here,' observed Nattye sagely.

'I still just love Jackson Pollock,' Booby put in. 'And I used to know Willy de Kooning in East Egg.'

'Was he the one that did holes?' Flordiligi inquired.

'Jets of sperm, dear,' the old Etonian puffed.

'Close your ears,' warned Aunt Vera, passing with the wife of the managing-director of Wacky-Packy orange drink.

'My nose as well,' sniffed her companion, downwind of one of the unwashed. – Her wattles were spackled with pearls.

In such an atmosphere, it was a marvel that all Oliver's paintings sold. They were quite serious art, after all, especially in execution – all those shades of light and colour and half-*pointilliste* slashes, which only struck the eye when you got close. But somewhere beneath the frivolity and trivia of London life, a serious side lurked: a collective semi-consciousness that was too advanced for sentiment or even cynicism. This is where his work hit a mark, and penetrated. The paintings were emotional and cool at the same time. He could see through our illusions, they seemed to say, yet not miss enjoying them. A wiser eye seemed to be looking; sex and wryness cut the seriousness to expose the precise mix of import and inconsequence we seemed to be living through. – Anyhow, that's how I imagined it, and congratulated myself for my part in it.

I needed to.

At nine o'clock, a flutter passed through the crowd. Eyes moved to the door like filings to a magnet. Margot went pale.

'Has *he* come after all?'

We'd been told at the last minute that Ollie had to stay in Catania with Magdalena. Her pregnancy had become complicated, and he had to wait by the bed in his new, improbable guise as Dad-to-be.

'It's a Rent-a-Kent!' whispered one of the paparazzi who turn up at every chance for a Face. 'Watch out for the goods, mate!' He elbowed a breast-plate of Nikons toward the door.

Carine, who had glimpsed the new arrivals, came up to me for the first time. 'Listen, dwaling, I'm going with Vera. She's worried about Harold: he doesn't answer the phone.'

Her expression said more. 'Are you OK?' I asked.

'Who me? I'm fino-de-bino.'

'Should I come too?'

'Well –' She glanced at the suddenly magnetic doorway. 'You'd better stay now, don't you think?'

'I don't see why. I've done my bit.'

'But there's What-not Lewes. You have to keep him organized, no?'

The gallery-owner, only superficially involved at first, had looked like he'd need constant prodding. By this point, however, following such success, he was more likely to need to be held back.

'Maybe,' I sighed, though the last thing I wanted was to be separated from my darling – the exhibition could have no better result than to justify my vagaries and restore our cooing state.

Did Carine understand this? Could it've been why she wanted to leave me to deal with the situation by the door, which she knew about but I didn't; or was it truly that Harold had become a concern?

'You stay,' she concluded. 'Vera's in the cab; must run. By-eee.'

'I'll be home early,' I called to her vanishing curls.

It was only as I watched them disappear through backs of heads that I recognized Gisela's face, brash and striking, chatting animatedly at the magnetic spot.

'Fucking hell!'

Godfrey and Margot were passing. 'Charming language,' she said. 'What's the matter? has your wife decided to run off to Italy and become a groupie to the new Lord Byron, like half the trendies and horses' hoofs in this place?'

She was perspiring under her rouge. Godfrey, looking like a put-upon spouse out of Waugh, supported her by an arm.

'Sorry,' she amended. 'I'm not feeling my best. Get my coat, will you dear. I'll just have a last word with our *mâitre des fêtes*.'

My eyes remained on the point where Gisela's head had appeared. Now it was gone, but I was sure it had been no mirage. The hair was swept back and sprayed like Erda's in the new *Das Rheingold* at the ENO. In fact, she'd looked like the earth-goddess herself, dropped out of starry space into this land of all-too-human Gibichungs.

'Are you going to listen?' asked Margot, 'or does our recent *froideur* mean you're too proud to be a friend when I need one?'

I would've turned then, but Carine's curls reappeared, moving at the far side of the room, out the door. In the same glance, I caught Oskar's head, slick-haired and distinguished in a slack, continental way, with Gisela's nodding beside it. A crowd had formed around them, at the front of which Booby Vaander appeared asking questions. Then all bent out of sight.

'Go and buy a plastic table-mat,' Margot mocked. 'Bargain prices. They'll be gone if you don't hurry. A second edition won't arrive from the printers in Bratwurst for weeks.'

'Pardon me?'

'Go on,' she repeated, eyes under make-up looking like topazes floating in oyster sauce.

Of course I wanted to break off and go over. What the hell was Gisela up to anyway, and why was Oskar with her? But something in Margot drew me more tightly. There is mesmerism in need.

'I must trust you,' she resumed, having got my attention. 'Come see me in the morning. Godfrey's waving; must go now.'

'What is it, Margot? Of course I'm your friend, or will be.' – A hand went to her side as if to locate a pain. I recalled the gesture; but the hand now looked gaunt, as if ageing, elegant with blue veins, red nails and gold rings. 'Are you OK?' I asked.

'Of course I'm not OK!' Grinning to her husband across the talking heads – 'I am four months bloody pregnant!'

City life whirls and swirls. So full of surprises, triumphs and defeats, it hardly gives you time to recover from one before another swells up to confront you. This sets it off from life in the suburbs or country, where every event is played over for its melodrama until the next one lopes onto the scene. Newcomers in great cities feel like they're going to drown in a sea of neurosis, whereas adept veterans grow used to the churning and look for the next crisis like a surfer looks seaward for the next wave. Gossip, scandal, backbiting – the successful rider simply bobs up from the last wipe-out and paddles out through the brine to get into the next.

Where did I fit in? I'd lost my cool when I shouldn't have. It had been a fine evening: all Ollie's paintings had sold; a great time had been had by most. But then came that spectacle of Gisela *mit* Oskar gate-crashing and taking advantage of the event to market their old inventory of airbrushings!

'What is the problem?' she'd protested as I cut through the crowd and knocked a stack of posters out of her hand.

'This is not cool, man,' Oskar remonstrated, making '60s values seem like universal orthodoxy.

Unfortunately for me, that went down well:

'Let a thousand flowers blossom!' repeated Jim Jolly, admiring Luke Skywalker gazing at a time-frozen Darth Vader.

'I think they're wonderfully *kitsch*!' schmoozed Booby. 'So Teutonic! And I can afford these!'

It was apparent that what she would've liked best would have been Oskar himself. Wearing a diamond stud at the neck of his collarless shirt and baggy black suit to go with shoulder-length hair, Gisela's ex looked like a *perestroika* rock-star.

'I wonder, though, is it art?' asked Flordiligi, half taking my side.

Her dog barked as, with an aggressive gesture, I tried to rip a stack of space-station placemats. Inconveniently, they'd been laminated.

'How exciting!' yelped Soraya Fawn.

'How did you get here?' I demanded of Gisela.

'That is a very nice greeting!'

She managed with Oskar's help to keep me from crumpling the star-station 'Déjeuners'; whereupon I desisted, having been caught by a whiff of familiar perfume. In fact, in close struggle, to my shame and surprise, I felt a leap of desire for her.

All I wanted now was Carine. Gisela had gone off for me long before. So what alchemy made her attractive again? some pheronome of triumph at having got Oskar back? Whatever, she looked as radiant as a rock-icon herself, done up in purple and black, with blonde hair flying round those exotic cheekbones, which make continental women at forty look better than at twenty-five. This is the same creature that disgusted you on a second visit to Munich, I recalled, and damaged your marriage. But people can change for the better as for the worse; and the reverse of what had dragged Gisela into unattractiveness during the summer had dragged her back now.

So did taste and desire follow cycles, like the seasons?

We were outside the Gallery, strolling down the Mall, snow having begun to collect on the trees... The worst part of it, I grumbled on to myself, was Oliver's role in it.

'Who do you think told me to come?' Gisela reprimanded once I'd calmed down enough to listen. 'He is not about to let you determine everything about his career, with your bourgeois pretensions and selling to rich Jews. "You have a right to earn money off me too," he told me. "Go and sell your airbrushing if you can."'

I saw his moon-face, insouciant, laughing at us: Oliver, for whom I – we – had just made £25,000 so he could pursue his art and free life with young girls, etc. – he simply, finally, *did not care*... Well: this was the last time I was going to put myself out for him, I resolved as I let myself be swirled down in the post-party flow to that den of well-heeled seediness, the Whistler and Wilde Club.

Dinner there was Booby's idea. She had used money to become a member where only talent should've applied and used being a member to underpin the one talent she had: organizing social butterflights. La Vaander was an indefatigable hostess of an East Coast type. Introductions from her sounded like agents' blurbs promoting bad screenplays to impatient moguls: 'This is Flordiligi Dorabell. She's the Barbara Cartland of the pet world. She appears on all the chat-shows before Crufts.' Or: 'Jim Jolly, meet Oskar. Oskar, what was your last name?... I'll never pronounce that; we'll stick to Oskar. Oskar's fascinating, Jim – real '60s person. Oskar, Jim was the King of Bohemia here in the '50s. You two have lots to talk about.'

In the event each turned his back on the other, as introductees of Booby's often did. Jolly chatted up Gisela who, being blonde, had also attracted the attention of Grip Nattye, even though he had a blonde on his arm. Nattye's blonde (I forget her name, or maybe never heard it) followed Booby in playing groupie to Oskar, who now launched into his chief party-trick, the lecture on *Heilige Kunst*:

'Modernism, you see, was of the era of Mass Man. It believed that technology could solve all His needs. In architecture, it produced the great faceless tower-blocks –'

'Which everyone wants to dynamite!' Booby chirped.

'Aren't some of them being refurbished now?' asked Nattye's girl, who had grown up in a council flat.

'That is very Postmodern,' Oskar murmured. 'Because Postmodernism, you see, is about inviting Pleasure, not providing Function. It is about seducing Consumption – your Mrs Thatcher: we love her in the East. Postmodernism is more oriented to Beauty: more appealing to your inevitable Narcissism; more thrilling, gratifying. Shall I give you a history of our time in two chapters? In the '10s we had the First War; in the '20s, sad Weimar; in the '30s, Depression; in the '40s, the Second War; in the '50s, rebuilding. It wasn't until the '60s that we began to be Liberated from preoccupation with populations being exterminated or thrown from their homes and having to fight for theories they did not believe in. All the Pleasure they had was eat-drink-and-be-merry – Bogart in a bar on the edge of *Apocalypse Now*. The Cry of the Victim roared in their ears, so who could remain a comfortable Existentialist-Aesthete?'

'Isn't he wonderful?' Booby respired, hand on breast.

Nattye's blonde looked him down. 'Not 'arf!'

Despite age and girth, Oskar radiated the style of Mick Jagger stepped off a chopper. He had, I realized now, surely been the muse of Gisela's sci-fi fantasies, whatever his intellectual pretensions.

We were standing in the Augustus John bar. Fallen aristos in paint-dappled jeans drooped over wine glasses, cigarettes in hand.

Fed-up with the other women's slavering, Flordiligi launched a challenge: 'Well I'm tired of this term "post-modern". Why do we have to define what we are all the time? It's just another form of mental wanking."

Despite new eyes on her, Gisela was not about to let a rival usurp her place as chief critic of her man. 'Yes, Oskar, how many times must I tell you you are wrong to try to define every *Zeitgeist*? If we are really postmodern as you contend, why all this unfashionable talk? Oliver, for example, rarely talks; he just paints. He is the real thing, not a leather suit full of theory. And maybe there is no Spirit of the Age as such. Maybe the Spirit of Place is *passé* too, except in a decorative sense. Now we are in London, but couldn't we be saying such things in München? Nationalism is discredited; only neo-Nazis and Jean-Marie Le Pen types advocate borders and this definitionizing.'

Oskar smirked. 'Watch you don't get out of your depth,' this said.

'We'll all be European by 1992,' Flordiligi offered.

'But all the right people've belonged to one global village for years!' Booby said, lest as an American she be left behind. 'So let's go in to dinner while they still have seats.'

'I'm sure we will be able to deal better with acid rain that way,' Gisela concluded on the One World idea.

'Unless Mrs Thatcher blocks it,' observed Nattye, to whom conversation was simply a verbal jigsaw.

'Nationalism is undead,' opined Jolly, concerned to maintain status as surrealist-in-tow. 'We have General De Gaulle in drag.'

The crowing cock who had started this clucking trained his mes- -meric gaze on the female most likely to become his new hen. 'I won't argue with you,' he murmured to Flordiligi. (Her Pekinese squirmed.) 'I don't believe in isms: they're just a Game which, being a Postmodernist, I'm happy to play. I am not a Messiah: I don't need to impose my Dogma on your Karma; it's a pleasure for me to discover the *défférence*. And when my ex-wife is lucky enough to find a way to make money on the airbrushing I once taught her, well – I am not too proud to take my cut.'

So: he had gone back to her as meal-ticket, eh? via Ollie's art, thus me, thus Carine, thus Margot, thus Godfrey, thus Bleistein-Sloman... The serpent of our lifestyles bit its tail.

'For a moment, I thought you were a fanatic,' Flordiligi said. (Her Pekinese sighed: seduction commenced.)

'I thought he was a radical anarchist,' Grip Nattye put in.

'Not a chance,' cried Jim Jolly, speaking up for the ersatz patriotic tendency in the place. 'All Germans are overcommitted to order. Just listen to the ideological blocks he speaks in: Schopenhauer filtered through Brecht.'

If this was meant as an insult, Oskar was a leering masochist.

'I don't know about any of that,' Booby intoned, taking her latest pin-up by an arm. 'I only know he's the dishiest thing in sight!'

'Let a Thousand Flowers Bloom?' Oskar tossed back to Jolly as she led him into the Dante Gabriel Rossetti dining-room. 'We don't have to Overcultivate the Garden, only sniff the Blossoms, *nicht wahr*?'

We traversed a corridor filled with sketches. Nattye's girl, Flordiligi and the rest oohed and aahed at what Gisela whispered were 'typical of the Bloomsbury amateurism'. She and I brought up the rear. Meanwhile, in front Booby concluded:

'And he isn't German anyhow, Jim; he comes from Bohemia – the real one. So let's not have anymore of your public school prickliness. You all're my guests to-night; and World War II is *over*, hear!'

Maybe it was. The evening was, at any rate – best part of it. Or maybe it was just me who was becoming jaded. The exhibition had been my show; this was someone else's – a preview, I feared, of life *sans* Carine: a freefall through the last bourgeois net of safety into a real demimonde; nest of will o' the wisps, where theory was hissed as if dream-speak and 'Luv' buzzed around whatever warm body was at its side... An unreal world. Puff from a hookah.

Carafes passed. 18th century grandees gazed down from walls on a 20th century beggar's banquet. Oskar as Macheath waxed mock-heroic about the type of our New Age: an androgynous He/She who was Creative yet not Fanatic, Order-Loving yet not Absolute, Loose but not Dissolute, happy with the Past but not Reverent about it – nor about the Future either.

Jim Jolly rolled a protuberant eye.

'Why *say*?' Grip Nattye ventriloquized for him. 'Why not just *be*, and leave all the theories behind?'

Flordiligi nodded. Booby ordered food. Nattye's girl stared as if in a trance. At last Gisela spoke up – rather touchingly, I thought – for a golden side to this New Age. In her vision there would be no war and everyone would enjoy the freedom to express her- or himself through his/her chosen art-form. We would wander through landscapes of neo-Arcady; need would vanish; no privilege would be allowed to accrue to any individual or group. There would be no Neroes or rapacious ruling classes any longer, Al Capones or underworld avengers to upset our collective *dolce vita*.

'You know how you seduce a woman like that?' Jolly whispered. 'Put your prick in her hand, your head on her shoulder and weep.'

A few moments later he tried this. Gisela shrieked.

The long, Mad Hatter's table of the Rossetti dining-room groaned under elbows of youth and age, dandy and scruff, roseate and wrinkly. There did seem to be some strain of liberty here; you could no doubt enjoy (if you called it that) the long summer's afternoon of prosperity and *diletto* that spin-doctors and ad-men had sold our world on – so long as you didn't think about it too closely.

'We are too lucky!' Gisela proclaimed. 'We sit here in our First World while no more than a thousand miles away Zionists and Fundamentalists of Islam rip each other apart. Marxism is undead; and there are neo-fascists. We cannot just have all as we wish!'

None of the rest could have cared. Falling about with drink, flirtation and gossip, Oskar fondled Flordiligi's Pekinese, while Booby appeared to be swatting Oskar's flies. Grip Nattye smirked oleaginously at a couple entwined like Siamese twins, while his girl ogled photos of naked African women flashed at her by an eighty-year-old brigadier. Jim Jolly, spurned by Gisela, wandered back to the Augustus John bar leaving me alone to imbibe her recycled Faith of the '60s:

'That's what makes me a Green,' she averred. 'I still believe we must work to get back to the Garden. It is not enough just to see and play like Oskar. He calls me puritan and says Germans always have been. "*You* be vigilant," he says; "I'll be content to let you protect me while I enjoy." Dynamic Hedonism is his Ultima Thule. "What is the point of your efforts to pacify the planet if no one is happy to just sit under a Bo Tree and listen to the voice of the breeze?"'

Yes, Oliver must have learned much from his time in Munich. Going to school to this lore may even have been what released him from an over-culture of words to become a journeyman artist at last. Because in this form words were an opposite of Living, I thought: a swamp of self-indulgent displacement activity where Instinct, Biology and Beauty could hardly breathe – unless you raised or lowered them, as Oskar did, to a level of Ironic Seduction.

Gisela I felt for. Still in thrall to her ex, it was clear that we others had been only shadows to her. An instinct of compassion warned me it would be heartless to ignore her completely while Oskar fiddled with Flordiligi's bodice in full view. On the other hand, it would've been a disaster for me to have given way to temptation when she put her hand on my cock, her head on my shoulder and started to weep. So I got up and went home as soon as we'd totalled the bill.

It was two a.m. and my darling was not there. I stood at the window gazing down, undoing cufflinks and puffing a fag. Snow fell but melted as soon as it hit the street: provisional snow just like provisional winter in England: a climate as unabsolute as the culture, always ready to turn to bluster under a warm breeze up the Gulf Stream... Throwing myself on the sofa, I turned on TV. The rhetoric of Central Europe was gradually drowned by Anglo-Saxon debunking – some post-historical, comedy talk-fest in which sixty-year-old female writer, mutton dressed as lamb, told a ribald story to a teenaged, bisexual male m.c. dressed in a magenta zoot-suit.

Watching this tosh and borne down by post-party remorse, I dozed. It could've been any hour when the sound of the latch brought me up, dim still except for telly blaring rock-videos. I switched the noise off to watch my darling trip in, a slim shadow.

Carine never cried but I saw a gleam in her eye as she sat, tiny, exhausted. 'Googly-dabbly-doodahs,' she sighed.

'I'm awfully glad to see you,' I said wrapping an arm around her frailness and drawing it over to me. 'What time is it?'

'Haven't the foggiest.' And then: 'Poor Vera.'

I hadn't foreseen what was coming. 'She was wonderful tonight,' I said. 'Or is it last night by now? Anyway, she did her bit.'

'She wanted to pitch in. That was really nicsch. But when we got back to Serpentine House…'

The tear was real, I could taste. 'When you got back…?'

'Harold was on the floor.'

Time passed.

After a considerable space of it, I asked: 'What was it? heart?'

'Blood clot, on the lung.' – Her head now settled between my arm and my breast. 'He was always my favourite.' You could hardly hear. 'And he liked you so much…'

This was reality, I thought, this life and death, not the glimmering demimonde.

Carine let out a small, unadorned sob. 'They said he might've lived if someone'd been there. I guess he couldn't get to the phone.'

I kissed her hair and forehead. Among many shadows, the idea that stood out was that it was for times like these that marriage was made.

'My sweetheart. I'm so sorry.'

'It's not your fault. He told Vera to go to the exhibition; he wanted you to do well. He felt it was important in proving your worth to the Family.'

As this sunk in, I felt terrible, happy and apprehensive all at once.

'He did that for me,' she concluded softly.

Maybe, I thought. But as with the rest of our efforts, the chief beneficiary was Oliver Murrie.

6.

Around this time I was overtaken by an idea that really creative people operate like gods. Events seem to happen because of or for them, though as often as not they remain indifferent, detached. Or maybe these exceptional people operate more like ancient heroes, with *amor fati* their religion and oneness with destiny their chief weapon against an outer world. Whatever the truth, it seemed to me that I'd never been intimidated by Oliver Murrie before: most of the time I'd been able to think of myself as vaguely superior. But now a change had crept in, half-imperceptibly. Maybe it had begun with my marriage. Anyhow, as I rose in material terms and superficial powers of manipulation, I seemed to diminish in relation to him.

London life, crowded with incident, may have been part of it. But I'd lived in London for years now and it had never affected me so. I felt out of joint, put-upon, adrift. A spirit was at loose here; it had to do with my efforts but was hardly operating for my benefit. Really creative people have more than superficial powers, I thought; their creativity is like some electro-magnetic force attracting us beyond safe moral realms. How else could you explain these circumstances: Harold dead, Gisela back with her ex, Margot pregnant, me given over to promoting him, Carine malcontent? It would've been daft to ascribe all these things to Ollie: he didn't think about us any more than God might've bothered with each petty mortal's daily hygiene. Still, his behaviour reverberated through our lives, affecting them in the present and beyond.

A kind of superstition had gripped me, making me imagine him, and people like him, to be more than they are. I had equivalent 'powers', of course: anyone who puts his mind to it can radiate out to warm or singe other lives. But was it the same? I had affected Carine, Gisela once or twice, maybe some others up to a point; but had I ever come close to transforming their essential attitudes or penetrating their dream-lives to such a depth as to make them bite their cheeks and wonder why they were here, why Time was passing them by and how on earth they were going to give meaning to what remained?

This power he had. Maybe he wasn't conscious of it; if he was, he was doubtless indifferent, even hostile, to it. Oliver did what he did; what we did was not his problem and possibly not his fault, even if we did it for him. To be a master artist is something I, we, half-forced upon him. An extension of our egos is what it had become: a vicarious means to glory. He hadn't asked for that exhibition; if he had an ulterior motive by this stage, it was only to get money for Magdalena and child. His encouragement of Gisela's airbrushings showed how little he cared for decorous reputability. So wasn't it unfair of me to see him as cause of so many effects?

Life, as Margot Wingfield might opine, is hardly ever very fair.

Margot, alas, I would only get to once Uncle Harold had been put in the ground. Poor Carine. Her father had died years before of the pneumonia I feared was going to take her away, and her mother had retired to a rest-home in Kent to escape chronic attachment to barbiturates. Bleistein-Sloman was not all fun-and-games, as Gisela had warned. Nonetheless, for Carine family remained a stand-in for religion. And I loved her the more during this period, drying her eyes and supporting her spirits while she bucked up Vera, who comforted everyone else.

A fleet of black Daimlers made solemn procession to Highgate. Under a headstone carved with an axe binding twigs the favourite uncle went to join numberless cousins and uncles stretching back to Isaac Bleistein and Heinrich Sloman, cousins themselves from the Hanse who had come to Manchester following Nathan Rothschild during Napoleonic wars. And Bleistein had married Sloman and Sloman begat Bleistein, until now around the grave bowed a vast clan with huge ears, diminishing chins and high spirits – a unit so large yet so tight that death, like birth, could always be taken in stride.

Harold was gone; all mourned and consoled; then it was back into Daimlers, sniff tears and be off.

'I must tell you,' Vera confided (she had some particular message for each), 'you were Harold's favourite in-law. He was so happy you married Carine and so impressed by the way you handled those galleries. I'm sure you'll think it dreadfully sentimental but he instructed me that when I die, I'm to will you his cigarette-lighters. Apparently you're one of the few who was polite about them.'

I felt touched and said so.

'You can use them to throw at the barricades when the revolution comes,' purred Arnold once Vera was out of earshot.

'I can find you a buyer,' said Uncle Nigel. 'Humphrey Twayne, my pal on the board of ICX, collects the things too. You could trade 'em for good lifetime seats at Glyndebourne.'

'Have we told him about the bank yet?' Lionel asked, coming up.

These snippets passed over brunch at Serpentine House, where all collected after interment. Bleistein-Sloman was out in force, as per norm on ritual occasions. It was family-life as you knew it from high-gloss soaps, only without American psychobabble and outbursts of angst, those being traits of families travelling up or down the scale: families who didn't, and wouldn't, ever have it absolutely made.

'Didn't Harold tell him?' asked Nigel.

'Harold had bridge tournaments all last week,' Arnold pointed out. 'No time for anything so trivial as a bank.'

I looked at them – the Three Stooges who otherwise might have been the first triumvirate of Rome; only they were too genial by half. Why would anyone want to rebel against a world they'd created? Maybe George Sloam in a more rebarbative era, but not Carine over her Trust as Gisela maintained. There was no credit in that.

'We've been worried about Godfrey,' went on Lionel.

'Seems a bit fond of his tipple these days,' Arnold explained.

'I had him to lunch at the Albemarle,' Nigel said. 'After three carafes of their best hock and a decanter of port, he went up to Hartley Victor, the American literary biographer, and said that his wife had recently told him that all great Yankee novelists had been alcoholics because they were closet-queens.'

A few of them had been women, I thought, but kept it to myself. 'Godfrey did that?' I asked.

'I'm afraid we had a similar experience,' Lionel lamented. 'He came to dinner the other week and made one or two remarks about Jews which Sir John Finkelstein, who was there also, thought in bad taste. It's true that Godfrey laughed rather loudly, which perhaps meant that he meant to amuse. But...'

'He's become rather unpredictable,' summed up Uncle Arnold.

'His wife didn't come with him,' Lionel mused, 'though she was invited. It was a sit-down dinner, and Valerie was rather put out. It messed up her numbers apart from anything else.'

'We were wondering,' Nigel clarified, 'if you knew any reason he should've become so erratic?'

'We took him on highest recommendation,' Lionel pointed out.

'Is it something to do with his home life?' Arnold asked.

At this point Carine joined us and conversation moved on to how Vera was coping, leaving me to ponder on Margot's pregnancy – yet more of Ollie's blasted effects. Praise was voiced for Carine's daughterly support, then inquiries made re how the property boom was affecting her 'little gem of a business'. Finally, as if with inevitable magnetism, the exhibition came up and Oliver's reaction to it.

'He was chuffed, I expect' – Arnold.

'Bloody grateful, I should hope,' Nigel grunted. He would never forget his *contretemps* years before with Carine's penultimate ex.

'Who was that German woman by the way?' asked Lionel. 'Most unusual having her sell plastic placemats.'

'Did he really invite her?' purred Arnold, whose smile mimicked the irreverence of Ollie's ambiguous act.

Carine disguised discomfort, and I did my best to deflect blame. What could they think of us if an artist they'd sponsored for our sake had been happy to subvert his own show?

'I'm sure it'll never happen again,' I averred.

'I should hope not.' Lionel was sympathetic, yet firm.

'We have a stake in his career now,' said Arnold, in subtle warning.

All fell silent. No one was willing to return to the matter of Godfrey so long as Carine was there.

'That reminds me,' spoke up Nigel. 'I was talking to Julian King the other day – he's on the board of the Royal Academy – and I wondered: d'you think it's time for something like that?'

Here was a turn-up for the ego of an ambitious young artist: just the sort of patronage these neo-Renaissance princes would like to bestow, and just the sort of establishment string-pulling a proud colt like Ollie would love to reject.

'What Nigel means,' explained Arnold, 'is do you think the young man could be mature enough to accept such an honor in the spirit in which it's offered?'

There was irony here: Arnold was doubtless the best judge of character among them now that Harold was gone; nor had Ollie's bolshiness been lost on him. That old *contretemps* with Nigel had gone Family rounds, as had the circumstance of his breakup with Carine. It was typical of their methods that they should notice all, complain of little and lean over backward not to take umbrage. Indeed, they were willing to go to great lengths to make amends for any offense they may've given, however inadvertent, thus such *actes gratuites* as sponsoring exhibitions; and only a person with a chip on his shoulder could have ended being uncharmed after dealing with them.

'It would probably mean portraits,' Lionel mused. 'Lots of money in that – and kudos.'

'Perhaps even a royal portrait one day.' Arnold whistled.

I couldn't bring myself to say that none of this was likely to cut the mustard with Ollie. But maybe they already knew. Maybe they meant the offer to be taken with a pinch of salt. It cost little to make it.

'If he was going to paint portraits,' Carine said, surprising us all and bringing the conversation to an apt resting-place, 'wouldn't it've been nicsch if he'd been able to start with Uncle Harold?'

'Oliver painting portraits? Don't be absurd.' – This was Margot's reaction. 'That takes respect and his idea of respect is to catch his friends with their pants down.'

We were in the drawing-room in Ladbroke Grove. Over the mantel now hung the picture of him with me and Gisela *in flagrante*. Since Carine had kept the one called 'Déjeuner sur les rochers', Margot had decided to keep this one. Once entitled 'Postcard to Carine', it seemed an odd choice. Margot could have had any picture of his she wanted, so why had she decided on this?

'Colour and composition,' she claimed.

It sounded false. 'Is that all?'

'Darling' (and it was the first time I noticed her using this endearment with me), 'you aren't suggesting that I have a secret desire to stare at you naked, are you?'

I made a suitable riposte; but la Wingfield was not showing her usual leg this morning – she was wearing a long Indian or Afghani skirt with multi-coloured bands and little mirrored beads sewn into it. Along with cowboy boots and an oversized man's shirt, it seemed most uncharacteristic.

'No,' she went on as we passed into her office, 'it's the one canvas of his where somebody other than him plays god. You and whatsit – his *gnadige Frau* – clearly have his fate in your hands.'

I suggested that it might equally be said that he, as artist, had ours, as timeless images, in his.

'Too deep for me,' she lied. 'I take these things as they appear on the surface. There is Ollie; there are you and his woman of the moment making love – sex anyway. His face may not imply torture, but it's hardly in calm repose. I'm thinking of retitling it "Just Desserts".'

She shifted her torso into a chair. Pregnancy had made her plump in an odd, reassuring way. If not for a glimmer of wickedness in an unmade eye, you might've taken her for a female Western Buddha.

'I like the concept,' she added, 'of betrayer betrayed.'

That she felt betrayed was implicit. That she had been betrayed in effect was unclear. That she had changed recently was apparent. Why she had done so could only be guessed. For the first time she looked like she might have belonged to him in some inner way. But I did not comment on it.

'You've taken your time in coming,' she observed.

I explained about Harold's funeral, etc.

'How's Carine coping?' – This was also the first time I'd heard her refer to my wife as other than 'thingie'.

'She's quite sad. But the Family's extraordinary.'

'Yes. I gather Jews don't cry.'

This brought to mind Lionel's disquiet over Godfrey's Semitic, or anti-Semitic, jokes. Unsure of what she was after or why she had asked to see me, I sipped her Nescafé in silence.

'I haven't been to a funeral in years,' she went on, 'only christenings.'

'Are you religious?' – It seemed appropriate to ask.

'God, no! At least not recently. My mother was Catholic; sent me to convent school and all that. We used to go to the Oratory too sometimes; but Godfrey's a normal C of E pagan, and I got fed up with the *Brideshead Revisited* snobbery.'

Godfrey a pagan? An image of him dappled in woad cavorted across the mind's eye, like some send-up of Oliver on the beach. And Margot fed up with snobbery? If that were the case, then what were class and achievement to any of us?

'You've always imagined me grand,' she went on, sensing my scepticism. 'It's your un-Englishness. I can put on Lady Muck if I have to; it's like riding a bike, one's done it for years. Your mistake is to imagine it's *me*. You don't know where I come from; I'm not the conventional middle-class schoolgirl you think. Godfrey may have that in his background; but I don't belong with the Waugh crowd in their private chapels anymore than you do with your in-laws at synagogue.'

'They don't go to synagogue. They've fallen, thank God.'

'Where I belong is out on some Celtic moor, in the elements, wildly in love – or in passion.'

Could one believe this? If so, it might explain the clothes, and her thraldom to him: a sort of Blanche Fury streak under the veneer which made this type of Englishwoman flirt with destruction.

'So that's why you did it?'

'Did what?'

'Slept with him.'

She looked at me as if she didn't like me anymore: as if I'd become just a necessary evil. 'How do you know I did that?'

'Didn't you tell me you did?'

'Why would I've been so indiscreet?'

Was she going to deny what she had once said plainly in this room, or one very like it? – Our little colloquies were getting less fun.

'It doesn't matter,' she said. 'You can't say a thing. You don't know any details. And who'd believe you anyway?'

Why would I have said a thing? And why had she bothered to confide in me, dammit, if she found me so untrustworthy?

'Godfrey's more interesting now, as I predicted. He drinks. He once hit me. He tries to be sweet.'

'Does he know?'

'That's the problem. After Johann was born he said, "That's it". He hadn't wanted more than two children; four at the outside. But six? There was no question of him putting himself in danger of a seventh.'

I began to see an outline. 'So he stopped making love with you; which drove you back to Ollie?'

'I'd hardly call one brief encounter on a divan "driven back". It was for old times' sake – the anxiety of his situation, speed of his trip to London. It was a nothing, a hello and goodbye. Unfortunately, even at my advanced stage, I'm still the kind of woman who's able to get pregnant when a man looks at her.'

That I could believe. Fecundity had always been part of her attraction. It was even more apparent now in this unpretentious, country-girl mufti than the old Joan Collins armour.

'Why didn't you just get an abortion?'

'Ah, darling,' she sighed.

'Was it "love"?'

'Isn't religion enough?'

'Religion?'

'I told you I was brought up a Catholic.'

I gaped. How could such an intelligent creature invite this folly: not the fucking – I was too much a child-of-my-time to condemn that – but living with the consequences of it? I didn't believe in her Catholic ruse: she knew that people are more interested in you when you're either losing or regaining your faith and so pretended to waver, that was all. What was true was how little I knew her, I realized. What was she capable of next? giving up her agency along with high heels? And what would become of church schools and holidays and nannies if so? lunch-parties and coffee chats, prime ballast to her status in lit London, whose denizens were no less pleasure-driven than the art-world glitter brigade? What would happen, *was* happening, finally to her marriage? because Godfrey, for all his implied irrelevance, remained the rock on which this establishment rested.

'I know what you're thinking: that I'm a fool. Well, it might please you to know that I think that myself on occasion, and am appalled and glad at the same time.'

I finished my mug.

'I'm not going to be melodramatic if I can help it.' – She stood and went to a window, hand on belly, looking like a Flemish wife or further development of some nude of Oliver's phase with Carine. 'But I must tell you that, rash as it seems, I'm terribly grateful for that last fling with him. It was wrong, of course; it may bring on catastrophe with Godfrey, who knows? All I know is, I'm one of the luckiest people in London right now. Something's happening to me. I've broken the law, as it were. Everything tests me and the people around me. It brings all the fundamental questions into focus, the great life issues of survival, fate, God. I fear but adore what's happened.'

I sat pinned to my chair wishing I could crack a joke. Aware of my smallness all of a sudden, I wondered again why she'd chosen me as confidant to this apparent madness which she and Ollie, or perhaps all of us, had conjured. Because madness it was in a conventional sense. These 'great life issues' and 'fundamental questions' were what people feared most – as pretentious, if not dangerous. To dare them was why he had gone to foreign shores in the first place, wasn't it?

'Jon and Lucius'll be back in ten minutes,' she said, changing tune. 'You'll have to go.'

She looked like a madonna in that moment, with low, oblique light from the window haloing her. 'I don't mind seeing your children,' I countered. 'Carine and I haven't done well in that department; I'd be happy to know them better.'

She stared at me as if trying to assess my true character at last. 'You can't,' she added succinctly.

It sounded ridiculous: severe. Nor was there any way I could've anticipated what lay behind it.

'By the way,' she went on, to avoid explanation, 'did you hear that Magdalena's baby died? No? I would've thought Carine would have told you. Ollie phoned me immediately; he must've phoned her – he needs us all terribly in crisis, his ex's. That's why it's essential I don't let anything break communication with him. He needs me; his work needs me, needs us all – you're the one who made us aware of it.'

Too many elements, real and imagined, seemed to be swirling around. 'Wait a minute, Margot –'

'A minute's all we have.'

'I didn't know the baby had even been born, let alone died.'

'It was born in Livorno, a boy. Oliver had been reading *Faust* and called it Euphorion in that Pseud's Corner, neo-classical way he goes in for – but they *are* living in romantic squalor. It was born at home, of course; Magdalena had 'flu and was ill during labour – I imagine the whole scene as terribly unhygienic. Anyhow, the poor thing struggled for ten days before what can only be referred to as cot-death.'

'How unfortunate,' I mused feeling oddly insincere – as if, 'betrayer betrayed', my subconscious thought he deserved this.

'He'll need a new woman in time,' she concluded practically; 'Magdalena'll run off. Don't look at me, though. I have six children, and Godfrey would cut me out completely if I took one step in that direction. He – Godfrey, that is – is still wildly jealous of our affair five years ago. So that's where you come in.'

'I?'

'Sorry, darling.' – She turned aside, so that her body was backlit and profile silhouetted. 'I've taken the most terrible liberty with our friendship, which is why you must be out of here before the children come in – they might tell their Dad. I rely on you to forgive me: I'm sure you'll understand. But even if you don't now, I believe enough in your better nature that you'll protect us.'

Protect them? who? Ollie? Godfrey? Margot and child? children? Why was I of all people being cast as *salvator tutti*?

'Have you twigged yet?' – She angled me to the door.

'Twigged? You have me totally bemused.'

'I told him it was you.'

'Told who it was me what?'

'Godfrey. That you were the father. That you were my lover, not Oliver.'

'…!'

But what if Carine heard? What if Godfrey fell into the abyss and went after her money? What *if*?!

'You're white as the wall, darling. I'm appalled at myself too, but there it is. Go away now. Don't call me or come here; I'll handle God. And don't look at me like that. One day you'll realize it's hardly so bad. You're still more or less alone in the world, you can take this. It gives you a connection; makes you more interesting too.'

What a monstrous embodiment of intrigue and rationalization she could be. Yet, in that moment I realized what Oliver must've seen in her and how she might have been the only one for him after all. Sinister as she appeared, her instinct was spot on: in Time, I would forgive and accept – her sheer audacity would assure it. Meanwhile, for the first and perhaps last occasion in our acquaintance, the extraordinary creature threw her arms around me and wept.

Women like Margot have a bottom line: the children. They are capable of almost anything in the name of survival and can hardly be convicted of such man-made crimes as 'cruelty'. Instinct is their motive-force, morality only a utilitarian disguise. Though it would've been easy for me to have railed against her, what would've been the point? Margot would carry on, rationalizing her situation; and I would just seem a suppressive Yankee prig. Besides, she hadn't done what she'd done to protect Ollie and herself from Godfrey so much as to protect Godfrey and the children from himself.

She knew her husband was reeling. He propped up the bar at his club every night and came home to pass out in front of TV. I thought about phoning him but recognized that, if what she said was true (and there was no reason to doubt it), talking to him could only make matters worse. For his sons, he managed to pull himself together; this gave her hope that his conduct wouldn't spin into some irreversible decline. A bad reaction that would pass in time was how she described it a day or two later on the phone:

'The birth may help too. Godfrey's not about to let the world know the child isn't his. And once a chap begins to pose as a father, the role soon takes over and carries the poison away.'

She seemed so sure about this that I almost asked if any of her previous pregnancies had been by others. Didn't one have red hair? Wasn't he slightly moon-faced? I could hardly go back to Ladbroke Grove and check it out: that door had closed on me for the time being. Oddly enough, I hoped it wouldn't be forever.

Did I feel hard-done-by? It would've been shallow. Margot's survival instinct hardly meant parking the kids on the street or even moving back to 'tatty' Shepherd's Bush. In the upper middle-class world she moved in, it meant keeping up to the level of siblings and neighbours come what would. I might've ranted a bit, like Ollie over the Miners' Strike; I might've pointed a finger at the House of Wingfield as symbol of the pathology of Thatcher's Britain, or something Gisela-like. But I had my own progress to get on with. Besides, little though I liked it, I was a symptom of the same *Zeitgeist*.

Gisela would tell me this when she phoned, as she did from time to time. Meanwhile, far from resenting being banned from Ladbroke Grove, my principal reaction was to miss the household, especially mistress of it. I had no choice but to report favourably on Godfrey to Lionel-Arnold-Nigel. (This may've been one reason for Margot's plot.) I would also have to confront extraordinary risk with Carine if chatter seeped out: rumour could hurt her and ruin us.

Those were the 'downsides' to use a term from Uncle Harold's New York stockbroker, whom I contacted on Vera's behalf. The upside grew apparent as I imagined the rot that could set in if I didn't bring Carine in on Margot's lie. London would learn of my 'liaison'; and if I reverted to old persona and wanted to publish a new Rough Guide, she would no longer be in a position to help.

'I would have done that anyway, darling,' she claimed in the course of what became almost daily phonecalls; but this was not so certain as she pretended. What keeps people committed, as Ollie had long realized, is need; and sharing a secret is how this is created when blood, money or passion aren't involved.

Margot needed my discretion; so did Godfrey. That I needed theirs was less apparent. But so long as serious damage could be avoided, it was comfortable to think of them in my hands.

By this train of logic I came to rationalize what might otherwise have seemed a scurrilous turn-of-events. But everything hinged on being honest with my wife. And when I told Carine as directly as possible what Margot had done, her reaction was shock, then annoyance, finally wistfulness. – 'I must be so naïve,' she exhaled.

'What do you mean, my poodle?' – My main worry was that she might not believe that Margot had lied.

We were in bed then, trying to make a baby: Harold's death had provided the cue to re-attempt it. Carine lit another ciggie: I'd tried to get her to quit – the Bleistein lungs were the least of Family attractions when thinking of genes. But she had cut down on hashish and drink, which was perhaps all you could ask for at one go.

'I'm so silly, aren't I? I always expect people to be like I was told when I was five – fall in love, get married, make a home, have children, live happily-ever-after, et cet.'

'There's nothing wrong with those things,' I said cuddling up. 'If you weren't like that, why would I care for you so?'

'You're nicsch,' she gurgled, affectionate as ever. 'But I know now that people need something else periodically. Maybe I should've taken Ollie back when he first skived off with Miss Nazi. He didn't want to go to Munich – only did it to make sure how he felt about me, and knock something creative loose. I feel terrible about having thrown him out. Nearly destroyed his career from what you say.'

She had pulled herself up against the pillows. I pulled myself up too and lit a fag, though I hadn't been a smoker in years.

'Do you want to go back to him?' I asked, but what I really wanted to know was whether she had faith back in me.

'I didn't mean that. I'm with you now; everything's changed. He's with Magdalena. We have different lives.'

The implication was half-crushing. Could it be that Carine, who I'd been sure of to the point of taking for granted, was becoming as fickle as the rest of us? Or was it just that she believed that, if she were going to have the kind of marriage she wanted, she could no longer afford to let me rest so sure of her? Either way, I'd lost something precious. What a vain little prick I had been!

'I always thought I was like my family. Bourgeois, Ollie called me – he was a bohemian; I never would be. Where did he get those terms: bloody Gisela? It got rather unpleasant. I never want rows like that again. But he was right, then. Now I'm not sure. Sometimes when I see how you all fawn over his work, I wonder what's the point of this life I'm meant to be living.'

'You mean marriage and babies?'

'I mean business, family, London – all of it. So I have a posh car, a big flat, an attractive husband, money, one of the most successful agencies in town – so? My car I can't take out without risk of being done for drink driving. My flat could revert to the Family whenever the Members say. My husband is lovely, but half the time I wonder if he wouldn't be happier with someone else. My money isn't mine: it's an accident of birth. And my agency will crash along with the others as soon as this bubble-economy bursts.'

There was no certainty, was there? not in marriage, not in bed, not in many things other than love, forgiveness and a commitment to keeping on.

We lay in silence. Night in the city throbbed out the windows.

'Wanna go back to Phuket?' I murmured; and visions of a hot south rose – a landscape where all complications might melt, thaw and resolve themselves into an existentialist stew.

It seemed a solution. But Carine was sensible now. She recognized escape for what it was and could differentiate between self-indulgence and legitimate quest.

'Lovely idea, dwaling. But I was thinking about going to the continent. You seem to like it, and Ollie's apparently got a lot out of living there. I was thinking about going back to old haunts in Paris. Haven't been for yonks – since you and I got married. And maybe in spring it would be nicsch to cross the Alps and visit him and his new other half... Would you mind terribly, just a few months? to clear the old head? We can have a baby if you want after that.'

I hadn't expected this – not in my remotest fears, or fantasies. But though I felt crushed by it, I could see the sense. And I said so, and that I respected her resolve.

It was for me she would do this, I tried to tell myself, as a person in love with being loved will. Having made her aware of her limitations, I'd set her on a path toward expanding into the dream of full womanhood she had come to believe I needed in a wife.

So I rationalized, loving her more. But when morning came and she got up and went off to work, worry crept into the sheets behind her; and green as the demon out of the depths, it brought jealousy and fear. Wasn't the real reason she wanted to go that, in her characteristic honesty, Carine knew she couldn't keep on with me so long as she was still, or could be, in love with somebody else?

7.

I felt wild again: wild in sorrow, wild in love, wild in wanderlust. London seemed blasted – damn February! Despite my wobbles and protests, Carine duly left. One morning she drove to the hovercraft at Ramsgate, and that was the last I was to see of her for two months.

I felt abandoned, judged against – but this was absurd. My darling had not given up on the marriage; there had been no real talk of separation. She'd left me smothered in luxury; the freezer was full of a month's chops and stews, and our joint bank account was five thousand in the black – no mean feat considering it was usually that much in the red. Her trip would be paid for with ten thousand cajoled out of Lionel from the Trust, not out of our funds.

Carine had arranged everything nobly. As a result, I felt even more like what the little boy stepped in.

What to do? adopt penitent celibacy? screw my way out of depression? My life was mine to determine: 'Freedom's just another word for nothin' left to lose' and all that; 'Nothin' ain't worth nothin' but it's free…' At first I dithered with an idea of taking myself off to Bali or Phuket. I called my old editor at the Rough Guides; he said he'd see if they had anything for me, but he knew as I did that I was beyond Rough Guides now – what did I know anymore about how the young got around without dosh?

I was making my passage out of freewheeling youth. I was starting to yearn for some absolute, predetermined role, as people in middle-age do. This had been building in me through marriage and vague intentions of having a child, but now it came with a gathering rancour as events threw me back towards existential indetermination. Like any un- or underemployed person, I asked: what does one do in this life?… Please yourself. Watch soaps on TV.

I called Lionel Sloman. Were there any favours left to do for the Family? The bank, it appeared (so he re-implied), had been more or less a sham, created to shift Members' assets to avoid death-duties. This I'd suspected but tried not to know. And what were the implications for Godfrey Wingfield?

'We'll keep him for now,' Carine's godfather assured. 'So long as we can trust in his discretion, better not to invite attention by changing personnel in mid-stream. Don't you agree?'

'So long as you can trust in his discretion?'

Pause. 'Are you trying to warn me of something?'

'O no,' I retracted; still, I dialled Margot as soon as I'd made the requisite verbal genuflection and rung off.

Her voice came on the line dark as a storm. On recognizing mine, it shifted and became bright, as if I were a suitor she wanted to keep from seeing how despondent she was.

I passed on Lionel's drift: she affected unconcern: 'Darling, Godfrey pitches in sleep every night cursing the day he put himself in a position to "take a mafia hit". Honestly, don't worry. He's scared shitless, as your countrymen have the grace to say. Wants to get back to the Hong Kong and Macao the first chance, despite money. Of course I'm worried: he's not doing much better and I'm afraid, if he becomes truly unhinged, he might make himself unemployable.'

'Surely not, with his connections.'

'It happens, even to the best. Fortunately, I have a business too.'

'Yes. That could see you through, couldn't it?'

A croak of laughter. 'Success in my walk-of-life is nine-tenths facade. Now, if I could find time to begin my own novel –'

But with six children and another on the way…

'No,' she concluded. 'Recently, I've begun to wonder about Ollie.'

I wasn't aware she'd ever stopped doing that. 'What about him?'

'Whether he might not take responsibility if things got tough.'

'That serious, is it?'

Her line of thought was as transparent as a single mum's in a damp council flat. 'I've been generous with him, haven't I? And I still have some of his drawings, and the watercolours which I haven't flogged. One might reckon some debt for the encouragement I've given.'

'Margot! What an unexpected twist.'

'One gives when one's got and takes when one needs. I'm not as falsely proud as I once looked to you. Besides, families produce cunning. Seven mouths to feed – you should try it!'

From this, I took a practical purpose for what was already a subterranean urge: to go to Italy and see the grand panjandrum myself. This had been growing in me too, along with frustration: an idea of confronting this hero, or nemesis, at last. Anyhow, Carine would be there, or just coming or just gone; and without her, London was dead as the dodo for me.

I turned my head south. But before I went, two more phonecalls delayed me, adding further purpose:

The first was from Simon Lewes of his St James's gallery. The George Sloam exhibition had been such a success that he was thinking of doing another. Did I know where any more Sloams might be found – portraits of his/her demimonde of the '30s? – and would I like to help with arrangements?

This overture might have been tempting a few weeks before. Impressed with my performance at the Mall, Lewes was evidently offering more than a one-off. With my 'connections and peculiar talents', he implied, I might become more than just a friend of the gallery – a colleague or even partner in time.

In time, I allowed, this might be worth mulling over. For the time being, however, my main objective was to go to Italy and give support to new work by Oliver Murrie.

'O dear,' he said, tetchy. 'You aren't going to let yourself become a one-man band, are you?'

I asked what that meant and he suggested that Ollie's success may have been inflated by 'peculiar efforts'; also that, despite general critical welcome, his work might encounter difficulties in future.

'What sort of difficulties?' – My hunch was that Lewes was only rationalizing his lack of foresight re Ollie's appeal.

'For a relatively new painter, he's dreadfully overpriced. Of course, given the amount of work that goes into each canvas, he pays himself a low-ish hourly wage; but that's hardly the point. In selling art as opposed to creating it, the bottom line is what the market will bear.'

'It's borne him to date.' – Was he trying to lay ground to get new work on the cheap?

'Yes, but don't you see? in some ways, he's rather too good – too classical, painstaking, too unamateur, if you know what I mean. This neo-classical lark he's rowed himself into: it could be over in weeks, and then what? If you're going to see him, take my advice: warn him off too much intellect, too many *pointilliste* dots, too much personal allusion and the touch of the twee.'

'The touch of the twee?! In Oliver Murrie?'

It came to mind then that Simon Lewes, though in his forties, lived with his mother, had never married, was gobsmacked by titles and never said a word against anybody to his or her face. With the right feathered cap, he might've made a perfect popinjay, like Osric in *Hamlet*. As it was, the one bit of tattle you heard about him was that he had once got tipsy at a dinner of Booby Vaander's and regaled the table with the joys of being spanked.

'All those bowls and tiresome things,' he went on. 'Interiors of churches. It's all right if it's Veronese. But I can't tell you how hard it is to sell that traditional subject matter in contemporaries.'

I was annoyed but, on reflection, might not have been. Gisela would say something similar in Munich. – She of course was the other person who phoned. On hearing that I was off to Italy, she demanded I come see her en route.

So it was in Munich again that I began to shake off this notion that the spirit at work in our lives was some emanation of Oliver Murrie. He was just a point of reference for it: an incarnation or 'objective correlative', wasn't he?

This was Gisela's opinion, though not in so many words. There was a pattern: each of us followed our designated path in it; each path was different depending on where we started from. The common denominator was this element of wilful self-determination: this spirit of bohemia finally compelling us all, freed in our own ways from too much necessity. It was what made our paths oddly congruent: Margot had Godfrey's turmoil yet Ollie's seed; Carine had my devotion yet her wanderlust; Gisela had her dogmatic idealistic attitudes yet her vulgarity and 'hopeless' new Spanish boyfriend. All of us oscillated between the steady and wild: the apparently certain, which was unpredictable, and the volatile, which was paradoxically constant.

That's how she looked at it.

Oskar was gone again, our flare-up in the Mall Gallery behind us. We sat on her roof, taking the first blaze of spring coming with unseasonal warmth across the Alps. Jaime, the new boyfriend, plucked a guitar and gazed at us sullen from the far side of her aerie. I drank tea as she studied winter-blasted skeletons of plants, pruning here, snipping there. So: what was the purpose of her getting me to Munich?

Jaime was part of it, surely. She wanted me to take the message to Italy that, in spite of rejections of recent years, the sex-goddess of Starnberg was not yet incapable of a renaissance.

Poor vain Gisela! Poor vain all of us, I thought. But then, with the next thought that passed at the speed of a cloud over *blaue Blumen* skies, I reminded myself that – given our health and our spark and freedom – we were quite rich. Lying out in the sun wearing naught but a gold chain on an ankle, Gisela was far from finished. Her body, that weapon and source of pleasure once, had reached a state where decay meets ripeness but doesn't yet dominate the conversation. Her breasts were quite large still, soft but hardly turning to slush. Her belly was flat, the skin slackening, but only so much as to become restful, not loose. Her legs had that tendency to swell that I'd noted before, but this seemed to hesitate now. Jaime was giving her incentive as well as exercise, it was clear. In fact, all you could see (along with other aspects recalled) combined to make the woman seem a classic incarnation of Indian summer of female sensuality.

The Spanish boy, dark and louche, did not take this all in. Young man rampant, he was a less brain-endowed version of the Oliver Murrie who'd sold airbrushings in Heidhausen. Gisela complained, bossed him about, sniped at him behind his back, generally tyrannized over him in a way Oskar had once done over her. He spoke little English, so it was easy for us to remove ourselves to a 'higher plane' as it were in his presence. Gisela claimed he was abjectly in love ('He wants me all the time: three times a night and more! This is like no man I've ever had: this is a demigod.') Thus pretending or fooling herself that he was not just a randy twenty-year-old with a mature woman who knew all the tricks, she made up for her most recent blow: Oskar having left her for a nymphet once the profits from Ollie's posters had run out. What was good for the gander...

'I always loved you best,' she lied on the second night, when – after a passionate row resulted in Jaime going off to busk at the Schwabing U-bahn – we poured back two bottles of Liebfraumilch.

I recognized this for the mix of drunk-talk, nostalgia and compensation it was. Still, a touch of desperation may be forgiven in a person so dependent on wandering instinct. Gisela was my sister; making love with her was no longer much more than incest; animal urges passed, only affection remained. But then, affection too can be tried.

Jaime did not come back that evening. Some evening in future he would not at all. In anticipation of this, Gisela's eyes became sockets and her rhetoric full of angst. Out of self-fear or maybe even remorse, she flailed about, trying to do harm: 'Oliver has stolen my daughter! my child! He is a demon! I have told him: one day, she'll have his head on a platter and I will dance on his grave!'

I doubted that Hérodias was Magdalena's destined role or Salomé hers; but *la vie bohème* is all about flair for the dramatic, *nicht wahr*?

'He is so phoney. And you – what is it about you Anglo-Saxon males? You must be so pious in the end: why? All this religion of Art: he denies he has it and makes a joke – but how can one believe a man who reads Goethe and names his child Euphorion and lets it die? He doesn't care about life really, or human beings. I told Magdalena. Now with the child gone, perhaps she will see. He reads your Lord Byron and rents a villa which he says belonged to the poet Shelley; but what do such things matter in this day? What people want is muscle, and this thing, not historical reference. They want youthful flesh, not reminders of dead *romantische* tradition: these pretentious allusions to Masaccio or Giorgione. As I used to tell Oskar, Life is not a university. Oliver must break his art now and then. He becomes middle-aged if he goes off to paint the domes of San Pietro and San Marco. He must do things that appeal to Jaime – eh, *Leibchen*?'

The young man had re-entered during this speech. It was dawn now and, zippered up in his leathers, he looked as surly as Brando in *The Wild One.* Mercifully she and I were no longer *in flagrante.* '*Komm hier. Komm zur Mutti. Ja, mein Schönheit,*' she said, wrapping him in her duvet; for tired and petulant child he then was, if in body a man.

As I watched, a sensation came over me of how we all long for comfort: he for Jocastan arms, she for lips to suck nipples, each of us for the art or quasi-religious image best-suited to our capacity for comprehension, all finally for someone who knew us better – knew everything better than we knew ourselves. And then Ollie came back to me in full significance; because in this world *faute de mieux* he had more essential knowledge than the rest of us... Or was it just my own need that painted him in those colours: my need for a being outside of the normal – a hero or god?

'Your wife is there with him,' Gisela announced the next day, a touch of malice returned. 'Will you see him even so?'

She had just made a twice-weekly call to Magdalena.

'How do you mean, "with him"?'

'She stays where he does.'

We both knew I could take this how I wanted, and how I did would be a test. Carine passed my mind then: Carine not in city mufti but wearing a bandanna and digging hands in the earth like some middle-aged peasant matron. Was that what I wanted in my subconscious, or was it just a result of linking her to him? Whichever, it pained me. Still, I had to keep on – go see them; pursue her, whatever it might cost in pride.

'Of course it won't stop me.'

'You mean, you can stand sharing her like he once shared me?'

'Like he once shared you?'

'You'll be a better man than he if you don't react with aggression.'

She smiled. It seemed to me almost impossible in that moment to recall what she referred to: that I had once had sufficient power to take a woman off him.

'You were a god then,' she continued, reading my thought. 'So sure of yourself, so independent. You lived in a castle; he was in the street. You wrote a novel, he sold the airbrushing like Jaime must now for our money – ja, *Liebchen*? You intended to "save" him. You saved me for a time by that means. Do you think he'll save you?'

If so, and by the same 'means' – wild sex with my woman – I felt sure I would rather be damned.

*

As I got closer to the reality of Oliver in Italy, I tried to fix this idea that I'd made too much of him. This business of erecting heroes or nemeses: it was about time I grew out of it, wasn't it? It's natural enough in a young man, and maybe none of us ever entirely gets over the wish for a higher grade of human, not even in a cynical era where everyone falls over himself to pretend that striving for stars is pretentious. First, we are mortals, then heroes, then gods, then *ricorso*, Ollie would say when I mentioned the these things to him. Quoting Vico, he went on to cite Michelet, Marx, Spengler and various changes between 18th, 19th and 20th century approaches to aesthetics. That's what interested him now. Reading had become a result of his expatriation: he'd had time to pursue knowledge – *real* knowledge, as he put it, not just the 'theory' Oskar ate out on, or liberal orthodoxies we're socialized in or the seat-of-our-pants clevernesses we end up flying by in great cities.

'I went to an English public school,' he pointed out. 'You learn to suppress hero-worship there. The group is the law – family, class, nation – even at a knit-your-own-violin place like Bedales. But I came unstuck somewhere. Started at Cambridge. Byron was at Trinity too, and Aleister Crowley. Germany may've helped: that Nietzschean individualism hidden back in their souls. The fact that I was an only child also contributed: I was always a loner, until recently.'

He did seem as much on his own as any of us, with little need for status like Godfrey or audience like Oskar. Still he struck me as being the brain-child of others' needs: Margot's for a notional lover, Carine's for a guide independent of family, mine for a person who could become fully realized on his own. At that moment, I oscillated back under his spell. And he *was* living like Byron, though in a rambling *casa* at the water's edge near Livorno which may have been

Shelley's – no one could say: quite a bit of modern Med holiday development had taken over since the poet's watery end.

I'd arrived on a gorgeous, delicate spring morning, with light high and full of anticipation. He was up already and at the edge of a shingle beach working on a new canvas, now nearly composed, entitled 'According to the Adventurer'. This depicted the tale told by Trelawny of how Byron jumped into the flames of Shelley's funeral pyre to grab out the heart, which refused to burn*. The subject was Gothic, but Ollie treated it with the order and control of French neo-classicism, a Gros or David. Something Beethoven-like was there too, paint laid on so thick you could no longer complain of the shimmering, *pointilliste* fuzz he'd gone in for in an earlier phase. Every stroke seemed sure now, the overall impression of cleanliness, clarity, precision and rapid approach towards a fulfilled intention.

'What will they say back in London?' he asked, nonchalant.

'That you bestride the world like a colossus,' I wanted to answer, though the petty arbiters of that *monde* – Simon Lewes and so on – would be put off, I knew. The whole undertaking was too ambitious, too unsmall, unjoky and eccentric; it could hardly relate to the kind of stuff being produced by other graduates of Bedales in converted vicarages in Sussex, day-dreaming of a latter-day Bloomsbury set. In fact, everything Lewes had warned me about in Ollie's work was here, including the personal and 'twee'; and even I was put off by an autobiographical urge which had moved him to project something like his own shape in all three principals – the blazing corpse, leaping poet and 'adventurer', Trelawny, who stood to the left of the central frame, back to view, regarding the action as if lackadaisically. 'Genius yawns while talent sweats,' he might've been saying, blowing a raspberry at the whole art thing.

Meanwhile, the real Ollie asked: 'Who is this narrative figure?'

His tone teased. Did he mean who could be so preposterous as to be a lying Boswell, or who had been the physical model for the figure on the canvas? I didn't ask; he didn't enlighten; he simply stared with eyes much bluer than I remembered, Mediterranean brilliance reflecting up in them.

* When I eventually got back to London, I read Trelawny's book and discovered that Ollie had got it wrong. It wasn't Byron who was meant to have jumped into the flames but 'the adventurer' himself – a clear case of the lesser man making his own myth by a momentary upstaging of genius.

'What a monument of ego you've become!' I almost answered, oscillating back to the view that I didn't like him much, or recognize my hand in the making of him.

Awe in the proud is chased by disquiet, the Margot in me said: it breeds repulsion out of self-contempt.

We sat in the courtyard of the tumbledown palazzo he lived in: a villa divided into semi-autonomous cells filled with random northern types long attracted to these parts. It was mid-morning and a mélange of stray dogs, cats and Italian teenagers loped around on no particular purpose. The human element among them exuded that aura of undervalued merit which seems to cling to anyone who takes up a laid-back attitude in such climes. It reminded me of a motel in Palm Springs I used to go to during Easter week as a teenager and Ollie of a 'cool' avatar in a crowd of would-be rebels-without-a-cause.

A boy brought us coffee, then sloped off as if star-struck.

My host was dressed in a baggy, colourful mix of red trousers, white shirt, salmon waistcoat, sashes, buttons and beads. Though little more than thirty, his hair had turned to wisps. Sunburn had brought out freckles on his face, which looked less like a moon because of the tan. Craters of hunger and fatigue of Munich had been replaced by happy pockets of flesh. The fingers and wrists had thickened and sprouted bracelets and rings. Hair grew on the backs of his paint-stained hands and down his neck. He wore his shirt open in the style of con-men, a V to the sternum, below which buttons strained over a preview of Falstaffian girth.

Ollie had become middle-aged. In fact, he looked a bit like Godfrey Wingfield, only more Celtic and comfortable in his skin. The same Church boots were on his feet – must've been fifteen years old. Apart from them, there was no longer a trace of a style you might've expected in Margot's ex-lover, let alone Carine's. He looked like an aspirant Picasso or Onassis, even the demonic Crowley. Something bull-like was apparent, as if the physical man had come down to earth at last. A stray glint in the eye was all you could see of the bird-of-prey wheeling, as if still searching for something beyond mortal sight.

While I sat studying him, a commotion began in the gallery above; our eyes leapt to where a door burst open. In a farrago of motion, two teenaged girls tumbled out wrestling.

'*Chè bella diavolessa*!' shrieked the first.

'*Du bist der Teufel*!' hissed the second.

Much cursing in languages I didn't know, having even less Italian than Deutsch. One of the two I recognized as Magdalena; she was wearing a blue shift or night-dress ripped down from one breast. The other, a blonde, equally tall, was Italian. She slapped Magdalena's face with the violence of Sylvester Stallone delivering a knockout in *Rocky XV*. From this Magdalena reeled before catching her balance and retaliating with a heave of a shoulder into the girl's bust. Oof! The two clasped claws around each others' throats and were about to tumble over the rail on top of us when a fair-haired James Dean wearing black briefs came through the door they had burst out of, pushed the Italian girl back and positioned himself between her and Magdalena so that neither could get at the other.

A crowd had collected below – shouts, whistles, cheers. Scuffling took place; on the other side of the yard, two dogs began growling; cats ran and leapt on perches to watch, erect. And what was Ollie's reaction to this event, which you could only suppose had something to do with him, involving his erstwhile woman as it did?

'*Basta*!' he called, muscles tensed and ready to hurtle body up stairs; but then, as things calmed, dogs' growls turned to whines and the young man strong-armed the Italian girl back to the room, signs of tension passed out of him too. '*Das ewig Weibliche*?' he shrugged.

Meanwhile Magdalena straightened her shift, entirely buttonless now, and flounced down the stairs.

'And among the things eternal,' he added, turning back to me, 'is the ferocity of a woman scorned.'

Arriving at his side, she wrapped herself into one of his arms, the picture of a ten-year-old taking comfort from Dad. Her black hair had been bobbed since the last time I saw her; she had the pouting lips of a Milan model and eyes to launch a thousand ships.

'Do you remember this man?' he said to her of me.

Nodding, she looked away. At this moment the Italian girl burst out of the room above; curses poured over the rails, until her man or boy – young James Dean – yanked her back. A flutter of more scowls, heartbeats, tension... then the courtyard, and Magdalena, subsided into its pristine state of somnolent languor.

'*Willst Du fur mich heute morgen sitzen*?' Ollie inquired.

Nodding again, she broke away and, drifting off to the sunniest corner, threw herself down on an empty seat. Lifting her face to the light, she shut her eyes and shortly was surrounded by dozing kittens.

He looked to me but said *nada.* The boy brought more coffee.

'And what about a man scorned?' I asked, only able to surmise.

Ollie sipped. Did he catch the significance for us?

'They fight too, in their hot youth.'

'And when they get older?'

'One has other weapons.'

'Such as?'

'You have money, I have talent,' he shrugged and, draining his cup: 'Alora, amico, let me show you my studio.'

He stood. I followed him in.

I had money? I'd heard this before, principally from Margot, half in jest. There was a touch of middle-class know-it-all-ism in it, also Cockney envy having to do with Carine and the myth of Jewish lucre. Ollie had a chink left in his armour, it seems: the heiress who'd got away. – So where was she now?

'Gone to the Franche-Comté,' he said as if reading my thoughts.

To the Franche-Comté? I wasn't even sure where it was*. And why on earth would she have gone there? – Clearly he only intended to tell me in his sweet time.

We passed through a bedroom: his, I guessed. There was a huge canopied bed in the centre, surrounded by dog-eared, second-hand paperbacks. The bed-frame was gilt and looked surprisingly tacky, as if it came out of a bordello. Whose taste did this reflect? Magdalena's? his? I remembered his *Star Wars* phase and realized with dismay that the touch of the vulgar was still essential.

The walls were sketched over in preparation for a *trompe d'oeil.* Of what? It was then that he told me about the ideal earthly landscape I've already described – 'There's the river, there's the beach, there're the people and town on the bluff. Here's where the sun shines through the trees, and there's the villa on the shady side... Can you locate it? You've travelled around. I've searched through Italy and haven't found it, though sometimes I've felt close.'

I said I'd never seen anywhere like it but didn't add that it probably only existed in his mind, and this bedroom, if he ever got around to

* Neither was Ollie, as it turns out. I finally caught up to my darling in the Lot-et-Garonne – nowhere near those foothills and valleys below the Jura which go by the name of Franche-Comté.

slapping paint on the walls, before restlessness carried him off.

'Carine said she thought it might be in France.'

'Oh?'

'Yeh. She's gone to find it: Rodez, Sarlat, the Massif Central – that's the route we mapped. I told her to look at the cave-drawings of Lascaux while she was at it. Seemed to fit in with this interest in brass-rubbing she took up when she was here.'

Brass-rubbing? Carine?!

A kind of sullenness welled up in me. I wondered if, in the warmth of the south, I might be prompted to stick a knife into this arrogant ponce who seemed quite content to steal my wife, even to turn her into some kind of servant or disciple like I saw in the next room he led me into: one more naïve soul to do his bidding; scour the continent to find some new coven for his self-centred antics. Creep! It made me recall another painting from his time with her: a version of a 17th century lithograph in which a diabolical magician led a group of youths toward an Egyptian shrine in the woods. It was his most insinuating work from that phase; and now in this new room – studio, as he called it – a fresh version of it was hung prominently; only now the shrine was a pyre overlaid with sacrificial bull and the devotees, leader-less, a cavorting troupe from *commedia del' arte*.

Another girl, Italian, *serio*, applied paint to the leaves in the background while elsewhere in the room, carved out of a catacomb or vault, two or three student types, male and female, worked on smaller canvases, all reminiscent of things he'd done before, especially in his time with Carine; only now they were Italianate, not Flemish in mood. Bowls – what Simon Lewes had disparaged ('He would've preferred balls,' Ollie joked) – were in plentitude, as well as church interiors. But the bowls were cracked now ('breaking perfection,' he explained) and the churches bisected with shadow as if to say that for all glorious light there must be equivalent gloom.

'Sit down.' – Ollie gestured towards a chair by the lone window, a simple metal thing like in schools.

The room was a workplace not entirely unlike his bed-sit in Brook Green; only this Ollie seemed to have devoured the shy chess-player of yore, along with other personae. Picking up a sketchpad, he studied my face with the vague disinterest of a caricaturist on Charing Cross Road. Throwing down one crayon, he took up another; grunted; whistled a tattoo against his teeth; glanced up; drew. I felt as if I had gone to the dentist ('Fine incisors, weak canines, loose filling here'), a barber of old times or a shrink. Yes, shrink; because, guru that he was or aspired to be, what could he could he tell me now – about myself, about him or about this thing I was burning to know?

'She is a baby doll, isn't she?' he pre-empted before I could bring it up. (The phrase seemed inaptly American.) 'Don't move!' he added (I'd shifted irritably), then went on in the half-sleep-talking way of a man preoccupied with technical work, like pulling a molar or changing a spark-plug... Bleistein-Sloman: oppressive, fascinating; always a love-hate for 'em; wanted to rip her away from 'em; got to detest bloody Jews; can't get on without 'em, tho'; more fun-loving than most. As for the money? infuriating the way she had to go cap-in-hand to 'those non-entities' to get tuppence out of her Trust: 'I like people who make money on their own,' he summed up in a formula any good Thatcherite might've bowed down to.

I didn't ask him how he subsisted, or point out the Bleistein-Sloman role in it; I just let him ramble, curiously old-mannish, in the style of someone who's lived apart from his people for too long and has begun to sound like the village bore.

After exhausting more or less what Gisela had told me, he returned to the bone of contention: 'That's why I'll always respect her.'

'Who?'

'Carine, of course. Who do you think I've been on about? Margot?'

'I see,' I nodded, though I didn't entirely. 'Why?'

'Pietà? Schadenfreude? Guilt?'

They didn't sound like the words of a man who's just re-seduced your wife, or about a woman he'd been in absolute passion with. So had Gisela just meant to upset me with her speculations? Had he never intended to re-seduce my darling?

'I'm worried about Margot now that you've brought her up,' I said, taking an oblique tack, and went on to describe Godfrey's behaviour since the pregnancy.

Ollie concentrated on drawing – 'Just hold that', etc. Only after a time did he answer: 'You've been helpful, she says.'

'Who?'

'Margot. Were you still on about Carine?'

I chuckled. He knew, I could see.

'I owe you thanks by the way,' he added, after another pause. 'It was a mistake, you realize: mutual error... Remember the time I came to

London in secret? I'd been warned to get my paintings from Carine's before some bastard sold 'em on me.'

He said this lightly, but it didn't alter the question of who had warned him: which one of the bloody amorist's conquests? It must've been hard for him to keep them apart, I thought crossly instead of applying logic and realizing it could only've been one.

'That was a misunderstanding,' I defended, though he hadn't quite accused. 'I never set out to sell your stuff just to aggrandize *me*.'

'Don't get shirty! I trust you; that's what matters. So does Margot: we have to. We're all part of the same union of egoists, no? bound by the same web of self-interest – isn't that how it works?'

The way he pronounced 'interest', in three syllables to mimic my accent, made me wonder if this weren't some elaborate attempt to mock away genuine hurt. But then, as if reading my mind again, he went on to admit what I believe to be true, though you can never be sure: that Margot Wingfield had been the love of his life, as he of hers, and this pregnancy (he admitted to no part in another, though use of the word 'this' may have been a hint) was a 'gift from the gods' – not only because his child with Magdalena had died, but also because it tied him to England and her: tied him to that 'life-current' forever.

'I have no other relations,' he summed up matter-of-factly, though matter-of-fact was hardly how he felt.

Looking around the catacomb-like room, I contemplated a few apprentice students, numerous canvases, odd rented space in a foreign country resonant with time past. He had these now, and his girth and his spirit, and only what he was able to make otherwise. I had a wife still, as he would point out; and now my worry that he had re-seduced her fell away. Of course she'd been the one who had warned him about me and the paintings; no doubt in return he had helped her clear her head about *us* and get on a new path. But now I was ready, maybe even too eager, to accept that that's all there had been.

'She came down here from another ex-life in Paris,' he went on. 'Paris makes her thoughtful. She lived there as a student, you know: garret on the Left Bank, lectures at the Sorbonne – *la vie bohème*, till the Family yanked her back. Carine's never been as bourgeois as they make out. We took a walk by the water here and talked about you. Central France was her idea. Said she hoped you'd settle down and finish that novel finally, if she could find the right spot. *La vita artista*, mate – the only answer these days, i'n' it?'

The hint of Cockney again: he was still too English to say anything heartfelt without prophylactic irony. But the way he was handling me is a good example of how he could deal with the world at his best: listening, reflecting, giving a gentle nudge, letting you believe you were guiding yourself to your proper art-form or whatever – that was his credo. He'd shared it with others and now was applying it to me. Meanwhile, biting his tongue, he kept concentrating on what had become a most elaborate *opus*. And sitting before him in a model's enforced silence, I felt a rare, pacifying glow begin to suffuse me, a kind of spiritual endorphin which muffled the old, half-acknowledged envy; because by some odd transference, I realized that I had my girth too, although leaner than his – I had my essential self and what I wanted to give the world. I had many things he had and one thing he hadn't: the love of a sensible woman, or at least hope of it, and all the 'bourgeois' comforts that entailed.

Thinking along these lines, I felt alarmed for him suddenly and began to mock up possible futures... 'You won't catch me becoming Joshua Reynolds doing likenesses of the Great and the Good,' he grinned when I told him about Nigel and the Royal Academy. 'But say thanks when you see him.'

He went on in silence; then reverting to ruminative tones, rehearsed the fixed elements of his persona as he saw it – outsider; bohemian; a destiny forced by events, the *Zeitgeist* and one's 'body of fate', as well as choice... the trick was to make the most of it. 'Just relax and enjoy,' he summed up. 'Life'll take care of the hindmost; it does with us all. I learned that from Carine: a sort of careless, unconscious faith. Just do what you will and the Devil take the other fuckers!'

That was right. That's what you *did* learn from Carine, with her spirit and the security of Bleistein-Sloman.

But the prospects for his future without this support system made me feel a genuine shiver. 'What if you fail?' I wanted to ask. 'What if Margot and I and all these helpmates stop devoting their efforts to you? What if the galleries can't sell you, or for enough?'

'Those who serve shall be served,' he added overhearing my thought again; and out came a wave of powerful, partly insincere indifference, quite annoying – it seemed too easy. 'What I do doesn't matter. I could become a pornographer like Gisela half-tried to make me. Art isn't the be-all and end-all, you know, mate. As *Il Duce* said, "When I hear the word culture, I reach for my gun".'

So there it was: the stone wall up against which you smacked: an ultimate, nihilistic, almost narcotic lack of care, even for himself.

Silent, I wondered: did Rubens hide behind such above-it-allness, or Byron for all his posturing? Had they too not cared in the final analysis? Was that part of what greatness meant? a kind of Beethoven-like capering: a more-than-human insouciance like I'd been trying to sum up in him, or project onto him, in these post-modern, post-post-*romantische* days? But how could art not matter if you devoted your life to it, even at risk of making yourself *déclassé*, cut off from your kind? These things hadn't happened to him absolutely; but they could. He could fail. As a matter of fact, looking at him – at his body of fate, if you will – you could almost see failure waiting to pounce.

No, you couldn't think of him for long without sensing an approach to the unknown: that abyss which, once arrived at, was not going to be easy to cross. But then, these ideas led back to gods (even God) and the question of whether the Ultimate wasn't some kind of artist as well, devoting His life (our eternity) to things which hardly mattered in a larger sense, if there could be a larger sense than that. If so, wasn't this Artist also be fated to be doubled up in ambiguity? in joyful, pain-disguising mockery or mirth?

Oliver seemed blissfully unoccupied by the matter, at least so far as this outsider could see. Peeling the page from his sketchbook, he declared: '*Eccola*!' Holding it up to me, he added, '*Ecce homo*?'

I'm not sure I caught the allusions quite then. The sketch – clearly of me – looked simultaneously, even more disconcertingly, like him.

'*Andiamo*,' he went on not giving me time to react; and following him into the next room, I saw in progress the most enormous canvas of his I'd ever laid eyes on – one of the largest paintings outside of a gallery I'd seen anywhere. 'La Scuola di Londra,' he announced; and I won't soon forget him grinning at me like a circus-master, extending his hand toward – well, it was a panorama like I may have dreamt of in some unconscious moment: an apotheosis for the aspiring young man and point at which our destinies met.

Raphael's 'School of Athens' merged with Peter Blake's collage for the cover of the Beatles' *Sgt Pepper's Lonely Hearts' Club Band*. The superficial setting was steps by the Mall Gallery; only instead of the Duke of York's pillar and Regency terraces behind, the right vista faded into buildings of the City, while the left became leafy and wild, like a patch of the West Country vanishing into Celtic space.

At the lower right corner stood Ollie in front of an easel painting, while above him swirled the *dramatis personæ* of his fifteen minutes of fame: the Bleisteins-Slomans, Wingfields, Simon Lewes's crowd, Gisela, Oskar, Magdalena and various street-people of Munich and Italy. In the centre next to but slightly above these, were figures out of story – Hamlet, Rosalind, Pierrot, Harlequin, Columbine – poised and draped on the stairs, along with Shakespeare, Turner and other poets and painters finally aligned to give pride of place (like Plato and Aristotle for Raphael) to Byron and Shelley. Two further figures hovered faintly above them: Faust in a beret and Mephistopheles in trickster's cap. Above them even fainter, laughing in the clouds, was a face of indistinct identity: a kind of will o' the wisp, like Jupiter in Correggio's 'Rape of Io'. At last, flickering on the left side, were evanescent shadows – creatures of the forest as yet unfilled in. I had a feeling that only some passage out of *A Midsummer Night's Dream* could explain them; but maybe that was because the closest figure nearby was the Thinker-like Shakespeare on the stairs.

I looked to Ollie. At the far left-hand corner he stood grinning at me still, hand out presenting the tableau.

'And who is this narrative figure?' he repeated, indicating a space for human head and shoulders left blank in the trees.

In the hand not gesturing, he reached the sketch of me out to the apprentice types. The Italian girl, *serio*, put down her brush (everyone in the room, I noticed, had been painting in forms and faces from a mass of photographs and illustrations in old books) and, coming over to us, pale and rather angelic, took the sketch from his hand, studied it a moment, exchanged a look with him, then returned to her seat and started to fill in the features.

'There you are, mate,' he concluded, turning me to the door. 'What do you say now to a baptismal dunk in our crystalline, polluted sea?'

II

The Paper-Pulper's Wife

Miranda was not happy about reaching her thirty-fifth birthday. Everyone told her she looked twenty-five. In fact she looked thirty, but that was scant consolation. Miranda wanted to be eighteen again. She tried not to be jealous of her eldest daughter, who would reach that age in three years' time. Lucinda would be a bright young thing: the Cravin family name assured that. All it had achieved for her, Miranda believed, was to make her a dull old rag.

She had been eighteen when she'd met Valentine Cravin. He had been over thirty, yet seemed glamorous. To be the second son of Lord Melot, who owned so many acres in Hampshire, could not help but impress a young woman whose early memories included her father complaining about the waste of leaving one choccy bickie half-eaten by the bath in their semi-detached 'villa' on the outskirts of Oxford.

Miranda's father, Ralph Evesham, came of lower middle-class stock but had made good. Blessed with a photographic memory, he had distinguished himself in Intelligence during the War. Good-looking in a Celtic sort of way (his mother's family had come from Gwent), he had attracted the daughter of a celebrated New Zealand academic and eventually succeeded his father-in-law as world expert on secret societies since the Renaissance. On taking the chair in history at Arimathea College, he had compiled a definitive work on the genesis of the Enlightenment in England, a book which had so interested a high-ranking Royal that he had been awarded a knighthood.

The knighthood was recent: Miranda had been twenty when her father had kissed hands. In fact, the honour may even have been influenced by Sir Ralph's daughter's choice in marriage – not only was Valentine's father Lord Melot and his mother a lady-in-waiting to the Queen Mum, but both sides of his family boasted courtly bowers-and-scrapers stretching back to that moment of *Aufklärung* which Sir Ralph was expert in.

All Cravins were born to great expectations; Valentine, however, had not quite lived up to the promise of forbears. At the time of his marriage to the pulchritudinous daughter of Professor Evesham, he was a mere designer of texts about rare fabrics at one of the many presses which grow up in the environs of great universities. Now, at age forty-five, having been through two equivalent jobs at two other recently-defunct presses, he was attempting to succeed on his own as a paper-pulping merchant.

Paper-pulping was less distinguished than publishing – the kind of thing a gentleman did for money, if at all – and Valentine looked on it as his last throw of the die for success, which for him equated simply with what he called 'respectability'. One had to make a pile, do charitable works, get a knighthood or at least CBE; and waste-paper merchandising, as he preferred to call it, seemed to him the 'coming thing' the more he saw of the other end of the business. Publishing was a 'twilight industry', Valentine liked to aver. Some whispered it was because he had been so indifferent at it that he had become a pulper at all; others maintained that this turn marked his revenge towards a business which had failed to reward his merits as he thought they deserved. But whatever the truth, whatever the bitterness in Valentine's soul (his mother had once termed him 'a non-entity' and a first wife had left him for being 'a bore'), he was determined to make the new business succeed.

His financial partner, the erstwhile banker Godfrey Wingfield, hardly pulled his weight; thus Valentine had to work hard – much harder, indeed, than a scion of his class was supposed to, especially at an almost unmentionable trade. But ignominy can inspire; and Valentine, working hard, was making a go of it. He had a plant in Ayrshire which was the second largest in Europe and contracts to pulp books from the North Cape to south Spain. His firm was listed on the USM, and a deal was being mooted for a merger or acquisition (City rumours suggested both) by his most formidable rival, a cool ruthless Swede – unless he could find a White Knight to forestall it.

The anxiety this caused him was making her husband grow old, Miranda fretted. It was another reason why she was uneasy, studying her face in the mirror.

Her own looks she took care of. 'You're not getting obsessed about staying young, are you?' Valentine would chide when she complained of him wearing a coat and tie, even on weekends – even practically to bed. This was not how he had dressed when she'd first met him: when they had married, he'd had longish hair and worn colourful shirts and interesting boots, 'hip' in the style of the times. He had been slim still, so that with his great height and sandy looks (flawed only by a diagonal slash over the lip), he might've been taken for the lead-singer of Zane, the pop group, rather than a mere commissioning editor for a pictorial study of fleas and flukes. Now with his hair thinning and clothes as they were, Valentine looked even more conventional than Godfrey Wingfield – and Godfrey at least had the bohemian grace of getting tipsy and voluble.

Valentine was, alas, (dare a second wife say it?) a bore.

('Worse sins than being boring,' Margot Wingfield might muse.

'What are they?' her husband would wonder.

'Give me an hour and I might think of one,' she'd retort.)

The Wingfield pair were chaotic, it was true. 'At least we have *some* order in our lives,' Valentine would point out when Miranda made invidious comparisons; 'look what's become of their sons!' The Wingfield boys were naughty, perhaps; but their father didn't have a pot belly (Godfrey swam at the RAC three times a week), and their mother didn't have a husband so career-obsessed that he hadn't been able to get her with child at the rate of one every other year. Life was not passing by for the Wingfields, though they were older by far than her (Margot was forty-five if a day). But I'm being horrid, Miranda pouted at the face in the mirror, pencilling in eye make-up. For she did wear make-up nowadays, even though, as Margot persisted in saying, she was 'the most natural English rose'.

Margot herself had once worn make-up like war-paint; now she disguised her envies by expressing them outright. But Margot was brave: she had a name on her own merits and some success. Long the most chatted-about literary agent in London, she was rumoured to be writing a novel as well, despite having whelped all those boys. Margot had a life; Miranda, like other women, felt small by contrast. With only three children, two of them daughters, and no career to speak of, unless you counted the classes in life-drawing she went to on Tuesday evenings, she might well have challenged the face in the mirror – what do you have? greying hair you dye amber? green eyes you claim to be blue? round cheeks which you paint to seem arched? a nose you long to have 'done'? You are no beauty, she might have concluded, and half thought she should – though deeper inside,

Miranda agreed with the many who thought her a knock-out.

She'd had some success with men (well, boys actually) before marrying Valentine Cravin. Memories from that era sometimes caused her real pain. Why didn't I marry Andy who'd loved me, or Martyn who wanted to have sex all the time? Why did I let myself be seduced by this boring, upper class English prig when I could've had anyone I fancied? – Don't think about it... Should I put on red lipstick? She studied the feature everyone thought her best: the mouth shaped like a bell. Her lips looked 'like a kiss', Godfrey Wingfield had once blurted; and in private, she had cherished the phrase, though, as Margot had said, Godfrey in his cups would flirt with a bar stool. Oddly, Margot didn't seem to mind these vagaries in her husband: at least he had spunk. That's why people liked being invited to the Wingfields. All sorts turned up there, in Holland Park, unlike at the Cravins in grey Islington.

Why did they live in Islington, Miranda had asked Valentine early in their marriage: he wasn't a journalist and didn't have to be in the City every day – why didn't they live in Holland Park or at least Notting Hill like the Wingfields? 'Find a better place and we can move,' he had said; but Miranda knew he never would, willingly. He had bought their narrow, four-storey Georgian terraced house as an investment with money his father had given him on coming down from Cambridge; it had cost £14,000 then or something preposterous; now it was worth £350,000 and had been up to nearly five before the Crash. Miranda had lived there ever since her marriage; her children had grown up in rooms she'd redecorated. She'd redone everything except the sitting-room, which remained in the style of Valentine's first wife, a woman whose aura was expunged otherwise.

Miranda had washed the kitchen blue and playroom orange and hung circus scenes on the nursery walls. These touches marked the place off as her own. Not least among them was the marital bedroom which she'd had built on top of the roof. This fairy-tale chamber had an 18th century four-poster bed in it, a Regency settee under the sash-window and an en suite loo behind a hand-painted, Bloomsbury style *trompe d'oeil*. The bathroom contained free-standing enamelled basins; the dressing-table she sat at had been transported from her gran's in New Zealand, just as it had once – in the dimness of the turn-of-the-century – been shipped out to that far-flung end of the world. Ecclesiastical prints decorated the walls, these a contribution of Valentine's. As a matter of fact, they were among the few presents he'd ever given her, and he'd done so in part because they'd come as a bargain through his father, who had more or less entertained himself as honorary consul at Siena during the year of their marriage.

Italy had seen their honeymoon as a consequence of that – Lady Melot had a friend with a villa outside of Empoli, which she'd been willing to let 'for a song'. It had been September then too, and Miranda had been charmed. Whatever the status of her father as academic, youth in Oxford had hardly been grand; holidays had been to relations in South Wales, or environs of this academic conference or that. Never had she been anywhere so other-worldly as Sentinale, which struck her on first sight as the perfect wedding between the aristocratic and the sensual: an atmosphere she had not known in any moment of her life before or since…

The breeze had been gentle, the mountains in the distance blue. The red earth was so fertile: every plant seemed to grow to twice the size of in England. London, Oxford, Gwent – all she had known seemed grey and old by contrast; dead and embalmed by suppressive civilization. Italy had come as a revelation to her. If only she'd had a soulmate to be ravished by it with!

Valentine had wanted to see frescoes. He'd sought out the intelligent, the chirpy, the getting-on. It was their honeymoon, but had Miranda been able to get him to bask in the sun, let alone draw himself up again to bed in long afternoons, as lovers were meant to do? She might have realized then from the extent of his indifference (he had not initiated sex once), that she was entering a disaster.

'You're marrying out of class,' her mother had warned in one of the few personal remarks that lady ever made; but Miranda hadn't listened. She'd hated the mean atmosphere of her parents' home, which persisted even after her father started lecturing across Europe. She despised too her mother's defeatist attitude; also the origin of it, which she'd discovered at age sixteen – that her father had a female colleague at Lady Anne's College, expert on Mme de Staël, as his 'alchemical bride'. Never would she allow herself be treated like that, Miranda had resolved. Never would she let herself grow plump and sexless like her brown bird of a mother: she who had been whistled at by boys hanging out of their college windows – she would distinguish herself with what she married and make a success out of Love!

A 'corker' they'd called her. In particular, she'd dazzled the eyes of one American student who rented a room in her parents' house. He'd been the first to undress her – and what pretty, sharp little breasts she had had! and what thighs! What a shape to make everyone stop and gawp as she'd strolled down Woodstock Road in hot pants... But then, she'd been seduced by Valentine Cravin – not by *him*, so much as an idea that in one swoop she could arrive at a point on the ladder of reputation that her parents had only reached through her father's currying of favour with a Royal. In one swoop she could become the daughter-in-law of Lady Melot and attender at garden parties of the Queen. In one swoop, she could go off for the most romantic kind of honeymoon to 'a spot of real old European cachet', as her father had dubbed it. Yet in one swoop, having done so, she could also lose all the fun, the sensuality, the freedom of expectation and movement that being an eighteen-year-old corker entailed.

Miranda recalled:

Most hurtful had been the night – third or fourth at Sentinale – when she'd inadvertently, half in a dream, begun to fondle his genitals and he'd started up: 'What are you doing? Never do that! Don't you realize that to do anything to somebody when they're unconscious is as bad as putting drugs in their coffee or taking advantage of a child?'

She had been stunned. The next morning she hadn't known what to say when, after breakfast, he'd set off with his hat and his stick to find a 12th century hermitage up in the hills. O, she had wept. There she was, hardly twenty, not much more than a demi-*vierge*, and this was to be her sex life?

To be fair, he had tried to be kind to her that evening, explaining Palestrina through dinner (early music was one of his passions), drinking more wine than usual and snoring like a congested baby in bed. The next morning he'd even offered 'a treat', as he called it: he would take her riding for the first time: 'All Englishwomen worth the name know how to ride. We'll teach you here so you needn't be embarrassed at home. Much less expensive anyway.'

Miranda had been terrified. The Italian guide, a mere boy, had kept looking back at her with an impish (she saw it as devilish) grin. He'd cast his eyes at Valentine too, who sandwiched her in from behind. Valentine had declined to smile back presumably, because halfway through their hour the boy had stopped his nods and winks and simply lashed them on hell-bent. By some miracle Miranda had not fallen off; but that night her bottom felt like it had been spanked for a week. Her calves had sores on them and inner thighs ached as if she'd been doing what she and Valentine ought to have been doing, were it a real honeymoon. And, strange to say, no sooner had she thought this than they *would* have been doing it, had he had his way. For as she lay there examining the red spots on her body, his blood had come up. What had caused this? the ride? the Pan-like grin of the guide? her pained whimperings? Without explanation, for the first and only real time in their marriage, Valentine had wanted to make love to her – to rut with her, act out the animal inside him, however pinstriped or incongruous the exterior. And with Valentine Cravin, she would have to admit, the exterior was frankly that.

She'd had an inkling of this the following morning when she'd gone to the stables again and, while waiting for the guide (his name was Bernardo), witnessed a sight which in her relatively sheltered town life she'd only heard of, never seen. Florio, the handsome but dozy young stallion she'd ridden, stood by the wall fully saddled and stamping – and got an erection. First it was a dangle of black; then extending, black and pink; then expanding, not a dangle but a branch as thick as the leg or the arm of a child or small person (or not so small). Twitching and hard as the rubber of some industrial hosepipe, it nearly smacked his belly; and Miranda had to look away.

After a while, she peered back and saw that the trance or mad spasm had passed and thing begun to vanish. Snorkling itself back up, it disappeared so entirely that, if it hadn't've been for the shrivelling sack behind, she might have taken him for a mare. Then Bernardo arrived, quite dozy himself. Miranda had been sent back to him because Valentine had to go into Siena to see his mother, a woman Miranda already felt irked by. On their arrival at Pisa, Lady Melot had announced that her son's second wife struck her as 'another social climber' (her fatal verdict on his first); and feeling that his bride ought to have some occupation while he paid diplomatic court to this *grande dame*, he'd arranged for Miranda to 'continue her lessons'. Miranda had complied, though she'd wanted to know what these lessons were in aid of: she hardly longed to ride to the hounds back in Hampshire; and did he really imagine that a child of the 1970s from Oxford, howevermuch a 'social climber', would go in for blood-sport?

Such thoughts rose and faded as Florio, recently so proud in young maleness, trotted underneath her like a baby falling asleep. '*Avanti!*

Avanti!' Bernardo cajoled, winking back; and shortly the lulling gait of the horses, heat and so forth sent Miranda into a daydream in which she perceived subliminally what she later would know, acquiring a teenaged son of her own – how this kind of male energy *did* rise and fall in peculiar spasms. She would realize many things about the male of the species later on; but at this stage, she could hardly construe why the Italian boy kept winking at her. In general annoyance, she too tried to coax Florio to go faster; at which Bernardo smiled like what Valentine had called 'a *cinquecento* angel mixed with a trickster by Frans Hals'. He had not shaved the down off his chin that morning... and when Florio bolted (three pack-mares laden with faggots startled them by appearing suddenly out of a wood, driven by an ancient ghoul), he galloped after her and caught the stallion's reins before she could be pitched down a crevasse.

There is something inevitably intimate about two horses coming together on a deserted Tuscan meadow; about a boy of sixteen and woman of barely twenty bouncing to rest side-by-side in such a heavenly place. Disaster averted, Miranda could hardly help but look at this angelic visage with more tenderness. She could not but believe that the demonic grin *did* belong to the illegitimate grandson of some prince of the church (another of Valentine's speculations). And for fifteen years after, she would dream about what might have been then but had not, because she'd been scared... because she'd been married to Valentine Cravin and half-realized that, on that fatal night before, he'd got her with her first child.

Ardently, she would wish during a long winter of first pregnancy that it had been Bernardo who'd sired the growth inside her. For mixed with the sun and the stallion, censoriousness of her husband, Lady Melot and the rest, an image of this boy as lover grew in her mind, until it became a semi-divine apparition – an incarnation of sweet, free young maleness, so trim and so pure that it was almost feminine, yet endowed in body and spirit such that it might have belonged to a *condottiere*, a soldier of fortune or highwayman of old tales; a Heathcliff of the sun or cowboy of old Europe; a thief of Baghdad or rock-star on horseback... Miranda's mind whirled. Indeed, her body still ached for that dream-lover and father of her child who might have been her secret twin.

*

But this was 'woman's magazine stuff', as Valentine would have said had he been privy to her thoughts. And with such words loud in her mind, Miranda's imaginings began to detumesce.

Lucinda had been born; then out of maternal instinct, not passion came Hugo and Anne. Miranda had sustained herself on babies' love: 'cupboard love' as with all children, Valentine would say. Be that as it was, something had gone. As the children had grown, her bonding with them diffused; so that now, as she sat looking at herself in the mirror, Miranda wondered if she were *ever* going to have that thing she had longed for for herself, or if she could even recall what it was.

Fifteen years had passed.

She put on pale lipstick, a bit of powder, some earrings she'd bought in the Portobello Road. She straightened her black skirt – the style that year was short: nearly back to the mini. Underneath it, she wore fishnet hose; over it, a false silk fitted top of *eau-du-nil*. She looked a touch vampish if truth were told: the opposite of her normal incarnation between Safeway and school-run.

'How do I look?' she used to ask Valentine once done up thus.

'How do you look?!' he'd retort, as if the question were a joke.

'That's what I asked.'

'Well, if you really want to know...'

She didn't bother anymore. 'Mutton dressed as lamb' he would say; and since it was now her thirty-fifth birthday, it seemed too close to truth for comfort.

Hurrying down the steep stairs, she encountered Anne, her youngest, just twelve. 'You look brill, Mum.'

In the sitting-room lounged her two others, spellbound by a soap-opera on TV. A hunk of a young man was pleading with a gorgeous blond whose accent resembled a barmaid's.

'Think so?' she answered, half-appalled at herself – did she need affirmation from her children of all things?

If so, she could hardly expect much. Hugo, fagged out from a teenaged boy's covert activities, cast a guilty glance at her, while Lucinda, deep in speculation about how to break hearts, busied herself painting her nails. How cruel life was! You married a man: he lectured, chided or ignored. You produced children who hung on the teat until they grew into these beauties ripe for every pleasure yet for all the world acting embarrassed to know you.

Hugo lifted his bum and passed wind.

'Of course you do,' Anne repeated so sweetly that Miranda could only conclude that her youngest was lying.

Still, she kissed the child, who was too plump to be pretty but too good-natured to nag about it. 'I'm meeting your dad there. You're all invited. Are you sure none of you want to come?'

'Muuuum!' Lucinda brayed. 'Those Wingfield boys're disgusting. I wouldn't go there again if you paid me!'

What did she mean by 'again', Miranda wondered while negotiating the family Volvo through traffic around King's Cross. Was Lucinda seeing the eldest Wingfield boy still? What was his name? Augustus? Gus? She couldn't keep track. Swarming hellions all. At least her own were polite, in public.

That was their father's influence. Valentine loved Form. Keeping it up was the real responsibility, he would say. 'I don't care what you do,' he had once let out in a row over their sex life, 'just don't disgrace the family'; and that was what he had taught the children. Well, it was perhaps a good philosophy for children; but for a marriage? It sounded like the rationalization for a non-marriage, Margot Wingfield had remarked in one of those unbuttoned moments when Miranda had confided in her: 'I can't stand it. I hate him!'

Calm as the Queen in her throne room, Margot had offered tea. 'You poor dear. Of course half the time I hate Godfrey like the plague; but what's one to do? He *is* the father of my sons.'

She'd made this sound as if perhaps one or two people thought he wasn't, at least not of all of them. 'Yes,' Miranda had whimpered. 'Sometimes I think it would've been better to have had one on the wrong side of the sheets. Then maybe I'd feel some independence.'

Margot had pondered. 'I don't think it would've worked in your case. You're too much the perfect English rose for such evil secrets.'

Miranda had faintly disliked Margot's tone. In fact, she had wondered if she really liked her husband's partner's wife – Margot had grown more and more lofty with success. On the other hand, given children and life galloping by as it was, what time did one have to go make a new friend? And there was something quite mesmerizing about la Wingfield: the way she listened, considered and delivered her *mots*. Going to her saved on going to a shrink. Besides, Miranda was drawn to the upper-middle class artsiness of the house in Ladbroke Grove, though Valentine loathed it, or claimed he did. She felt there was Life there as well as Form, whatever the sons got up to.

Fighting rush-hour in Bayswater Road, she was just turning into Margot's street when her lights caught the eyes of a figure crossing. This was her first glimpse of Oliver Murrie, though she had no idea who he was then, nor what role he would play in her career afterwards. Often she would think back on this moment, cherishing it as a turning-point in an otherwise dull existence. But the moment itself seemed quite ordinary – perhaps *coups de foudre* always do. What Miranda saw in her headlamps was simply a glint of eyes still as glass: then as she passed, a well-boned, slightly sunburnt face above a Shetland wool sweater.

He was leading a child by the hand. Nor was it his looks that arrested her in afterthought so much as the child's. Wasn't it one of Margot's? Didn't its eye have a gleam (she would return to this later) similar to that in the pair above? a spark of wonder made sad by fatigue, or to use a phrase he would teach her, made soulful by *hiraeth*?

'Did I see just one of yours in the street?' she asked Margot once arrived in the Wingfield kitchen.

Margot was enthroned in her spot by the fridge. A wine bottle and glasses, two boys and two adults were in attendance.

'That would have been Lucius. I asked Oliver to go to the off-licence; Luke wanted to go too. Why, is something wrong?'

Miranda might have asked who this Oliver was, but Margot pre-empted her by introducing Carine and Tony Thomas, the adults, a married couple. Meanwhile the boys, Marcus, 10, and Matthew, 12, argued over a last round of sandwiches set out for tea.

'Neither of you can have more,' mama officiated. 'There won't be enough for supper, and I'm not cooking again tonight.'

Protesting, the two trailed out. Perhaps another drifted in; Margot paid scant attention. There was a flurry of wine-offering, superfluous in Miranda's case – she'd given up drink on taking up aerobics; besides, she had never drunk much anyhow. At one time Margot had not drunk much either, back in the days when she'd been pregnant all the time. But pregnancy had now been replaced by *la vie artiste*; and Miranda had long heard of the sodden state this led to from Valentine's complaints when a publisher:

'I can't stand bloody artists and writers, that's my problem. They're nothing but a bunch of whinging, egotistical sots!' (Colleagues in the paper-pulping business were not turning out much better: 'egotistical and whinging' had been replaced by 'guffawing and wheedling' but the 'sot' part remained – thus Margot's husband, Godfrey, as Valentine never tired of describing him.)

Margot, however, in recent weeks seemed to have another, more obscure reason for the tot of gin in her tea. Nothing had been said: la Wingfield rarely confided in Miranda the way Miranda felt compelled to in her. But she did show stress, if one looked closely; and she was showing it now, mascara smudged slightly, hair subtly askew, like her red lipstick and shoulder of a low-collared blouse. Though grand still, if heavy from having borne all those sons, Margot looked somewhat loose nowadays – as if one of her shapely legs were itching to kick down the door and trot her off like a bag-lady into the street.

'What is the "modern religion" then?' she asked drily, returning to a topic under discussion when Miranda had stepped in.

There was always a topic under discussion at Margot's table: high-blown talk with young chatterers eager to show off. Tony Thomas was one of these evidently, though like many who paid obeisance at the Wingfield court, he was perhaps not so young. American, though softened, Miranda heard in the accent, he had shaggy blond hair and was a child of the '60s, she supposed, or perhaps, like her, shortly after. For a moment, she felt herself half-fancying him, though his nose was too thin. Then the thought came that he'd probably enjoyed more of the '60s than she had, and resentment rose.

Carine, his bright-eyed wife, was clearly Jewish.

'It depends on which country you're in,' he retorted.

'In America it's money, I should've thought,' went on Margot.

'That's their old religion.'

He said 'their' as if it were not his. What was he then? Canadian?

'Oh? Do they have a new one?'

'Not unless it's being culture-philistines.'

This was not a term Miranda was familiar with. Fortunately Margot put in: 'I'm not certain what you mean. As a matter of fact, I'm not sure I understand Americans at all or much want to – barring your dear self, of course.'

He was American then. So why did he refer to his people as 'they'?

'What's the English religion?' Carine piped up.

It seemed that she had no more interest in the topic than in being cut off from her wine, but obliged her man by pretending. Must not've been married for long, Miranda concluded. She herself had given up pandering to Valentine years before; with Godfrey, Margot never had bothered.

'I'm not sure,' la Wingfield mused. 'What do you reckon? Class?'

Margot and Tony's wife seemed as opposed as you could get: the one round, fertile, superficially pessimistic, the other brittle, tousle-haired and chirpy as a flea.

'Class is too facile,' Tony suggested. 'I think the current English religion is children and country-life.'

Miranda wondered how he had come up with this. His wife was little more than a child and looked as urban as the spires of St Pancras Station. Did it mean he had a lover?

'You mean family and flowers – that sort of thing?'

Margot made a point of not looking at him as she said this, and Miranda's mind leapt: was she having it off with *him*?

'Yes. Anyhow for the "best people". English public schoolgirls, etc.'

He spoke far too knowledgably. And how dreadful, Miranda thought: how could Margot?! Of course, she'd suspected for months – years even: ever since, following a particularly self-indulgent whinge over Valentine's bed-manners, Margot had speculated that she, Miranda, ought to consider a lover. But a lover in Miranda's view had to be perfect. He had to be physically right, which this man was not – at least not for Margot. He had to be uninvolved with anyone else, also not the case here. He had to be a Lancelot, a Lone Ranger, a kind of stallion or Italian farm-boy with a spark of Pan in the eye.

'Are they the best people?... Miranda, what do you think?'

What did she think? Children and country? English public schoolgirls? What had been the question? the 'real religion'? Yes, she loved children, or said she did, her own anyway; but who didn't? who admitted to hating the little demons half the time? The country, well: she liked going to Hampshire at weekends. But the place belonged to Valentine's family, who were country-people in only the most exalted sense. And she was sick of 17th century gardens and the hunt.

What else was there?

'Sex,' Tony filled in, surprising her with anticipation of her thought and unnerving her with a look.

'What about sex?' – this from Carine, who squeezed a mitt around her husband's arm.

'It's religion to that type,' he said irritably.

Miranda was disgusted. So was this what marriage did to everyone, even Yankees and Jews?

'Sex is religion?' Margot queried. 'I should've thought it was one of your American vices.'

'Not really. You don't know Americans well. They don't understand sex like you do. Like so much else that has to do with living, they're still in a pre-civilized stage.'

'Why do you say "they"?' Miranda asked. 'Aren't you one of them?'

'Tony's an expatriate,' Carine said, as if proudly.

Miranda looked to Margot. Margot avoided her eyes.

'All the best people are,' Tony tiresomely quipped.

'You mean like Oliver?' murmured the hostess. 'He's an expatriate too, isn't he?'

'He's come back now. Depends if he stays.'

All of them went silent, though perhaps for different reasons.

'Why, where has he been?' Miranda took up.

Margot turned to her dinner preparations.

'Italy,' Carine answered and looked to Miranda so beseechingly that another, even more incongruous thought arose: the little Jewish girl was this Oliver's lover as well!

Clearly her own lack of love was making her unhinged, Miranda reflected as they went up for dinner. She saw 'subtexts' (a word Tony had used) in everything. Most likely, there was nothing in any of these lives more extraordinary than in her own. Or was there?

Anyhow, Godfrey and Valentine now came in: and if anything could cut off romantic speculation, it was the appearance of the English husband home from his day of the extended business lunch he called work. Godfrey was lit up; Valentine exasperated. Both looked like characters out of Wodehouse or Waugh: fogeys in the hinterland between youth and age, exuberance and bile, callowness and self-suppression into the code of their tribe.

That tribe was, of course, the English public-school, an institution which extended into middle life, or perhaps the grave. Like the mass of the English who had not attended one of these august institutions, Miranda felt the mixed emotions of the excluded: a combination of admiration and contempt which public school-boys themselves are so trained in fending off that it would have only surprised them if the reaction had been favourable, or indifferent. From their women, they expected no less. And from Margot no less than Miranda, it's what they got. It was perhaps what the two wives had most in common.

'Who's coming for dinner?' Godfrey demanded. 'It's Miranda's birthday: that's what Valentine said. Miranda, is it really your birthday? Who'd want to come for one of Margot's horsemeat pies on her birthday? Valentine must be having me on.'

'It's not a good joke, Godfrey. Miranda does not eat meat.'

'Happy birthday, darling,' murmured Valentine and made a show of pecking his wife on the cheek.

He did this sometimes, in public. But the real answer to Godfrey's expert thrust was that no woman would have chosen to come for one of her friend's 'horsemeat pies' on her birthday if her husband had organized to take her somewhere more suitable. One needn't have done more than read a woman's magazine to know that. But Valentine never read women's magazines and had been too busy to organize anything appropriate. So Margot had stepped in.

'Sorry, darling,' he whispered as if just realizing. 'I should've taken you to that place in Upper Street you fancy, shouldn't I?'

'Of course not,' Miranda snapped, afraid of upsetting her hostess, though Margot hardly seemed to care who turned up at her table.

'Who's sitting where?' burped Godfrey, gravitating towards his carver. 'Who else is supposed to be here?' he put to his wife.

'Pipe down, dearest. You're as loud as the boys.'

'The boys? What boys? They aren't very loud now, are they? Where are they? You haven't finally got fed up and diced them into the pie, have you?' – Laughing at his macabre witticism, he plunked himself down at the head of an incongruously formal dining-table.

A ghost of grandeur lurked around *chez* Wingfield. It was not only in the house itself, which would have fetched twice the price of the Cravins, but the furniture, which Godfrey had inherited from his mother when she'd fled England after his father's death. He was French on her side, ex-colonial on the other.

'What a positively revolting thought, sons in the pie,' Valentine mused, glancing to his wife. (Why on earth must we have dinner here, the glance said: I have to endure him all day. Isn't that quite enough?)

Miranda straightened her fringe.

'Let the birthday girl sit next to me!' Godfrey brayed.

He was horrid, she thought, settling beside him but taking care to avoid his attempt to buss her lips. Stocky, balding, with clown-like orange clumps on his temples, Godfrey Wingfield was much less attractive when full of an afternoon's ration of whisky; and he was hardly God's gift to women when sober.

'Valentine, sit next to Margot,' he commanded.

'I'm not sitting, I'm serving,' Margot pointed out. 'And do try to be a gracious host.'

'Try to be? I'm always gracious!' – He turned to Tony and Carine. 'Hello, Godfrey Wingfield, pleased to meet you. You are – ?'

'Godfrey! You've known Tony and Carine for years. Stop being rude. No one but you thinks it's the slightest amusing.'

In fact, no one did, though Tony tried to snicker, while poor Carine blushed to the roots of her salt-and-pepper curls. Godfrey had once worked for her family's merchant-bank. It was a phase of his career few any longer mentioned.

All sat, except Margot. Besides her chair, two others were empty.

'Who's meant to be there?' her husband inquired, pointing with the wine-carafe stopper.

'Banquo's ghost,' she said blandly, 'I'll get soup', and turned to go.

'Honestly, sweetheart, do prepare us for whatever other odd creature you're going to inflict on us. It's not more bloody paint-dabblers or word-merchants, I hope.'

'It is not.'

'Well who is it? We're dying of curiosity.'

'Just turn up your toes then.'

Exit.

Miranda, Valentine, Tony and Carine unfolded their napkins and put them on their laps. Godfrey glared after his wife.

'Probably Booby,' he muttered.

'Booby Vänder?' asked Miranda to be polite – she'd often heard Margot speak of this American adventuress but had never met her.

'Bloody Booby! Margot feels sorry for her. Apparently her lover stood her up because his wife'd arranged a dinner he'd forgot about. He gave Booby some cock-and-bull about why he couldn't meet her under a bush in Regent's Park or wherever these types do their jiggery-pokery, what? But when Booby found out he was lying, she drove to his house and ran the car back and forth over the rose-bushes while the wife and guests watched from the window.'

Tony chuckled.

'Rather good, isn't it?' Godfrey guffawed.

'Adulteresses like that ought to be put down,' Valentine observed.

'It was the man who was committing adultery,' Miranda corrected.

'The woman too.'

Carine took it up. 'Can an unmarried lover be called an adulterer?'

Nobody seemed to hear her. 'That's another part of the English religion,' Tony said to Miranda.

'What's part of the English religion?' Valentine asked severely, religion being one of his topics.

'Adultery.'

Godfrey burped. It did not sit well with Miranda's husband:

'I'm sorry,' he said across the table, 'I didn't get your name. You're American, are you?'

It was going to be a long evening, she could see.

Valentine interrogated Tony and Carine on the religions they'd been brought up in, this with the loftiness of one who had sung for years in amateur choirs and actually believed in the C of E, or said so. Miranda took to gazing at the empty chairs and wondering where one could find a still point in the universe or, barring that, a wild horse to ride away on.

Margot returned.

'Who's missing?' Godfrey repeated to her, pouring wine.

She busied herself ladling soup.

'Well?' he demanded, arriving at one of the empty places. 'If you don't tell me, heart, how am I to know whether to fill these glasses?'

Margot passed bowls. 'Booby's not coming after all,' she admitted following a lengthy silence.

'I knew it was Booby! What's happened? Has her lover left her now that his wife's rose-bushes're crushed?'

'Other people's misfortunes are not funny, Godfrey.'

'That's all very well; but what's one meant to do in this life, weep?'

Valentine finished his soup almost before the others had been served. Hoovering food was one of his holdovers from school. Wiping his lips, he now weighed in:

'I agree with Margot. Adultery's not funny; it's pathetic.'

'Indeed,' said the hostess, rising to his posture of offended dignity.

She did not look remotely towards Tony Thomas as she said this, but Miranda did. He was smirking. Carine meanwhile kept her eyes on her soup.

'"Indeed",' Godfrey echoed sardonically. 'Valentine's always right, isn't he? I'm sure if he ever caught Miranda with another man, he'd stuff them both into one of his pulping machines.'

This produced another guffaw. Ever since he and Valentine had gone into business together people had been getting stuffed into pulping machines. It was humour worthy of a six-year-old, Miranda reflected. Yet did he perhaps know about Margot and Tony? Could his guffaws have been hiding the tears of a clown? Had Godfrey once been sufficiently in love with his wife to be hurt? Had he once been a swain to Margot's shepherdess? Had passion been the reason for all those pregnancies? Wasn't this man pouring wine really the wreck of a kind of husband Valentine Cravin ought to have been for her?

Starved for love as she was, Miranda felt she could throw herself into anything rather than more of her own husband's cold, pompous respectability. Maybe he wasn't a bad man ethically; still, time, hurt and indifference had made him so unappealing to her that even poor Godfrey's slobbery kisses might have been preferable. Shocking herself with this thought, Miranda nonetheless continued to sit there perfectly decorously, polite as a prim wife, until, at last, Carine's eyes brought her back. They were gazing at her, beseeching; and she realized, or thought, that the woman was worried that *her* husband was going to leave her.

Tony, meanwhile, was still looking covertly at Margot. Imagining Carine to be asking her to distract him, Miranda began, 'Tony?' – Yes, that was right, the eyes said: keep him from looking at Margot and thereby Godfrey from making a scene.

'Yes?' he answered, so willing to be diverted that Miranda half-wondered if she should make a play for him – but with the eyes of both Margot and Carine on her, she could hardly consider bringing about *that* amount of complication and betrayal.

'You mentioned – ' What had he mentioned? What could she say? 'The English religion.'

'Bloody religion!' Godfrey muttered, plunking back in his chair.

Margot vanished to get the main course.

'Children, country, sex – and sex, preferably as adultery. That's my theory,' the American obliged.

He sounded terrifically proud of himself – almost as bad in an opposite way to Valentine, who now put in with affected amiability: 'Why is it that some of you ex-colonials assume that only ideas that shock can be interesting? One used to think rather a lot of your country. Nowadays one wonders if all that freedom hasn't made even the best of you lose your sense of proportion.'

Tony smiled, false amiability evidently being a mask of his too. 'Don't judge them by me. I'm sure out of the 250 million you could find one or two still to your taste.'

Miranda saw the knuckles of Valentine's hand go white. She began to feel a touch ill. Fortunately at that moment, Margot came back in with the pie. 'O I do wish Oliver would get here,' she murmured. 'They have been gone rather a long time.'

Godfrey, who'd started to fall into an inter-course sleep, sat up as if he had been slapped across the jowls. 'Oliver? Good God, not Oliver Murrie. He hasn't come back to haunt us, has he?'

'I get rather worried about you when you're like this,' Margot observed, his face having gone crimson. 'Valentine, how much have you let him drink today? I won't have him apoplectic.'

'I take no responsibility for your husband's ingestion of spirits.'

'Why not? You're his partner.'

Miranda had never seen Margot like this: masterful as a monarch over not only her brood, some wannabe or her husband, but *her* husband as well. She was picking a fight with Valentine, for godsake.

'Don't change the subject!' cried Godfrey. 'I do not wish to have that man in my house, as you know.'

'He's not in your house.' – Margot passed Carine a plate of pie and potato. 'He's gone to the off-licence with Luke.'

'With Lucius?!' Godfrey stood up and threw down his napkin. 'That does it! What do you take me for, heart?'

'A rude host. Do please sit.'

These words were exchanged in a space of seconds, while Carine's, Tony's and Miranda's heads swivelled as if at Wimbledon. Valentine fumed over Margot's swipe at him; Miranda intuited that Godfrey's reason for dislike of Oliver Murrie must have been great indeed for Margot to have tried to deflect him; Godfrey, still standing, practically panted down the table as his wife passed plates to the rest with *froideur*. At last Valentine spoke up:

'Oliver Murrie. I'm not sure I'm familiar with that name.'

'Shut up, Valentine,' Godfrey snapped.

Margot repeated, 'Godfrey, sit!'

Carine blushed.

'It's too bad you have it out for Ollie,' Tony observed in his host's direction, forking his crust to see what was inside. 'Maybe you had a reason to dislike him, but he's lost everything now. Until a few weeks ago, it wasn't even certain he still had his wits about him. We're lucky he isn't six foot under.'

Godfrey ignored this melodramatic assertion; he was still glaring at his wife, who blandly replied, 'Tony's right. Carine's organizing a place for him: somewhere in the country, to recover in. And I'm not about to turn out someone who's been through what he has, whatever scene you wish to create.'

Miranda was on edge to know what, where and when. In fact, this was the moment when the image of the man in her headlamps first began to have more than passing interest for her; it may even have been when the dart of Cupid first pricked her parched spirit to suggest that he was her twin. Gazing at the empty chair, she wondered: could he be a still-point among all these wagging heads? an oasis of silence in the midst of incipient violence? Because violence is what it felt like when Valentine put in:

'I should think if the man's had recent mental problems it's rather a rum idea to let him out with one of your sons.' – His pomp made it sound as if he had a personal stake in the matter.

Margot glanced at him oddly.

'But Ollie loves children,' Carine said. 'Whatever condition he's in, he'd take beautiful care of a child.'

Miranda was all ears.

'Well I'm not letting him do it to my son!' Godfrey erupted again.

'To whose son?' queried Margot.

'To either of yours's,' intervened Valentine, as if the Voice of Reason. 'Do sit, both of you; you're as bad as Miranda – far too emotional. What's needed here is tact. Shall I go out and find them?'

'Fuck off, Valentine,' breathed Godfrey.

'Pardon me?' he inhaled.

'You heard him,' Margot muttered, making Miranda's husband look at her in shock.

'They're right,' summed up Tony. 'This is their business, not yours.'

Miranda was spellbound. Here was Valentine, risen from his seat, ready to adopt the pose he liked most, Grand Arbiter of Dignity; and there were Godfrey and Margot daggers drawn, Tony Thomas and apparently even his sweet wife adamant that they were not going to let him interfere with what they all for some reason saw as their personal affair – this Banquo of Oliver Murrie.

'Don't you think,' Carine seconded, 'that we all might sit? Ollie's been back for an hour almost. I saw him upstairs with the boys when I went to have a wee.'

Everyone stared at her.

'Why on earth didn't you say so?' Margot asked; and the sharp little Jewish girl took on depth in Miranda's eyes.

'Because nobody asked me and, even if they had, I couldn't've got a word in edgeways, as per norm.'

Silence. The men looked to their plates.

'Well I'm still not eating this bloody horsemeat!' muttered Godfrey, tossing back wine.

'Suit yourself,' concluded his wife. 'But this is Miranda's birthday, and it *is* rather hard on your partner's spouse not to behave properly.'

In so saying, Margot was of course being subtly rude herself; but Miranda hardly cared. Her mind was already halfway up the stairs.

It was Valentine who gave back: 'Well you are being rude to her, not to mention me... I think we'd better go, darling. What do you say? fancy an Indian or Italian, just the two of us?'

Perhaps it was the word Italian, or 'horsemeat!' again on Godfrey's lips as he cut into his pie. Perhaps it was some subconscious emotion, or just an inner knowledge that she needed to manufacture an excuse. Whatever the trigger, Miranda swooned at that moment. For a brief second, she fainted away into a dream of galloping on Florio, the stallion, with Bernardo, the guide, leading her towards a stable where Oliver Murrie waited, smiling at her.

'Must go to the loo,' she murmured.

Had the others noticed? Certainly not Godfrey or Margot, still serving. Tony or Carine?

Valentine stood, as if gallant. 'Shall I get your coat?'

'Don't be an ass, Valentine. Margot's cooked for us. Eat!'

Leaving him non-plussed, she hurried to the stairs. But it was not a loo she was looking for; it was the man she now glimpsed, reading to a circle of tousled-haired boys on the floor of their playroom – even sixteen-year-old Gus, who'd made a pass at her eldest. He had a voice of such timbre, she fantasized, that it might have mesmerized the sea.

*

Miranda was in her blue kitchen clearing up plates, Valentine upstairs rearranging inventory on his computer. The children were doing homework or supposed to be (she would see to them later) when the telephone rang.

The phone in Miranda's kitchen was next to an old wing-backed chair which she loved and Valentine hated; its stuffing was coming out, and she had to mend the upholstery every other week. The kitchen was as much *hers* as the sitting-room upstairs *his* – that was the way these London houses worked.

'Hullo?' she said throwing herself down (a puff of stuffing blew out) and picking up the receiver in one motion.

Clearing plates had made her impatient. Anne had offered to help, but it was a job Lucinda was meant to do, as eldest. Lucinda, however, was washing her hair or something: she'd certainly not rushed from the table just to do maths.

'Miranda? This is Tony.'

'Tony?'

'Tony Thomas. I met you at – '

'Yes, I remember. What can I do for you?'

Usually a friend phoning would get smooth tones once she had recognized who it was. Miranda loved phone chats: they'd been a principal pastime of hers for fifteen years and cause for more than one dispute with Valentine over bills. Tony Thomas, however, did not get the smoothed-out Miranda: he was not a friend, only an acquaintance, and foreign at that. Actually, he was worse: a 'cultural half-breed', as Valentine had judged after Margot's party. Miranda had gone along with this. Invariably she went along with her husband's opinions when they had no evident consequence for her. Anyhow, she had a suspicion of what Tony was after; and since she'd fantasized about Oliver Murrie all through her plate-clearing, as through every mindless activity of her week, she was not disposed to encourage him.

'I was wondering if you'd like to meet for a drink.'

'I don't drink, Tony.'

'Well, coffee then.'

'I drink tea.'

He chuckled amiably. 'Tea then. Where would you like? The Ritz?'

From her point of view, tea at the Ritz were for Arabs, Americans and other socially insecure types, which is how she had pigeon-holed him. For a moment she wondered the more how Margot could have to do with this man.

'I'm not sure,' is what she answered.

'How 'bout Fortnum's then? It doesn't matter where. I just thought we might meet up.'

'Why?'

'"Why"?'

There was a point beyond which brusqueness could only be taken as rude; and Miranda, having reached it, went on more politely, 'What I mean is, what about your wife, Tony? I don't think it's a good idea.'

He chuckled again. 'For goodness sake I was only suggesting a cup of tea, not a roll in the hay. I should be so lucky! How presumptuous do you think I am?'

She did not field that.

'It's Margot's suggestion. She says Valentine needs a White Knight; and I, or Carine and I, might be able to help.'

This was unexpected – perhaps even a blow to Miranda's amour-propre. 'I should've thought if you wanted to talk to Valentine you would've asked for him directly.'

'Sometimes one has to be a bit indirect, don't you think?... I didn't feel he took to me at that dinner, and it struck me to try the power behind the throne first.'

'What power is that?' she asked disingenuously.

'You are his wife, aren't you?'

Indeed, her servitude in his kitchen proved it. But Miranda was too proud to admit as much to a stranger, especially a stranger bearing gifts or claiming to. She would call Margot and check him out. Meanwhile, she agreed to lunch, not tea – tea was 'too twee', as he remarked; besides, she turned up her nose at all the places he offered. So they agreed to a date in a week's time at a wine-bar over a gallery in Holland Park.

This was at her suggestion. Miranda loved Holland Park now even more since she'd met – at least glimpsed – the object of her fantasies there. In fact, Oliver Murrie was staying with Tony and Carine in Knightsbridge. So her host let drop in the initial small talk as they took their seats.

'Oh?' Miranda inquired as if the matter were of no more than conversational interest.

'Yeah. A bit close. We just bought a new flat, but only two bedrooms… Did you know Ollie and she were once lovers?'

Miranda refused wine from the carafe that almost instantly came. They had been placed at a small, octagonal brass table; the wooden chairs had Indian or Arabic designs carved on their backs and carpetbag cushions to soften their seats. A palm plant rose beside. Briefly scanning the menu, Miranda ordered ratatouille.

Tony chose smoked mackerel.

'Ollie and who?' she inquired, once the waitress was gone.

'Carine, of course.'

'Ah. That's your wife, isn't it?'

'Who did you think I meant?'

'Who did I think you meant what?'

The wine-bar had a dated, middle-class hippy feel. It made Miranda long for the 1970s again; she would be twenty still and sitting here with her soulmate.

'Who Ollie had been lovers with. Not Margot, I hope. That's a vicious rumour; been around yonks. Godfrey still half-believes it, which may be why he behaved badly. By the way, I wanted to tell you how sorry I was. Were you able to get the wine out of your blouse?'

Tony Thomas could not be a soulmate. No one who probed so professionally could. And Miranda had hardly been thinking about the claret Godfrey had jetted over her *eau-de-nil* top when he'd slammed down the carafe for the umpteenth time.

'Who is this Oliver Murrie everyone seems so bothered about?' she asked, spreading a bit of ratatouille over a cold potato and putting it between those bell-shaped lips.

'Thought you might be interested.'

'In what?'

'In Ollie.'

'Why shouldn't I be?' Lest this should sound too bold, she added: 'But we can drop him, if his relationship with your wife makes it too painful. It was Valentine you wanted to discuss anyhow, no?'

'Is that what you wanted to talk about?'

'I can't think what else would've brought me here.'

'Bit wary of the truth, are we?'

She found this man even more annoying *à deux* than she had in a group and for the rest of the meal treated him with cool *hauteur*. Of course, she would've preferred not to have done so: it made her feel like Lady Melot; and unlike that *grande dame*, Miranda longed for relations to be sweet. But with the world she inhabited as it was – sharp, direct, competitive – sweetness was out: those who gave it were vulnerable and got crushed – Tony's wife for instance, from what she could tell. And maybe it was just because he seemed to be offering contacts to this poor girl's family (the Bleistein/Slomans were as near as you could get to Jewish aristocracy) while evidently quite willing to cheat on her that Miranda felt so hostile to his charms.

He tried to draw her out about Valentine's financial background and business, matters she'd long since been trained not to mention. Even if she couldn't stand her husband, and couldn't stand him in part because of his preoccupation with such things, Miranda knew it would be less of a betrayal of him to sleep with another than gossip about the meanness of his mother or state of his bank balance. The latter she had no clue about in any case.

'Why don't you ask Godfrey?' she said over coffee. (Actually she drank tea while Tony stuck to wine). 'You know him, don't you?'

'I'm not quite sure Godfrey's well-disposed to me either,' he stated, a Cheshire cat grin giving away nothing and everything.

It was the smile of a male sphinx, a type Miranda knew instinctively a woman like her had to avoid. A woman like her needed a victim or semi-innocent like herself, she thought, failing to register the truism Valentine had often tossed at her – that such types are the most dangerous. Tony Thomas seemed dangerous. Anyhow, in her mind Miranda already felt loyal to Oliver Murrie – absurdly, of course. He had never come down to the table at Margot's, and her glimpse of him reading *The Jungle Book* to the boys was the sum-total of her first-hand knowledge of him. Still, the 'relationship' had progressed so far in her psyche that she felt faithless taking lunch with this stranger, who seemed too clever by half.

In truth, there were things she might have liked to talk over with Tony; but with the sun burning through palm fronds beside them, she felt more and more eager to get out of her seat and flee. Women at other tables had begun to laugh too loudly as their men muttered ribaldries. She would go to Margot's and find out all the 'subtexts', Miranda resolved. Yet no sooner had she struck on this plan than something in the buzz of low talk in the place, in Tony's too-knowing gaze and fragments of light snaking through oriental filigree on the chairs, made her think of Oliver's voice again and, from that, India... It was a place she'd wanted to travel to more than any other. In her years with Valentine she'd suggested it more than once; there or back to Tuscany was where her mind wandered always. But now she was glad that her husband had been too busy to take her. She would go with her soulmate and sit under a Bo tree; they would become the still-point in the universe, locked in one of those Kama Sutra poses she'd glimpsed that morning in her son's wank magazine when tidying his bedroom. On which lurid, wholly unexpected image, she snapped back to attention:

'It's awfully nice of you to offer to help Valentine. I'm sure he'd be happy to talk with you if you had something serious to offer. I'm afraid that's all I can suggest.'

The American studied her features. What on earth was his game?

'Do phone him when you're ready,' she added.

He shrugged off any hint of rejection. 'And you phone me when you need to,' is how he concluded.

Cocky twerp.

Margot was sitting at a rattan desk in her conservatory. She was wearing half-glasses, an accessory Miranda had rarely seen on her. Smoke rose from an incense-burner behind as she hastened a purple pen across a page, making a vertical, oddly Cyrillic-looking script. Silent, serious, seeming ageing and sexless, she had lines of compression around the mouth and a vulpine elongation of nose and chin. Miranda was shocked. Not being a working woman herself, she felt threatened by the sight of vanity vanished.

'Hello there,' Margot intoned as if in a trance. 'Put on a kettle. Shan't be a minute. The Muse, don't you know.'

Miranda did not. Having not been exposed to writers as her husband once had, she simply referred to his judgment: that like all artists – indeed, creative people – they were egomaniacal shits. It did not occur to her to sympathize; composure is necessary for balanced reactions, and a woman in love – or in need of obsession – is hardly a balanced reactor. Desiring her best friend as mother and sage, it annoyed her unduly to find Margot so preoccupied.

'Oh Christ!' – she laid down her pen and let the glasses swing on a cord round her neck. 'I think we're all coming unhinged. You know my friend Booby? She's been trying to write a book. We've experimented with the lot: thriller, bodice-ripper, straight novel, screenplay. She's terribly clever, but we don't seem able to find the right thing. I suggested a hot historical, and she said what do you mean? So I swotted this up:

> In the dead of winter, the Grey Knight came home. He awakened one morning in a puddle in Jerusalem with complete amnesia. Gradually, through wandering, he began to piece together some sense of who he had been. Leaving his lances and broadsword behind, his Saracen catamite and scenes of derring-do, he made his way to Malta and back through Italia. At the edge of an Alp he stopped to collect his belongings from an ex-amour, the Contessa of Plütz, who was cavorting with her new lover, the Baron Tweedledum, who had lost out to him once for the favours of La Belle Dame Sans Souci. Among velvet doublets and pointy-toed slippers, he found copies of ballads in his hand to someone called Adelaide. Reading them over, he tried to remember who she was. What did she look like? What had gone on? From the passionate words, he was forced to realize that this mysterious woman had been the Love of his Life.
>
> He made his way up through Burgundia, seeking. Gradually, in abbeys, castles and inns, he began to hear her name. Apparently she was famous now, a sort of uncrowned empress. Was this the reason, when he arrived at her demesne in Bretagne, that his passage was blocked?
>
> The way led across a broad field. On this bright winter's morn, it was staked out at four corners by young men in rough doublets with wild-haired damosels at their sides. In the features of one, the Grey Knight thought he saw something familiar. Something even more familiar dwelt in the look of the Lady who stood in the gate of the château at the back of the field, a child held between her white hands. The Grey Knight might have recognized her as a trim, ageless Adelaide had he had a chance to gaze unmolested. But not only were the four with wild-haired damsels blocking his way, but an indistinct presence behind seemed to loom up, a kind of black nemesis. The Grey Knight was frightened for the first time in his career as a few sharp blasts on a horn made him turn to confront –

Miranda could hardly disguise her impatience with this. She'd been fiddled with mentally too much for one day to sit around considering the 'subtext' of some dashed-off piece of drivel. So full was she of questions – why Godfrey disliked Oliver, why Margot had put Tony onto her, what had gone on between Oliver and Carine, what above all had happened to Oliver in Italy – that she hardly stopped to consider any hint Margot might have been trying to convey.

'Gracious me. No good either.' – The half-glasses remained on the page, but intensity drained out of la Wingfield's features, loosening them back to her softer, if somewhat artificial, brand of attractiveness. 'Too portentous. Rather depressing as well. I must've felt you coming and lost the magic circle.'

'Magic circle?'

'An artist friend taught me years ago, a painter: creativity is nothing but black magic really. You set up a space, arrange your implements – pens, pallets, whatever. You stand back, make notes, wipe brushes on your smock, put on a piece of music, turn it off, lock the door, et cet; then you're ready. I say it's bosh. I tell my clients you can write in the bath, on the tube, in the kitchen with five screaming heads all around; but maybe my painter friend's right. Or is it just the quality of what's occurring in your space, as they say? whether it's making direct demands or not, if you see what I mean.'

Delivering this speech (it sounded rehearsed), Margot put down the paper, dropped the glasses once more and transformed completely into persona as mother-of-house.

'What can I do for you, dearest?' – She shook tea into a pot. 'You seem fraught. Is Valentine being beastly again, or did you want to warn me about Lucinda and Gus?'

'Lucinda and Gus? What about them?'

'It's nothing, I'm sure.' – A grandfather clock in the corner struck three, and the lady changed tune: 'Good God, what a muddle! I've got two artists, a writer and photographer arriving at half-past from Hull – only time they could come. I can't get a soul to take my school-run; so Lucius and Jon, the neighbour's boy and two others are going to be stranded at the Hill. I'd put off the authors, but they're *en train* already. Either you could stay here and let them in for me, or... but then there's Matthew and Marcus home at a quarter-to-four. Oh deah!'

'Why don't I just pick up Luke and Jon,' Miranda offered, not even trying to evade Margot's ruse.

'*Could* you, dearest? I'd be in your debt to the grave!'

'But what about Lucinda?'

'Ah that. Phone me tonight. Not to worry; but we should keep each other informed. Never quite sure what to do in these things.'

'What things?'

'That silly teenaged institution Mills & Boon have a monopoly on.'

'Mills and Boon?' echoed Miranda, exasperated.

'What us '60s idiots used to call "Luv".'

What '60s idiots used to call Luv is what Valentine's wife craved. But she had no desire for Lucinda to experience it before her, certainly not with one of the Wingfield boys. Christian, the fourteen-year-old, was not bad, just bashful; but Gus had a reputation from Chelsea to Highgate, and Marcus and Matthew, though younger than her Hugo, had already been found bumming fags and drinking cider in the tube. Valentine would have to hear about whatever it was, Miranda mused, speeding her Volvo through High Street Ken. He had more influence on Lucinda nowadays anyhow.

Actually, Miranda wasn't speeding; she just felt that she was. The traffic was stop-and-go. As if because October brought night down more early, rush hour seemed to have got earlier too. Idling, she wished she could get out of London. They were meant to go to Hampshire at the weekend – Valentine's brother's birthday, Cravin family gathering – but that was not what getting out of London meant to her. Italy came to mind again, a vision bathed in sun, colour, youth, bliss, the stallion and so on, as ever; only now Oliver Murrie was mixed in with it – one of the few things she knew of him was that he'd just come from there.

What had he done? where had he lived? who (she was sure there was someone) had broken his heart? Miranda hadn't connected Margot's tale of the Grey Knight with him. Nor had she given herself over to fantasizing enough yet to blot out all other sensations, such as of traffic, rain, the encroaching dark, oncoming winter and state of her children. Hugo had been her principal worry that morning: disgusting to have found that magazine under his bed. To think that her son, the babe whose cuddles she'd cherished, could sit in the loo exciting himself over *that*! She'd only glanced, but. She'd have to have a word with Valentine about it as well.

Life was a martyrdom (the word was his: he used it to mock her when she grew particularly fraught) – so she told herself now as she veered her car into the queue of school mums hooting their way through Hans Place. The Hill House run had been one of the staples of her life for years; here, High Street Ken – all Cravins went to the best schools. She'd driven Hugo along this route morning upon morning, until the most posh section of London held no romance for her. All those Dutch Gothic villas made one feel as if one had eaten too much marzipan, Margot had once said.

Thinking of Margot again, Miranda marvelled over how she had managed to con her down here – and without so much as a word about what she ought to have heard about Lucinda and Gus. Mothers had to be shrewd to offload the endless nuisances children thrust on their days. Miranda's own were old enough to take the bus now; but poor Margot with so many!… Mustn't be mean-spirited, she remonstrated pulling her Volvo up to the kerb and glancing in the rearview before getting out to mix with other dyed heads from Chelsea to Hampstead.

Her eyes froze.

Beyond them, to one side of an amber fringe, stood a man with a pale, moony expression. His own hair was a mélange of orange and white, quite sparse, though charming in the inadvertent way it was combed. He wore cracked leather shoes but a new pair of jeans: the sort some concerned female might've purchased for him – Carine Thomas, for instance. His arms were thrust deep in the pockets of an old Barbour jacket, its collar turned up, half-obscuring his face. One hand reached to take a cigarette out of lips as thick as a cut of prime beef. The eyes stared forwards, absolutely intent on a stream of boys trickling out of the Hill House doorway.

It was of course Oliver Murrie.

The effect on Miranda was sudden and extreme. On recognizing him, her body seemed to convulse: at the armpits, in the crotch, between toes. She felt sure that she reeked; as if every orifice were suddenly giving off a neurotic scent. This was in part fanciful; what made her panic truly was the way she was dressed. There he was as cool as some poster, Jean-Paul Belmondo or James Dean, while she was prim as a Girl Guide in the cords and baggy jumper she'd put on to not look fetching for Tony Thomas. She was prepared to be embarrassed in front of other mums; but if she were going to see *him* – ?

Miranda had never felt so inadequate, she imagined. In fact, with the rush of blood to her face, she looked inspired as she hurried past the corner on which he'd planted himself. Far from a stench, the scent she trailed was so subliminally sweet that any alert male might have been jolted to attention. But swathed in cigarette smoke and with his responses atrophied by recent experience and eclipsed by his present object of obsession, Oliver Murrie did not even notice the woman, though she threw her eyes at him in a way which made one of the other mums murmur: 'Bit of all right, I'd say.'

She rushed through the door, up the stairs, into the vestibule, tossing hair back and wishing desperately that she'd washed it that morning, hoping it wouldn't go slick and bedraggled because of the rain. Searching for Margot's boys, she tried to check how it looked in a window and rearranged the fringe while they collected their bags. Feeling weak, weedy, drained of all marrow, she led them back down the steps, one on each hand, Luke just seven, Jon not yet five, and out the gate as if readying herself for Judgement Day.

'Ollie!' exclaimed Lucius and, pleased as a bird taking flight, started towards him.

A Merc had to brake: Miranda just managed to collar the boy back. Once the car passed, they carried on towards the man smoking, each step feeling like a coal burning under her toes.

'Ollie!' Luke repeated and, disengaging himself, ran until – noting the rock-star cool – he tried to disguise his excitement.

Oliver flicked his cigarette into the road and reached out to rough the boy's hair. Meanwhile, pale eyes roved to the face of the minder.

Miranda, hyper-conscious, couldn't prevent a smile from spreading over her lips. She was sure it looked like a rictus of inanity. Her palm squeezed Jon's hand till the younger boy cried.

'Sorry, dearest,' she intoned, sounding Margot-esque.

Oliver's glance dropped. A line of doubt creased his brow as he turned to Luke, who was saying,

'I went skateboarding yesterday, Ollie. Brill! I zoomed down that big curve around Lansdowne Crescent without falling off once. Will you come with me?'

'One of these days.'

'Why not now?'

'Can't.'

'Yes you can. Please?'

The child tugged at his sleeve, reiterating the request in a happy chant. Oliver's eyes searched out Miranda's again. 'Ouch!' Jon repeated as her hand resqueezed. 'Sorry!' – She gathered him up in her arms and waited, ostensibly for Luke, only semi-conscious of her posture as madonna with child.

The pale eyes seemed to question.

'Hello,' she murmured, feeling much too aware.

He half-nodded.

Lucius pulled at him still. 'Come on, Ollie!'

'Can't today, my son. Just happened to be passing, as it happens. I'm staying a street over. See you soon.'

He gave the head a final shake and was off. When the boy started to whine, he spun round and added:

'And don't squeak like that, or I won't. And by the way, don't mention to your parents that you saw me.' – This with a final, almost pleading look to Miranda: 'We'll keep it our secret, OK?'

Lucinda was lounging in the wing-backed chair. Dangling her legs over an arm, she was listening to the phone. As soon as her mother walked in, she straightened up and rang off.

'Sorry, Mum. I was just talking to Helena.'

Helena was the Cravin grandmother, Lady Melot. Miranda knew from her daughter's colour that *she* was not who had been on the line. Normally Miranda might have chided her eldest about Gus Wingfield, say, or warned her not to use the phone as her 'personal toy' (Valentine's description). On this occasion, however, she did not even ask Lucinda to help with the three bags of shopping she lugged in, nor to peel potatoes or boil a kettle.

'O? and how is your grandmother?' she inquired, a picture of affectionate unconcern. 'Goodness, don't you have to get upstairs, darling? Isn't it time for *Neighbours* on TV?'

Lucinda was non-plussed.

'You're happy tonight, Mum,' observed Anne, who'd been trying to hide a supply of bickies she'd coated with blackcurrant jam.

Miranda gave her youngest a peck and said not a word about not eating between meals. Anne followed her sister up to their soap.

Miranda swirled around the kitchen as if to some 1970s pop tune. She made a fish-pie, chopped carrots, mashed swede, dressed a salad, put cheese on the sideboard. She even went to the cellar and brought up a bottle of claret for Valentine's supper. 'Is that you, Hugo?' she called when the front door slammed louder than necessary.

'Hi, Mum. Sorry, didn't mean to make so much noise.'

'I'll forgive you this once.'

She wasted no spirit brooding about the lecture her son deserved for his magazines, nor any of her complaints with her home. She set the children's places and rushed to her life-drawing class, not minding that she had to park two streets away and walk through a torrential rainstorm to get there. Her imagination was soaring; her hand flew over the paper; her teacher expressed himself as amazed at the progress she'd made since last session. She could get shoulders all of a sudden, nor did buttocks look like blocks of ice; there were curves in her lines now and warmth in her shadings – the model turned heroic on her page compared to how he appeared on the dais, alternately too proud or diffident about his physique, shivering in spite of two coils. But of course it was not the model's physique Miranda was contemplating; that was a mere palimpsest. She was revelling over how she'd cracked her problem and what she would do in the morning.

When she got home, she phoned Margot to say she'd be happy to pick up Luke and Jon as often as needed. 'I'm lonely for children these days,' she explained. 'Besides, I have to go to SW1 three times a week now and have to come your way to pick up Anne, so...'

'You blessed angel!' Margot replied, almost too complacent to ask why Valentine's wife should have to go to SW1 out of the blue.

'Oh – ' This required split-second excuse-making; but surreptitious romance is a spur to invention. 'I've decided to start consulting a shrink. She lives in Pimlico.'

'A shrink? I say, that sounds ominous. Valentine hasn't started beating you, has he?'

'No. And as a matter of fact I'm sick of the way I've been complaining about him and the rest. I have a fine life, or will if I can just get my attitude straight.'

Margot appeared to accept this, credible or not. So now Miranda had an excuse to do what she'd determined: to stake herself out for Oliver Murrie. Margot's child would be the pretext: it was plainly his obsession – their 'secret'. Through it she would bind him and make him her lover. She would enter into her own secret world with him; wind down the corridors and through the dark places, until they came out on the other side, as it were – to sunny uplands, glorious and free: to a new life where they could ride wild with the wind in their hair and collapse into each other's arms under a Bo Tree.

Miranda had no doubt that she could accomplish this. Her will felt as hard as a luminous crystal inside her. She was eighteen again, as gorgeous as starlight and destined for brilliant success!

2.

If April is the cruellest month, then what can one say about October? In England at this time it was a season of storms, sudden changes. Margot Wingfield called it a season of relief, and Miranda knew what she meant. There was no compulsion to be cheery as in summer or at Christmas; many became downright depressed, which was acceptable up to a point. Miranda's mother was an example: when birds flew south, they took away her sole interest, in sky-gazing. Miranda's father on the other hand got energy from autumn: start of a new term, new students to impress, old lectures to swot up, academic teas to attend. Sir Ralph found rebirth in the dying time of the year – in which respect, during the October in question, Miranda was her father's daughter.

She loved the flickering light in the leaves and high winds. She adored the colours and fact that it was still warm enough so you could go out in no more than a jumper, yet cool enough so there was no longer the eyesore of too many white legs. She liked the sound of geese honking as they set off for Africa and sight of sudden sprays of swallows against fading gold. She even tolerated the fact that evenings began early, though not too early yet. Most of all she cherished a memory of students flooding back to Oxford and young men's eyes on her, making her feel quite striking as she hurried along paths behind colleges on her way to and from school.

She recalled how it felt to clutch her books to her nipples and self-consciousness over how she walked: not too slowly, nor with too much sway nor too little, never to be obvious, always to be seen. She felt their eyes on her: the blue ones and grey ones, ovoid brown ones and squinty blacks. She felt them caressing and relived the tension of wanting yet not wanting it to go on for too long. Two or three pairs had made a point of looking for her each day, she recalled: one whose rooms she passed under, another at a bus stop, a third who circled on his bike to see her cross Woodstock Road. She saw their checkered scarves and red cheeks and noses; their hair flying in spikes as they rushed between classes; their eyes going sad as they realized they could look but not touch; their shyness at making a move.

How stupid she'd been then! As with Bernardo, she wished she'd had them all now. How vain to have just wanted them to want her, like Lucinda with boys after school. All that make-up and primping, hair-washing and practicing facial expressions – the only good it did was to keep Hugo from sneaking into the bathroom with some horrid magazine up his shirt. Teenaged girls were tarts, Miranda concluded with a self-righteousness that only superficially tinged her recollections. She'd been a terrible tease, allowing the American tenant in her parents' house to undress her but not have what he begged for. She'd even taken pleasure in the way he'd been forced to retreat to the loo like poor Hugo, only not with a magazine but frustrated visions of her.

She should have had him. How futile the puritan prejudices of her teens! Fears of pregnancy? there had been the pill. How loathsome the lower middle-class snobbery and envy that made her wait for undersexed Valentine Cravin... Well, that was over, she reflected now as she drove. October was death-in-life: the changing time of the year. All was churning inside her. She was proceeding towards her destiny, she believed as she sped towards a sun shining through silver clouds in the west. She'd made a decision: the most fateful of her life – most rash anyway, if brave and potentially full of pleasure. She was going to live out a fantasy and lock herself away with him for the weekend. It was going to be a real honeymoon; and unlike Tuscany, it was not going to lead to disillusionment!

Consciousness of lying and extreme expectation made her spirit even more frenetic than usual. 'If you need any help settling in...' she'd said when he told her about the place Carine had organized for him. God, it had been daring! They'd been sitting in one of those coffee shops in Brompton Road one morning a week after she'd first seen him outside of Hill House. Just as she'd expected and hoped, he had turned up again; and after she'd delivered Lucius and Jon, she'd made a point of casting eyes to where he'd stationed himself on the corner.

Two days later, the same happened. At last, a third time, once games of eyes had made everything clear, she'd driven up behind him as he'd loped off and, rolling down her window, asked if he wanted a lift.

'Well,' as if indifferent – 's'pose it can't hurt.'

She'd dropped him at the Thomases: another gingerbread Gothic a few streets away. He hadn't said much. She'd wondered if it weren't a bit crowded, living with Tony and Carine. He had observed:

''s only temporary. I'll be going to Hampshire soon.'

'Hampshire? That's where we go at weekends.'

'Carine owns some property there.'

'What a coincidence!'

There had been a thousand things to add, but it wasn't time yet. She'd had to wait till the next chance; and it was killing, the suspense.

A few days later, getting him into her car again, she'd blurted:

'I could murder a cup of tea.' (She cringed now recalling: why had it come out so vulgar? Had she struck him as some frightful, suburban housewife?)

'There's an Italian place up there,' he'd said, hours later, it seemed.

So relieved had she been that she almost shrieked: 'How lovely! I'll bet they have wonderful cakes. I could kill for one. Like to join me?'

'S'pose it can't hurt...'

'Is it terribly wicked?'

'What?'

'Eating such fattening things at my age?'

'Don't be absurd.'

He'd looked at her then as a woman for the first time, she imagined. She might have burst into hysterics had he not smiled. In fact, getting him to smile was as hard as getting an upset baby to laugh, she reflected, driving towards the M3. The pale, tired eyes; the large, generous face with broken veins in the cheeks – years of living in the elements, she supposed. Doting on these things already, she reheard the way he had spoken: quite sparsely, taking long pauses to think. It was not like Londoners, not like the types she'd been stuck with: no sharp retorts as from Valentine, no 'woman's magazine stuff', even if it was. With Oliver she felt free. She didn't stop to consider if she weren't merely projecting a private mania on him. She'd found herself telling her life story from that first cup.

He had lived so much more than she that he could understand all, couldn't he? He could endure her silly witterings-on and come up in the end, having listened acutely, with some fresh, simple philosophy to turn everything right. 'Just look at this big sky,' he had said, for instance, the next time, when, after coffee, they'd gone for a walk around the Serpentine. 'Sometimes when I'm overwhelmed with my problems, I just look at it and remember how in the face of the All, they don't amount to anything as big as that cloud.'

It was so simple. He was so comforting, heart-warming. What Valentine would kill with ridicule, he would accept without the lift of a lid. Accepting, he'd said, was 'what it was all about'. He'd accepted what had happened to him, hadn't he?

'What *did* happen?' she'd demanded, ravenous to hear all.

'Doesn't matter. Past is past. No use wondering if it was good.'

'I always do.'

'Whatever happens must be for the best. Can't be changed.'

Valentine would have branded this 'worn-out existentialist tosh'. For years she had heard him embarrassing her friends with set-pieces against New Age consciousness, organic gardening, biorhythmic life-planning – 'Dreary middle-class panacea-mongering,' he'd disparage, sounding like Godfrey Wingfield, only with upper-class pomp rather than bohemian tipsiness. 'Bedales!' he might have added about Oliver's school, had he known; 'what do you expect of a person whose parents sent him to a place like that?' And: 'Trinity? It's always produced oddballs. The only decent college at Cambridge is Peterhouse.'

Valentine would have turned on Oliver Murrie the same sort of *hauteur* he used to put her in place. (To give him his due, he'd never said a thing overt against her father: that would have been rude, which Valentine believed he was not. Yet if Peterhouse were 'the only decent college at Cambridge', what on earth was one to make of a new college at Oxford called Arimathea?) The difference in this case was that, whereas over the years Miranda had let Valentine's prejudices colour her own, now she couldn't have cared less. Oliver Murrie was no thrusting Ralph Evesham. Though he may have lived in Italy and other places, he wasn't even a 'cultural half-breed'. His parents, like her father's, had their origins in the Celtic fringe (this particularly pleased her, making her feel as if they were long-lost siblings). His father had been an author and his mother's family owners of a country-house; so even on the snob basis, where Valentine customarily won, he could – so far as Oliver was concerned – get stuffed!

But her husband was of no interest to her now, not even as object of spite. All her nerves, all her tension were directed elsewhere. She was flying up towards the light, she believed, not flapping her wings in the shadows. Being in love, or in obsession, gave such energy! It blasted up through her, making her feel that she might explode with joy, or trepidation. Did he like her? That was all she'd been able to think as she'd raced through everything to do with Lucinda, Hugo, the house, even Anne, who'd stared at her on the morning when she'd first made love with him as if she were stark raving mad.

'What's happened to you, Mum? You look like you've put your finger in a socket.'

Among cosmetic touches, Miranda had used curlers on her bangs.

('Valentine's wife is the only one I know who can make real hair look like a wig,' Margot had quipped to Godfrey over breakfast after Miranda had picked up Lucius and Jon; 'I'm not sure I like the effect that analyst is having on her.'

Godfrey had belched. 'What "analyst"?' throwing down his *Times*. 'The woman's all painted up like you used to be. She's obviously having an affair.'

'Miranda?' Margot had paused. 'I doubt it. On the other hand – '

'Of course she bloody is. You don't think she gets any satisfaction out of Valentine, do you? especially now that that Swede's made a hostile bid.')

After dropping the boys off, Miranda had rushed to meet him at their Italian place. They had talked desultorily: it was the only way with him. Then, in an attempt to keep up momentum, she'd suggested another walk in the Park.

'S'pose it can't hurt.'

Halfway through their amble, it had started to rain. Taking shelter under a tree, she had murmured:

'Shame we have nowhere to go.'

He'd stayed mute; her spirits had dropped to the mud; at last he had said: 'S'pose we could try Carine's.'

And so...

Entering the Thomases' penthouse, she had remarked: 'What lovely cornices!'

Lighting a new fag, he had gazed at the ceiling.

'What a lovely balcony!' she had added, feeling absolutely daft.

Exit to the kitchen, to put on a kettle.

Carine's kitchen was done up in posh-hotel, ersatz marble.

'Are they both out in the day?' she had inquired.

'Guess so. Mostly.'

'Where do they go?'

'...Work?'

'I thought they were too rich for that.'

Filling mugs with tea-bags, he had not answered.

'Where do they work then?'

'She runs a property company, I think.'

'Ah. That's how she found you this place in the country, is it?'

'Two sugars?'

'Don't s'pose it can hurt.'

A half-smile at her irony. She loved the way he talked, but for wit it was heavy-going.

'What about thingamajig?' she persisted.

'Who's thingamajig?'

'Tony.' – Touch of gossip, relief for the nerves.

'What about him?'

'Where does he go in the day? Out to pull birds?'

But Oliver was no gossip. – 'Wanna sit?'

The sitting-room was spread end to end with white leather sofas: Hollywood décor out of a Sunday supplement. He had squished down on one of them, looking incongruous. In the oversized dimensions of the place, she'd felt minute settling as close as she dared.

Silence. She'd had a thousand more questions, of course. They surged up like the adrenalin shooting through her system, making her fear she might give off some frightful stench.

'Fancy music?' he'd asked.

'Lovely!'

He put on *La Bohème*. She asked him to tell her about what they were singing. He gave one or two details, then called the story silly.

'Mimi – that's her now – is dying of TB.'

'How dreadful!'

She'd meant it with irony but, taking it as dead serious, he vanished into himself. This made him even more compelling, she thought. And maybe because of the music, which seemed awfully tragic for something so 'silly', or the awkwardness of the situation, which must have been as bad for him as for her, it being someone else's place, she gradually, after another long passage of silence, squeezed the world into a ball and moved closer to him.

The first kiss was not long – it seemed quite unsuccessful: as if flesh-and-blood were an illusion and Oliver Murrie not a live man, but some spirit she'd evoked who had incarnated in semi-robotic form. Lip to lip, she tried to press the initial opening into a deeper impression. Feeling an awkward teenager again, she wondered how they must have felt, the boys who'd tried to kiss her, only to get the mouth of a stone. She was sure she was failing until, pulling back, she noticed that sad, faraway look in his eye.

The gaze came into her, and through her, while, as if in a trance, a smile began to turn up the corners of his lips. Then suddenly she came unstuck and it was all she could do to keep from screaming with joy and rage, fear and compulsion to abandon herself. (My God, she realized now, driving through Basingstoke, how close she'd come to ruining it, wanting too much! Nor was it a mistake she was going to repeat, she resolved, adrenalin constricting her throat.)

'I'm not very experienced at this,' she murmured.

Another kiss; then –

'I hope you don't think I do this all the time, or ever! I've never done it before; you're my first at this sort of thing. Was it all right?'

In fact, it had been less than perfect. She had just missed, she imagined, what she had read about for years but had no personal knowledge of.

He'd sat and lit up a fag. She longed for him to cuddle her but was unable to speak. He got up and strolled across the room to where several happy-faced photos of Tony and Carine stared from the mantel.

'Don't feel right here,' he murmured.

'You'll be moving soon.'

'Not soon enough.'

What was the 'subtext'? 'Don't you know when?'

'Next weekend, Carine says.'

'That's not far off.'

She'd grown aware again of the other woman's generosity. It made her jealous: she longed to be his protector and have him all to herself.

His body as he stood there looked big-boned, yet lean; no excess on it. She might have said it was perfect, if not for that vague, somewhat sunken look around the eyes.

'Would you like to see me again?' she'd asked, feeling crushed yet in love, huddling still at the far end of one sofa, mackintosh over her goose-pimpled midriff.

Exhaling a plume, he'd answered: 'I think I would. But would you mind awfully if it wasn't here?'

*

There were warnings and reasons not to hurtle on too quickly; but aren't there always in 'Luv'? Miranda had read enough woman's magazine stuff to know that. She had also learned that a woman who didn't want to end life in abject domesticity better take Chance by the throat. She might have been cautioned when Margot phoned to cut off the school runs; she might have paused when Valentine came home with his back to the wall because of the Swede's hostile bid. She might have deflected her attention to Lucinda, who'd started wearing white lipstick and not reappearing from school in time for *Neighbours*, or to Hugo, who by Margot's report had started 'hanging out' with the middle Wingfield boys. Anne's sad little face might have arrested her motion (the youngest Cravin helped her Dad with his computer every night rather than Mum with the dishes). Above all, she might have taken a closer look at Oliver Murrie before throwing herself at him. But Luv is a fever, a hallucination of escape; and Miranda was delirious with it.

Reason told her she was becoming a caricature and that resistance might save her from what she knew could become a nightmare if she didn't wake up till too late. But Luv is a deceiver; it wears an innocent, tricksterish grin, like Bernardo before the stallion had bolted. It pretends all is possible and lights up the spirit with such a blaze that all the dark corners seem remote. Miranda, in short, did not stop to consider the real Oliver Murrie. The real Oliver Murrie she did not even see again after their first love-making, she only talked to him on the phone. They made plans for a fugitive weekend in Hampshire; the sound of his voice compelled her to such flights that the real Oliver disappeared into a series of 'Wells...', 'Uh-huhs...' and cigarette puffs, around which she filled in the blanks.

Luv is an inventor, a fiction-maker, a shameless bad artist with no respect for Reality or Truth. Miranda's mind skittered. It jumped back and forth between past and future without rest. The present, meanwhile, held no interest for her unless his voice filled it, or thoughts of him. Their tryst in Knightsbridge burgeoned into an annunciation of the New Life. The weekend in Hampshire would be the most transcendentally charged event since the Second Coming. Anything was possible; Oliver was a god, and Miranda rapidly imagined herself into apotheosis beside him – Heloïse and Abelard, Tristan and Isolde, Antony and Cleopatra would have nothing on this. Beware, good sense might have told her (Margot certainly would): those starved of 'Luv' until middle-aged will be the most consumed by it. But good sense was hardly at hand.

Margot she avoided. Oliver's passivity, his relations with Carine, his obsession with a Wingfield boy, his history and future – all things she'd longed to know about paled beside what had broken loose in her as she drove west. He might have been a mass-murderer for all she knew; she had risked too much already to dwell on doubts. How *he* felt she assumed, letting herself imagine him as full of the fever as her. As for his reticence? She put it down to style and some sorrow that, far from flashing an amber light, made him even more attractive.

How could she help but adore him, she thought as she pulled up in front of a Jacobean manor which he stood beside, gazing at sunset through a brace of beech trees?

Turning at the sound of her door shutting, he smiled in that sad-happy way. 'How was your drive?'

'Ghastly. My mind spun the whole time. I should've waited till Anne got home but with Friday rush as it is, I would never've arrived to see *this*.'

The sky was azure, blood-orange, gold, with just enough cloud to make it Turneresque. It was brightened as well by a moon climbing over the village to the east.

'So...' she went on, rearranging her shawl over her blazer.

Why didn't he kiss her? The reserve drove her mad. Still, she couldn't complain: she was here now. And didn't he look lovely where he stood, a few steps down the terrace, half into the trees, silhouetted except for his hair, which appeared like a halo in fading light?

'This is where you live?'

'There.' – He pointed to a small building detached from the manor by a patch of lawn and low wall.

'How charming!'

Stubbing a cigarette under a toe (he was wearing the same cracked leather shoes as before, making her wonder if he had any others), he followed her look. The building was a grey stone dovecote with a steep, pointed roof and deep-set windows, like an old person's eyes. This hint of anthropomorphism made it seem ominous.

'Carine owns that?'

'She owns it all.'

'You mean that as well?'

He followed her look now back to the manor, which was low and long, laid out in an L-shape and quite stately in its mouldering way. Construction was apparently going on inside; piles of brick sat on the yellow gravel of the drive.

'Yes, that as well,' he said tapping out a new fag. (She wished he wouldn't smoke but took it as a sign of lover's nerves.) 'Conversion into maisonettes. Didn't you see the placard as you drove in?'

'Placard?'

'All Inquiries Bleistein-Thomas, Exclusive Agents.'

His tone seemed cynical. So was he not so attached to Carine after all? Miranda hoped not but hardly dared ask. It was not what she had come here for.

On the inside, the dovecote had been modernized. All its walls were white-washed but the bird-holes not filled in; so that, though monochrome and block-ish, it had atmosphere. On the ground level was a bedroom, an enormous bed in it covered with pillows and duvet; also an *en suite* loo. On the first floor was an open-plan kitchen and dining-area with round, bare wooden table and chairs. At the top, under a steep, equilateral ceiling was a sitting-room fitted with sofa, television, compact-disc player – the mod cons. Its ceiling was crossed with termite-eaten beams. Carine or whomever had done quite a job.

'Welcome to yuppy historicism,' Oliver said.

Miranda smiled. 'It's not so bad,' she replied in a tone of aren't-we-a-happy-conspiracy-of-two?

He lit a new fag.

'Aren't you going to kiss me?' she added, eyes watering. 'You have no idea what I've been through!'

So he kissed her. And she kissed back… It wasn't much.

A kind of rage rose inside her, and she burst into tears. 'I'm sorry. It's just that I've had to make such preposterous excuses. I've never lied before, not like this. What on earth must Valentine think? If he found out…' She dug in her bag for a tissue.

'What did you tell him?'

'It's so far-fetched. But he has such a crisis on now that he may not even notice I'm not there. I've farmed out the children, all except Anne, who wants to cook for him. Hugo's at the Wingfields, and Lucinda… But this is boring you. It's just that I feel so guilty.'

In fact, she did not. She wanted him to make a show of passion, that was all.

'So what did you tell him?' he repeated.

'That I was going to my analyst's for the weekend. I said that she – a woman I've heard of – has a cottage in Wiltshire, on the estate of

Lord Frome. Do you know him?'

'Used to.'

Frome was a celebrated 1960s figure, the archetypal hippy lord; Miranda's tears tapered off into gossip about him, a staple of chat at Cravin/Melot houses, which were not far away. Some instinctive reaction to weekends in Hampshire encouraged her to revert to this sort of trivia. Oliver listened politely.

'How do you feel about lying?' he asked when she was done.

'Lying?'

'To your husband.'

'Dreadful!'

As soon as she'd said it, she realized that, on the contrary, she'd half-enjoyed the rush of invention and element of going through the looking-glass in it. How had she tread the straight-and-narrow for so long? 'Making things up is fun!' she almost blurted in a phrase Lucinda had used on her once cheekily. But was this what her host wanted to hear?

For a moment again, she felt something really deep inside him. Excitement abating, she saw herself being drawn into his strange fabric of silence. Some magnetism seemed to pull her towards a kind of Zen moment, this re-enforced by titles of books scattered round: *A Journey in Ladakh, Fantasia of the Unconscious, A Celtic Anthology…*

'I love being here with you!' she ejaculated as he led her back down to the kitchen.

He is the still-point, she thought. He won't let me rush as I've been doing for weeks. Everything will be gentle, ritualistic, caring. For the first time since I've met him, I can be calm.

'I don't make you nervous, do I?' he asked, as she flapped doors to cupboards; and the timbre of his voice made her desist – she was *there* now, she told herself: there for that night, and another, with no need to escape anywhere anymore… for the first time in her life she was truly *there*, as he added, 'Why not just live in the present now?'

'Now and forever,' she gushed. 'You're so wise!'

'Not really. Not yet anyway.'

'Yes you are! And subtle and sensitive, and so handsome. That's why I love you.'

'… You hardly know me.'

'But I will!'

'… Two sugars?'

For himself, he'd poured out a glass of wine – more lover's nerves, she supposed. 'I brought some supper,' she ventured. 'It's in the car. Shall I go get it?'

She wanted him to take her on the spot, of course. Again she felt like some romantic caricature: one of those women in novels Margot mentioned: 'Thrills and Swoon', as Valentine scoffed. – Was she absurd? She wanted to laugh or to cry but told herself there was no hurry: she would go at his pace simply and learn.

They ambled to the car and brought in her things. She unwrapped two poussin and set out smoked salmon to start.

'You haven't you used this cooker yet. Why? Didn't want to spoil its yuppy pristineness?'

He poured himself a second glass and hesitated, bottle mid-air. 'Sorry. Would you like one?'

'I don't drink.' – A moment later she added, 'Except on special occasions. Oughtn't we to have champagne?'

'Yes of course. You must think I'm very unprepared.'

'Never mind. If you were waiting here for me with champagne and caviare, I would've thought you did this with every frustrated wife who throws herself at you. Which of course you do, I expect.'

She felt a crass Londoner, though, in fact, in town life, among the snobs Valentine had grown up with, she'd always seen herself as shy, prim, not very knowing: a silly Oxford girl. Here, in his silence, she felt almost garish. You must shut up, she told herself, just feel and take cues, as he went upstairs and put on some slow blues guitar.

'God I love you! *La Bohème* and this, not just Palestrina and a lecture on the values of the 17th century motet…' She sipped at the wine, and crass London slipped off.

There was a painting on the wall. She found herself staring at it after putting on courgettes to parboil.

'What do you think of it?' he asked, coming down.

It was clear and full of light and had been created in some sunny place, one could see, though the landscape was covered in snow. In the left foreground stood a man in a shaggy fur coat. From the centre and progressing off to the right ran a series of diminishing mirror-images of another man, slightly epicene, and a mature woman having sex, having sex, having sex until finally, in the last image, they turned into a swan.

'Who hung it there?' she asked, unwilling to voice an opinion that might conflict with his. (She felt sure he had one.)

'Carine, I expect. Tony.'

Miranda was attracted to it but somehow didn't want to be. Maybe it was the stress she was under, but didn't the figures look oddly familiar? The man in fur resembled Ollie, while the two *in flagrante* seemed like a younger Tony Thomas and punk-haired version of herself. Of course that was unhinged: how could she have stepped into a picture obviously painted by no one who'd ever seen her?

'What do you think of it?'

'Rubbish!' he exclaimed with more passion than she'd heard from him. 'Pretentious, derivative, postmodernist crap. The artist finally gave up. That's the sole thing to his credit.'

'... Giving up?'

'Of course. When you're mediocre, you should admit it and get on with something else, not go around trying to impose your pathetic ego on the world.'

Miranda was taken aback – his bitterness sounded so like Valentine's. 'Well I like it,' she ventured, returning to the stove. 'I take it you know who painted it?'

He poured another drink. 'Uh-huh.'

Conversation with him could have its edge: its own kind of shadow across the light.

'Someone I used to know. In Italy.'

The penny dropped. 'You mean – ? You're not an artist as well?!'

Oliver glared at her. 'As well as what?'

'As well as being utterly perfect!' she cried and, rushing to him, perched on his lap and pecked him on the cheek. 'I adore it! And it is yours! I knew it must be.'

Spacing his words slowly, carefully, he said, 'Do me a favour. Let's not gush on about art now, OK?'

'But I love it. I draw too – take a life-drawing class every week.'

'Please!' he insisted, no longer so calm. 'Let's just live for the here-and-now, OK?'

'OK,' she mimicked, really happy for the first time; because her lover (she should've known it – *did* know by instinct, of course) was a genius as well!

He opened another bottle of wine over a dinner which neither ate. She told him about her life from the beginning – that is, every detail up to and since Sentinale, which seemed wrong to mention. Bernardo's grin slipped in and out of view as she worked to be entertaining. Oliver seemed adept at listening.

'You're so lovely,' she effused. 'I've had such an unsatisfactory time, though no one would suspect it. I have a house in town and one in the country, three lovely children, two cars that work and a marriage that was once written up in *Chatter*. But you know all that; let's not talk about it, ever. Let's talk about you. Tell me about Italy. Did you live in the mountains?'

'Yes. And by the sea. And in Rome.'

'How romantic. And you painted great paintings and loved beautiful women? Tell me all. Or don't – I'll get jealous.'

'You shouldn't.'

'Yes I should. My life's been ghastly; I can't think what I've missed. Why've you come back to England? Was it to find me, my twin? When can we leave again, just the two of us? Will you take me to India? That's where I want to go. And other places.'

'What places?'

Sentinale. 'Oh – everywhere!'

He poured out more wine, in fumes of which Miranda realized she was getting tipsy. The mirrored images in the painting seemed to flutter, as if a breeze had blown through the room: a cool breeze across blinding snow. The bodies seemed to move, those bare torsos making love. Her head and spirit began to reel slightly; the blues guitar upstairs sounded like ululations of the sea.

'All right?' Oliver asked.

'... bit dizzy.'

'Want fresh air?'

'I think maybe I should lie down.'

He stood up. 'We can do both.'

More than anything, she wanted to go to the bedroom, sprawl out and let him stroke her. She felt like a cat or some animal covered in fur. Was that why he was leading her outside?

'Are you magic?' she wondered, tripping, feeling bewitched.

The moon sat above the manor, poised between beeches, looking like the emblem of some secret cult. It shone out bright and brave between phallic pillars, making Oliver appear in silhouette again, his hair a gauzy halo. Miranda felt as if she were being transformed into a sylvan goddess, her body like mercury.

'No,' he mused. 'But you are.'

'I am what?'

'Magic. Look at you.'

'No, look at you!' she wanted to cry, 'my lover, my hero, my brilliant sad failure – why did you say those things? I'm not going to let you put yourself down, ever. I believe in you. Whatever's happened, you don't need to tell me. I'm going to make everything right!'

Did he think her unhinged? She couldn't care. And where was he leading her, stumbling through grasses, down from the dovecote towards where sun had set.

A small clump of fir trees half-obscured a shed which she recalled glimpsing as she'd driven in. 'I don't sleep in the house,' he explained.

'Why not? too nice?' Or too twee? or too much Carine's?

He shut the door behind them. Through windows facing back, moonlight shadowed the dovecote: tall, strange, old, inky.

'Looks like a witch's hat,' Miranda murmured. 'My children would be scared of it, the way the roof points, almost like a steeple, only shorter and thicker and – '

'Not so religious?'

'O what are we talking about *it* for? Put your arms around me. Say you love me. Tell lies!'

'I don't tell lies, or try not to.'

'Then just do things. Do everything to me. Make me a woman, my beautiful prince. Tell me you like me a little. Put your hands here – both of them… If only you'd been around when I was twenty… No, don't stop. You think I'm pathetic, don't you?'

'Maybe a bit pissed.'

'I don't care. We have time. I'm never going back.'

A Valentine voice said: 'Don't talk nonsense. What about your kids?'

'I don't care about anything but this, you're so lovely – it's lovely. Please. Oh – come in to me – isn't that what one should say? I don't know what to say: I'm no good at this; teach me? Promise I'm not just another frustrated, ageing, middle-class housewife you've seduced?'

'Shut up,' he murmured.

'I'm sorry… What's this we're lying on?'

'A futon.'

'How exotic. I'm so ignorant.'

'*Basta*!'

'What does that mean?'

'It's Italian.'

'O speak Italian to me.'

They made love. It went on longer than in Knightsbridge and sobered her up. She heard the wind sigh and his breath coming harder; then it was over, only she didn't want it to be. Again, she felt as if she'd just missed that moment she'd been dreaming about.

As he rolled off, she rolled on top and gazed at his face in moonshine. It was silver-white, with dark craters.

'Speak to me,' she demanded. 'You seem remote. I'm not sure you even like me.'

'Sorry?'

'Don't be sorry; just speak. I want everything.'

'You've just had a good bit: I'm not twenty-two anymore. Nor thirty-two either.'

'How old are you, my lover? I feel eighteen.'

'Do you?'

The way he said it made her feel a fool: mutton dressed as lamb, indeed. She was not eighteen, she was thirty-five – perhaps older than he? The thought so alarmed her that she rolled off.

'Shouldn't have done that,' she muttered, looking at the witch's hat.

'What?'

'Joan Collins says that no woman past thirty should be on top. Wrinkles show, and your breasts sag.'

He gave the first laugh she'd heard from him. 'You're absurd.'

Her blood jumped. 'It's true!' – She felt like a child defending some fact it's just learned. 'I read it in a magazine.'

'What magazine?'

'*Woman's Own* or some rubbish.'

'Why read that crap?'

'That's what Valentine says. Only he doesn't say "crap".'

Oliver had meanwhile cupped one of her breasts. Now took his hand away.

'I'm sorry. I'll never mention him again. I never want to see or hear of him, now that I've met you; I wish he were dead. I wish he'd fall into one of his pulping machines and come out as the page of some woman's magazine; it would serve him right.'

She cupped her hand over the tip of his penis. 'Don't say that,' he gave back. 'Hatred is evil. It shrivels everything, even love. If you hate one person, you can't love anybody; it's the same kind of passion. It takes over and obsesses.'

'You're so wise,' she said, kneading. 'How do you know things?'

He fumbled for a cigarette.

'I feel passion,' she went on. 'Don't you?'

When he still didn't answer, she took her hand away and rolled onto her back to look at the dovecote again.

'You don't, do you?'

'Don't what?'

'Feel passion. For me.'

She heard him light up. '"The best lack of all conviction, while the worst are full of passionate intensity."'

She thought her heart would crack in that moment. Tears swam in her eyes, making the witch's hat shimmer. She felt so absurd, as he'd called her – as Valentine had so often called her, and Margot and sometimes even her children had thought her. So hopeless was she that briefly she wondered if she should throw her*self* into a pulping machine and be turned into the slick page of some sordid magazine, to be read in secret in a thousand loos, then tossed away.

Why had she come here? Did this man really want her? He seemed half dead. It was worse than being a picture on a page for some randy teenager to wank over.

What should she do now? Could she leave yet?

A tear rolled down her cheek. Wiping it with the back of a hand, she asked: 'Who said that?'

'Who said what?'

'What you said, about lacking passion.'

'I didn't say anything about lacking passion.'

'That's what I heard. What did you say then?'

'I said, "The best lack of all conviction, while the worst are full of passionate intensity."'

'I see,' she said, though she didn't quite. 'I'm of the worst, am I?'

Rolling eyes, he gazed at her. 'You *are* absurd,' he repeated tenderly.

'No I'm not!' Having dared this first sound of anger, she added: 'And I'm not going to stay here another moment if you insist on talking like Valentine.'

She started up; he caught her wrist. 'Don't be like that; I didn't mean *you*. I was trying to explain myself, or beginning to. I thought that's what you wanted.'

Instinctively she wrenched her hand away and covered her breasts. 'Don't bother!' she cried, and with a furious sob – 'I know you don't like me. I was a fool to come here. What on earth was I thinking?'

'Hang on a minute – '

She let the tears flood.

'Poor thing,' he murmured.

'I am not poor, and I'm not a thing; and I'm not a sex object. All I am is a housewife whose husband couldn't care less and garbage-collector for my children.'

'Don't say that,' he echoed. 'Come back here. You're exhausted.'

'No I'm not!'

But she was. And after a spell of sobbing, she did lie back. And as he stroked her, things started to happen again; until, at last, with her body taking over, demons of fear slipped away.

He pulled her on top. 'Fuck your Joan Collins. You look terrific.'

'No I don't.'

'Yes you do. Turn your mind off.'

'I can't,' she lied; but in a moment she was far, far away, into some fantasy landscape of the soul, riding a wild horse towards she didn't know where.

Miranda was not an original thinker: people who get churned up by Luv rarely are. It might have been easier had she been less sophisticated: less exposed, for instance, to the idea that there was something wrong with the abject emotion and sentimentality Valentine would mock. But it was not only Valentine's voice which inhibited her: there was Margot's female dandyism, equally if differently scornful of 'Luv'; there were also her parents' puritanism and work ethic, her mother's quiet suffering and father's belief that affairs should be conducted only if they contributed to his own open-collared version of intellectual progressiveness. Miranda's children were perhaps products of a permissive age, but that did not make them sympathetic of her; permissiveness had gone only so far as to breed a kind of hardness in them – she could not imagine Lucinda and Gus, for example, making love with much less barking gusto than Godfrey Wingfield with a barmaid.

Thus by instinct she had sought out a victim: an innocent and sensitive like herself. In lighting on Oliver Murrie she thought she had found one; and to the extent that she had, it made her feel powerful. She had almost exulted throughout the night, letting herself go, nearly falling in love. She had fluctuated between throwing herself off the cliff and standing back to watch waves roar below, thankful she stood in a high place. Was he a raging sea then? Not exactly. The half-dead thing in him gradually held the waves back; and though more drenched in passion than she ever had been, she got less wet than she hoped. By morning, it was clear that the tide was in full ebb; so that even with strokings and kissings and other paraphernalia of encouragement, she could see she'd had all she was likely to get.

'My poor darling, have I worn you out?'

'A little. Must not be very fit.'

'You look like you are. Your body's lovely.'

'Not half as much as yours.'

This appeased her and set her off again, though she did not quite believe it: he'd said the same to thousands, or anyway dozens. He denied this; still she half-believed it, not yet realizing that she was projecting on him an ambivalence all her own. Indeed, Miranda was only beginning to realize how truly maimed her feelings had been through years of not having what she'd longed for, yet pretending she had. Oliver seemed so experienced that it did not occur to her that, in this situation, he could be the naïf and she the victimizer. All the risk, thus all the vulnerability seemed to be on her side: she was the adulteress, he merely a chap who could find a girl on any station in half a dozen countries and take pleasure without consequence.

This made her terribly jealous, yet attracted her too. And it gave her odd satisfaction that in the morning she was up with the lark while he lay there sprawled and diffuse, mouth open, snores greeting each shift of duvet or sound of her feet on the floor. Her body felt lovely. This was a change. She couldn't recall when it had seemed so energized: strong yet lithe. For the first time in years she looked at her breasts and thighs without feeling anxious that they were going to turn to flab before anyone could admire them again. Granted, they were hardly the swells and curves of the 'corker' who had let her parents' American tenant undress her; but they'd worked. They had passed the audition: a man had liked them – even her belly, which she'd tried to not let him see.

'A woman who's had three babies may not be what you're used to,' she'd warned.

'You don't know what I'm used to,' he'd said, pressing to come in her for a third time. (She'd made sure he had to press hard to approximate the relative virginity she felt.)

'O God,' she had sighed. 'O darling, don't, please...' Somehow, starved of experience as she was (or because of it?), she had known all the lines: 'I don't think I can again. I'm getting so sore.'

'You want me to stop?'

'O – God – Yes – No – Yes. Keep going. Oh that's lovely – '

Et cetera.

She felt a little chagrined now remembering, in daylight. But at least she had done it: taken the risk and accomplished a change. If nothing more came of it, at least she could feel less bound, less crushed under the weight of her marriage and family and fictions of that existence. This was her real life, London an illusion, she told herself, as she went out in the morning and smelled the damp of the trees. All those talking heads and frustrations and duties – what she was really was a woman alive: mature yet young still; sturdy, if volatile emotionally; not so different from most other female creatures ever.

Nor was her discontent new. Women had felt it since the days when they'd dug hands in the earth, dressed in furs, been raped by strange men, whelped fatherless babes, stirred earthenware pots full of root vegetables and perhaps a skinned rabbit or two. 'I've always loathed the back-to-the-Primal-Goddess brigade,' Margot had once said when pondering Booby Vänder's fantasies of living 'a fecund country life': 'If God had meant us to rut and grunt all the time, he wouldn't've burdened us with brains.' And every summer when hippies clogged the road by Stonehenge on the way to his parents' place, Valentine would complain: 'Aren't they perfect asses? All this sun-worship and back-to-nature amounts to is fornicating and defecating in public.'

'What's defecating mean, Dad?'

It meant something that in the Cravin/Melot version of country life was hardly acknowledged. Cheveley House claimed a dozen of the oldest still-operative water-closets in England, owing to a marriage in the previous century of one of Valentine's forbears to an heiress from Buffalo, New York; and it had always been Miranda's duty to make sure the cottage apportioned for her and Valentine remained perfectly up-to-date in amenities – *comme il faut* for inspection should

Helena, Lady M, and milord happen down from the big house... But she suppressed these errant, annoying reflections as she walked across a dewy lawn to the dovecote. Nor did she glance north to where Cheveley-Cravin-Melot carried on in accustomed manner no more than fifteen miles away.

She put that out of mind. This was *her* weekend. Once more she puffed herself up to determination that she was going to make the most of it. – 'I deserve it, don't I?' she said to herself.

'You deserve all you can get,' Oliver had murmured in the night when she'd wondered if he minded making love yet again. 'You poor thing. Starved all these years.'

He was so tender. But was he worthwhile?

Up in the dovecote, clearing dinner plates, she entertained sober morning thoughts. What would they think of him: Lady Melot, Lady Evesham? What would her children say if she suddenly left Dad to live in a borrowed folly with a self-confessed failure? Of course he was heart-warming, but was that enough? The sex was lovely, or could be in time; but what sensible middle-class wife would give up a 'good' marriage for that? No, she chided herself gazing out the window to where he lay on his 'futon' (why did he sleep down there? a perfectly good bed was up here): she could not imperil her children for this. Perhaps, if he'd had the manic energy of her father, up every morning at six to bicycle to college, or even of Valentine, up equally early to go to his ration of worry. But Oliver was slow, dozy, half-broken, like all failed artists and hippies. So what had she been thinking?

Miranda grew sad then, wiping the counter. Tender in the womb still, she recalled *that* energy. He'd given her more there than she'd had ever; and that was worth something, wasn't it? And he was sweet, if abstracted and distant. She was not sure he loved her but felt she could make him in time. More confident than at first, she still had lingering doubts – what about Carine, for instance? And what about whoever had inspired that painting, which she now took time to study properly.

It was not good light for inspecting art. The window was on the west side, looking down towards the shed. Morning sun shone there, upstairs, out in the beech trees, everywhere but here. Even so, Oliver's large, ambitious canvas seemed more radiant than on the evening before. Internal light poured across snow towards the lovers and swan, illuminating the right half of the narrative figure where he stood peering out of a flipped-up collar. From the beige of his stubble to pink of bare bodies, the green of pine needles to shadows of gold on the snow, colour danced and pressed at every edge of a circumambient darkness, daring the whole to sing out. It did this while at the same time hinting that much in its subject was painful to its creator.

Was it about sexual betrayal then?

Miranda now got a different impression of her lover than she'd had a moment before, a sensation her own little English experience could not quite pin down. In the light and colour, pain and potential, she saw things she'd glimpsed only in Sentinale: a red earth and bronze sun, vast blue hills with cities of God in the distance, the ambiguity of Bernardo's tricksterish grin. She was riding again, galloping, feeling frightened, being free. And again she regretted not taking what had been offered, and reminded herself that what she had longed for was now at hand. Nor was everyone so lucky as to get a second chance. Thus in making a cup of tea, she concluded that – other things being equal – she had taken the right risk after all.

'Still asleep, my hero?' she asked, presenting the cup.

'Hmmm.'

'Would you like some brekkie?'

'Umm, not yet.'

Pause. 'The day's lovely. I thought of taking a walk. You?'

He stretched an arm towards her. Exhausted he may have been, but the arm still felt strong.

'Not now,' she resisted, though surprised and delighted to be wanted again – how had she missed this all those years?

Resentment against Valentine grew as she tiptoed out, shutting the door softly behind her. What did it matter if he were lethargic?

She loved him.

She imagined now a magical, earth-bound existence where she would determine all, like some female goddess, while he came and went, rose and fell at her bidding. Wind blew through the poplars down by the river; from atop the bluff, the manor gazed over her as she strode through a field where sheep munched in silence (spring lambs with their baaing were now long gone). Wind made a thunder against her exposed ear; far ahead a duck quacked; in a further field several other species replied. Nature seemed to her perfect this morning, holding no undercurrent of discontent such as she felt when Valentine and the rest took their regimental walks through the plantations at Cheveley. Here all was hers: no one else would intrude. Up there sat the dovecote, warm and benign in a sun flickering through leaves of tall beeches, grey and green haloed in gold. God, it was lovely! God, life was lovely! Oh Oliver, I love you, she almost prayed, gazing back at his shed, humble and unpretentious under a heavy-branched, protective yew. I want to live with you, she thought; and for a moment all obstructions seemed to pass.

Her children were school-aged: they could go to Bedales – there were good schools down here; why should they stay in town? How could it be right for them to grow up in a house where the parents obviously didn't love one another; where no touching or hugging or kissing went on, except on occasions of crisis when a teenager became a child briefly again? But even those moments were gone for the most part. Her children needed her less and less; soon they'd leave home, and then – ? Bloody Valentine and his lectures? an ice-age to contemplate. The future gaped at her, stony-eyed, hollow-faced, blue as the edges of Lady Melot's best china, thin and brittle. She couldn't face that. Here was her chance.

Wind brushed the leaves back. From the river came a cry of geese lifting off the water, wheeling; to the west stood a cloud bank – the brilliance of morning would turn. Oh Oliver, I love you, she repeated, desperate to utter these words as she changed direction and started back up the hill... Gone further than intended, she realized. By the time she reached the top, the sun was dead south, just above the beeches, fighting a rearguard action against clouds rolling in on the wind. She'd been gone an hour, perhaps two – time was distorting again as it had in the night, past mixing with future, muddling the present. She felt a touch mad. What were her children doing? what Valentine thinking? Try as she might, she could not get London to fade. Going through the looking-glass was for fantasy, a voice seemed to say; what was real was that illusions had to end.

Her weekend was half-done. What had she accomplished? What did he think of her? – Sun now vanished completely, then flickered back. On the lawn by the dovecote sat a chair, empty, a book on it opened, face down. Did he think her a fool? had he just pretended to need sleep to get rid of her half-hysterical presence? What an ass she had been! All that over-the-top talk, the Luv stuff and lies; all the squeezings and pumpings and strokings – hadn't he just been trying to put on a good face for something that struck him as crazed?

Must collect myself before he sees me, she reasoned and, to do so, picked up the book and sat down. Wind whooshed some more; a branch of a yew banged the shed; the sun fought its way free. Miranda shut her eyes. Then as the warmth and light again disappeared, she opened them and looked at the page.

> '*Hiraeth* [it read]: That typical Welsh word which we can but inadequately render as 'longing': an intense, passionate yearning for that which we have not, for dead friends, vanished youth, the peace of heaven, some satisfaction which life can never give... Delicacy united with the power of bare, direct, seeming-effortless and infinitely significant expression, heartrending in its perfect simplicity.'

In the margin a heavy pencil had written M.

Miranda's stomach turned. She longed for him. A surge of sweet, sad, sexual aching roiled her body, making her faint. Her senses expanded, contracted, went purple with woman's magazine stuff plus, plus, plus. She would retire from that censorious London which understood nothing; this man was what she wanted – *all* she wanted. He thrilled and moved her like nothing since the birth of her last child. In her imagination, she was now running for him: racing towards him on the stallion as wind roared and swept the leaves, turning them on their backs.

Overcast. Clouds swirled in over the beeches. Miranda unlatched the door of the dovecote and, as she stepped in, heard a voice. For a second she thought there was someone else with him, then realized he was on the phone:

'Yes... Yes... Well that's the main thing... Of course... Of course, you sweet noodle, that's all that matters... No, we couldn't be doing without you, could we? I'm sure he'll be all right... Yes, you will too: just keep warm and concentrate on what the doctor says... Call me when you get back. Or call me from over there... Yes, well I'm fine here; don't worry about me... Love you too. Bye.'

She'd stopped dead in her tracks.

'Miranda, is that you?'

She spoke not a word. She heard him light a cigarette, cough, then pick up the receiver again:

'I know I'm not s'posed to call but couldn't help myself. It's just that something splendid's just happened, and it's made me feel so much better I had to tell you I forgive... Well, I'm sorry. I won't again – call me if you want: you can get the number... Yes, a wave of reconciliation with the world and wanted to tell you I still felt... Course not. We go on. But I thought you should know. You have someone to thank... No, I can't tell you. Anyway, bye now... You too.'

Silence. She heard him smoking and pacing and, after a time, whistling under his breath. Then he ran up to the sitting-room (he'd been in the kitchen) and on came music – a symphony, Beethoven: stormy, uplifting. Finally he dropped down the stairs, breathing to tempi and, thundering down a last flight, discovered her at the door.

'Miranda!' – his face a portrait of pleasure. 'Didn't hear you; music's too loud. The wind getting on your nerves?'

She gazed at him as if through the wrong end of a telescope.

'You shouldn't've gone out without eating. Shall I make an omelette? What would you like in it? We've got – '

Should she dissemble? It was too sordid to confront him. She had no rights, no contractual reason to demand or even expect him not to have another woman – even two or three. She felt dizzy and ill. What a child she'd been to imagine that anyone could want to lock himself away in a *cloitre à deux* with her!

Gathering her sang-froid, she asked what he'd been doing while she'd been out. He went on about his dreams and reading and didn't mention the phonecall. She felt resentment welling and collected her thoughts for how she was going to deal with it as he rattled on about things she had wanted to know for weeks: how he'd succeeded, then fallen on hard times; how his paintings had sold, he'd made a pile, then lost it through speculation, hangers-on and outright theft; how he'd had troubles in love and lost several 'good women' and a child. Miranda ignored questions she would have asked had she still meant to make him her twin: what child had he 'lost'? who was the mother? what 'good' women was he referring to? why, having succeeded, had he not kept on with his art; wasn't there still a market for it? Most of these answers he might have given. A few he would've reserved for honour's sake, but even them she could have winkled out of him if she'd still been focused on what she'd imagined she wanted – a relationship that went all the way. But Miranda's mind felt frozen. She'd risked so much that she expected the worst now. She didn't mention the phonecalls; the fact that he neglected to mention them too she took as proof that he was a happy-go-lucky, two-faced Don Juan. Nor did she quite register the significance when he said:

'If you love one person, it spreads out to all the other people and places you thought you'd never look back on with anything but dismay. It reconciles you to the world. That's why it's so good.'

'What?'

'Love.'

'Oh that. Valentine calls it "woman's magazine stuff".'

Quite kindly, he said: 'Must you be so hard on him?'

'I hate him!' she exclaimed.

'Then how can you love me?'

'Who said I did?'

He studied her for a spell, trying to understand. 'You've really had a terrible time, haven't you?'

'I'm not asking for sympathy!'

'Of course not... What do you want?'

'For you to take your trousers off and fuck me!'

They were in the shed again; it had gone dark. Darkness came early now, but this was earlier than expected. A yew branch banged the roof, syncopating with their motions. The wind roared like a chain-saw through leaves. A hurricane was coming, and Miranda rutted as if it were to be the last sexual act of her life.

'My God, you're crazy.'

'I love you!' she lied.

'Don't say it unless it's true.'

'It is!'

'Then love everyone else.'

'Even Valentine?'

'Especially him.'

This man can't love me. How could he and tell me to love another man too?

'He's your husband, and the father of your children.'

'I wish you were.'

'... You're lovely.'

'Am I? Am I driving you wild?... Are you going to come now?'

'You want me to?'

'Oh darling!'

'Now?'

'Yes.'

'Are you sure?... Right now?'

'Yes. Yes. Oh Oliver. I think I'm – doing it too!'

But she wasn't. She was lying again, and now the lies were less fun than perverse. The childlike imaginativeness had gone out of it. As she lay under him panting, she saw with contempt just how powerful she could be in this new version of her old attraction as 'corker'. Bang went the branch against the roof; howl went the wind. Roar went the sorrow and anger inside her as he kissed her and she knew she could not love him really – could not love anyone, she feared.

Up she sat to a crash and sound of breaking glass.

'Tree's down,' he breathed.

A window was shattered. Wind hissed through and yowled; a spatter of rain almost hit them.

'Let's go to the house.' – She started to arrange herself, but he kept hold of her. 'I must call home!' she insisted, breaking away; then, crash! a beech branch hit the lawn. 'Aren't you coming?' she demanded, the harshness of tone surprising even her.

Reluctant, he sat up.

Wind was raging now. Out by the manor other large branches heaved to the point of breaking, then broke. Rain smacked down on the witch's hat of the dovecote while up through the grasses they struggled, pelted by sticks and leaves.

Mud oozed through her toes as she clung onto him, duvet flapping around like a bedsheet in the wind; only this was no mere wind anymore. Another branch came down, just missing the manor; then a beech cracked at the trunk with a sound out of *Revelations*, and she half-imagined them as Adam and Eve being thrown out of the garden, or Lot's wife and so on being cast into deserty exile. But there was no time for what Valentine might call blasphemy; it was all they could do to reach shelter.

Miranda fought her way through the door, a wet shred of duvet clinging to her legs. She tried the phone in the bedroom as he struggled to shut out the wind.

'It's dead,' she announced.

'What?'

'The phone.'

'Of course it is. The lines will have come down.' – He stood there shivering, shrivelled, the last thing but heroic.

'What do you mean "of course"?'

He stared at her strangely, almost imploring.

'Don't you realize what this means?'

'That you can't call your children.'

Peeling off the duvet, she said, 'I'm going.'

'You can't go in this.'

'Well I am. Let me get my clothes.' – She tried to pass.

'Don't be stupid. You – '

'*Don't* call me stupid. Look what you've made me do!'

'What I've made you do?'

'Come out there, get caught in this – what if Valentine finds out? What if I can't get back to London until – '

From the driveway came the most terrific crash yet. A crunch of metal and bursting glass made it apparent to even the most distracted ear that somebody's car had been crushed.

3.

Nobody was there when Miranda got home. The house was tidy, warm, dry; the Aga, sink, kitchen counters and cupboards were all as clean as a pin. In the fridge, remains of a Sunday roast were put away neatly in bowls covered with cling-film. The table was clear of plates and crumbs; in its centre was a small vase filled with apricot roses. At Valentine's place sat a stack of Sunday papers, three of them, plus a document entitled Eurofibreworks, Ltd.

This was the new brochure of Valentine's company. At the Wingfield dinner, Miranda had suggested to Godfrey that they revise the logo and add colour to indicate that, however boring, the paper-recycling business was not strictly a black-and-white affair. The cover accordingly was a rainbow of three shades of blue, red and yellow, two of green, one each of brown, purple and black. It looked almost lively. It also had a function: the colours denoted various hues of stock which the company's mills could produce.

Miranda glanced through the brochure almost fondly. Its insides included photos of the Ayrshire works: the delivery of waste paper, the pulping, rolling and pressing of new papers, the dyeing, cutting and warehousing. There was a progression from chaos to order: tubs of shreds became a vat of pulp soup, which became gargantuan kitchen rolls, which became piles of thick-fibred sheets in jolly shades. The final warehoused stacks looked like freshly laundered bath-towels folded and stacked neatly in cupboards. Next to the stacks stood a balding workman, wearing an engaging smile. Underneath him was a last bit of copy, also at Miranda's suggestion: 'Prime Recycled Papers – for a Greener Environment'.

Making a cup of tea, she was idling over the colour supplement of *The Observer* when the front door opened and feet clambered in. Some went upstairs, attended by girls' voices; two pairs came down, delivering Hugo to the kitchen, along with a fair-haired, sweet-faced adolescent whom Miranda knew to be Christian Wingfield.

'Bring me the papers,' Valentine's voice called. 'And don't mess up Anne's table. She'll be cross if it isn't tidy when your Mum gets home.'

'She's already here,' announced Hugo.

'Nonsense. Her car's not in the street.'

'It's a ghost otherwise.' – Hugo nudged Christian: *Ghostbusters* was a teenagers' film of this era, a favourite of theirs. 'You haven't died and come back to life, have you, Mum?'

'I might have for what I've been through.' She collected herself. 'I thought you were staying at Christian's, not vice versa.'

Valentine appeared in the stairwell. 'I picked them up after lunch. The girls wanted to go to Hyde Park to see the trees that had fallen. Lucinda suggested we might as well pick up Hugo then too, as we were in that part of town.'

'She just wanted to see Gus,' Hugo put in, ransacking the fridge.

'Is that so? Christian, are your brother and Hugo's sister keen on one another?'

She was almost too weary for stratagems. But with Valentine hovering, ready with questions, she had to catch her breath and organize her story; and it was only logical that she should try to deflect attention.

Christian had blushed. He had seraphic, almost feminine features, quite unlike those of his elder brother, the dark, prematurely manly, sixteen-year-old Gus, whom Miranda imagined Lucinda to be keen on. 'Guess so,' the boy murmured.

'Sure. They snog the whole time.'

'Hugo, words like "snog" are vulgar.'

Her son ignored her. ''s not all they do,' he added towards Christian in a tone that made the boy blush rather more.

'What do you mean?' Miranda demanded, sounding severe; in fact, she was pleased for this hint of sexual worry to cover suspicion of her.

'Nothing, Mum.' – Hugo grabbed a yoghurt. 'Let's go upstairs.' Slamming the fridge door, he plucked Christian by a sleeve and clattered past his Dad coming down.

'Hugo, you know you're not to eat except in the kitchen. Bring that yoghurt back. Valentine, do something. What's got into him?'

This deflected attention yet more and, when Valentine said, 'Never mind; let him go', she instinctively launched into a pre-emptive strike:

'He's too cheeky by half. Obviously I can't risk going away; you're too lenient with him.'

Valentine took off his Burberry. He was wearing a cable-knit jumper his mother had given him and a pair of corduroys Miranda had purchased in a failed attempt to make him look casual.

'We were worried about you,' he surprised her by saying.

She'd expected some barb, to which she would have responded by fleeing to the bath under cover of a row. His tone was almost sweet, though; what's more (this almost stupefied her), he looked rather handsome for a change.

'Well I'm worried about Lucinda,' she returned. 'Must call Margot. What are we going to do about it?'

'About which?'

'This "snogging" business with Gus.'

'I wouldn't make much of that.'

'No? And what are we to say when she turns up pregnant? That's not going to delight your mother, is it? scandal with a Wingfield boy?'

'I don't see what my mother has to do with it.'

'She wants Lucinda to marry a Royal,' Miranda averred.

'What nonsense.'

'Of course she does. Just like she wanted you to marry Cicely Fitzhoward-Leighton or whoever that girl was who was the granddaughter of the Duke of Telford.'

She was lining up ammunition lest he chose to attack: his family's snobbery, her feelings of being snubbed.

Valentine did not rise to any of it in specific. 'Your weekend doesn't seem to have calmed you,' he said.

She had to be careful. 'It might've done if we hadn't been in the eye of the storm.'

'But you were in Wiltshire. The real damage was in Hampshire.

Cheveley had several windows blown out; the cottage took a branch through the roof. I was on to Father this morning; we'll have to go at the weekend. Perhaps you should drive down earlier to see.'

Here came the moment. 'I can't,' she stated.

'O? And why not? I didn't see the car outside. Has something happened to it?'

'Yes.' – She let tears well. 'A tree fell on it. It's an absolute wreck.'

'Good God. In Wiltshire? Gracious me. I hadn't realized the storm got so far north. Some freak air current, I suppose. You poor thing. What did she do? put you on a train?'

'Who?'

'This analyst of yours. What did you say her name was?'

'I didn't. And yes. I got into Waterloo an hour ago.'

'Waterloo? Paddington, surely. Waterloo's the south, not the west.'

'O, *don't* be pedantic. Can't you see how gruesome it's been?'

'Yes, it must've been frightful. Darling girl.'

A brief silence.

'You got on where?'

'Got on where what?'

'The train. What's the station for that part of the world? Beyond Swindon, is it? Warminster? Bath?'

'For goodness sake, Valentine, isn't it enough that the car's been wrecked? Do I have to recite the time-table of British Rail?'

'Of course not, I was only thinking: I'll send a man in the morning.'

'Send a man where?'

'Where the car is.'

'What's the point of that? I've told you: it's flattened.'

'There must be something to salvage.'

'There isn't.'

'Darling, you're not expert in these things. Anyhow, we can't just leave it wherever it is. There'll have to be a claim against insurance.'

'I'll take care of it.'

'What nonsense. You're no good at that kerfuffle. I'll send a man down. You've been through enough as it is.'

'No I haven't.'

He stared at her. 'What an odd thing to say.'

'O I'm so tired...' More tears.

'What's this analyst been doing? I thought she was meant to make you as happy as you were in Sentinale, but you're more upset even than on Friday. How much is she charging for this therapy?'

What a mess she was in! If only he weren't so uncharacteristically solicitous. He never sat with her like this: it was always barked orders and titbits *en passant*. Fortunately, at that moment the phone rang.

'Hello?... Hello...?' Putting down the receiver, he said: 'Funny... Perhaps it's Father trying back. They say the lines are going to stay dicky. I got through this morning – must be interference now.'

Miranda knew that wasn't the problem. It was Oliver, of course.

'Must just go to the loo,' she breathed and dashed up the stairs.

In her bedroom she pondered, then picked up the receiver and dialled. Line dead; service was still erratic in Hampshire. Even so, she knew it had been him. Must have tried from a call-box. And what would she do if he tried again?

'Hi, Mum.' – Anne's chubby face peered round the door-jamb. 'May I come in?'

'Of course, poppet.'

Miranda was splayed over her canopied bed. Her youngest ran and hung on her neck like a dreamy child half her age.

'Did you have a fun weekend?'

'OK.'

'What did you cook?'

'Nothing really. Bacon and eggs. Things like Dad likes.'

'I'll bet he was happy. He complains I don't cook him anything he likes anymore.'

'No he doesn't. He said we missed your cooking. The joint was overdone today. I thought it was my fault, but he said the sermon went on too long.'

'You went to church?'

'Yes. Lucinda and Hugo hated it, but I thought it was fine.'

'Where did you go?'

'St Paul's.'

In her mind Miranda saw the nave of the great cathedral. She'd only been there on a few occasions, always with Valentine. The most recent had been the marriage of the Royal who'd revered her father at Oxford. It was one of the few times Evesham and Cravin families had appeared together and certainly the only one on which Eveshams came out more favoured, because of relations of Sir Ralph with the Royal in question. The fact had made Valentine, and even his mother, relatively respectful of Miranda and her lot for a change. Miranda recalled it as one of the few satisfactory days of her marriage.

'Will you let me help cook for the party, Mum?'

'What party is that, poppet?'

'The one Dad has to give.'

'Dad has to give a party?'

'Hasn't he told you?'

'Not that I recall.'

'He found out Friday. Somebody named Tony rang to say that someone named – I can't pronounce it, French or something – was over from America and did he want to see him because of his business so Dad said why not bring him to dinner.'

'O?'

'Yes. He said you knew about it already. Used a funny phrase. He said it was going to be a White Night. Does that mean it's not going to be fun?'

'I'm not certain.'

'Even if it does, I'd still like to help with the cooking. OK?'

Momentarily Miranda recoiled into complex thought. 'Of course you can,' she said and, kissing her youngest, implicitly dismissed her.

'I'm glad you're back, Mum,' the girl turned to say from the door. 'Lucinda and Hugo make jokes about you, but I think you're the best mum in the world.'

There was hardly time for a tear and snatch of further wonder about this 'White Night', or Knight as she supposed, before the phone rang again and she pounced:

'Hullo?'

'Miranda?'

'Why are you phoning here? Don't you know it's the weekend? Valentine's downstairs. Was it you who rang off when he answered?'

'Yes, I just wanted to – '

'What are you playing at, Oliver? This could wreck my family. I could lose custody of my children if – '

Valentine came on the line. 'Sorry, darling. You've got it, do you?'

'Yes,' she said breathless. ''s all right: it's for me.'

Her husband clicked off.

'Don't you see?' she demanded.

Oliver's voice was subdued. 'I don't mean to put you in jeopardy; I only phoned about the car. Should I have it towed or what?'

'I don't know!' – She felt disgust and despair, confusion and a good deal of fear. Still, there had to be some answer.

'You just want me to leave it here?'

'Of course not.' She said in a flash: 'Have it towed up to Wiltshire.'

'To Wiltshire? What for?'

'Oh for goodness sake, do you want to help me out of this muddle you've got me into or ask questions?'

'I don't know what to say,' he answered at last, deflated.

'I'm sorry.' – For a second she felt a genuine wave of remorse. 'It's just that – ' Then Valentine walked in.

He glanced at her with no sign of suspicion and went to his bureau to pull out a drawer. Such resurgence of affection as she might have begun to work up for her lover now flew out the window.

'Listen,' she concluded, flat, efficient, non-committal, 'I can't give you an answer tonight. Let me discuss it with my husband and call you in the morning.'

Oliver was non-plussed. 'Miranda – '

'I'm sorry, I just cannot think at the moment. I'll phone tomorrow. Thanks again for the weekend.'

'Is someone else there?'

Thank heavens he twigged. 'Of course. Bye.' She hung up.

Valentine pushed his drawer shut and, clean socks in hand, went to the bathroom, leaving the door ajar. From an angle in the mirror over her bureau, Miranda could see him sitting on the edge of the tub and unlacing his shoes, which had got wet in the park.

'What's this Anne tells me about a party?' she inquired, as if the phonecall were an aeon away.

'Ah yes of course, that. I suppose we could talk about it. I'd rather hoped to spring it on you after you'd had some rest. You've had a wretched time, haven't you, dear? I do wish you'd let me take care of the car; it's the least I could do. I should be paying this woman as well, shouldn't I? There's no reason it should have to come out of the cheque your father sent; some small bit of psychological treatment ought to be covered by BUPA anyhow.'

Tossing damp socks in the corner where dirty clothes lay, he came out wearing dry ones and lay down on the bed. Stretching an arm out, he appeared to be inviting her to nestle her head in the crook of it. What on earth was this in aid of? Valentine never behaved like this, especially on a Sunday afternoon.

'Darling!' she exclaimed, trying to sound light. 'What's come over you? Isn't *Grandstand* on TV?'

'The children're watching a video,' he explained.

He had hired a video for them? This was truly abnormal.

'I promised it as payback for going to church,' he added.

'Ah.'

'The music was Vittoria. Lovely. Shame you weren't there.'

She had to think quick. Not wanting to nestle up to him exactly, she nonetheless recognized its usefulness. So laying her head on his shoulder, she breathed: 'Saw your new brochure.'

'O? And what did you think?'

'You and Godfrey did everything I said.'

'Well, we appreciated your suggestions, darling. Women's instincts are often best for that sort of thing. Like a job handling PR?'

Was he flattering her now?! She felt thoroughly chilled. 'Love to,' she murmured, yawning. 'But I do have a bit on my plate, don't I?'

'I guess. Especially with this therapy you're taking.'

Silence. She tried to feel warm and happy beside him, but was scared nearly out of her wits.

'I'm not being entirely facetious,' he went on. 'You've already done more than any PR person I could hire. Why didn't you tell me you were seeing that American chap?'

So was that it? The penny dropped, or at least *a* penny. Miranda saw, or thought she did, what – or part of what – he was thinking. Tony Thomas, lunch at the wine bar, the White Knight – it all fell in place. Valentine thought she'd been flirting with little Carine's husband!

Complications flowed from this, of course: what would Margot think if she heard? would Valentine be angry or merely watchful? was it in her interest to disavow the American instantly, or might economy with truth be a useful cover? Still, it was handleable.

'You mean Margot's thingamajig?' is how she responded.

'If that's what you call him. Yes, he rang. Said you suggested it.'

If truth were told, Miranda could hardly remember the lunch now: it seemed like a year before. 'Did I? Maybe. I can't think why I bothered; bored I guess. But then he said – yes, that was it – that he knew someone who might be able to help you.'

'A White Knight, did he put it? Well, he does. Or at least is proposing to come up with an extraordinary possibility. Why didn't you tell me you'd seen him?'

Here it came. What to say? – 'Oh, it seemed unimportant. I think he's quite awful. You have no reason to be jealous.'

'Jealous?'

It had hardly occurred to Miranda till then how much benefit might be got from the fact that Valentine couldn't care less what she'd done, or not done, with Tony Thomas – or anyone for that matter. It was his business that concerned him, that was all. Only now as he talked on, did she realize she was safe; and her tension subsided. Almost immediately, however, it was replaced by the more usual drift: dull, resigned disappointment, sliding into resentment.

'Your little friend has an acquaintance called John DuRocher. Mean anything to you?'

She shook her head, though of course she'd heard the name. Few American families had more renown: after Rockefeller, DuPont and, say, Getty or Hearst, DuRocher was as royal as those colonials got.

'I don't know what he does or why he should be interested in Eurofibre, but your pal's offered to introduce him. Godfrey's checked him out: apparently the real thing. At the moment I can't afford to leave any stone unturned.'

'Poor Vally,' Miranda murmured, trying to obscure what spun in her mind by seeming to fall off towards sleep… Oliver Murrie, Tony Thomas, crashing trees, now her husband – 'Has it really been as ghastly as they say?'

'What as who says?'

'Your business. The papers… Margot tells me it's all over the City page of *The Times*.'

'That bloody Swede. The problem is, if he gets the firm, I'm out. And he's on the verge. With the Single Market in Europe and Sweden not in the EC, he's willing to pay a premium for a London listing. He's put out a story that his company's the oldest in the world, as if that made any difference. He's banking on snob appeal, and my backers might not be able to resist. I tell them it'll just end in tears, with all our assets stripped and profits poured back into Stockholm, but. The one hope is to find another bidder who can beat his price, a sympathetic one who'll keep me on.'

Miranda did not pretend to understand this. She only knew from her husband's tone that he needed her support now more than she could recall; and it touched her slightly. Under the circumstance too, it made her sigh with relief.

'What can I do for you, darling?' she asked, cuddling closer; and for a moment, in memory of comforts in the night, she was half tempted to wrap her limbs around him.

*

This impulse didn't last. By the time of the dinner, there had been several rows. In the first place, any temporary affection she'd felt for her husband was not met by genuine response: the small ration of niceness he'd cast towards her was merely to get her operating as hostess and cook. Then there was a row over the table: should they clear the children's playroom and make it into a dining-room 'as it was meant to be' or go with the normal arrangement and have the guests sit in the kitchen in front of the Aga? Miranda naturally plumped for the latter: it was less work and more charmingly English; an American might appreciate it from a touristic perspective. Valentine, however, did not wish to take chances:

'This is too important for country-cottage stuff, darling. Can't we just have a formal, sit-down dinner for once?'

'I wasn't intending to make them stand.'

'You know what I mean.'

'Why don't you get your mother to organize it if you want a Cheveley House sort of thing.'

'Please don't let's have words.'

'Well what's wrong with my kitchen?'

'For goodness sake, nothing. I just want a proper dinner!'

Similar discussion was held on the menu. This came over breakfast; Anne brought it up by suggesting roast chicken. Miranda tried to explain why that was not posh enough; Valentine declared that, considering time of year, it ought to be pheasant or venison. Miranda said she did not know how to cook pheasant or venison. Hugo asked if he could go hunting with the Wingfield boys when their father next took them. Lucinda said that pheasants and all creatures of the kind were too pretty to shoot and hunting was immoral. 'What nonsense,' Valentine replied. Miranda said it was not nonsense. No firm decision was reached.

As these matters were rehearsed, so too was the subplot of the car. Oliver, dutiful and unoccupied in the country, had the wreck towed to Wiltshire despite his confusion as to why Miranda should want it there. Miranda found out the location of the therapist's cottage and told Oliver to go along with the AA and find a neighbouring lay-by to leave it in; he was then to go to the cottage and knock on the door: if the woman were home, he was to tell her that a friend had run off the road in the recent storm, that the friend had just managed to escape with her life and that he, Oliver, had come to check on the wreck and could he possibly use her phone to call London and have someone haul it away?

'I did all that,' Miranda's lover in due course reported. 'I felt a right berk. Your therapist woman couldn't've believed a word. Why did you have to dream up such a complicated story?'

'Never mind,' Miranda retorted.

She wasn't entirely certain why she'd engineered all of this, or if she'd got the details right. But whether or not, the car was now in Wiltshire; Valentine could send his man if he insisted; and if he were suspicious and checked the facts, he would find that it had been parked rather close to an analyst's cottage on the estate of Lord Frome.

'What was she like?' she asked in passing, thinking it prudent to know at least the colour of hair of this woman she was meant to have spent a weekend with.

'Who?'

'The shrink, of course.'

'Oh, you mean Gisela.' – The analyst was called Gisela Cohn-Burton ('What on earth kind of name is Gisela?' she could hear Valentine mock.) 'Asked me in for a cup of tea,' Oliver said.

'And?'

'And, so I had one.'

'You usually do. And then what?'

'Not much. We chatted. She's into Klein and things.'

'What on earth does that mean?'

'Not just psychoanalysis. Metaphysics – that bit. Interesting.'

'Made a new conquest, did you?' Miranda quipped.

He muttered something she didn't quite hear. Now that the thought had risen, she almost wished that he *had* made a new conquest – it might have made things easier on her. She went so far as to wonder if she should push him. How was she going to handle it, after all, if he phoned every day and grew as attached as he seemed on the verge of? She'd been cruel at the dovecote: her leave-taking had been downright rude. So shocked had she been by the car and mortified by his phone conversations that all she'd been able to think of was to get back to town, her family and even husband, the *known*; thus the extraordinary passage of affection she'd felt for Valentine when first home. But now, with his usual rejection of her in bed (she'd made the mistake of touching him in the night; he, feigning sleep, had shrugged her hands off and, when she'd failed to move, kicked her so hard that she'd had to spend the rest of the wee hours clinging to the far side of the mattress, fearful that she might fall off) and the usual rows at mealtime, complicated by his veiled accusation that she might not be able to produce a 'proper' dinner, Miranda had no more affection for him than for an inmate in Pentonville Prison up the road. Thus Ollie's stock had gone up.

'Aren't jealous, are you?' he asked.

'Should I be?' she inquired.

'Of course not. It was you who asked me to see her.'

'But you didn't have to have a cup of tea with her, did you?' Miranda teased.

Oliver hesitated. It was almost as if he did have something to hide. But Miranda was hardly suspicious.

'This is silly,' she concluded. 'I don't know why I'm asking: I have no rights over you. Besides, I'm the one who's unavailable.'

So saying, she half-consciously wound him up to replying: 'You don't have to worry. I'm not interested in anyone but you anymore. Not in that way.'

'What way is that then?' – And so on.

This conversation passed while the children watched their soap on TV. It was Monday evening. By Tuesday morning, after more bad nerves from Valentine about the dinner ('Call Margot if you're not sure what to do; I have enough on my plate without having to figure out menus as well – why can't one have a wife one can rely on?'), Miranda began to wish for him to call back. London was safe maybe, certainly when the country was torn up by storms; but London was eternally frustrating as well. She could feel desire returning for that still-point. It was like the echo of a melody heard at the right time with the right person at twilight in a transcendental landscape.

Out the window she gazed at November day in her garden. Ordinarily the view evoked little but itself: a tight, tidy urban scene, gorgeous with flowers or depressing with stems depending on time of year. This morning, however, in the thinning of leaves on the copper beeches and last blooms of the tobacco plant, in her snapdragon and the blue and fleece over roofs opposite, Miranda glimpsed something that took her back to the dovecote and his sweet ways. The yearning and restless romantic impulse which had driven her there returned, covering up her shock at his intimacies with other women (who were they?) and disappointment in his character in general (how could she replace Valentine with *him*, at least publicly?) and concentrating her spirit on the tender excitement he'd evoked. She still wanted a soulmate. But now she had this blasted party to get through. So, though fed up, she did phone Margot:

'I'm in a rush, dearest,' the *grand dame* declared. 'My friend Booby's here. We're trying pornography now. How can I help?'

'The menu's the main thing.'

'As long as you've got the right food and drink, you've done your bit; everything else is up to the guests. Who's coming by the way?'

There would be Valentine and her; Godfrey and Margot. She would have to invite Tony and Carine too, she supposed, considering Tony's role in events. Then there would be the White Knight.

'What did you say his name was?... American, is he?'

Miranda could hear the name being relayed to Booby: a hand went over the receiver while the women tittered. Lately, Godfrey's wife had started reacting to gossip like a naughty schoolgirl. Success had made her more trivial, Miranda reflected; and since she, Miranda, had scant sense of humour herself, she sometimes wondered if the tittering weren't about her.

'Booby wants to come too,' Margot returned on the line to say. 'I think you should have her. She knew some DuRochers in New York. Says this one's a crashing bore but has a funny story about him. And you need an extra woman, don't you?'

'I guess,' Miranda was forced to admit. 'I was thinking of – '

'Two,' Margot corrected, 'you'll need two; I doubt Carine can come. She's been ill, you know: doctors have said she must go away.'

This was not something Miranda had known or suspected. Nor was she agile enough to put two-and-two together and reflect that it had been the reason for the first of those phonecalls at the dovecote which had so upset her. Too many things were on her mind now to allow all connections. She had a vague recollection of the skinny little Jewish girl coughing and instinctively liked her husband even less for his apparent Casanova-ism.

'Are you sure she won't come?'

'No. You'd better ring them. But do think about Booby; she's awfully keen. Good value too. Every party needs certain types. Look at what you've got: a rigid bureaucrat, Valentine; a buffoon, Godfrey; a sexy man, Tony; an ingenue, Carine, if she turns up; an upper class rose, your dear self; a balanced female, me; a balanced male, that must be your guest-of-honour – you have to build the thing as if he were, even if he's not. What's missing?' Margot answered her own question: 'Someone over-the-top. A woman preferably. Loud and crude.'

'Why on earth should I want that?' Miranda demanded Valentinely.

'Balance, dearest. One always needs someone for others to detest, especially someone of the same sex; it sets oneself off. Like having a social lightning rod, as Booby puts it. How do you imagine I've been able to put up with dear, inadmissible Godfrey all these years?'

Miranda could hardly believe Margot's cheek, especially when one of those she was maligning was in earshot. Could Booby really have been 'for others to detest'? She thought she heard more titters and concluded that her erstwhile best friend now inhabited a world too fanciful for a simple soul like herself. For she was a simple soul, Miranda insisted inwardly as she pondered options for the menu, which Margot noted with bland assurance. She, Miranda, did not calculate personality for its value around her table or various courses for their capacity to impress. She did not have funny stories to tell and often found it an effort to laugh when others did. Unlike this new Margot, she was embarrassed by earthiness; sex was a topic she hardly spoke of, name-dropping unknown to her beyond the confines of the English class-and-merit consciousness she'd grown up in and had deepened by marriage to the son of a lord. A great name in the City would have been lost on her; the fact that Tony's wife was a Bleistein or Sloman evoked no background of Edwardian catering, Bow Bells, grand hotels or any of the other items that people in the know might have associated with such London Jews. DuRocher was a name she may have heard of; but if you'd asked her what the family did or had done, she would have been at a loss to note lumber interests in Oregon, oil in Ohio, steel in Pittsburgh, banking in New York, distribution and mining throughout Latin America – all of which Tony Thomas detailed in spades when she rang to ask after Carine:

'Margot says she's been ill. I hope it's not serious.'

'We're going to America next week. She might be able to come if it's Thursday: she sees the doctor Wednesday. Can we leave it till then?'

'Of course,' said Miranda, though it put out her numbers; but Valentine had been clear – cultural half-breed or not, Tony Thomas had to be treated well now.

She thought to probe more, but he was uncharacteristically mum. Whatever Carine was suffering from must have been serious: the glibness had gone out of his tone, despite an all-knowingness in his run-down on John DuRocher:

'He's the salt of the earth for someone so wealthy. You'll like him... By the way, how's your subtext going?'

'My "subtext"?' – Had Oliver been indiscreet?

The American chuckled. 'Still the princess of candour, I see. Never mind. Like I said when we lunched, the time may come when you need someone to confide in. I'll be happy to oblige.'

Miranda was non-plussed and hung up at first chance, concluding that she did not like Americans.

This was hardly convenient, given she was throwing a dinner to impress three. Tony Thomas seemed intent on undressing her figuratively; Booby Vänder, whom she had agreed to include, seemed on Margot's description intent on undressing herself; goodness knew what one could expect of this John DuRocher. Tony said unpretentious; Booby, via Margot, talked of a 'bore' with an odd story about him; Godfrey via Valentine reported that he was 'the real thing'. Miranda conjured a picture of some rather overbearing, vulgar George Bush, her image of the U S of A being limited to what she knew from TV: J. R. Ewing or a hairdresser's model like some of those who ran for President. In fact, she did not understand America well and, like many of her kind, was not sure she wished to. Though having no political consciousness to speak of, Miranda preferred Europe of the two continents Britain was pulled between, she believed. Yet more and more as she prepared the event, she longed for a third thing: escape: Oliver's next call, *faute de mieux*. In the background, however, even that seemed imperfect. A phantom of the Italian boy's grin lurked about. Youth and hopes are receding, a voice seemed to whisper as, putting her head down, she cooked.

'Buckling with horseradish cream. Petit Royales au Parmesan. Prawn Cocktail – boring. Smoked Eel Smetana,' Anne read from a cookery volume. 'Do you like eels, Mum?'

'Certainly not, slimy things.'

'What about Royals?'

'Your father might enjoy one, but I don't think they'd appreciate being cooked.'

'I guess that leaves Buckling.'

'What on earth's that?'

'I don't know. Shall I read on?'

The actual preparation was fun. Even Lucinda helped: she came to Safeway to carry bags. This was after Miranda had had a word with her, the upshot of which was that Lucinda be allowed to invite Gus Wingfield to come eat in the kitchen while the grown-ups carried on upstairs. To get Hugo to help clear out the playroom, Miranda conceded that he could invite Christian too: the second Wingfield boy was becoming her son's shadow, a development she approved of rather more than Lucinda's relations with Gus. Thus a formalish children's dinner was arranged for downstairs. – Anne looked forward to 'playing mum'.

After Buckling, they would have Savoury Game pie – this on Margot's advice – for vegetable, Leeks *à la Niçoise*; for pudding a special trifle. 'Keep it simple,' Margot had warned and went along with Miranda vs Valentine on the idea that Americans were charmed by Englishness. 'He'll adore you,' la Wingfield had added. 'How many Americans ever get a chance to know the real English? Booby was just saying so the other day. That's half the reason she's keen on coming – I described you: the perfect, most inviolable rose.'

Miranda had once been flattered by this epithet; now she wondered if it weren't some kind of put-down. Certainly Booby Vänder puffed it like a gust of hot breeze when she sailed through the door. 'The perfect English rose!' the Americanne enthused.

She was first to arrive, as she would be last to leave. Nor was Miranda likely to see such a sight outside of a film or in Manhattan.

Though 'relocated' to London years before, la Vänder had not lost her native expressionistic verve. Some said she'd left New York because 'if you can make it there, you'll make it anywhere' yet pedigree had kept her from making it as she'd wished. Others believed that she'd had more positive reasons – i.e., to teach London 'real' civilization, as New Yorkers of her vintage imagined they had attained.

Booby's vintage was 1960s. Her persuasion had been to be 'a card-carrying member of the studio of Dandy Rawhol': 'I was *there*!' she declared over drinks. 'Where do you think I picked up my nickname?'

'We'd all been wondering,' quipped Godfrey, who arrived second with Margot, 'but were too polite to ask.'

'Godfrey Wingfield, you've never been so polite as to give me the time of day! But then I've lived in Blighty long enough to know what to expect, or not in this case, from an old Wykehamist.'

'What's a Wykehamist?' asked John DuRocher, who'd arrived last with Tony. (Carine had come too, after all.)

Tony eyed Booby sardonically: clearly he could barely abide this fellow expat. In fact, by the way he looked at her, Miranda was moved to wonder if Margot hadn't been playing some obscure prank by prompting her to invite the creature in the first place.

Unquestionably, Booby was over-the-top. Her dress looked like it had been new when Queen Victoria was old; her pearls were so numerous and large that they might have draped around the neck of Mary of Teck; the neck was cantilevered like the Queen Mum's; on top of it sat a face so vividly overbred that it might have belonged to a Habsburg. Booby's nose and chin almost touched. Indeed, had she not been preoccupied as hostess, Miranda might have paused to consider how any man's lips could have been so protuberant as to reach the mouth in between.

Once there, they would have found a gap prodigiously opened: 'A Wykehamist went to Winchester,' Booby explained like some social estate agent. 'Winchester's an English boarding-school, like Andover; only they still haven't reformed it to let in women or real blacks, or anyone but the precious English upper-middle classes. The English upper-middle classes are a club: everyone knows everyone, or is related to them, or sleeps with them, or went to school with them and was buggered by them in the loo. Winchester's the lawyers and civil servants: they're shits. Eton's the grandees and players and poufs: they're polite, powerful and immoral. Harrow's for cads. That's all you need to know. Where did you go?' she ended by asking Valentine.

Miranda was astounded. She'd heard of characters like this but never believed they existed outside of 1930s novels. Booby made Helena, Lady Melot, seem like a middle-class suburbanite. Valentine was non-plussed. Glancing at Miranda as if to say 'How could you invite this baggage?' he answered: 'To Winchester. And Godfrey was at Harrow, as it happens. What did you say your name was?'

'O don't pretend you don't know who I am: I know that one from way back. And don't bother to ask the next question: I'll just say. My real name's Marianne. Like Johnny DuRocher here, I'm part French – at least some ancestor wanted to think so. I got the name Booby because Dandy used to photograph me when I was young and gorgeous. He'd put me on a plinth and wrap me in a sheet like the Statue of Liberty. I'd stand there for hours with my arm in the air and a crown of thorns on my head or whatever. Then one day when Newman Revolté and that crowd were sitting around smoking pot, Dandy asked if I didn't think it'd be better to pull down half of my top, see, like this. "You've got it wrong, Dandy: that's not the American Liberty who does that, it's the French one, Marianne." "Oh," Dandy said, "sorry, I've pulled a boob." "No, I've pulled a boob," I said, doing this; "anyway, I *am* her, Marianne, so why should I mind?" "That makes us a couple of boobs," he said. "A couple of boobs?" I asked, doing this. "Ah yes, just hold that – perfect dear! a pair of boobies."'

During the narration, she had unpinned the black rose which held up her bodice and let fall what Miranda thought the most disgusting sight imaginable: a pair of pale, sagging, pumpkin-tipped teats. Valentine gasped. Tony drew frail, embarrassed Carine to his side. John DuRocher chuckled gently, whether out of amusement or chagrin wasn't clear. (It wasn't clear yet what he was altogether, except a most unlikely-looking possessor of countless millions.) Margot, who was wearing a tight violet frock with velvet flounces, tittered, putting a hand to her mouth.

'Sweet potatoes, my favourite,' guffawed rude Godfrey. 'Do put them away, Marianne: I'm hungry enough as it is.'

Excusing herself, Miranda fled.

They were a threat, Booby's breasts, a death casting, a mockery and negation of everything feminine, she thought and had a devil of a time getting them out of her mind as she beat a retreat to her kitchen. As a matter of fact, they made her go off her dinner; and she stayed down with the children as long as she could, feeling dirty and out-of-place in the company above.

Carine was one gentle spot. It was almost touching the way she smiled at stories that were not funny in order to keep a semblance of good spirits. Smoking cigarettes end-to-end, she coughed; each cough contracted her narrow chest; the chest itself was sheathed in a grey silk blouse and suede Chanel jacket, simple but *chic*. Though dark and sharp in the way of her race, she had a delicacy Miranda admired; and though still a touch jealous of her pre-history with Ollie, Miranda nonetheless began to think that if her lover had to have a past, better with this woman than most.

Thus Margot's system of contrasts had at least one good effect. And Miranda's jealousy diminished further as she realized just how unwell Carine was and how genuinely dependent on her husband. Tony for his part seemed less objectionable as the evening wore on, this partly by contrast to Valentine and Godfrey, the one perfectly rigid, as Margot had previewed, the other a buffoon who was only too pleased to match each one of Booby's off-colour tales. Tony seemed withdrawn; seated next to the Americanne, he declined to look at her; he did not seem eager to contemplate Margot either, who was a shade too obvious in her violet get-up. Once or twice his eyes came to rest on Miranda's; she almost imagined sympathy in them. But then they would move off rapidly towards his wife, and she had to conclude that he was wrapped up in her now.

Illness had attraction, Miranda reflected, though only if the ill person were as sweet as a child. Imagine Booby under the weather! More than once through the meal (not least during a graphic description of what the woman did with her lovers) it crossed Miranda's mind that she should have let Anne cook chicken after all in hopes that the creature might choke on a bone. Her verbal domination was indeed indefatigable. Booby barely stopped to draw breath at the table; and when the ladies excused themselves to powder their noses upstairs, she launched into an assessment of the men they'd left below passing round cigars.

Miranda loathed this rite of the sexes, but Valentine had insisted on all formalities. So as la Vänder warmed to her topic, Miranda's consciousness drifted towards the window, as if in search of her lover out on some moonlit tor.

'What do you think of John? He's a terrible dullard, but I'd rather be married to him than what you English girls have to put up with. Godfrey's one thing: at least you can laugh. But Valentine – darling, I don't know how you do it: you must take a lover; or maybe you have one already. Why not take John? he's divorced again and terrifically rich. I know he looks like an eel or something, but what do you expect of a man whose father was the one of the five DuRocher brothers who had to squat to take a pee? And *Maman* was definitely a fag-hag. Lived between Capri and Cap Ferrat and only came to Manhattan in a very blue moon. Despised kids. John was brought up by a nanny a month; that explains him. I say show me a man who's been brought up by nannies and I'll show you a man who's a cinch to control: praise 'em for all their little successes and let 'em be naughty whenever they feel, and they'll come back to you forever.'

Coughing, Carine offered Margot a cigarette. 'I wish you wouldn't smoke in here,' Miranda muttered, surprising herself.

They were standing in her bedroom, Booby in front of the mirror, she by the door. The other two had perched on the edge of the bath.

'Smoking's terrible, I agree, hon. Health is one thing we have in common. Margot's an artist: what she does may be forgiven. Carine, sweetheart, I don't know what you do for a living, but you're obviously killing yourself. Is it that husband of yours? he's way too attractive. Playing around? You've gotta accept: certain types do. We're all fated, especially by looks. Why do you think I'm so disgustingly flamboyant? It doesn't take genius to see that if you look like a female Tyrannosaurus Rex, you have to perform; otherwise people would never invite you to their parties. Margot can go anywhere on poise. Carine, I imagine it's family for you – like for your Harrovian husband, Miranda; Wykehamist, sorry. You get invited because you're gorgeous – don't deny it; look at that blushing skin. Tony's the perfect WASP, they fit in anywhere. Godfrey makes people laugh. As for John – who could refuse someone with his bank balance?

'Honestly, Miranda, if you need a lover, there's your bet. He's worth forty million on a generation-skipping trust alone. Made another fifteen or twenty in the Reagan market. Now his mother's died and left it all to the Anglo-Uruguayan tap-dancer she married after his father started pushing up daisies. He was a pansy too, the second husband; John can break the will, no problem. His mother was eighty and had lost her marbles; the tap-dancer was forty and only in it for the dough. John could be worth a hundred mill with one lawsuit, and he's already filed it. All he has to do is go back to Manhattan and tell a few outraged lies. What jury outside of Montevideo is going to decide against a DuRocher in favour of a tap-dancing woofter?'

'Shouldn't we go back down?' Carine inquired.

Having watched Miranda throughout this speech, Tony's wife had clearly picked up on her discomfort. It seemed a trait in Carine to keep an eye out for others' responses. No wonder Ollie had loved her, Miranda thought with a twinge. Now she realized too how, on hearing of his need, Carine might have set him up in that dovecote without ulterior motive.There could be genuine care in the world.

'But my point,' went on Booby, gathering her handbag to prepare for further assault on the males, 'is that DuRocher's a catch. I don't care who you are or what you're into: he's the most eligible thing around. So he looks like a fish: what person of breeding is a movie-star? a few times in the sack and you'll be worth half a million. That type treats women like they oughtta be. I'd take a fling at him myself, but like I say it: takes a man of particular discernment to spy the attractions of a female Tyrannosaurus Rex.'

Down they went.

'Poor dear Booby,' Margot whispered to Miranda on the stairs. 'You do see the point of her now, don't you?'

Valentine did not. On the other hand, he would not call the evening a failure. Cigars had brought the men's conversation round to business, and John DuRocher had expressed some enthusiasm for Tony's suggestion that they set up a group to buy shares of Eurofibre out from under the Swede's nose.

'If we put on enough pressure, we can drive him out in one account,' Godfrey had said. 'Swedes haven't had the spirit of adventure since the days when Charles XII was buggering Mazeppa!'

Valentine dismissed Godfrey's 'typical swagger'. What had impressed him was when DuRocher had replied:

'I don't like to be rushed. If a thing has real value, it's worth as much as you need to pay to get it. Why not play a long game? The more you spin it out, the more you see everyone's hand and the more likely you are to be able to raise serious capital.'

This Valentine repeated to Miranda in the kitchen once the guests had decamped. It was one a.m. and he helping clear plates, a fact which surprised her. It felt almost like a good marriage.

'What did you make of him?' Valentine mused.

'Of who?'

'DuRocher. He is the real thing, isn't he?'

Miranda had not been impressed with the guest-of-honour

instantly. Though he hadn't look quite like a fish or an eel, she could see what Booby had meant. Thin, sharp – a good deal more so than Tony Thomas who was already too angular for her taste – he seemed to have subsisted on a diet of flint. The slipperiness of water-creatures and hardness of ferrous metal combined in his skin, which was oily, and hair, which was dark and tight, as well as his overall posture, which seemed lithe and rigid at the same time. Miranda had an impression of someone so foreign as to be extrahuman. Maybe this was an effect of his mother's blood: Creole, he had said. On the other hand, he had been familiar, easy, laughing without affectation, not like Godfrey too much nor like Valentine too little. Nor like Tony Thomas had he seemed preoccupied. He'd shown no side against anyone nor for a minute seemed to wish to be elsewhere.

'How old do you think he is? about fifty? Looks extraordinarily like pictures of his great-grandfather, the original John Du. He lived to be a hundred, if I remember correctly.'

There did seem something about him which defied age. Stress and mortality went out of Miranda's mind as she recalled him coming down to the kitchen. She'd been sitting with the children; Lucinda had been arguing to Gus that game-pie was immoral – wildfowl should not be shot; hunting and things like that should be banned, and Gus was a macho bully to approve of them.

'You're as bad as your dad,' her eldest had concluded; whereupon meek Christian, to Miranda's surprise, had seconded her.

'Sounds like my daughter and me,' John had quipped. 'Only with her it's nuclear weapons.'

'They're horrible too,' Lucinda had added.

'You're so wet.' – Gus had shook his head.

'No, you're just a bully in your black leather jacket and hair slicked back. Who do you think you are, some kind of mafioso?'

Aggression had not necessarily meant that Lucinda was not head-over-heels over the eldest Wingfield, Miranda had mused. Yet what had intrigued her was the way his younger brother had continued to stand up for Lucinda in the debate. Christian was the gentle presence downstairs, rather like Carine above.

John's approving glance had also appealed to her. 'I was just looking for the bathroom,' he'd explained.

'Ah. It's up one flight, not down.'

'Thanks. Sorry for barging in. Or actually I'm not. It's always a comfort to see mothers getting along with their children. I wish the mothers in my life had. Which are yours?'

She'd introduced them. Each had responded politely, thank God. She'd felt proud.

'Well, I don't want to disturb you,' he'd concluded; and after a quizzical pause – 'Maybe see you again sometime?'

'He was nice to the children,' Miranda recalled for her husband.

'He was "nice" to everyone – even that beastly Booby or whatever her name was. What on earth were you thinking of, inviting her? I've never been so appalled.'

'It was Margot's idea.'

'Ah. And what's she up to this time?'

'Said we needed contrast,' Miranda repeated, though as explanation it seemed inadequate.

What *had* her erstwhile best friend been up to? Given Oliver and the rest, Miranda hadn't had time to think much about la Wingfield recently, nor plumb the depths of that fascinating psyche. If she had, there was no guarantee she would have got to the bottom of it, nor very far. Margot was more and more obscure to her these days: so much so that Miranda wondered half-consciously if she didn't mean some kind of harm.

'The food wasn't bad,' Valentine went on. 'Though I'm not sure pies are the thing for occasions like this. And minced herring or whatever it was for starters – bit down-market, don't you think?'

But if Margot had meant harm, why? Miranda's relative youth and good looks? She had nearly ten years on her, it was true; still, Margot was hardly some female Tyrannosaurus Rex – poor Booby showed what real unattractiveness was. Even Carine in her strange, Levantine way had made Margot seem alluring, despite years. Of course Tony Thomas had hardly glanced at her, though she had worn that extraordinary dress. And was *that* it? Had Margot perhaps heard about Miranda's lunch with him? Had Tony gone off her since about then? If so, had Margot blamed it on *her*? But that would have been unfair! Tony had made no further passes at her; in retrospect, his whole object appeared above reproach. He'd organised help for Valentine, and for all one could tell that had been his sole motive. Why he should have wanted to help Valentine was of course odd, though maybe it was a simple matter of a commission or to be in the good books of an American plutocrat and son of an English lord –

people did more for less. But coming back to Margot: it did seem far-fetched that she could have been jealous, and certainly not over Tony Thomas. Still, jealousy was what Miranda had felt from her erstwhile best friend – there was a drift; women sensed things. She got the distinct impression that Margot was fighting her at some dark level, and the fight seemed as if over a man.

Valentine, meanwhile, continued to be abnormally helpful. After straightening the dining-room ('Thank you for getting the children to give up their playroom, darling – so much more presentable than in front of the Aga, don't you agree?'), he stepped into the drawing-room and put on a cassette.

'Valentine, what's got into you? It's nearly two a.m.'

'I know.' – He flopped into what was known in the family as *his* chair, an odd relic from days of his first wife, one that Miranda would have thrown out long before had she had her way. 'I just thought it might be nice to sit here together for a bit. We do so so rarely.'

This was extraordinary. No less was the music he put on: Vaughan-Williams – one of those 'Celtic' English pieces favoured in the Evesham family yet derided by Valentine as 'pleasing romantic stuff'.

Sitting on the sofa, Miranda stared at him.

He looked haggard, she realized. Rarely did she study her husband nowadays: the lines and angles of his face had long since passed through familiarity into contempt for her, until they had arrived at a kind of oblivion. Normally she looked at him with little more recognition than at the windscreen of her car. He was a habit, a necessary evil. Could he have also been evil in fact?

This thought rose errantly, unbid. Miranda dismissed it forthwith. If he had been a bad man, a really terrible one, his looks might have affected her still, mightn't they? As it was, all she saw was a blank.

'You've done well for me, darling.'

'How do you mean?'

For a second she wondered: was the Great Unexpected going to occur? After years of neglect and foul-tempered shovings in bed, was he going to break down and make up to her?

'You've helped me this evening. It may tip the scales.'

'I thought you thought the menu was Margotish and the choice of guests appalling.'

'It doesn't matter what I thought: I wasn't the one who had to be impressed... You still haven't said what you thought of DuRocher.'

'I hadn't imagined you required an answer.'

'Would I have asked if I didn't?'

'I thought it was one of your rhetorical games, Valentine – a prelude to dismissing someone as "a cultural half-breed".'

He looked vexed. 'Am I so awful?'

'I'm sorry,' she said and for a moment was. (Was he going to break down and for the first time show real vulnerability?)

'May I take it from that that you were annoyed about my comments in regard to Anthony Thomas?'

'I don't really care what you say about other people; it's gone too far for that, long ago. It's a general question of tone.'

The Vaughan-Williams was moving her subliminally. The deep swells of piety and emotion put her in mind of Magdalen College chapel, punting on the Thames, the stream under the dovecote and inevitably Oliver. Who else did she have to project these feelings on? How else could she respond to the sad beauty of the horns, the weary longing inside her but by wishing to be with the one person in the world closest to approximating her soulmate? *Hiraeth.*

'Are you having an affair?' Valentine stunned her by asking.

Without thinking, she answered: 'With who?'

'The cultural half-breed of course, who else?'

'Don't be absurd!'

A pause: 'I wonder why he should've taken up my cause like this?'

'What like what?'

'The White Knight, why should he've wanted to help me if not for you? The only other time I met him I was quite rude, if I recall.'

The shock of her husband's question and lateness of hour made Miranda answer yet more snappishly: 'I don't know why he should've wanted to help. I wondered myself for a moment but frankly haven't had time to give him, or it, a thought. And now if you don't mind, I'm going to bed. I've done quite a job today – even you've said so.'

'But I do.'

'I beg your pardon?'

'I'm sorry. What I mean is, can't you just sit here a minute more? I have something I'm trying to say.'

What was up now? He couldn't've known about Oliver, could he? For God's sake, he hadn't had her followed to the country?! She'd been careful not to give the analyst's name. Surely he'd been too preoccupied over past weeks to track her movements.

'The reason I asked you about Tony Thomas is because, thinking back, I seem to remember that he quite fancied you at Margot's.'

'That's hardly my fault.'

'Of course not, darling. Still it made me wonder, given his motives are obscure.'

'People's motives are often a muddle,' she found herself saying. 'How can I help it if some man fancies me? Several did before I got married; it doesn't mean I have to do with it. I'm insulted you should make the suggestion.'

'I didn't. Calm down.'

'Well what do you take me for, Valentine? I've been faithful to you for sixteen years and have little enough to show for it. In this day and age, people have a right to expect a sex-life: it's not the Victorian era anymore, though it's humiliatingly obvious to everyone that some people wish it were.'

'Dear girl – '

'I think the least you could do, however you behave with me in private, is to show some affection in public. Even that horrid American woman told me I must take a lover.'

'Who?'

'How many American women were here?'

'No, who did she tell you to take?'

A trickle of recognition began to dampen her temper. Could he be leading up to what she began to suspect?

'She said that John DuRocher is the "most eligible thing around". I think that's how she put it.'

The music swelled again. She felt almost sick. A simple, straightforward marriage was all she had wanted, Miranda believed. It was desperate, what so-called civilization did to people.

'He may be, from a financial point of view. What did you say back?'

'I'm going to bed,' she repeated and this time stood.

In the same motion, Valentine rose. Indeed, his motion was so abrupt that in her subconscious, Miranda had a premonition of violence: one of those strange, disjunctive images that loom up in deep, disturbed dreams.

'I need your help,' he said.

'Help yourself,' she retorted. (Oh Oliver, how could I have treated you badly? You were my chance, my one chance to escape this mercenary demon! What have I done but drive you back to previous loves on the phone, or on to future ones like that exotic analyst? I must call you tomorrow; must race to you like the wind – like the silly heroine out of some woman's magazine that I don't care if I am!)

'He fancies you, this DuRocher. You know what Americans are. They come over here and think they're in a fairy-tale.'

'I don't see what his fantasies have to do with me.'

'Darling, stop playing the dim ingenue; this means millions. It means all I've worked for. For our children; for you.'

He took a step towards her.

'No, for you!' she hurled back. 'You and your Cravin family pride. You just want a way to impress your parents and get back at your brother because you'll never have a title and he will. Tell the truth, Valentine. And don't ever ask me to do what you're proposing.'

'What do you think I'm proposing?'

'It's too horridly sordid. And if you raise the subject again, I'm moving out of our bedroom and filing for divorce!'

With that she burst into uncontrollable tears. 'Miranda!' she heard him call as she fled, but all she could think was where on earth could she go? who could she turn to?

'Mummy, is that you?' she heard Anne murmur in sleep and realized she had to get a grip. (Oh please God, my children!)

'What's the matter, darling?' Valentine pursued, finding her where she lay in a heap on the stairs. 'What on earth's happened? All I was asking was for you to indulge him a bit.'

'Will you stop tormenting me?!'

'Tormenting you? Are you coming unhinged?'

'If I am, it's because of you!'

In the calmness of morning it should have been possible to interpret his overture less hysterically. Miranda, however, was not to be calmed. She'd slept on the sofa, locking the door to the sitting-room to prevent him from coming back in. She might have reasoned that what he'd been trying to ask her was less sordid than she'd made out; she might have reflected that she hadn't actually let him state what he'd meant to. But *might have* seldom obtains in this kind of marriage: signals pass in shorthand, sentences aren't allowed to spin themselves into finely-wrought paragraphs. Perhaps Valentine had the best motives; no doubt from his perspective he did. Somewhere, indeed, a story might be told in which his inner workings are explored and he ends up looking like a long-suffering saint and Miranda a whinging shrew. Valentine might have found solace in the kind of high-brow fiction he had sometimes fancied writing: some public-school novel like, say, Piers Paul Read's. But to his wife there were other perspectives. And chief among them was her tear-occluded own.

Miranda, in short, imagined the worst. Besides, her habit of blaming her husband was too ingrained now to be evaded. Under stress and fatigue, all she could see was that he wanted to pimp her to John DuRocher. Why she believed this had to do with his coldness, her instinct and a resentment that went to the core. It did not occur to her yet that the principal matter was her own self-interest; what she focused on was a certain belief that her husband did not love her – he loved form. Marriage meant that to him, full stop.

Perhaps this impression was muddied by guilt. A worry did lurk about what he might say when her car was found at a lay-by instead of the analyst's cottage; then too the whole matter of making love to John DuRocher had not been entirely uninsinuated into her psyche by the amoral Booby Vänder. Booby was American, but ruling class was ruling class; and it struck Miranda in her middle-class subconscious that there was something in common between the Yankee millionairess and her husband, however much Valentine may have deprecated her. Both he and Booby could tell in a flash what was above them in order of rank; both snapped to attention to it. John DuRocher in his khakis and trainers was no more Valentine's idea of an aristocrat than an African chief; but money spoke, and to truckle to it was as natural to this scion of courtiers as to bow to the Queen.

So Miranda reflected as she woke up; in these reflections lay the seed of her eventual throwing of caution to the wind. Meanwhile, she felt like a child who's been beaten and sent to her room without supper: tired, sad, disillusioned, alone, melancholic, listless, without a friend in a world which had revealed itself as unspeakably cruel. She was a 'damsel in distress', Oliver said when he heard her whimpering on the phone – he called at ten-past-nine, as soon as he was sure that Valentine and the children were out of the house.

'O I'm so happy to hear your voice,' she blubbered.

'You poor thing. What can I do?'

'You've done so much already – the weekend, the car. You must think I'm frightful. You'll be off to one of your other ladies before long. Maybe you have been already. Don't tell me; I couldn't take it this morning. You haven't, have you?'

'Miranda… It's you I want.'

'You're just saying that.'

'No. I'm a new man since I met you. Restored to life.'

She loved hearing such words, though caution and training forced her to answer, 'Woman's magazine stuff.'

'Maybe so, but it's true. You're bringing me back… Can I see you?'

'O Ollie, I'd love it.'

'Come down then.'

'How can I with the car wrecked?'

'Take the train and a cab from the station.'

'I wish I could; but – what about the children? I have to be here when they get home. And I do Anne's run today.'

'Make an excuse. You managed before. What about the analyst?'

'I can't use her again. Valentine's suspicious as it is.'

'… You aren't going off me?'

She felt thrilled – 'Of course not!' – and sniffed back tears.

'I long for you,' he said.

'I do for you too.'

She surprised herself again by the ease with which she used phrases she'd read but had never expected to hear from her lips. Maybe that's part of what incited her to go on, propping herself up on a pillow:

'Look, Ollie, can you be very discreet? It would be a huge risk, but I hate Valentine so just now, I don't care. Could you come here?'

'What, to your house?'

His tone expressed such disbelief that she half-recanted. 'It's awfully immoral, isn't it? But where else is there? We couldn't go back to Carine's, could we?'

'No. They're leaving for California, but they have a friend staying.'

So: he *had* been in contact with them. 'What friend?'

'Some American, I think. Has a foreign name… Isn't there anywhere else you can think of?'

'Not unless you can afford a hotel.'

She regretted these words as soon as they'd come. Why introduce the question of money when all she wanted was to see him so much that she was willing to violate her family's home? She didn't care what he could afford or couldn't – or did she? His poverty and failure – they were part of his charm, weren't they?

In her subconscious Miranda faintly recalled why Oliver could not be her ticket to long-term escape, whatever she thought of him as lover. And now the idea of escape was growing in her truly: real escape, not a through-the-looking-glass kind. She worked not to allow this to rise intrusively as she dressed in a scarf-skirt from the '70s, put on white lipstick and waited for her lover in an alarm of euphoria. 'I thought you'd never get here,' she gushed four hours later when a cab deposited him at the door. 'Here's the money for it – just take it: Valentine has loads, or will have. I've closed the curtains so the neighbours can't see. Go on – all the way up, to my room.'

'Doesn't he sleep there too?'

'I don't care,' she proclaimed now; and she did not.

She made sex with vengeful exuberance.

'I'm getting better at this, don't you think?' she asked after a second time, though she still hadn't quite reached the plateau of ecstasy she'd read about; but it hardly bothered her now – what you've never had, you don't miss, she told herself; besides, how could she be sure the growing surge inside her wasn't all any woman felt ever?

Oliver burst this thought-bubble. 'Gettin' there,' he replied.

She knew, or thought she did, that he hadn't said this to hurt; still, in her present state it enraged her. 'Look, I know you've had more women in your life than hot breakfasts, but do you have to flaunt it?'

'I'm sorry. I didn't mean it that way.'

'Well maybe you should think before you blurt out things that can be taken horribly.'

'Miranda, please – '

She might have interrogated him then about the phonecalls at the dovecote, but already it was a quarter to three – no time for an argument. 'Well I'm sorry too!' Abruptly changing tone, she kissed him. 'You're lovely. We have to get up.'

'So soon?'

'My children start to come back in an hour.'

He looked at her disappointedly, almost with pain. 'I wish I could meet them.'

It touched her. (The phone rang.) 'I wish you could too,' she said and for a moment loved him entirely. 'I wish you could take us all away to live a fairy-tale with you.' – Phone ringing still, she was unaware of using a phrase Valentine had once used with her.

'I'd like that too, I think.'

The 'I think' broke something. And though Miranda hadn't

intended to answer (nine or ten rings had been reached), she muttered, 'O for goodness sake!' and picked up the receiver.

John DuRocher… thanks for dinner; house, food, children and hostess delightful; hope to meet again soon – would she like lunch one day, etc? – Miranda hemmed and, saying she'd phone back, took down a number.

'Who was that?' Ollie asked, striking a match.

'Some friend of Valentine's.' – Jumping off the bed, she crumpled the number so that he couldn't recognize it. 'Would you mind not smoking in here? It's bound to smell.'

'How silly of me.'

He looked so handsome and touching, deflated, she thought. 'I hate to leave it like this,' she added, tears welling. 'In bed, bang, bang, then off.'

He gazed at her body as it hovered by the bathroom door. 'You don't think *I* like it?' His eyes were pale and still.

In a spontaneous motion that shocked even her, she leapt back through the air and onto the bed. 'Stay to tea?' she demanded.

'How can I?'

'Who knows you're not just some friend who's popped by for an hour? My children won't suspect – they're far too self-absorbed. I'd love them to meet you.'

'You're amazing… I think I adore you.'

And in that moment Miranda imagined she'd triumphed over the world and that no one ever had been quite so happy as her.

4.

No more than a week later she was sitting across from John DuRocher in a posh Italian bistro in Beauchamp Place. Dressed somewhat vampishly as on the night when she'd first met Oliver, she felt as attractive as she looked now, unlike on that occasion. Her lover's journey to London and subsequent phonecalls had contributed to this, as had her husband's solicitude since she'd agreed to 'stop being hysterical' and 'at least humour' the White Knight. Miranda felt like a war-bride being asked to be friendly with Yank soldiers: in cause of King and Country, she was meant to keep the man up. Contemptible as the role seemed, she was determined to enjoy it. The battle-lines of marriage were drawn: it was get for 'us' and oneself as one could.

John DuRocher, poor man, seemed abashed. No doubt he had known *grande dames* before, which Miranda was not (or not yet); but had he ever entertained a 'corker'? For corker is what Miranda felt in relation to him. On the far side of fifty, John was bound to regard a woman of her age as fresh and unspoilt; and this was an elixir. If you wanted to feel young, hang around older men – that was the principle. It hadn't quite worked with Valentine, of course. But Miranda had married Valentine, and marriage always made one feel the age of one's spouse. An older lover, by contrast, ought to make one feel young out of sheer gratitude.

So she imagined, gazing at John's thin, ovoid skull. No doubt the atmosphere in the bistro encouraged such thoughts: Casa Nuova catered for businessmen with their bits on the side. Idle rich women lounged at the tables, glances roving, nails flashing. Would she become one of these, Miranda wondered in a rush of nerves. Her image of herself in recent days had reverted to a fantasy of a country girl living in fairy-tale bliss with her hip, well-travelled lover.

Meanwhile, John talked. He seemed a content enough character, though his life-story was a bit worrying. How could a man be secure when his mother had disinherited him and father (viz. Booby) had had to 'squat to take a pee'? John had had a lucrative career on Wall Street, Miranda was told, but had been pleased to give it up.

'What do you do now?' she inquired, taking a bite of melon and recalling Booby's remark that this DuRocher was a bore.

'Loaf.'

'Sorry?'

'I loaf. Mooch around. Get into this and that. Take pretty ladies to lunch, when they let me.'

He said this with diffidence, not flirtation, and Miranda was sufficiently charmed to listen with half her attention. He went on to tell about how he'd once taught a course in science at Yale and wrote an article entitled 'The Ecology of the Puffer-fish'. Then came an account of his love life. (Americans did talk!) He'd had a wife or perhaps two – it was unclear whether Mary-Claire was Mary and Claire or if one were the name of his daughter. Anyhow, they, or she, now lived on an avocado ranch in California, while John divided his time between a flat in Manhattan, a house in Mystic, Connecticut, and a villa on the coast of Tuscany.

'Oh?' Miranda asked. 'Where?'

'Near Castiglione. Ever been?'

'We don't travel as much as I'd like.'

'You should.'

Polite conversation. He liked his place in Connecticut best. It was the equivalent for New York of a West Country cottage for London; only instead of being a converted rectory, it was a barn. He kept a monkey and a parrot which flew around loose.

'How eccentric!'

It was the first direct evidence of his wealth, she reflected. He didn't dress like money – but then perhaps serious money rarely did, as Margot or Booby or even Valentine might have claimed. Serious lifelong money thought about things like having played chess with Jean Cocteau as a boy. (Miranda could not quite remember who Cocteau was – not part of Bloomsbury, at any rate.) Do you like art then, she was thinking of asking – something witty like that – when the waiter arrived with her linguine and his sole.

They raised forks; she was famished. 'Hope I'm not boring you,' John went on. 'I'm sleepy today.'

'O? Late night?'

'Yes. Usually I'm in bed by ten.'

What an extraordinary admission. He must have been either less sophisticated or more eccentric than she'd imagined.

'It's Marianne,' he explained and, when Miranda looked blank, added: 'Marianne Vänder. You had her to your party.'

'You mean Booby?'

'That's what she calls herself now. She must think it makes her seem just one of the guys. But that story she told about how Dandy Rawhol used to paint her half-naked isn't true. I wonder why she feels compelled to lie? My mother did too: her thing was age. Used to claim to be forty when she was sixty; and when she was eighty and going senile, she began to think she was twenty – which may be why she married a second husband half her age. As for Marianne – Booby, as you call her...' He shook his head.

'What about her?' Miranda probed, listening now with more than half of her attention.

'I knew her back in the days when she claims to've known Rawhol, the '60s. She was skinny and shy and almost pretty then – a little like you, in fact. I was stuck on her; but I'd gotten my wife pregnant at college and'd already been married for years, so... Anyhow, last night she invited me for dinner and I went, even though I was surprised by the way she behaved at your place. Her guests were a strange set of ghouls. There was a playwright who kept making suggestive remarks to a young member of Parliament who'd fallen out with the Prime Minister over a joke about handbags; a man from Oxford who's an expert on Evelyn Waugh and his wife, or girlfriend, who knew all about those English aristos who end up living around Florence. There was a round man in a green tie who Marianne kept calling an Anglo-Catholic, whatever that is, and a doped-up woman with dyed blonde hair who claimed an exotic title from an Eastern European country which hasn't existed for sixty years. I was sitting between a Spanish bond-trader and his Venezuelan wife, a cute little thing who'd lived in New Haven, Connecticut and wanted to become a commodity broker. They were the ones I liked best – I have a soft spot for young couples: that's why I'm so fond of Tony and Carine. What is it one of your great cynics said? "Sentimentality has been the ruin of many a promising American"?'

Miranda wiped her lips and took a sip of Pellegrino.

'I'm not boring you, am I? How's your pasta?'

'Delicious. Not at all. Do go on.' (He hadn't touched his sole.)

'Dinner was in Marianne's conservatory – ever been? It's not a thing like your pretty kitchen; cramped and conspiratorial as a hot-house. We were stuffed along a bench butt-to-butt, which isn't so bad if you like who you're rubbing up against. But what made this especially uncomfortable was that every time the conversation started to get interesting, Marianne would interrupt in a tipsy voice to say "Ash'lly" and go off on some tangent that meandered into gossip, usually about sex. It was like being beaten around the head with a wet dish-rag, the gay playwright said. I wasn't able to talk to the Venezuelan girl till past midnight – the're all sorts of things I wanted to ask her about the Orinoco: I want to go there next year and see what's been happening to the marine life. By the time I got the chance, the Waugh-Italian expat couple were leaving and I was supposed to hitch a ride home with them. I'll take a cab, I said, but somebody told me it was hard late at night in that part of town. Then Marianne asked why didn't I just stay in her spare bedroom and like a fool I agreed.'

'Is this going to be suitable listening for a lady?' Miranda inquired.

'You see what's coming. Should I stop?'

He told a story rather well, for an American. 'S'pose it can't hurt,' she answered, having a small joke with herself.

'Her spare room turned out to be a frigid postage stamp hardly wide enough for a single bed; but it was way past my bedtime, so I didn't care about anything but getting to sleep. I took off my pants and hopped in in my socks and squeezed up in a ball to get warm and was just dozing off when there was a crash through the wall next to me. That was the bathroom; Marianne'd flushed the toilet and was banging cabinet doors, humming, brushing her teeth, making all the noise you could. She's drunk, I thought and put the pillow over my head; but the next thing I knew – shunk! – the door opens and she pokes in to ask if everything's OK. I pretended to sleep and, after some heavy breathing, she went away to have more brandy or whatever. Then when I was just getting into a nice dream – shunk! – the door goes again and she's shaking me by the foot asking if everything's OK. "Yes fine, thank you, I'll just get some sleep" So she goes out and turns on the TV – there's loud laughing and singing. I assumed she'd pass out in a chair before long but – shunk! – in she comes a third time, sprawls at the foot of the bed and asks if I'd like to watch *Lolita* with her. "No, I really need my sleep"; but this time I was sure I wasn't going to get it, not in Marianne's place.

'I was bracing myself to get up and put my clothes on when – shunk! – she's in again and saying, "Lissen, Johnny, you know an' I know what's going on here. I tried to pull you" – that's an Englishism, huh? – "but don' worry: I'm gonna leave you in peace now, OK? Friends?" Meanwhile she was pawing and slobbering over me, drunk as a skunk and not smelling much better. As soon as she went out to brave herself for another assault, I got up and put on my clothes.

'I didn't imagine going out at that hour was going to be taken as the most gracious of exits, but I never expected her to react like she did. "I'm so homesick, Johnny!" she screamed and begged me to stay. Then she ran to the door and locked it from the inside and dropped the key in a pocket of her robe, which was all she was wearing and was coming undone. She folded her arms over her boobs and stood there blocking me. What's a fella to do? I didn't want to leave a woman scorned, but Marianne, bless her, is so much bigger than she used to be so, after a few minutes, I realized I wasn't going to get her to budge. I tried to make a joke of it, but she just got this evil little grin across her face like my wife used to when she was threatening to sue me for all I was worth; so I realized I had no alternative but to *take* the key from her pocket... You don't think I'm a bad man, do you?'

'Not yet,' quipped Miranda, by now listening with all of her attention and alarmed as well as amused.

'I had to wrestle her. Finally, I got the key in the lock and pried the door open, her trying to hold it back. Then I slipped out and she started screaming, "Bastard!" Apparently in the tug-of-war, one of us knocked a Francis Bacon sketch off the wall and the glass broke and scratched it. "Cunt!" (Why do the English use that word as a pejorative? we never do.) "That's one of my most valuable pieces. You'll owe me thousands!"'

At this stage, the waiter returned and asked John if there were something wrong with his sole: he still hadn't eaten a bite, though Miranda had finished her linguine long before. 'I'm sorry,' he said. 'It was delicious; I'm just not hungry today.' Seeming embarrassed, he added: 'Can you bring us the dessert menu?'

The waiter cleared and went off.

Miranda hesitated. 'Poor you,' she observed. 'Do you always have this effect on women?'

He seemed more embarrassed still. 'The irony is that the ones you want are too young and beautiful; the ones who want you are too old and ugly; and the ones you get end up after your money. That's the cliché anyhow. Poor Marianne! She must feel mortified this morning.'

While digesting this tale, Miranda had drawn back from the role she'd imagined herself playing. Of course she couldn't change out of her mini-skirt then and there, but she could act prim and try to forget that she was the same woman who'd had her lover in her husband's bed a few days before.

'I can't get out of my mind her saying, "I'm so homesick, Johnny!" It's probably not true, at least not all the time; but it must be awful now and then. I'm sure my mother felt it, spending all those years on the continent. Tony and I talked about that...'

The dessert menu came, and Miranda was torn between profiteroles and tiramisu. But though she loved anything sweet, she took her cue from her host and ordered only a tisane.

'So you walked home then, did you?'

'How'd you guess? All the way from Ladbroke Grove to Knightsbridge. But it wasn't bad. No muggings, like in Manhattan.'

'You must be exhausted. I'd be longing for bed.'

He made no attempt to eke something suggestive from this as a flirt like Tony Thomas might have. 'I'll take a nap later. I feel too guilty now boring you with this silly, sad subject. I was thinking of going to the Natural History Museum; someone last night said I'd like it. You wanna come for a half hour? make sure an old man doesn't fall over?'

Now that she'd mentioned it, all Miranda wanted to do was race home and bury all trace of vampishness in a nap, then get into her usual mufti as school mum. What had she been at? How reckless her fantasies of breaking loose! What would this man think of her if he'd known about Ollie? (She was not yet quite conscious of wanting John's approval.) What would the world think if, say, her lover went berserk like Booby when she'd driven over her lover's wife's rosebed? Thank God they were English and Oliver too well-bred for that!

'Personally I prefer the V & A,' she murmured, 'though I have almost no time.'

Her host's face lit up.

'The Natural History Museum scares me: all those slimy reptiles. I used to have to take my son every week. Fortunately, he's grown into other things.'

The Victoria and Albert it was then.

In the museum she found herself as reluctant to take off her raincoat as she'd been eager to in the restaurant. Her raincoat was the sole part of her outfit that avoided the vampish; and while she'd often been annoyed that Valentine hadn't recognized it as a cast-off of her mother's and bought her a new one, now she was quite pleased to be wearing it. Looking at her escort's worn trainers and unironed trousers, she realized that – even if it had been her intention to attract him – she'd taken the wrong tack. Wealth of this kind was not motivated by glamour. Indeed, as they wandered through rooms of armour and effigies, she began to imagine that John was compelled by something deeper, more heartfelt. At the least, he was not like Americans the world knew from TV: J. R. Ewing, etc. had been off the mark. He was more like the person she'd glimpsed in Ollie: a free spirit or lonesome traveller of the road. In his gentleness there was a quality that almost moved her: the way he'd put his hand to the small of her back, for example, as they'd crossed Brompton Road; the way he now asked if she liked this statue or that form of beauty – not too much, just enough as they passed through the rooms. Of course it was phoney, a Valentine voice inside warned: what was the point of galleries in the afternoon? weren't they a cliché of where prospective lovers had trysts? The voice coaxed her to inspect others surrounding them: tourists hand-in-hand; students in ill-fitting, rag-tag inventions; arts-and-crafts types; bohemians deliberately frayed. How could the daughter-in-law of Lady Melot feel at home here? Why did she perpetually long to revert to an Oxford where young men swerved on bikes to watch a girl amble to school and an American lodger was reduced to spying through keyholes to glimpse a fragment of her?

'You like that?' John asked, and she woke from her reverie to see that they were standing in a room of old fabrics.

Wall-hangings, tent-covers, cloths for skirts, headwraps, sarongs... all came from the East – Persia, India, Nepal – and were dense with flowers and leaves, trees with fruit on their branches in symmetrical patterns, birds and beasts, dancing women and warriors momentarily subdued into postures of love. The one she stood facing was predominantly blue, with a symbolic tree rising through its centre in stitched gold, its branches zigzagging strangely towards a helmeted tip. Now why should she have stopped here? The tree was phallic: had it caught her through subliminal ideas of sex? She remembered a crude representation of the Tree of Life from the Kama Sutra which she'd seen in one of Hugo's wank magazines; she recalled too some image from her father's study – a medieval line-drawing of the Path to the Stars in the *grimoire* of some magician he'd scoffed at, while at the same time arguing that he had been 'one of the first true liberators of the individual consciousness which characterizes our Modern Age'. (Sir Ralph had spellbound his students with this sort of speech, not least the young Royal who had got him his title.) Looking now nervously to her watch, she replied:

'I really must go.'

'So quick?'

'I have to pick up my youngest. May I drop you somewhere?'

'No need.'

'You're not going to walk over half of London again, are you?'

'Why not?' he shrugged.

'We can't have you killing yourself with exhaustion.'

'That was last night; now I feel great. Must be lunching with you.'

'You didn't touch a thing.'

'Sometimes a guy can be revived in other ways.'

She was tempted to ask how but knew it would be fishing. Pecking him on a cheek, she dashed away before either could make some Tony-like *double-entendre* that might have embarrassed them both.

The mind is like an Indian fabric, she found herself thinking as she drove: her mind, at any rate. Birds and beasts, little flowers and fruits, demons and lovers – all the natural world seemed to swarm in it, becoming so supernatural at times that it gave her a headache and made her half-fear she might be going mad. This happened to everyone, she knew; but like everyone she forgot it when it was happening. Sometimes indeed when thoughts came too intensely, she half-wondered if she weren't some kind of magnet for all the forces in the universe. This was a delusion mothers were particularly prey to, Margot had observed: with so many psychologies to deal with – such conflicting aggregations of thought, forces, supernatural emanations, transcendental or banal – mothers became an almost separate category of creation. Thus a voice spake. Then, out of nowhere, her father appeared.

This was incongruous. Sir Ralph was lower-middle-class and mean, unlike John. He had been in love with respectability, about which John couldn't have cared less. His love of respectability had been what led her to Valentine: the original sin in her life. Meanwhile, as for Valentine – how had he become as he was? too little love from his mother? bullying from his brother? the fact that he'd gone to Winchester, not Eton, as Godfrey would claim? Maybe it all had to do with his first wife (Miranda had a soft spot for this explanation); but more likely it was class. Secretly he despised her, and himself, for having married down on the scale. She, Miranda, had disappointed him by never going riding to the hounds, despite Sentinale. Nor had she ever warmed to the cottage at Cheveley, because it was Cheveley, though she'd longed for the country – some free countryside – as much as any 'English rose' could.

There were no open windows in her life with him, she reflected as she had so many times. Passing the towers of St Pancras Station and gas works behind it, across the Caledonian Road with its council estates, by black faces waiting for busses under a smuggy sky, she plied her daily route home to tree-less Islington. And was it just this that made her feel so desperate? this grey cityscape and anti-sensual atmosphere? Others survived it; but they had love, she imagined. If not that, at least they called one another 'darling' and half-meant it and were sweet to each other when times were hard. Working-class blokes sometimes even shopped with their women: she'd seen them crossing the road on Saturday mornings. Sometimes they even put hands to the smalls of their backs, as John had done with her, just to touch lightly, less to guide than to let know that somebody cared.

But did Valentine care? That was the question: her eternal question. Did he have time to? When was the last time he'd asked her to go to a museum? – 'Women's magazine stuff!'

In her empty kitchen, dark already though not quite yet four, Miranda saw the light of the answerphone flashing. Throwing her bag on the winged chair, she wound the tape back: a man's voice – no, a woman's, a woman's, a man's and a woman's. Would she be right? It was a game she played every afternoon, lending a tiny thrill to her days: the significant moment when she found out who cared enough to phone. First came a cough – that was Ollie: a signal they'd worked out – then in rapid succession Lady Melot for Valentine and Lady Evesham for her: the brittle followed by the bland. Then there was Valentine's voice, quite abrupt; then Margot, surprisingly – Margot never called, she was called: it was part of her grandeur. At last, as an addendum, came Ollie's cough again, reassuring yet nerve-wracking.

Miranda erased all so that Valentine or the children couldn't come in and hear, though none would appear soon. She'd lied to John about having to pick up Anne. Anne was ice-skating with friends after school; and Hugo, whatever he was up to, never got home before tea anymore – nor Lucinda, preoccupied as she was with Gus. So it was quiet, dead quiet in the house now. Sounds of traffic, hum of London, endless mechanical sea-noise – that was all. And that was all there would be in a few years' time, she reflected, climbing the stairs.

Dusk came weakly through windows on the landings. In a few years the children would be living in Spain or wherever, with their lovers and lives spreading out like the dawn. Throwing herself down on her bed, not switching on lamps, Miranda mused: was he so unattractive? What had Booby called him, an eel? He was slim and dark, true; not a bit handsome, though the way he smiled was – it could grow on you. But why did people have to be handsome anyway, or even young for that matter? Beauty and youth had meant almost everything to her till then. But there were other values, weren't there?

Going to her dressing-table, Miranda looked at her face in the gloaming. There was truth too, wasn't there? And goodness. Ollie had goodness, no? truth, at any rate – the authenticity of failure… and beauty at last. She wiped make-up off her lids. He had sadness too, which was what beauty was in the soul: the ability to make you cry; vulnerability that made you so sad it was all you could do not to hurl yourself into some stranger's arms and beg the world to go away…

The phone rang. She ignored it and, dressing in jeans, went back downstairs and out.

The air was dead damp. She drove to Safeway to do the weekend shop, which took nearly an hour. Through the check-out line, she had to watch a pregnant young thing stroking her belly. So dreamily did she do this that Miranda nearly cried, 'Oh Valentine, you bastard! Oh Oliver, I love you! Oh, oh – somebody please make me young again, unresentful, fresh and unruptured, ready to bring beauty into a world true and good!'

Driving to her life-drawing class, she felt Bernardo or some sprite like him slip into her psyche. (Actually, with the years, the Italian boy had become so idealized that it was not him anymore but some mirage of perfection with whom she was free and beautiful, naked and young again on a southern beach.) In her class, they were doing women till Christmas. She found it almost impossible to concentrate. Inevitably, she compared her own body to that of the twenty year old on the dais. As her pencil traced a protuberant belly and thighs, Marianne Vänder's breasts came back, then John DuRocher's story; and she thought: 'I'm not going to end like *that*, am I?'

Fear froze her hand. Ripping the sheet off her easel, she had to start over again.

Back home, a new cough on the machine…

'Did you call me?' she asked, re-ensconced in her dark bedroom.

'You know I did. Where've you been?'

'What do you mean, where've I been? You sound like my husband.'

In fact, Valentine rarely wondered. That was part of the problem.

'Are you cross with me?' asked Ollie.

'Why? Should I be?'

'Not for any reason I know of. But you sound cold.'

What would she reply? How could she tell him she didn't want to go on? She had to think, breathe, figure out what to do in this perilous situation she'd got herself into.

'Are we losing the magic circle?' he added.

Still in annoyance, she snapped: 'Did you call for a particular reason, or did you just want to say you adored me?'

She felt wicked cramming these words into his mouth, but truly it was all she wanted to hear from him. 'Just to say I adore you,' he obliged. 'But you make me feel lonesome.'

'Why don't you go out and meet some new people?' she retorted, harsher still. 'There must be plenty down there.'

She knew this wasn't what he wanted. 'It would only make me feel more lonesome.'

Sometimes it was better to leave the receiver in place. Talking could be worse than dreaming in silence. Words could hurtle you towards a crisis of 'Do you love me?': insecurity, mixed signals, exposure of different purpose and needs. Then she might have to rush to the country to see him, or he up to town where they had nowhere to go. All would take time and spirit and risk. But if she didn't alter her tone now, she ran the equal if not greater risk of losing the security his existence provided.

'I'm sorry. I can't think why I'm in such a mood. Perhaps it's my period. Valentine says I have the worst PMT of any woman he knows.'

The idea of Valentine being privy to the ups and downs of many women might have struck one or both of them as incongruous.

'Maybe it's something else,' Oliver answered cryptically.

'Like what?'

'Sometimes when I'm down here in a flood of thoughts about how you've brought me back to life, I like to imagine that maybe you're stuck on me too.'

'Well' – she changed tone – 'maybe I am.'

'God, you're lovely!' he gushed, and it was OK: they could go on normally now, him telling her what he had done with his day, what he'd felt, she saying where she'd been and so on.

She was wondering why she was so reluctant to mention John DuRocher and whether it wouldn't have been better if she did when the door slammed downstairs. 'Valentine's come in!' she breathed.

'Mum?' Anne's voice called.

'Must ring off.'

'Shall I phone tomorrow?'

'If you want. But Ollie, in the morning, only. I can't have them wondering what all these coughs are on the machine.'

'O,' he said. 'Sorry.'

Light came on in the stairwell. 'Bye now.' She clicked off.

'Mum? Are you there?'

'Hello, poppet.'

'Are you by yourself?'

'Of course. Who else would be here?'

'I heard you talking.'

'I was on the phone, to your gran.'

'Oh.' The girl entered. 'Mummy?'

'Yes, let me hug you, my sweet.'

'Why do you spend so much time sitting in the dark nowadays?'

Why indeed was she in the dark, Miranda might have wondered. It was the light she wanted: acres of open sky tinged in gold, mottled in cloud, warm and dappled with blossoms against the sun, green and fresh with young leaves. Colour she needed, and happiness, not grey winter: this trap of the old, going nowhere, in London… Christmas was coming. Valentine had said nothing about plans. They would go to Cheveley one day as ever no doubt, Oxford the other: the brittle followed by the bland. (Must call his mother and hers, Miranda reflected.) Hugo and Lucinda wanted to stay in London – that's what they said the next morning at breakfast when the matter came up:

'Let's go to the Wingfields,' Lucinda suggested.

'You just want to smooch with Gus,' chorused Hugo.

'That's not any worse than what you do with Christian,' elder sister tossed back.

Miranda might have been shocked had she heard, but she was packing Anne's lunch. ('Can I have bickies *and* satsumas, Mum?) Valentine for his part was upstairs, performing the regular man's morning rites. 'School-run today?' he asked coming down, stuffing *The FT* into his valise.

Miranda was now doing up her rain gear; Hugo and Lucinda had gone, Anne was pulling on her school jacket. 'Yes,' she gave back in marital monosyllable.

Valentine buttoned his overcoat. 'By the way, John DuRocher

called the office yesterday. Said you'd had lunch; most charming female he's met in years. Americans are quite over-the-top, aren't they? Anyhow, keep up the good work. We'll beat that Swede yet.'

Exit.

There might have been a kiss, Miranda might've thought had she not given up such thoughts long before. But then a surprise came. Just as she and Anne were getting into the temporary Volvo the dealer had lent her, Valentine reappeared and tapped on her window.

'Almost forgot, darling. You're meant to phone Margot. Something to do with the children. Godfrey told me.'

'What?'

'What do you mean "what"?'

'What did Godfrey tell you, obviously.'

'For you to ring Margot. Aren't I making myself clear?'

Rolling up the window, she noted with bored resentment how both Godfrey and Valentine took it for granted that anything to do with children was women's stuff.

'I'll bet it's smoking,' Anne opined as the ignition clicked.

'What do you mean, poppet?' – The loaner Volvo, being well-used, expelled a fart of black fumes.

'I'll bet Hugo's been smoking with Marcus and Matt. Christian's told on them; Gus's beaten him up; their Mum discovered. That's what usually happens.'

Good lord, what was the child on about? 'Gus beaten him up?'

'Don't worry,' said her youngest, 'Lucinda'll beat him up when she hears. She's potty about Christian. That's why Gus acts like he does.'

Here was a new subtext for mama to fret over. And it was the mother in her, not the lover (to say nothing of individual or friend) who sped over to Ladbroke Grove once she'd dropped off Anne.

The villas of Holland Park passed by unseen. Almost unseen too as she parked was the figure of Margot, hair freshly frosted and dressed to the nines, hurrying (Margot never hurried these days) in the opposite direction. She looked striking, majestic – what Miranda hoped to look like in ten years' time. The vision brought back a mix of envy and admiration that had moved her to try to make friends with Godfrey's wife in the first place.

Getting out of the car, she called, 'Margot?'

The other glanced back. 'Go inside, dearest.' She seemed almost as if to have expected this visit. 'You know where they key is. Make yourself a cuppa. Back very soon.'

Puce raincoat and multi-coloured scarf flared in the rush that led her round the corner and off. A flash of bouffant hair and crimson lips – Miranda stared as some odd echo of colour resounded. Then she located a key under a cracked, mossy urn and unlocked her way in.

Margot's kitchen was abnormally silent. On the butcherboard table sat a teapot, splayed paper and detritus of breakfast such as awaited her back home; only here was more to clear, there being more faces to feed. When would the char come? Unlike her, Margot had to have a char. In a physical sense, she had grown idle, Godfrey's wife. All that contemplation and chat, no rushing about like Miranda... It was another respect in which the sight of her hurtling down the road disconcerted.

What was up? Hugo? Lucinda and Gus? Which one or ones of these had done what while she had had her head turned? Must have been something or Margot would never've told Godfrey to tell Valentine to tell her to call. And it must've been important or Godfrey would never've remembered to tell Valentine, nor Valentine her.

Miranda felt guilty and cross: guilty because of Ollie, cross because of Valentine, as ever. If he'd been a proper support, she would never have had to become involved with a lover. And if he hadn't been so preoccupied, he might've known already whatever was going on with the children so that she didn't have to wait in Margot's kitchen like some supplicant to the Queen.

She thought of making 'a cuppa' but didn't. She tried to read *The Independent* but found herself grumbling at her husband instead. She decided to call him at the office but dialled Oliver's number.

'Hello?'

She rang off.

Why had she done that? What weakness made her so full of need? Couldn't she stand on her own feet?!

A glimpse of John DuRocher passed. What would he be doing now, came the question: sitting on one of those sofas at the Thomases where she and Oliver had made love? A mix of imagery followed: his body naked – Ollie's, that is – leading to wonder about John's.

Good lord, am I mad, Miranda demanded of herself and, fleeing up stairs, thought: I have one lover too much as it is; how can I be wondering about another naked – and a scrawny, funny-looking, fifty-year-old at that? Has some moral screw come loose? Am I going to turn out like Booby Vänder?

The Wingfield sitting-room was L-shaped. In the long part of it were a sofa, two winged chairs, an antique table – the expected set-up of upper-middle class London sitting-rooms. In the short part were a piano and desk: under the piano were papers, paintings, notebooks; on top of the desk sat a pile of memos and phone numbers – the bits a housewife collects in a vain attempt to keep up with all situations that seem to call for her attention.

Idly, inevitably, out of some idea that she might find a clue to what Margot meant to tell her, Miranda sat at the desk and looked at one or two items. After a while, her eyes gravitated towards the papers under the piano. '1979' said gold letters on the green cover of an A4 notebook on top of the stack. That was the year she'd realized she'd never have another child by Valentine: when he'd refused to make even perfunctory love to her after she'd recovered from being pregnant with Anne.

'Three children is quite enough on our income,' he had said. 'And if a man can't believe his wife when she claims to've taken precautions, he'd be a fool to go on providing her with chances.'

That had been it: the worst, absolute worst moment of married life. After it, she had ceased to manufacture the illusion that she loved him at all, or could ever. That he had never made a real show of passion she'd been able to rationalize – damage from his first wife, pressure of career, age. But to have her pregnancy made out as some crime against him was too cruel. From then on, she'd simply loathed him.

1979... The curious thing was that he'd never agreed to move out of their bedroom. Why? He'd insisted on the facade of marriage when all it had been was a death-mask. Sometimes he'd even seemed insecure, almost hurt: as if someone had battered him psychologically, not vice versa. Sometimes – not sexually, but in other ways – he'd even seemed to need her, and she'd almost been moved to reach out and touch; but... Why was she thinking these things for the millionth time, Miranda wondered, checking her watch. Where was her hostess? And what had *she* been up to in '79?

Taking up the notebook, she found it falling open to a fragment entitled 'The Leave-taking'. 'Think names – archetypes,' a pencil had scrawled. The text was in vertical black biro: an early, more readable version of Margot's familiar, oddly Cyrillic script:

> As the affair ended, he took to his sculpting with demonic energy. He couldn't bear the thought of being without her. Form and contour in stone had to substitute for the curves and warmth of her body. Substitutes, always substitutes. Hadn't he been doing this all his life: losing what he loved for the superficial superiority of what he could make out of himself? His mother's breasts and dreams with his first beloved – how many times did a man have to lose touch with the Grail? Did women feel compelled to drive men away only to see if they would crawl back? Did they force them to their knees simply to confirm that they themselves were essential to male happiness?

'No!' screamed the pencil (a different hand): 'Who is "they"?' And 'Why switch the sexes?'

Miranda turned a page. To read a writer's castoffs is always rash – so Margot might have warned her had she walked in. Experiments are made; reality is distorted; fiction is overlaid with fact in a way which a layman can hardly separate out. To Miranda, however, the notebook in her lap seemed no more than a diary. And wasn't it a commonplace (hadn't Valentine said over the years) that a diary left about is an invitation?

More passages were marked; then a new fragment, or continuation of the old one:

> 'How are you today?'
>
> 'A bit cheesed off.'
>
> 'Why?'
>
> 'Confronting what I have to, I s'pose.'
>
> He said, 'You mean Godfrey?'

The name was crossed out. The pencil had written, 'Basil?'

> 'That's part of it, yes. He's been frightfully nice. Did the boys' run and made the little ones an egg before going to the office.'
>
> 'And to you? Is he being… affectionate?'
>
> She hesitated. 'I tried to thank him; he looked at me as if I were mad. I am, I guess. One can hardly be nice to one's husband without raising suspicion.'
>
> He recognised the perversity he loved. 'Are you in bed still?'
>
> 'Yes. I got up for a while and watched a video with M_____. He has a fever now too, poor babe.'
>
> 'You sound better today.'

'Do I? I still feel weak. But mine's gone, I think.'

'Good.'

There didn't seem much more to say. That is, there was too much for either to begin, especially as it was ending, both realized.

'Well,' he murmured.

She couldn't answer.

'I love you,' he offered.

'Please don't,' she broke off. 'I think I'm going to weep.'

'I feel that way too.'

Miranda looked up. Was there a sound in the kitchen? Putting a finger in the page, she stepped to the door... nothing. Sitting back down, she was avid to read. Uncannily, it sounded like a conversation going on in her head with Oliver Murrie.

Was the affair truly over? Would he immerse himself now in the woman he lived with? Could he, or would he, wander the world dreaming of her in his soul, wishing for the day when she might have him back? Now they had to live like normal people. Wickedly, she wanted him to become a monk: a lonely, melancholy, modern knight errant doing deeds of daring under her sign.

Was it over truly? Did anything ever end? Weren't Time Past and Time Future always contained in Time Present?

Yes. And that was the Hell of it.

If only one could escape from consciousness, she thought lying indolent in bed. If only one could unzip one's body and step out for a week, or even a day or an hour. Drugs like her friend M_____ used. Or drink like her husband had come to rely on.

'No, no, no!' cried the pencil; 'everyone thinks this – can't do it – reader bored to tears – make people laugh!' But Miranda was not bored, nor did she want to laugh. She wanted an answer, or at least to know what had happened.

Turning a new page –

That night at dinner the woman he lived with said, 'You look tired.'

'I had a hard day,' he lied.

The woman he lived with was anorexic. She wore a bomber jacket and ironed jeans; she was twenty-two and a glorified shop-girl. Her flat belonged to her wealthy family and had all the mod cons.

'What were you doing?' she asked.

'Wrestling with a vampire.'

She looked irritated. He was reluctant to hurt.

'I think I won,' he continued, trying to shut off the subject.

The woman he lived with was the opposite of his beloved. His beloved was shapely and fair-haired, an English rose; the woman he lived with was angular and had the grape-clustered curls of her tribe. She had never been faithless and never would be. His beloved by contrast had had three men in one day the last time he'd slept with her.

Miranda breathed in. Was that a sound? She hardly cared now. The writing scratched on, more and more pencil marks, hard to decipher:

The last time he slept with her, she came to his studio dressed in a red sheath skirt, garter belt, stockings and sequined jacket with silver lamé collar that made her look like an old movie star. Maybe because of it, she seemed off to him. He made her some supper – prawn salad, her favourite. They watched telly – Fawlty Towers or some such. She didn't talk about her husband as usual, or what she'd done in the afternoon. When supper was over, he cleared the plates and put on some music – this had been their ritual. The music was some piece of jungle drums and pipes; he liked that sort and she'd gone along with it, even though she disliked it intensely. She would have preferred to have had just his voice in the silence. With the lights off, there would be nothing but shadows coming in from the skylight onto his work-space and divan, covered in a sheet. She said she was having her period, but he didn't mind. He made love to her, and it was like the first time – maybe because it was not in the afternoon, as per norm. Maybe it was because of this that she dug her nails in his bottom and dragged them up his back. 'Taking possession?' he asked, hoping against hope that what they knew had to happen wasn't going to. She didn't answer. He had her on top, then she got on top and went on until they were sliding off the mattress and she writhing on his body arched so far back that the crown of his head bounced on the floor. Finally she pulled him upright on top and reached down and squeezed his balls to make him come, which he had just managed to keep from doing five or six times.

After such Passion, what Hope?

'You don't mean you were with another woman, do you?' the woman he lived with had asked.

Oliver tried to drag his mind back to the dinner table. He remembered that there had been blood on the sheet and all over his belly as they had dressed. Not wanting to part, he had driven back as far as Notting Hill with her. 'Do I look all right?' she'd asked at the end of her street. 'What on earth must Basil think?' Then he'd taken a night-bus home to his woman's flat, feeling as empty as a meth-drinker's bottle and half-tempted to lay down on the kerb and expire.

'Miranda!' cried Godfrey. 'Fancy you here. Where's Margot?'

Her pulse fluttered. She felt flushed and hoped to a God she had never believed in that tears wouldn't spurt.

'I don't know,' she stammered. 'Valentine told me – '

'Valentine indeed!' – Godfrey stroked the red clumps on his temples, trying to flatten them. 'How's that husband of yours anyway? I see him at the office, but he's not your husband there, is he? Not a bad chap really, just a pedant, like all Wykehamists. Do you know the definition of a pedant? A pedant is someone who when you say "Life is short" asks you for five citations.' – He chortled.

Poor fool, she thought, sniffing herself into order. But what was he doing at home, dressed for work?

'Don't tell him you saw me. Thinks I'm in Fleet Street arranging to pulp returns of *The Star.* Actually, I overslept. That happens to insomniacs: sit up all night, then doze off at breakfast. By the way, he told me you had lunch with John Du. Bloody good if he puts money in. All have to suck up to him; decline of the Brits. Never mind.'

At this point, he seemed to half-notice the tear on her cheek: half-notice because, to an Englishman like Godfrey, tears were to be either unseen or run from.

'Reading her old diaries? Wouldn't advise it. Crashing bore, that. Margot once saw that Wilde play where a character says that if you want to read something racy open your own diary. Well, it's one thing to read one's own and bloody purgatory to eavesdrop on someone else's. I told her to burn 'em. She says they may help her write a novel one day. I say no good novel is ever going to come from anything but the inspiration of the moment, but then who am I?'

'Dear God,' purred Miranda.

He pretended not to hear, sentiment being as disconcerting to his type as tears. Hesitating at the door, he concluded:

'I wouldn't worry about whatever Margot wanted to tell you. When children get into trouble, it's rarely as serious as mothers like to think. If Christian cuts a finger, she goes hysterical. That's the problem with you women: all so bloody fragile and innocent, aren't you?'

He vanished, leaving her bemused.

Was it possible for a man to be so stoical, or unseeing, that his wife could get up to what Margot evidently had all these years and he still behave as if life had not gone stark raving mad? – Miranda looked back at the notebook. For some reason, she felt as if a stake had been driven through her heart. Then a door slammed downstairs – only Godfrey going out. Still, it made her realize that she couldn't face Margot's blonde, busty persona now. So ripping out the last two pages of the fragment, she slipped the notebook back where she'd found it and fled to her car like a thief.

> Three mornings later in a kind of trance, he told me it had to end. [Miranda read this round the corner, slumped in her driver's seat so that Margot wouldn't see her if and when she came back. Unlike the penciller, she was not disconcerted by the sudden shift to first person: by now she could hardly have been convinced that the story was anything but a confession.] I'd come to his studio again. He was trying to be manly but his resolution was no more than acceptance of the inevitable. I'd called to say it was driving me mad. We'd had the conversation before, but this time I cried and he told me I'd been working too hard and had a heavy period and wouldn't it be better to talk when the weekend was over and I'd had a chance to think. But he must have known that I wasn't going to have a chance to think on the weekend, with Basil and the boys. 'I wish you could get away,' he said; but marriage and family don't allow the luxuries of time he could have to his heart's content. Married lovers have to think on their feet, I pointed out, thinking about my other one. 'That's part of the aphrodisiac of adultery for you,' he said, which I thought a bit cruel. Of course I knew that he knew that on sober reflection I'd have to decide to go back to my married lover; but then he probably also knew that I'd be miserable if I did, because it had made me miserable before. But he must have known too how it had reached a stage where more than anything I needed somebody I could feel in charge of, which with him I never would. We'd been through that. He was just too demanding. Also, he said, he felt guilty about the shop-girl he'd been living with. 'I want to be a decent chap to her'; so the time had come for me to be 'an honest woman'. Even though that's what he said, it didn't feel like rejection because I knew it was me who'd done it to him, not vice versa.

There was a smudge, then a shift back to third person:

> 'Are you in bed still?'
>
> 'Yes. I don't have much desire to get up these days. Pathetic, isn't it?'
>
> In his mind's eye, he knew exactly what she looked like, pillowed up in the morning sun. Her room was the pride of her house. (He'd slept there once when Godfrey had gone to Singapore for the bank.) Her

bed was grand, with a canopy and crown-shaped, padded headboard, like something out of the 18th century. Catherine the Great and Count Orloff, they'd called themselves. And he would always think of her there, with sun streaming in through the window, just like in his picture of the Danaë. He would dream of her as in their first days he had fantasized about climbing the vine in her courtyard and slipping through the window like a ghost of Romeo.

'I tried to call last night,' she said.

He was no longer sleeping in his studio, she knew.

'Are you better?' He tried to change the subject.

'Bit.'

He knew she knew he was trying to change the subject and why. There was no reason he shouldn't live with Carine now, but they both knew he felt he was betraying her and was sick at heart.

'You sound better,' he went on.

They both wished she didn't, but it was true. Falling ill had been a way to cross the Rubicon, but would it be easy going on without him?

'I must get up today. The boys are beginning not to believe I've been sick.'

He wanted her to say that she wished he were there in bed with her, looking after her, waiting on her as her husband never would, except in perfunctory ways. He wanted her to want him to have his cock inside her growing hard, and she did. But that had to be over now, didn't it? Wasn't that the point of all this bravery and pain?

'Have you decided what you're going to do yet?'

He couldn't let himself be wound up to a point of rage again, she knew. And she couldn't let herself have a nervous breakdown.

'Have to go away, don't I?'

'I don't think I could stand you staying here.'

What she meant in her heart was that she couldn't stand him being with another woman here. London was too small for that.

'Italy?' he asked.

'You must decide, dearest.'

He was on his own now, I meant.

'I love you,' he repeated.

Not long after, in spite of his shop-girl, he left London and did not come back for years.

There are always explanations, Miranda might have counselled herself. If she'd ripped a further few pages out of the notebook, she might have noticed Margot's guilt, her grief, her turning back to religion – not the Catholicism of her Brompton Oratory youth, but a strict, more austere Anglicanism. She might have read scrawlings about how one has to mourn, mourn, mourn until mourning exhausts itself and a kind of sympathy spreads out to mother the world. But Miranda didn't read on. She allowed herself simply to feel betrayal and loathing, humiliation and near despair.

Something had been wrong with her lover; she had not known what exactly until now. *Hiraeth*, 'M' – the spell was surely broken; the 'magic circle'. To think all her passion had been no more than a shadow! replay and substitute for love of a woman she'd tried to believe all these years was, or could be, her 'best friend'. Women beware women. Margot had not seduced her to Holland Park to discuss children; she'd drawn her there to read about this past. She'd plotted it out: stage-managed life as dry-run for a novel. She'd planted Booby as warning and knew by a sixth sense that, if she left her house for long enough, Miranda would arrive at her desk and poke about.

Yes. All fell into place now. The Grey Knight recitation had been a warning too: Margot wanted Oliver back – at the least, she was not going to let Miranda have him: that was the gist. But two could play at this game, Valentine's wife now reflected. She would not be beaten: not by Margot or Valentine or even Oliver Murrie, who had been (to use one of her husband's favourite phrases) 'economical with the truth'. She had a secret weapon, she believed: a way to win over them all and escape this treacherous school of life they had thrust her into, this place where only the strong survived and to be strong simply meant to be cunning.

London was not for the simple, not at this level. It was no place for cooing and love-making, standing at a check-stand with a hand on your belly and having the check-girl give you a smile as your husband doted on you with all the warmth of a spring day. Women's magazine stuff. Being good here only led to stale domesticity. You became a glorified suburban housewife; a garbage-collector for ungrateful children; a dried-up, ageing slave to an unloving master, chained to a regime as stultifying as a smell of overcooked cauliflower on the air.

Miranda might have worried about Lucinda and Gus then; but so sure was she that Margot's alarms were a ruse that she disbelieved any crisis had blown up around them. Even if it had, Godfrey's line was the right one: children were children; especially in teenage, they did rebellious things; it was only abnormal if they did not. As long as they were fed, dressed, schooled and knew they had love at home if they wanted, a parent had done what he could. Besides, apart from Anne, her own children were on their own now effectively, at least in their estimation; there was little more she could do to control them, nor would it have been advisable if there'd been lots. She had simply to accept, she knew from women's magazines.

Meanwhile, she had to reorient her attention to building a new life of her own. For that had been at the base of everything, hadn't it? fear of ageing and the rest which had led to the affair. Her subconscious had drugged her: the weekend in the country, the way she'd thrown herself at him in previous weeks of driving Margot's youngest to school – all that had been madness: the madness of the great break. But now she had a chance be liberated truly. Oliver Murrie had been only a start; to her future, he would be an irrelevance. If Margot were his secret beloved, so be it: she was almost relieved to have discovered, Miranda lied to herself. The child had been his, of course, the one he'd been obsessed with. *That* was the reason Godfrey had been so cross on her birthday. Poor God!

Back in Islington there were two coughs on her machine. Well, he could cough till he choked!

Upstairs, she changed into her most innocent outfit: a Laura Ashley frock, very country lass; a pair of prim schoolgirl shoes, nearly flat.

Did she look vulnerable? Dusting her cheeks, she put on pale lipstick and dashed the faintest line of blue under her eyes: a colour to harmonize with the flowers on her dress. She played with her fringe, then went back down.

The phone rang – him again? She'd be damned if she'd answer. The tape clicked on – Valentine's voice:

'Sorry to miss you, darling. Wanted to see what you thought about going up to Scotland for New Year. I've been on to your American admirer again; that seems the best time to get him to see the plant – can't do it sooner. I thought perhaps we could take the children skiing before or after, or both. Godfrey's idea actually. Why not rent half a hotel together, Wingfields and Cravins? Think about it. And oh by the way, I just wanted to say again how grateful I am you went to lunch with him yesterday. He mentioned you again this morning – something to the effect of how lucky I was. I said English roses are as changeable as the weather, and he said isn't that part of the charm?

I think you must be the first he's known. Imagines you don't have a whiff of the earth about you, which I guess is quite true.' (A chuckle.) 'Do let him continue his fantasy, darling, at least till we get through this patch. I'm sure it can't hurt for him to imagine that he's become friends with "a great English matriarch in the making" or whatever extraordinary phrase he used. Bye.'

Erasing all, she exited.

'Miranda!' exclaimed John at the door of Tony's and Carine's marzipan Gothic in Knightsbridge. 'To what do I owe this pleasure? Is Valentine in the car?'

'Just me, I'm afraid.'

'How thoughtful of you. English version of the Welcome Wagon?'

'Sorry?'

'In America when a new person moves into town there's an organization of neighbours who come around to tell him about the local services and bring him a cactus, or something useful like that.'

'How silly of me. I left the hyacinths at home.'

'Well, I have plenty of plants here. A real jungle in fact. Maybe you'd like some. Come in.'

He was dressed in a tracksuit which gave off an odour of sweat.

'You'll have to forgive me. Been running. I was just going to take a shower – I mean bath. You don't have real showers in this country.'

'I can come another time. I was just passing and thought – '

'Please stay. I'd much rather talk with you than do anything so prosaic as washing my armpits. It's just your olfactory displeasure I'm concerned about.'

'My which?'

His grin was sheepish. Again, it almost reminded her of Oliver.

'I smell,' he explained.

'Do you? I can't tell.'

'Of course you can. Just been to Kensington Palace and back.'

'Do you run everyday?'

'Twice. My sex substitute... Sit?'

She perched on the edge of a sofa she'd huddled on in post-coital fear less than a month before. John hovered by the mantelpiece, wizened. That is, he was not wizened himself so much as in comparison to the ghost of Oliver, naked, which stood there in her mind's eye. A radio or stereo was on in another room.

'What's that?' she inquired.

The sound was drums and pipes. 'Some Peruvian thing I found in Tony's collection. Evokes exotic places. Does it annoy you?'

Somehow it did, though she wouldn't admit it.

'I can turn it off,' he said, picking up the vibe.

He went out and shortly the music stopped dead, only to be replaced with something that struck her as little better: modern, classical, spare and pinging, like a deranged harpsichord.

'What's this?' she repeated when he reappeared.

'A Boulez quintet. More your thing?'

'Much.'

In fact, it was a negation of music as she knew it: inhuman; as if composed for insects or creatures from outer space. But then John was so foreign to what she had known. And doing what she'd planned to might be a revenge, an escape, but it was also a leap into the dark. If she had little taste for Boulez or Peruvian drumbeats, how much was she likely to have in common with this man whose coffee-table held an art-book splayed open to a nightscape of nude women and a skeleton worshipping a crescent moon on the checkered pavement of a classical courtyard?

'You like Surrealism?' he asked following her eye.

'I'm not sure. If you mean this, I think I find it disturbing as well.'

'Look at the date. '44. Disturbed time.'

Why was she here? Her sense of purpose ebbed. She was only a simple housewife with three children: good at baking cakes but with no more knowledge of 'art' than a modest talent for life-drawing, nor of the Outer World than of an abortive Italian honeymoon.

'I've been trying to decide whether to buy some paintings,' he went on. 'Tony has a friend who's in trouble; wants to give him some money but's afraid the guy won't accept a handout. The idea is that Tony sells me a canvas or two and I sell 'em to relatives in New York who have big contemporary collections.'

Going out again, he came back in with a picture that was as large as the painting she'd seen at the dovecote and unmistakably Oliver's too. Its background was moonlit black-and-white similar to that of the classical courtyard in the book on the table. But here was a landscape instead of a courtyard, a rocky promontory over the sea; and instead of nude women and a skeleton, there were three figures, one a plump man in a tuxedo, another a thin one pouring champagne, the third a nude woman stretched out on slick stones. What particularly disconcerted Miranda was that these three, transposed to opposite sexes, looked like Margot, Carine and Ollie himself.

'It's got good architectural sense. It understands the tradition of European figurative and landscape painting and isn't cutesy like so many British artists, if you'll forgive what sounds like a slur; but so much damage was done to your people by all that decorative Bloomsbury stuff – girls going to the Slade and moving to Tuscany to daub a little between making babies and cooking pasta. They never really get beyond two-dimensional representation; lots of charm and colour and linear competence, but no depth of mass, or anguish, or real chances taken, and no very deep context. This has all that. It's more continental than British. I'm just worried that it doesn't have – well, what this has, or this:'

He flipped through the book till he came to two paintings so famous that even Miranda recognized them: 'Nude Descending a Staircase', a frenzy of jagged lines, gold, brown and motion; and 'The Secret Landscape', its red sun or moon behind green bushes and blue sky cloudy, with a mysterious box in the foreground – coffin perhaps.

'My people in New York are very tough. It doesn't matter how fine you are technically – these *pointilliste* slashes Tony's friend goes in for won't amount to a hill of beans unless they believe it's got genius.'

'And what is "genius"?' she asked with a hint of Valentine's irony.

'You tell me.'

'Me? How would I know? I'm only English. And no art critic.'

Staring at Ollie's painting, she burned with a mix of crossness and admiration which her host could hardly miss. Did he know about *them* then? 'Sorry,' he soothed. 'Have I insulted you?'

'No. I just didn't realize you were an art expert. I thought you only – how did you put it? – "loafed".'

Why was her tone bordering on insult now?

He chuckled again, unperturbed. 'An art expert's the last thing I am. That's why I don't know what to do about this. Probably buy it. Tony can have some money for his friend; and if they turn out to like it in New York, I've been smart; and if they don't, I'm no more stupid than everyone else and can take a tax write-off.'

Life was terribly smooth for the mega-rich, wasn't it? How gratifying it must have been to be able to go around the world waving your magic wand over people you didn't even know, making careers with a flick of the wrist, like Tinkerbell.

'When I was your age,' he continued, 'or a bit younger, everything was clearer – and more confused. I know that's a paradox; what I mean is that we knew when we didn't understand something that we were on to a winner. Take Jackson Pollock and the Abstract Expressionists: who could tell what was going on in their stuff? it was all that '60s "like, wow, man!" If something had movement and colour and looked outrageous, it sold; it was NEW; it was breaking through to the Unknown like a drug-vision or dream or a nightmare. Something sober like this wouldn't've sold then. Now I don't know. It may be just what they want: the Artwork of the Future. Like your husband's business, paper-pulping, recycling – waste-management, as we call it in the States – who's to say it won't be "the great growth industry of the 21st century" just like he claims?'

While giving this speech, he propped the painting against a wall and sat down across from her. In the huge space of sofa, he looked like a grasshopper. It was almost comic.

'Can I get you something? tea? coffee? The English are much quicker to offer refreshments. You must think I'm a bad host.'

'You're funny,' she said.

'Am I? My ex-wife used to tell me I had no sense of humour. She used to say all sorts of things about me. Like when I was writing my study of the puffer-fish, she told me I was like a puffer-fish myself.'

'Oh?' Miranda took up a mask of amusement. 'And how's that?'

'I used to tell my students that, along with the praying mantis, the puffer-fish is the main proof in the natural world that heterosexual men don't always have to be boss. The male attaches himself to the cloacal sac of the female and gradually stops doing anything on his own, even eating. He shrinks until he exists only to produce sperm to fertilize her egg. When that's done, he vanishes.'

Miranda tried to appear as if this tale didn't give her the creeps.

'As for the praying mantis... but you know about that, huh?'

'I'm not sure. Do I?'

'I wonder why the educated English always seem to forget what they learned about science? – Anyhow, when praying mantises have sex, the female bites off part of the male's brain so he's uninhibited enough to consummate. But I'm boring you, aren't I?'

'Not at all. Then what?'

'Once he's done, she finishes the meal. That way she'll have enough strength to give sustenance to her babies.'

'How perfectly beastly!'

It put Miranda in mind of Margot again. Was it natural for a woman to be so ruthless: to Godfrey – to Ollie too, if the diary was to be believed? Feeling a twinge of care return for her lover, she half-wished she'd answered his coughs… Meanwhile, what was *this* man up to with his stories? He was looking at her much more knowingly than she cared for, rather like Tony Thomas in the wine-bar. Did she seem transparent to him as well?

'How do you know Tony and Carine?' she asked, changing subject.

'He was one of my students. First semester I taught in New Haven. Used to go out running together on the river. He was wiry and fast – perfect male specimen, but in the European way; not bulky and macho like our American type.'

Two thoughts rose here: first, quite alarming, that John might have been gay, or 'bisexual' – weren't many Americans of the era before AIDS? second, possibly even more alarming under the circumstance, a train of images returning from Sentinale: first Bernardo, then the stallion aroused, then Oliver in this room naked, finally an anticipation of something she now hoped would never be: herself in bed with this man.

She went rigid with primness. And Tony's words came back: that Americans didn't understand sex really. What had he meant? What she wanted was love, she believed; or, barring that, to be on her own, to be free, to escape. Never had she wanted sex per se, she protested to herself – so why had she seduced Oliver Murrie? and (again) would she end up like Booby Vänder?

This fear froze her more.

'It's great he got back with his wife,' John went on as if unaware.

'Who?' she demanded.

'Tony – with Carine. They've had a checkered relationship. He went off with someone else like everyone seems to do nowdays: then she got sick and he came back. I'm sure she'll get well: TB's curable with drugs. They've gone to my ex-wife's ranch in Ojai. Do you know California? Ojai's very dry – perfect place. And Santa Barbara's close. My family's foundation's given a grant to a writing program at the university there; I've told Tony I'll help get him a job if they want to stay. He's a promising author – at least that's what your husband's partner's wife told me. What's her name? Marjorie?'

'Margot,' Miranda corrected as a welter of thought crowded in.

'Yeah. Seems a tough lady. But I'm told she knows what's up.'

She wanted to leave now. The aura of knowingness she'd disliked in Tony seemed amplified in John, if more subtle. Ironically considering how he appeared, he seemed more dangerous even than the 'cultural half-breed'; and she longed to phone Oliver. Whatever *he*'d done with Margot, wasn't he her twin still? an innocent and victim, unlike this man who could buy and sell people's futures? Tony's, Ollie's and even – now the thought entered and checked her – Valentine's, Godfrey's, her children's, her own?

Dimly, Miranda realized, or imagined, there was no turning back. She could run to Ollie, true; but that was half-wrecked, the innocence ripped away by Margot. Besides, where would it leave her? Would he even take her? Wasn't he in love with Godfrey's wife still? Could she ever have him completely?

'You're quite generous, aren't you?' she managed.

'Not really. I've gotten every job I ever had through connections, so I don't see why I shouldn't do the same for friends. Anyway, Tony's worth it. He'd do no university harm.'

'You're too modest.'

'Nah. The're several houses on my ex-wife's land – I bought it, after all: I pay huge alimony – it's not hurting her for them to stay there. In scale, Tony's been more generous to me.'

'You mean by letting you stay here?'

'That and putting me onto things that might interest me.'

'Such as?'

'This painter. Investing in your husband's business. You.'

'Me?'

He looked into her eyes quite penetratingly. 'I was expecting you'd show up. He warned me you might.'

She felt caught like a doe in the headlamps.

'Called you a "damsel in distress",' John went on.

'What does that mean?' she demanded, half-panicked.

'I have no idea. I don't know you at all really, though I'd like to. I thought your house and children were charming. Your husband's delightful; I look forward to doing business with him. No, I don't know what Tony meant, but he told me to keep an eye out for you. That's one of the reasons I wanted to take you to lunch.'

Should she flee? hold her ground? brazen it out? She started to stand but felt the tears come, threatening to overwhelm her.

John rose in reaction. 'I'm sorry, have I been offensive?'

She fainted away.

Margot had once told her she did not believe in fainting: that was what one did in a Jane Austen novel. Girls used to fake it in her school, Miranda recalled; and sometimes she herself had felt faint in the rush of her days, but that was because of having drunk too much tea or not eating. To faint in front of a stranger was humiliating: she would never've done so by choice. In fact, she could hardly believe she had done it at all now she was conscious. But how else could one explain being splayed on a duvet in an entirely unfamiliar bedroom?

The space was white and vast, like the sofas they'd been sitting on. There were cornices on the ceiling and a wall of windows leading to a balcony filled with midday light. Sun had come out for the first time in a month, it seemed. Spreading through bare branches in communal gardens, it lit up the leaves of house-plants by the balcony-door. Yellow and gold, it flowed across two paintings on the wall opposite the mass of swan's down on which John had apparently lain her.

The paintings hung side by side over a mantel. (There was a fireplace in this room too, filled with dried roses, reminding of mortality.) In the first, a nude man and woman lay under a tree by the side of a lake while a couple in bathing-costume passed in the distance and a girl, fully clothed, looked over her shoulder as she disappeared into a copse. The nude woman was half sitting, eyes closed and head back, as if relaxed or perhaps satiated; the man beside her slept, face turned, penis flaccid. Charcoal clouds gathered in a blue sky.

In the second painting (were they also by Ollie?) a chestnut-haired girl, slightly more than teenaged, stood in a sitting-room next to a window through which gold light poured in even greater profusion than it was pouring through Tony's and Carine's balcony-doors. This woman was naked also and had her eyes shut. Spreading her arms, she dropped a robe off her shoulders to let light gush up against her skin. The pose was vulgar as well as touching. The woman, or girl, looked Italian, not English. A female Bernardo?

But where was her host?

Rising on elbow like the woman in the first painting (though Miranda had clothes on and no man beside), she heard water draining not far away. Dizzily she dropped back. Then the door opened, and from outside his voice said:

'Thought I'd just step in the tub while you rested. Only be a minute. Feeling better?'

'A little. Quite mortified though. What happened?'

'You need food is all. I'll get us some lunch.'

He shut her back in. She lay there immobile. She would go now, she thought but felt stuck to the spot. It was as if, having melted, she had congealed into this new position.

Before long, he knocked gently and came in in a robe to collect clean clothes from a shelf. 'Blessed are the imperfect,' he murmured, 'for theirs is the kingdom of love.'

'What does that mean?' she challenged.

'Just a saying that came into my head.'

'Well I can't see its relevance.'

She thought: I don't love anyone but my children, and them I'm losing – no more cuddles and kisses. No one else really loves me, or has ever: not my father or husband, or Ollie as it turns out – I was just a stop-gap between Margot and whomever. Maybe Mum loved me but, if so, it wasn't enough. How can a mum love properly if she isn't loved? And if one isn't loved enough, and never has been, how can one learn to love oneself?

'You're right,' he agreed, socks and shorts in hand. 'You're perfect. It doesn't apply.'

'Me?'

'Of course. The perfect English rose.'

'I'm fed up with that phrase. Anyway, you must've had a good look at my wrinkles when you brought me in here.'

'You don't have any. I'll go and get dressed.'

His tone was kind, avuncular. 'You're a strange man,' she muttered; then half-inadvertent – 'You're actually quite kind, aren't you?'

'Not what my ex-wife used to say.'

'I should imagine that, if she couldn't see it, it has something to do with why she's ex.'

The light was shining around her and towards him. He seemed timid, small, like a boy.

'Maybe I would've done better with an Englishwoman,' he shrugged. 'You think Valentine and you could find me one?'

'I rather doubt Valentine would be much help.'

'He found you, didn't he?'

O for goodness sake, she thought in a kind of happy exasperation, *why not?* 'Do you find me attractive?'

He looked at her quite sweetly, undecided perhaps.

'Why get dressed yet?' she went on, a strange heat rising through her and smile parting those bell-shaped lips.

She felt vicious. She felt free. She felt powerful, then scared again... She was beautiful, wanton; youthful, sexy; foreign, exotic and rich... 'O take me away somewhere!' she demanded; but now she felt heavy and he uncertain.

'What about Valentine?' she heard him ask, silent. (And what about Booby, puffer-fish, strange music and paintings, trendy artists, Americans, gays, AIDS and things far from all she was familiar with?)

'I just want a simple life,' he observed. 'Being happy's enough.'

'I have chaos,' she answered. 'Nothing but chaos, it seems.'

Can you save me, she wondered. Have I betrayed myself?

On the door when she got back to Islington at dusk was a yellow heart with a question-mark in the centre. On the answerphone were two more coughs.

In the night she thought she heard someone trying to climb the trellis outside her window. Valentine was snoring. She lay on her edge of the mattress. The witch's hat of the dovecote shone out in her mind, blue-black against a crescent moon.

5.

She felt she was living in another century with John, and she didn't take long to realize that she didn't like it. She belonged to the past, he to the future, it seemed. Perhaps this was just another way of saying that Americans would always be different, foreign inevitably and not wholly congenial. As a matter of fact, John belonged to the recent past – the 20th century, as Valentine pointed out – whereas she belonged to all time or no time: her father's *Aufklärung*, Ollie's mists of *hiraeth* or even Valentine's regime of Victorian rectitude. She belonged to her son's world of tacky videos and skateboards as much as to anything to do with John. But the fact was that she had slept with him: the die had been cast. Events would take their course now, and there was little she could do to stop them.

In the dimension of space, he did have some appeal: that is, his money did. Against her will almost she found herself fantasizing about the old scenarios – going to India or back to Sentinale – as well as colourful new ones, such as riding a camel in Egypt wearing a broad-brimmed sun-hat, going to carnival in Rio and Venice, being seen at the opera in Salzburg by her father, wandering through a souk in Istanbul and buying every eccentric piece of fabric she fancied – that sort of thing. There were only two problems with these pipe-dreams. First, at the end of each she woke up to realize that it was not John she was travelling with, but her soulmate. Second, the actual journeys John did propose – to Cape Cod, Connecticut or the Amazon – seemed to her arid, arduous or too rationally accounted for in his scheme of 'loafing'.

It did not appeal to her greatly to get decked out in diamonds for cocktail parties in a Manhattan of Booby Vänders. It was perhaps unfair to pretend that John dreamt of this either, but it was what he came from. As for his barn in Mystic with parrots flying about: it sounded amusing, but was it her? His description of Yale and environs did not evoke punting on the Thames, Christmas carols at Magdalen or any of the sensual images she'd stored away from her youth. And that was the crux of it. John evoked nothing from her past finally: none of the secrets hidden in her soul, none of the dreams that she felt more and more to be slipping away. A future with him would be slow death to all that. It would transform her into one of the international rich: an artificial rose preserved by face-lifts, not a sad-happy love-child drowning in eglantine.

Miranda felt these things but did not articulate them. Having slept with him once, she had to play along with his infatuation, she believed, at least for a time. And it would only be a time, she assured herself: he had to get back to New York to take care of the lawsuit that would make him twice as rich. This was the point really, sex only a means. John had to bail out Eurofibre, Ltd. In obligating him to that, Miranda was only performing what Valentine wished for but could not request openly. By these mornings of sacrifice of her body, she was providing for his business, thus the wealth of herself and the children. By these frenetic flights down to gingerbread Knightsbridge, spreading herself across an oversized bed and granting her favours (that's how she imagined it) as if a goddess or whore, she was merely doing her duty.

'You're such a perfect English rose!' he would marvel.

'Do stop saying that or I'll scream.'

In fact, it was not so purgatorial as she pretended. Swiftly, Miranda became quite uninhibited. Though protesting primness, she grew enthused about stripping off for him, watching him react, then feeling him give his 'all'. He was not unattractive, she decided after vacillating on the subject. Dark, gristly, lean, he was diminutive but did have startling energy for a man his age; also a repertory of tricks she had hardly envisioned. With his surgeon-like hands, he somehow enabled her to have that long-sought-after spasm once, twice, until finally she was having them with spellbinding frequency.

What was the secret? Why could she explode with this man whom she didn't love and who didn't touch her in any way but physically? Miranda was at a loss. Was it a bit pornographic? Several of the things he did or encouraged her to do were acts that had repelled her when she had glimpsed them in Hugo's wank magazines. Here was a conundrum. She felt as if she were violating her *self* subtly, not just Valentine and Ollie, whom she still felt tied to. Yet she enjoyed it, and whisked the children off to school in the mornings so she could speed down to Knightsbridge to wake him, as he put it, 'with her tongue'. They would then rut for an hour or more – for rutting was what it was: animalistic, clinical sex, which seemed to go on and on.

'Don't you ever get tired?'

'Do you want me to stop?'

'Of course not; it's lovely. But I thought men always came quickly and went grumpy afterwards.'

'Not all men. Not if they know what they're doing.'

He told her about Dianism and *Carreza*; about the old Chinese doctrine of 'holding your Ching'; about the relationship between orgasm, longevity and Power. He put her on top of what he called his Jade Stem and asked her to meditate on the Fire-Snake spiralling up her spine. He made her imagine strange gods and goddesses in embrace, and temple maidens dancing with bangles and finger-cymbals. Images rose towards the sublime, then fell back to earth, taking on forms from the photos in Hugo's magazines.

What was it about this kind of sex that could give such release, then send one plummeting into disgust? A number of ideas flitted here and there in the aftermath of orgasm; Miranda might have liked to have worked them out with her soulmate, but somehow she could not ask John. Talk was more intimate than sex finally, and she did not want that with him. In any event, he chattered enough for them both:

'You English are more passionate than you seem. I guess that's what Tony was trying to get across. He said you come on as cold as Bostonians but are as hot as Italians at heart.'

'Are Italians quite "hot" then?' – Her tendency with these sallies was to respond with what he referred to as 'your wonderful, honest-making English irony'.

'I don't know. You should ask him. He's the man-of-experience.'

'I don't suppose I'll be running across your American pal soon.'

'Why not? Come to New York. We'll fly to California for the weekend. I'll make him tell you about his sex-life.'

Miranda didn't fancy an undercurrent here. As before, she detected too-fond feelings for Tony. Nor was she attracted by the hint of wife-swapping that floated over the image of a suburban sex confessional. Indeed, something in John seemed a touch overeager in the direction of vulgarism. Was it that he had come of age in the '50s and so had never really been part of the Sexual Revolution? She hadn't been either but wasn't drawn by such things – or was she? Recalling Booby, Miranda concluded that John's attitudes proved that the international rich could afford a more trivial approach to matters of bed than a heartfelt, soul-driven, middle-class girl like her.

Following this line, she half-decided that John's happy-go-lucky approach might not have appealed to Tony either, eager though John was to invoke the younger man as guardian-spirit. This in turn made her recall again Tony's words about real Americans not knowing about sex, and this time she felt that she knew what he'd meant. People like John and Booby couldn't feel in their bones what made the spirit ache; Ollie, by contrast, seemed to feel without knowing. Tony had noticed it in him and, glimpsing the same in her, had guessed her secret. The 'cultural half-breed' had appeared so knowing because – in straddling both worlds while belonging to neither – he'd made *seeing* his game.

This was so plain to her now that she wondered if Tony had not also foreseen what was happening to her now and the consequences that might flow from it. 'I wouldn't mind talking to him again,' she murmured; and for a flash it seemed as if he'd been the one man who'd bothered to look at her for herself, not as sex-object. This of course was not so; but the mix of emotions it churned up made her wonder further, almost hurt, if that were why he had never made a concerted pass at her. She'd put him off, true; but mightn't he have gone on? A 'faint heart' and all that. Of course there was Carine; and it did impress Miranda the way he'd pulled back to duty in the end – pulled back in soul as well as body when the chips were down.

'Were you fond of him?' John asked.

They were in bed still. 'Who? Tony? You must be joking.' It almost occurred to her then to point out that it was Tony's, or Tony's and Carine's, bed they were discussing this in.

'Why?'

'Why what?'

'Why must I be joking? He might be perfect for a woman like you. I'm surprised you weren't lovers. Why weren't you?'

Miranda could grow tired of John rapidly. In fact, she found herself enjoying the sex yet wanting to get up and go directly after. Not only did he talk, he burned up all mystery with his questions and psychoanalysing, his endless inspection of the whys and wherefores and perhaps unintended assault on secrets she'd tucked away in the nooks and crannies of consciousness which no one, from her point of view, was obliged to reveal.

'Or am I being "too American" again?'

Fortunately, he was tactful. '... bit.'

She meandered on then in her mind while he held her body by rubbing lotion into the lumbar vertebrae. (He practised quite naturally what any but the most 'alternative' Englishman might have found unthinkable: yogic massage.) If Tony had seen how she'd bonded with Ollie, why should he have encouraged John to 'keep an eye out' for her? And this business of 'damsel in distress' – was the simple explanation that, having known about Ollie and Margot, he hadn't wanted to see her to get hurt? Was it possible that he himself had been hurt when he'd discovered – that is, if he too had been sleeping with Godfrey's wife, which Miranda still felt sure he had?

How many men had Margot carried on with? – There was a spiritual similarity between Godfrey's wife and Tony, a shared asexuality of the observer. Beyond this, however, they hardly seemed right for one another – not symmetrical finally. That had been Miranda's first impression and was still. Margot and Oliver by contrast were right for one another physically: Miranda had to admit this, ill though it made her. But Margot and Tony? No, that affair seemed all on the surface now: a little plot hatched by two intellectual tricksters to pull wool over the eyes (or protect the feelings) of somebody else.

Who?

Ollie had been right for Margot, yes: more right than for her. Indeed, if one sized them all up on mere bodies (or bodies and 'auras' to use a John word), then Ollie and Margot were suited exactly, whereas she would have been better with someone like Tony. That was the truth. Tony was too good-looking for his wife, as Booby had noted, whereas she, Miranda, was too young for her husband. Margot in turn had too much pomp for Godfrey, whereas Godfrey, like Carine, had too much character to qualify as a romantic lead. Booby herself was out of it, as was John. They were the satyrs and witches you saw on the fringes of Renaissance paintings, depicting Primavera or the Birth of Venus. Valentine was on the side too. Give him a tonsure and he might have been a monk.

And would her husband have been satisfied with *that* existence? Yes, more so than in the role and place he was struggling to get through on his own. On his own... Valentine on his own – yes. Miranda hardly ever thought about him as himself now, only as her oppressor. But as she ignored John's chatter above the lotiony swish on her skin, she saw an image of him kneeling, hands clasped in piety. Dressed in a brown habit, he was facing something, an altar or icon – she couldn't quite flesh it out. While all the rest coupled errantly and recoupled, he was pledging his troth to something or somebody.

Who?

And what was Ollie up to really, Miranda asked herself, shifting back in her mind – that was all she wanted to know. Suddenly, with violence, she had ripped him away from Margot; for Margot was not right for him, her spirit protested. (That spirit was a runaway horse now: it could not be reined in.) What was right was this new picture of Ollie suffering: of him raising arms towards her across the night, of him coming to London and surreptitiously placing his tell-tale heart on the door (he'd done it again twice – and such coughs on the phone!) Because he loved her: Oliver Murrie loved her, not Margot Wingfield!... Margot was haughty, remote, like some sinister medieval intrigant: an Eleanor of Aquitaine, as she'd once called herself – or was it Valentine who had described her that way? Anyhow, Margot was not right for Oliver Murrie, and it was up to Miranda to save him: the one man who had truly loved her.

'Why're you sitting up?' John protested. 'I'm not done.'

'Oh, dearest,' she sighed (and vaguely understood how Margot could have adopted this false form of address for all and sundry); 'I can't stay another minute. I have to – '

'Don't be silly. I haven't gotten your legs yet. Anyway, you haven't answered my question.'

'What question?'

'Whether you're coming to New York.'

Had he asked that? She hadn't heard a word of what he'd been going on about. 'O John please, you know I can't do that. I'm a mother, with three children.'

'Just for the weekend. I'll fly you on Concorde.'

'You're sweet. But think what you're asking? What would I tell Valentine?'

'That you want to marry me?' he shrugged. 'That you want to escape, even though you don't love me. Love comes with habit. Besides, I have too much money for you to resist.'

He said this with perfectly bashful, American frankness; and for a moment, like some heroine out of a Woody Allen film (a favourite of his), she was completely at a loss.

'Or,' he continued, kneading, 'if you don't want to be that decisive, make an excuse. A sick friend. Your grandmother. The type of thing great ladies've always made up when they wanted to see their lovers.'

'But I'm not a "great lady".'

'Of course you are, or will be. Why else would I want to be a drone to your queen-bee?'

He was so exasperating. How could one crush an insect? an insect, moreover, that could fatally sting you, or yours, with one rescission of the wallet?

Again she sighed. Then, shaping the sigh into a sound of amusement, she leapt off the bed and fled to the bathroom.

'I'll let you go now on one condition,' he went on through the door. 'That you promise, if you won't go to New York, you'll let me take you somewhere before I leave. Paris, Rome, Reykjavik – name it. You have to give me at least that before I get buried in my lawsuit.'

She came back in, letting the loo whoosh behind her and began throwing on clothes that were heaped on the floor.

'You're mad,' she said lightly.

'Of course I am. I'm in love.'

'Don't be silly, how can you be? You've known me – what is it? – two weeks?'

'Two minutes can be enough for a *coup de foudre*.'

'I can't be that necessary. You've lived a long, eventful life without me till now.'

'More's the pity.'

He was inflexible at core, if impish twinkles on the surface. 'All right,' she sighed, thinking to herself, only this once; then he'll be gone, and by the time he gets back –

'You mean you agree?'

'I can't promise a thing.'

'But – ?'

'But I'll see what I can do.'

'Whoopee!'

'But John,' she added, thoroughly alarmed at the boyish enthusiasm with which he whisked her back onto the bed, 'I can't go out of England, do you hear? I may be able to come up with some excuse for a night here; but the continent's out of the question.'

'How would anyone know?'

'The telephone, of course.'

'What telephone?'

'I'll have to phone my children. And John, if I do this, will you promise one thing?'

'What's that?'

'To absolutely respect the fact that I'm a married woman and mother, unless and until I'm ready to be otherwise. And there's no guarantee I ever will be.'

He gazed at her with genuine fondness. 'I knew what you were when I met you. What makes you think I can't play by the rules?'

'I just need to make sure you know what the rules are.'

'I may be Americanly naïve about things, but you have to remember I lived half my childhood in Europe and learned about *cavaliere serventes* and all that when I was two. As long as one lover doesn't violate the other, or the spouse involved, these things can go on for ten, twenty-five, even forty years. Isn't that what you want?'

'I'm not sure.' – She got up again, trying to hide how tetchy this made her, even frightened. 'I'm a middle-class English girl, not some Italian countess.'

'Why put yourself down?' he retorted, seeming to miss the point. 'To me you're a natural monarch.'

She needed someone to talk to. Her mother would have been shocked; Lady Melot, who might have understood, could only have taken Valentine's side. Margot was implicated, Lucinda occupied, Anne too young. Teenagers in any case could hardly 'relate to' the problems of (dare she say it?) middle-age. Among men, the only one who knew her well, yet was not involved was Godfrey; but he was not the sort to advise on such muddles – the mere thought was absurd. Tony, who was and whom she might have turned to, had vanished. Older friends? They'd either been frozen out by Valentine's manner or grown weary of her complaints about him. Thus the problem. She had no 'support system', as Americans might call it: no means of gently jostling herself back onto track.

She could ring the woman in Wiltshire or some other analyst, but a voice inside said why spend fifty pounds an hour spilling words to someone who might at best listen and at worst advise some New Age solution that could only make a botch of your family and leave you even more on your own? In any case, weren't analysis and such sociological disciplines simply despiritualized, self-centred versions of the guidance traditionally offered by the Church? And wouldn't the Church still do for those who had the sense to turn to it?

'I thought you were finished with that,' Valentine retorted when, after dinner, she mentioned therapy as a reason for wanting to go to the country for another weekend.

'I've felt shaky for days,' Miranda extemporized. 'I called her, the woman in Wiltshire. She could offer the weekend but no other time.'

They were in the drawing-room, Valentine deliberating over a sheaf of bills, she sorting out her reticule. 'I wish you'd thought of this before,' he grumped. 'You know it's the Christmas hunt at Cheveley: I must ride even if you won't – that's embarrassing enough. How am I to explain why you aren't at the big house for dinner afterwards? And who's going to look after the children? me again?'

She took a stitch in the bum of Hugo's trousers, which she'd begun mending. There were a number of ways she could handle this. On inspiration she stood and went over to the arm of Valentine's chair. He looked down in alarm as, bringing tears to her eyes, she knelt:

'Please don't bully me, darling; I can't take it anymore. I know it's terrible for you, having to make excuses for me to your mum, but I'm in such a muddle – do please let me. It's for you and the children; you must trust me. I promise things will improve.'

Another man, an Ollie or John, might have swept her up then, heart pounding, spirit aching to save the 'damsel in distress'. Valentine, perhaps, just knew her or her type too well. For a moment, she thought she saw an expression suggesting he understood all. Then, self-protective, she reverted to the idea that he was simply the man-of-ice she had long pigeon-holed him to be.

'Well,' he sighed, looking back to his bills, 'just make sure you give me her number this time.'

Miranda stood. 'I don't think she has one.'

'I thought you said you'd called her.'

'Yes, but that was at her home.'

'I thought her home was where you were going.'

'Not this time.' She produced a lie on the spot: 'It's going to be somewhere else.'

'Oh? Where, for example?'

Miranda's consciousness swirled back to Ollie: her saviour as she envisaged him in her distress. 'Some manor,' she blurted.

Hadn't John said they could go there, to Tony's and Carine's place? Frightful prospect, putting her next to the dovecote as it would. But now, perhaps just because of that, it was all she could come up with.

'In Hampshire, I think.'

'A manor in Hampshire?'

'Yes, I think so.'

'Where in Hampshire?'

'I'm not sure yet.'

Valentine studied her through his half-glasses. 'Why?' he demanded.

'Why what?'

'Why a manor in Hampshire? Last time you went to her cottage, I thought, although I still haven't worked out why you should've parked in a lay-by a half a mile away.'

This was the first time he had brought *that* up: Miranda, unprepared, pretended not to hear. 'She told me to come to the manor because she's giving an encounter group there.'

Would he take this? Would it be the moment when all the lies and resentments blew sky high at long last?

Valentine looked non-plussed. Eventually, he said: 'So you're going to an "encounter group" in a manor in Hampshire – that's what I'm to tell the family, is it? Would you like me to drop you there on my way to Cheveley? But of course you don't know where yet in Hampshire, do you?'

She might have admired his mix of irony and decorum. Valentine could be rather fine in his way – sometimes even she had thought so. But at the moment she had no time to think before he nearly knocked her off her feet by adding:

'Margot's artist friend lives at a manor in Hampshire, I hear. Place bought by that American friend of hers and his wife. That's not where you're going, is it?'

Averting her face, sniffing back a tear, Miranda returned to her chair and Hugo's trousers. Wasn't American 'openness' preferable, as John had argued, to the mix of innuendo and subterfuge that went on in these Old World liaisons?

'Since when have you been chatting with Margot?' she countered as if Valentine too had something to hide.

'Since you failed to get back to her about Lucinda,' he answered, not raising eyes from his chequebook.

Miranda took another stitch. Echoing his unflappable sourness, she added: 'I went to see her last week, by the way. She stood me up. I'm not her lady-in-waiting, you know.'

Silence. Signing a cheque, he ripped it out.

'What about Lucinda then, if you've spoken to her?'

'Better let her tell you, darling. It's all women's magazine stuff.'

'What is?'

'O some theory she's got about "sins of the parents". That's how she put it, in that melodramatic, high church way she's taken up.'

If Miranda registered any subtext here, it was only of her own guilt. 'Valentine!' she covered. 'She's got under your skin!'

'Beg pardon?'

'Listen to you – your tone is positively bilious!'

He hesitated, as if unsure what to write on the stub. 'For goodness sake, darling, it's this stress I'm under. DuRocher's the whole game now. He's got to go to New York and his lawsuit and get back here with the dosh.'

'Well? Isn't that what he's going to do?'

'We hope so. Seems less than eager at the moment though. Godfrey says he's found some lady-friend. You couldn't possibly cosy up to him tomorrow or next day and make sure he gets off, whoever she is?' He glanced over his half-glasses.

'I'm not sure.' – Miranda felt uncharacteristically grand in the thought that she for once held more cards in her hand than anyone else. 'I'll have a lot on my plate getting ready for the weekend. But I'll see what I can do.'

So she did, and ended up embarking on her second tryst at the manor next to the dovecote in Hampshire; only that weekend she'd looked forward to, whereas this one she dreaded. That one had seemed a breakout for freedom, this a proof of increased entrapment. That had seemed glorious, heroic, with streaks of sunset illuminating her arrival and silver beams of moon lighting their love-night; even the hurricane seemed significant in retrospect. By contrast, with John she arrived in dank, wintry fog; the moon was in darkness and air still as ice – as if, like the bare trees, it were freezing to death.

And death is what it felt like to enter the manor with him. Here she would have to be for thirty-six hours, entombed. She could neither go out nor pass a window for fear of Oliver seeing her. And what would he do if he did? murder her? himself? all three of them?

John, of course, knew not a shred of what she was thinking. She tried to be cheery as they poked around the kitchen, sitting-room etc.; but she took in hardly any of the *faux*-Tudor mod cons. Was that *him* out by the shed under the clump of yews? Had he seen the rental car pull up and noticed who got out?

She'd taken care over that: 'Park here,' she had said, directing John as far as possible from his space.

'Why, what's that over there?'

'A dovecote. God, it's cold! Let's get inside.'

'A real English dovecote? I'd love to see how they've converted it.'

She'd been afraid of nothing more. And the thought struck her now that John might wander out in the gloaming, encounter Ollie and in that easy American way of his invite him back for a drink. Burning hell that conjured: swirling and drowning in the hot, viscous fluid of some medieval fiery pit.

Was there evil here, she wondered. Certainly inside her lurked guilt and fear. 'Let's go to bed, darling!' – She had to keep him occupied, narcotized, immobile.

'Miranda! You're so eager.'

'Well, it's what we've come for.'

'You make it sound as if you were being coerced.'

'O John please!' – She burst into tears.

He carried her upstairs and set her on a bed which looked through mullioned windows up the valley towards Cheveley.

'Don't worry,' he murmured, gazing into her eyes.

'About what?' She sniffed.

'I won't love you and leave you. I'll be back in a few weeks.'

My God, she thought, what a hideous fix I'm in! and, sobbing, she turned away. Meanwhile he, misinterpreting apparently, took his clothes off, then hers, rolled back the covers and began licking her parts, confident that this, and shortly his penis knifing up, would appease the pain, stop her tears and provide comfort; which in a perverse way is just what it did – but only by making her feel that there was no doubt: events couldn't be stopped now, and she was of the damned.

In the night she got up and was sick. It was not what she'd eaten: she'd hardly touched dinner. John had checked in a guidebook and offered to take her to a hotel nearby, but she'd said, 'Let's stay here; we have so little time'. So he had cooked ('You're tired; stay in bed; I love cooking'); but what he'd come up with had been frightful. In another mood, she might have found it amusing, or touching. He'd done what he could with what she'd brought for breakfast. 'Scrambled eggs *and* kippers?' she'd exclaimed when the tray appeared.

'Why, is that wrong?'

'In this country, we eat one or the other, not both.'

But John had not recognized gluttony or bad taste. He'd devoured both platefuls while she confined herself to a few mushrooms and a tomato. And now as she retched in the en suite loo (it was done up as if an American hotel), he snored, happily replete.

For his sleep, she was grateful. It allowed her to be alone and do the one thing that gave her a shadow of pleasure in this place: to stand by a window and watch the man pass to and fro in the light opposite.

'Oh Oliver!' she murmured, 'are you tortured, my twin?'

'Yes,' a voice seemed to answer; and every gesture he made allowed her to think on: 'He's just like me! He *does* love me! When Monday comes, I'll call him and end this charade – this sell-out to respectability, money, the Valentines and Johns. I'll come to you, my lover, and live in your nest here, or wherever. We'll fly away from this hideous world, just the two of us!'

Such clichés and more passed. But what in fact was he doing? Pacing, insomniac, lifting a bottle, he disappeared from view, then returned lighting a cigarette. His hair seemed grey now fully, unkempt.

'Oh my darling, let me soothe you as you soothed me!'

She recalled their night in the shed. It was quite dark down there, at the foot of the garden back in the yews, one of whose branches had almost crushed them. Something seemed to be growing out of its roof now: a tower? ladder to the stars? – Her eyes returned to the dovecote. Yet, as if connected to or programmed by her thoughts, his figure was now traversing the lawn, other-worldly as a ghost. At the door of the shed, the light of a match flared and she made out his lips, *those* lips, before it flickered out and behind her John's voice said:

'Miranda?'

She spun round. 'You scared me!'

'Sorry. What's the matter? Can't sleep?'

'Nothing.' – She burst towards him.

Did he notice the light through the window? Throwing her arms on his neck, she told herself *no*, the match had burned out and Oliver was no longer more visible than a dream.

'There's a man over there building a tree-house,' John said the next morning loitering at the same window, herb-tea in hand.

'Sorry, darling?'

'I said that man over there seems to be building a tree-house. Looks like fun. I built one myself as a boy – or our chauffeur built it for me.'

'What are you talking about?' she prevaricated. 'I thought you were coming back to bed. I'm cold.'

Had sex ever been such a purgatory, she wondered.

'Aren't you going to let me take you to lunch?' – Even John seemed a little turned off now.

'Why? We can make something here. How could I eat anyway with you going back to New York?'

'My Miranda!'

You poor man, she thought, and performed another of what he called their 'honeymoon' acts.

'Why don't I buy this manor from Tony,' he observed after a restorative nap and his favourite snack: fried garlic. 'And when we get married – '

'John?!'

'Sorry. But even if we don't, I could build you a tree-house.'

Oh you sad man, her soul cried. 'Just go to New York. Get your finances sorted and stop this mad dream! What on earth am I going to do with you?'

*

What on earth was she going to do with herself was the real question. But this she could only take up once he was safely on Concorde.

Sunday night, getting home, she found Valentine not back yet. A message on the machine: 'Bit of a disaster here at Cheveley. The children are all right; 'll be back tomorrow. Don't bother to phone, too upset at the moment – nothing you can do.'

Anyone not so preoccupied might have been curious; Miranda, however, had been so eager to get back to London that even John had seemed almost offended; and now, given breathing space, she realized that her first priority had to be to get him on his plane with no less than glowing feelings about her. How to dim the glow she could plan out later: unanswered phonecalls, cool letters – there was always some stratagem. Caught up in publicity back in Manhattan, he might even get picked up by some vamp in black diamonds. If not and worse came to worst, she could always say that Valentine had found out and demanded an end to it.

Meanwhile, in her empty house, her first task was to phone Knightsbridge and gush with more thanks for the weekend. This she did, and arranged to drive him to Heathrow in the morning. Come morning, she duly performed this second task and put him on his plane full of kisses and tears.

'If this is an act,' he said, 'I hope it goes on forever.'

That might have given her pause. So too might his comment in the car as he scanned *The Times* (some article on Latin American unrest) that, if he'd been in charge during the Vietnam War, he would have either nuked Hanoi or not bothered to fight.

'That's the way these things have to be handled,' he added. 'You either play to win, or get out of the game.'

For all his solicitude and massaging hands, John could become vindictive, Miranda might have construed. But Miranda forgot about

John the moment he disappeared through the Departures gate. By the time she was stuck in traffic back on the M4, her mind had reverted to Ollie – in specific, to why hadn't he answered the phone in the night when she'd called.

At first it had just rung, then been busy, then just rung. For a time she'd decided he was down in the shed; then that he was drunk; then much later, in the wee hours where worst fears lurk, that her neglect had driven him into the arms of some other female. Crushed by an image of what she might've thrown away, she had cried: 'Oh Ollie, my lover, my perfect one!' Overwrought from the hypocritical sex of her weekend, she'd demanded: 'Where are you? I want you! Please, my darling, forgive me!'

This had kept her awake until nearly time to pick up John. Her face had been blotchy; she'd covered it with powder, making him joke rather Valentinishly that she looked like a walking corpse. Before she'd been able to voice offense, he'd added that he would remember it as 'one more happy sign' of her grief at his going.

'Call me in Manhattan anytime, collect,' he'd concluded.

Had those been his last words? She could hardly recall. She had run, literally, from Departures to a phonebox: dialled Hampshire – still no answer. And now as she loped in the moribund traffic into town, it hardly occurred to her that the excitement of John had been the one thing in the last week to keep off the gloom she now felt descending upon her.

Coming off the M4, she crept towards Shepherd's Bush. Winter London; choking traffic – how could she, or any rose of her type, be expected to survive here one more day? I am like a corpse, or a ghost, she reflected catching sight of streaks over powder in the rearview.

A lorry sat on her tail. Clutch, brake – she inched forward. Holland Park Avenue – why had she come this way? she'd meant to go the Western Flyover but in the roundabout had missed her turn. But then the trees, the tall plane trees spreading up towards Notting Hill, began to cast their spell over her. Their huge, dangling branches canopied the road here, even in winter, when bare. Subliminally they evoked a happier London – Margot's London – not Islington or King's Cross; and for a moment, just long enough, Miranda had fond thoughts about her onetime best friend.

These led her half-consciously towards Ladbroke Grove. As she approached, she was mesmerized further by a thing that can happen in London, even in grey December: light beginning to change. A weak sun strained to climb to the rooftops; it gilded each lattice and pane as it passed. For a moment, Impressionist loveliness glinted around. The town went nostalgic for Whistler and Monet.

Meanwhile, from the Wingfield gate came a sea-green apparition which Miranda did not instantly recognize. Booby Vänder, however, could hardly miss Miranda as she clacked up the sidewalk, scarves flowing, hair coiled in thick, ropey loops:

'Dearest girl!' the Americanne chuntered. 'But what's the matter? You ought to be the most fragrant and radiant rose with your life!' – Her tone was salacious, but without malice. 'Everyone's dying of envy. But don't tell me: I can guess why you've been crying. Listen, hon: he'll be back. You're the kind of gal he's always wanted, not some warty old rhino like me. And he isn't two-faced like some of these old Etonians with their hip-swivel. If he's with you, he's yours. So don't give yourself lines worrying about what he'll get up to over there.'

Miranda was speechless.

'Really,' the extraordinary creature emphasized, squeezing both her hands and looking into her eyes with intense scrutiny.

Impressionism turned surreal. Great thyroidic globes burned over a mouth spread across a cartoon of disembodied, equine teeth. Another squeeze, significant. Then:

'Must run now, bye-eee!'

Clack, clack down the pavement.

Miranda stood staring.

'Come in, dearest,' a sweeter voice intoned; and she turned to find Margot gazing over her gate.

Between clasped, beringed hands, la Wingfield held a mug to her lips. Peering over this as if innocent, yet somehow wicked too, she looked like Princess Diana musing at the face of the Taj Mahal. In the pumpkin-and-green blur of Booby, Miranda had failed to notice Margot lurking there; if she had, she might have run like a doe from the headlamps. Now instead, she was trapped by a look of deepest affection. So: did Godfrey's wife care for her still? Had she remained her best friend all along?

Pathetically, Miranda felt new tears rise as the other lifted the latch. 'Brrr! You must come in – hurry. Quick!'

In the Wingfield kitchen, she heard a clarinet voice call from the stairs, 'Mum?'

'Make a cuppa,' said Margot. 'Chrétien's ill, poor babe. Must just go and tend to him.'

Chrétien, Christian, a young man's voice, the boy ill – these impressions passed half-consciously as Miranda settled at the butcherboard table.

Something hovered beside her. What? Sudden gold snaking in from Margot's garden seemed to lighten mid-morning with a false hope of spring. So rare was this here at this season that for a moment Miranda imagined she was in the south of France, or Tuscany. Then, muddled up with the clarinet tone, Sentinale appeared, and with it Bernardo – an emanation half-imperceptible, passing beneath full recognition, pleasing, confusing, obscure.

Meanwhile, her eyes roamed over a mélange of coffee mugs, uncleared bowls and newspapers till they struck on a familiar hand. Of course it was unhinged to imagine the page was meant for her. Still, what else could Valentine's wife think as she picked up and read,

> She was Queen of the Lilacs. She had green eyes and hair that varied from a bright baked bean colour to the sweetcorn hue of a haystack. The hair was dyed, but that didn't signify; something in her tired Time and made her seem younger year by year. Once she had been a Princess of nothing, shy and unremarkable as a newlywed wife. Her hair had been brown then: mousey, like mine. But I'd a proper job, whereas she'd made a 'good' marriage. That was the difference. There was the lie: that middle-class habit of not marrying for love – novels are full of it. A hundred years ago, it was the banality of the age; our century is supposed to be a history of individuals pursuing their true selves. But there were class reasons for her bad marriage – money reasons, then children. And so she dyed her hair yellow; became Queen of the Lilacs. Desperate inside, she worked to bewitch the world. And I was one of many who fell for it.

The next paragraph described a summer solstice party: the Queen of the Lilacs threw a bash for her set, a country-cottage do entirely at odds with her status as châtelaine of one of the great stately homes of Bathshire. This underlined the fatal wrongness of her marriage, all could see. She had tears in her eyes as she led them through rosebeds; yet everyone adored her, because she was 'an expression of their unexpressed anguish', a precious 'damsel in distress'.

Coming on this phrase, Miranda felt a wave of heat up the neck. Furious suddenly, she wadded the paper – it was only a page – and hearing Margot's hard, low heel on the stairs, stuffed it into her bag.

She was through with the subtle hints and twee feints of notebook posturing! She would not be someone's experiment: some rat injected with serum to see if it might keel over dead. For wasn't that the game here? And how many were in on it?

She was on the verge of asking when Margot observed: 'I'm so glad you're here, dearest. I've been trying to get through to you for weeks. There's something we must talk about.'

Did her eyes scan the table to see if the paper was gone? On not finding it, did they turn onyx-cold?

'Valentine said you wanted to talk about Lucinda and Gus,' Miranda stated.

'I did, but it's beyond that now. It's complex. Please sit.'

'I'll stand, thanks.'

Miranda surprised herself with this answer. Was she about to make a strike for independence at long last?

'I see. I'll be brief then. Gus is, or was, dotty about Lucinda; Lucinda, however, has developed an obsession for Christian. Christian is so holy that Godfrey's afraid he's going to turn out a pouf – we've kept a close eye on his friendship with Hugo. But the truth is that, like his father, Christian is simply as pure as the driven snow.'

Something was wrong here: Miranda could not quite locate it. 'Go on,' she answered, blind with rage that Margot had never told her about her affair with Ollie.

'The point is, we can't risk it. Godfrey thinks I'm just worried about teenaged sex and someone getting pregnant, and for obvious reasons I let him think that. But Valentine agrees with me: it's got to be stopped.'

'What?'

Margot fixed Valentine's wife with a look of humility, yet resolution. 'This calf-love Lucinda's developed for Christian.'

'Why?'

From Miranda's point of view there was nothing the matter with Christian. Of Wingfield boys, she had long found him preferable to Gus. Of all but perhaps Luke, whom she was sure was Ollie's, he was the sole one who moved her; and jealousy of her daughter was the only motive that might have prompted her to conspire to put him out of bounds.

'Don't you see?' queried Margot.

'Don't I see what?'

'Must I spell it out?'

At the end of her patience, Miranda exclaimed: 'I'm sick to death of your secrets and mysteries, "dearest"! Why on earth didn't you tell me about you and Ollie?'

Drawing herself up to the full height of high church piety, Margot explained: 'I've often feared you might not be able to handle what you were getting into. I've tried to encourage restraint without intruding on your free will. But in the end there's only so much meddling one is justified in. Your life is yours to make good or evil. We all have to come to grips with who we are, even if it turns out we're not very nice. I'm sorry for what I've done, Miranda. But as for the children: they're innocents still. We simply must draw a line.'

There was too much here to respond to, other than by glowering at her friend, or enemy, or whatever this woman had become.

'Have you never stopped to wonder why Valentine should've put up with the dead weight of Godfrey in his business?' – When Miranda didn't answer, she continued: 'They're chalk and cheese, dearest. So why should Valentine have taken him on after Godfrey started drinking and came a cropper with Carine's family bank?'

These events Miranda only vaguely recalled: Valentine had said little about them, and she'd always assumed that Godfrey had his uses or that her husband wouldn't have employed him.

'Guilt is the reason,' Margot concluded. 'That and a profound sense of responsibility. Now do you see?'

What was the woman on about? So distant was it from anything Miranda conceived of that she hadn't a clue. But before it could come out, a slippered foot on a stair announced the ill Wingfield boy.

'What can I get, child?' Margot asked, turning.

Christian wore a blue robe, frayed, hand-me-down. A bashful smile creased his face as he murmured hello.

'How are you?' Miranda rejoined, regaining a fragment of poise.

'We think he has glandular fever, poor babe. What do you need now, more juice?'

Christian nodded; mama served. Meanwhile, Miranda recognized that, though pale and swallowing awkwardly, this Wingfield boy did have something special about him, as Anne had remarked. Into her mind came Carine and the sympathy evoked when a truly good person is ill; she recalled Tony's attentions to his wife, then the love she'd imagined in Oliver's eyes when watching for Lucius at school. But gentleness was not all that struck her about Christian. Following a vague sense of his clarinet tone, she half-glimpsed Bernardo again in his pale face. They were about the same age, and didn't this smile hold a faint recall of her Italian's tricksterish grin? Not that Christian looked like her dream-lover really: he was taller already and less filled out; his skin was creamy and, in contrast to first impressions, he now appeared younger than the downy-faced adolescent she'd spent such fantasy on. On dispassionate reflection, Miranda might have concluded that Margot's child was not like her *condottiere* at all, rather his good double, or holy obverse. All that was the same was an uncanny, inadvertent attraction she felt towards him – so strong, indeed, that as he left the room with the glass mama had filled, it was all she could do not to reach out and touch him.

Meanwhile her hostess murmured, 'Well?'

'Well what?' Valentine's wife snapped.

'Can't you see?'

'Can't I see what? that Lucinda's not right for him? that she's some kind of bully like her father, and you're afraid he might be broken?'

Margot fingered the half-spectacles around her neck. 'Dearest, I have tried. I've kept it from you for so long… lately I've been dying to drop some hint. I've tried to get Valentine to face up and tell you. I've tried everything – it's my fault, of course. But what more can one do? They simply can't be allowed to see one another, not in that way.'

'What way?' cried Miranda, beating jealousy back. 'And why not, even if what you're intimating is true? It's Lucinda's business, not yours. And if I can take it, why can't you?'

Margot raised the half-glasses. 'You just don't see, do you?'

'Of course I see! See what?'

She studied Miranda's face long enough to be sure that Valentine had been right: the woman did not have a clue. 'Christian is your husband's natural child.'

On the back of the page Miranda had stolen, a different hand had scrawled:

'Her sense will have to open to the wrong. To what's called Evil – with

> a very big E. To the discovery of it, to the knowledge of it, to the crude experience of it. To the harsh, bewildering brush, the daily chilling breath of it. Unless, indeed, as yet (so far as she has come, and if she comes no further), simply to the suspicion and the dread. What we shall see is whether that mere dose of alarm will prove enough.'
>
> 'But enough for what then, dear – if not to break her heart?'
>
> 'Enough to give her a shaking. To give her, I mean, the right one.'

Miranda did not read this. Underneath it, the hand had added: 'From the laureate of our tribe.' That might have made her wonder. But as if to conceal any sign of muddle from herself, she left the page crumpled up in her bag, there to burrow its way under make-up, shopping-lists, receipts and other detritus, until sometime in the rush up to Christmas it would be tossed into the bin in a perfunctory, essential clean-out.

She did not want to think about her muddle rationally. On leaving Margot's, her instinct was simply to drive to the dovecote and elope with Oliver. That idea, mixed with tears, led her as far as a call-box in Westbourne Park; but as he was still not in, not even when she tried from a call-box in St Pancras half of London later, she realized she would at least have to go home first.

Would Valentine be there? The prospect made her look to the rearview again. Wiping off smeared mascara, she mused: have my eyes gone distorted? has the moment come when the last trace of prettiness goes? are my mouth and nose turning into grotesque cubes like in one of those paintings in John's art-books? – Fretting thus gave an odd comfort. It was steadying to think about the petty fears women of her kind indulged in every day. What Margot had told her was simply too much. Anyhow, she could hardly believe it, logical though it seemed. Valentine had never fancied her, it was true; her children had been bred virtually on her own. He'd spent years pining over his first wife, she'd always believed – but to think he had suffered for Margot as well?!

It was so shocking, and the result so compelling (Christian), that for an instant Miranda almost admired her husband. Certainly for the first time in fifteen years of marriage, quite against her will, she actually found him half-interesting. This was not entirely conscious: it mixed still with rage, resentment – all the old emotions plus several new ones. As she sped through King's Cross, Miranda imagined she was still going home just to pick up belongings and flee. But families have weight: one couldn't leave one's children just like that, little though they seemed to care anymore. Nor was she likely to turn from Valentine now without, as it were, a last look.

Who was this man who'd had a secret passion she'd entirely missed? Was it possible that he could become her new obsession? She did not contemplate this consciously yet either, at least not so long as she sat at the light at Caledonian Road watching Oliver Murrie pass.

She had to look twice to make sure it was him, not just one more phantom out of a daydream. 'My poor love!' was her thought; 'have I driven you to this?' For the man was drunk, evidently.

Studying him as he weaved, she was about to call out when he started towards her, only to careen into a woman crossing on foot. Dark, lank-haired, a product of generations of Cockney street-wandering, the woman smoked; and Ollie waved a fag in her face for a light. Miranda stared spellbound as the creature handed him a box of matches, which he duly dropped. 'Drunken sod!' she prated as he bent to pick them up, in process of which he almost fell. Bending to help, she let out a coarse laugh; and for a moment, the two swayed in a comic kerbside dance – a grotesque weave-and-bob so oddly harmonious that it was all Miranda could do not to recoil into primness and pretend to herself that she'd never met this man, not this Oliver Murrie who took his time straightening up and gave the woman a look so maudlinly out-of-focus in a drunk's mix of 'love me' and 'fuck off' that, shoving the car into gear, she sped away.

The explanation for why he'd been there (and it answered why she hadn't been able to reach him in the night) was apparent as soon as she arrived in her kitchen.

Valentine was home: he stood by the wing-backed chair listening to the phone. From the door, shattered glass was strewn in towards the table. By the Aga, a green bottle lay on its side, a yellow heart pasted on it.

Miranda crossed swiftly, picked up the bottle and, turning away from her husband, peeled off the heart. Crumpling it, she turned back and raised the bottle as if in question.

'Yes,' Valentine said to the receiver. 'Dear me, how frightful. How long do you think he can last?'

She had an immediate impression of Ollie hit by a car. *Mea culpa*, her heart cried: my lover, my hero – why must it end like this? But before tears could spurt, Anne had bounced down the stairs and was whispering, 'Mummy! There's been a terrible accident. Daddy's brother fell off a horse!'

Miranda sat. How much did one have to take in an hour? ('Bit of a disaster here at Cheveley…') Then Valentine was off the line and, glancing at the bottle, remarked: 'I've called the police. They may want to fingerprint it.' –With that, he proceeded upstairs.

Anne climbed onto her lap. 'They were coming to a jump when his horse got startled by some stray cow. It threw him into a crevasse, and he hit his head. Dad says he'd had a bit to drink after breakfast. Lucinda says this means you'll be Lady Melot one day. Is that right?'

'Get down, poppet.' She shifted the child off. 'What about this?' she asked, indicating the bottle.

'We think we saw who did it when we were driving home. There was an old man across the road – well, Lucinda says he was your age, but his hair was grey. Anyhow, he was staring at the house. Hugo wanted to go after him when we found the bottle, but Dad said he might not've been the one and anyway it was a matter for the police.'

Miranda wondered if Valentine had recognized Oliver and knew. 'Yes, he might've been dangerous.'

'That's what Hugo said. That's why he wanted to chase him. What if you'd been in the house by yourself like when we're at school, and there was no one here to protect you?'

'Hugo said that?'

'Dad says we all must look out for you, especially now.'

Miranda waited a beat. 'Why "especially now"?'

The child went to the sideboard and, without looking back, explained: 'He says you've been through a bad time.'

'Does he just?'

Miranda stood and, finding pan and brush, began to sweep up glass. 'Dad says we should leave that,' Anne continued, eager to change the subject. 'He says the police might want to see it too.'

Miranda felt more sure of herself in this posture. 'What nonsense. The police can't be interested in this. And is a future Lady Melot meant to put up with some madman's mess on her floor?'

Such a welter of thoughts flew around her head that she could only revert to an ironic tone. It was a tack she'd taken increasingly in recent months, even with her children.

'I know it's wicked,' Anne giggled, 'but I do hope you become

Lady Melot, Mum. Sounds grand.'

'It is wicked, child; and if you think such a thing while your uncle's apparently in a coma, I do not wish to hear.' – She chucked the bottle into the bin. 'I can't think why your Dad imagines the police should want to trace fingerprints. All the hundreds of drunks who might've wandered up from King's Cross – why even bother them with it?'

'It's for the insurance, he said.'

'Ah.' – So Valentine was still Valentine, despite the hugeness of his secret and glory of his sudden prospects.

'But Mummy,' continued her youngest, 'we were wondering about the label.'

'What label?'

'The yellow heart, on the bottle.'

Miranda hardly paused. 'Why, what about it?'

'I don't know. Lucinda said it might be some kind of sign.'

'What does your Dad think?'

'He didn't look at it. Just went to the phone.'

Miranda continued to bustle. 'Doubtless Lucinda is right for once. It's probably the sign of the Yellow-Hearted Vandals or some horrid gang. By the way, how's your gran taking it?'

'Taking what?'

'The accident, of course; what else matters? Don't you realize the death of a child's the only thing we mothers cannot survive?'

With that, she dropped all and embraced her youngest with such passion that the girl quickly broke loose and fled up the stairs. This left Miranda to potter round her kitchen as if nothing out of the ordinary had happened. And indeed, nothing looked much changed – a pane of glass broken, that was all. Methodically, she cut a triple thickness of *The Times* and taped it over the hole. She would get Hugo to buy some putty and fix it, she thought, and thought on warmly about what Anne had said about him having wanted to protect her. Then she thought of Valentine's solicitude about her to the children and what it might mean. The bottle through the window, the car in Wiltshire, his remark about Oliver at the manor – for some time she'd suspected that he knew more than he let on. Now that Margot had confirmed his penchant for secrecy, she realized all the more that it was not in his nature to state what he did know, however it may have infuriated him. Valentine was pious, this man she'd never quite fathomed. He had hidden his passion all these years and, out of guilt (or perhaps faith), had been beastly to her.

'He came to me shortly after his first wife left him,' Margot had explained. 'I put him off then; I almost always did. The only time I didn't was after Gus was born and Godfrey had gone off me in the way they do when we mothers are obsessed with our first. My body had stretch marks; I needed affirmation; your husband in his austere way seemed somehow right. He needed me too: you were obsessed with Lucinda. Besides, he felt you could never love him: you were too young and disliked his tendency to religion. He felt he'd made a mistake, which maybe he had. Maybe we all have; but there it is. Marriage is the shell, dearest. We must keep it intact for incubating our chicks.'

Was the hideous woman right? Was there no alternative finally but to put on a brave face and carry on? Was Family the one Truth? Had this glass through the window been an ultimate warning: give up your Mills & Boon fantasies and get back to middle-class sense?

After a time Miranda decided that, in preventing Hugo from chasing Ollie, Valentine had been sending her a signal as well. We must avoid scandal; must not have a scene; must adhere to the forms, call the police, inform the insurers, go through the rituals, keep up the facade. We must do these things properly, set an example for the children and above all not talk about any 'subtext' unless – as in the case of Lucinda and Christian – it threatened to violate some fundamental taboo. Yes, Valentine knew, Miranda concluded. He would not confront her, and it was up to her not to confront him. To speak would be vulgar; to be vulgar was what he feared most (she perhaps too finally). To pinch pennies like her father, to rut like an insect with John, to be drunk in the street like Ollie – these were so 'non-U', to use a Lady Melot term. With Valentine she had a union of guilt and suspicion. But there was too much self-interest to break it off. Passionless maybe, at least it was clean. And she needed that now.

I'll be what he wants, she determined. And if he continues to ignore me, hiding behind this quite proper concern for his brother, then I'll comfort myself with the role my children are already conjuring for me – becoming her ladyship one day.

*

It was midwinter summer. The Impressionist loveliness that had begun at Margot's that morning continued; and Miranda began to feel subliminally that she really was quite content. Christmas shopping and carol-singing lifted her spirits further; and though Valentine kept remote, she didn't take her usual umbrage. I have as much on him as he could have on me, she reckoned. Besides, why would he want to risk exposing her now that he was within a breath of the respectability he craved?

Thinking along this line relieved her of the fear and guilt she could have felt over Ollie. Regarding John, she still believed that Valentine had sanctioned that affair in part, though to reduce risk she didn't return his calls from New York. John was sufficiently discreet in any case that there were few burps (his signal) on the machine. Coughs were another matter.

'What is all this horrid hacking on the phone all the time, Mum?' Lucinda asked on the day when Miranda finally tackled her about her relations with Christian Wingfield.

'Some crank, I expect.'

To this her eldest replied, 'I hope we move to Cheveley when you become Lady Melot. London's sickening. Yesterday some creep tried to flash me in that parklet off Homerton Road, and this afternoon a drunk nearly peed on my foot.'

Hugo chuckled.

'Hugo, don't laugh,' Miranda chided. 'It is not humourous.'

Anne tucked into more bickies.

It was normal five o'clock tea at the Cravins.

On the subject of Christian, Miranda was surprised to hear Lucinda confess that his purity appealed to her. Like Godfrey, Miranda had half come to suspect the boy to be gay; but then she heard from Hugo (she refrained from asking how he knew) that Christian didn't 'have a clue' about sex.

'That's what makes him so much more attractive than Gus,' Lucinda averred. 'He doesn't drool over you; he's too bashful even to look. But he's so pretty, you'd just die to get him at it.'

'Well just don't!' said Miranda, closing the subject; and when Lucinda asked, 'Why not? I'll bet you used to feel the same about Dad', she covered by adding: 'I'll not have you bringing his glandular fever into this house.'

Miranda was not so naïve as to assume that this command would restrain anyone as self-willed as her eldest; but she was gratified too, if strangely alarmed, to hear that Lucinda had the same reaction to Christian as she did – it made her feel less divided by age from her sexy sixteen-year-old. As to the issue of incest: it wasn't for her to mention. She'd done her bit. If more were needed, it was up to Margot and Valentine.

Some moral passivity lay behind this washing-of-hands. In fact, in some Celtic recess of her psyche, Miranda wondered if incest were really so evil: hadn't it been quite common between brother and sister in mistier times? This impression floated in the part of her brain where she also wondered: if I do become Lady Melot and Valentine stays this cold, won't I be justified in taking a lover? In fact, wouldn't it be the done thing, along the lines of John's *cavaliere* whatever?

Such thoughts appeased her when in the night Valentine continued to be offish in bed, this despite the fact that she had modified her behaviour towards him. When a kick or a shove made her cower on her edge of the mattress, Miranda summoned his voice inside to remind her of what Ollie had looked like in the street; also to chide that becoming a bird-of-flight with John might end in a sad expatriation like Booby's. Independence was fantasy, she let the voice say: passion was no substitute for reason, or rightness. The lyricism of Ollie, the weekend at the dovecote, the sadness of his smile and sweetness of his lovemaking were nothing compared to the stoicism of a foursquare English husband, his hard work, his sense of duty to family and discretion above all.

And Valentine had things to offer her still, didn't he? Miranda was persuaded of this a few days before Christmas when an extended version of his college choir was asked to fill in at a gala of *L'Enfance du Christ* at The Theatre Royal. Valentine performed as one of the supplementary tenors; a minor Royal watched from a box; and afterwards Miranda's parents (Valentine had sent them comps, knowing how a Royal in attendance would thrill) congratulated her on him, though his had only been one voice in a hundred. The subtext here was that her parents did not want her to damage the 'good' marriage. Word had reached Oxford about Valentine's brother's mishap, and to have a daughter as viscountess could only be one more jewel in the crown of Sir Ralph's career of getting on.

One consequence was that on Boxing Day in Oxford (following a more than usually twitchy Christmas Eve at Cheveley) Miranda felt that she had real status in her vague, academic family at last. This was a happy prelude to New Years in Scotland, which is where the mood finally turned.

The fine weather broke; sky became haggard, clouds a colour of slate. The children didn't mind: it meant snow in the Cairngorms, which is what they'd come for. Amorous arrangements between Gus, Lucinda, Christian and so on gave a kind of soap-opera aura to their expectations too. Whatever parents might fear, the nexus of Cravin-Wingfield relations struck the young as no more than a home-grown version of *Neighbours* on TV. Thus they showed off or 'pulled moodies' with a continuation of the energetic glee they devoted to presents, parties and all other events of a festive half-term.

The families took a floor of a hotel north of Stirling. Two vans were laid on from Eurofibre works, one to transport children to the slopes, the other to take parents to Ayr on the day of plant-inspection. Miranda insisted on a rental-car too, arguing that with so many people – eight Wingfields, five Cravins and (in due course) John – there would always be one or two who needed to go elsewhere. Then there was shopping: they could hardly afford to eat all meals in restaurants, could they? Valentine appeared to appreciate this note of economizing, though renting a car would cost a good whack. But the principal result of Miranda getting her way was that, when the day for plant-inspection arrived, he asked her to go via Prestwick to collect John from his flight.

A touch of the ominous re-entered here. Part of the reason Miranda had been able to enjoy Christmas was her ability to ignore this *liaison dangereuse*. Now she would have to confront it; there was no escape. Valentine seemed as nervous about it as she, if for the more prosaic reason that the long-sought decision on John's investment was due. Why Valentine should still care about DuRocher lucre gave Miranda pause: with his brother a goner, he stood to inherit land in Hampshire and much else. Still, he was adamant. Perhaps his brother's death didn't strike him as such a sure thing as it did everyone else; or perhaps it only increased his desire to make a success in his own right before the world could accuse him of being just one more undeserving recipient of easy wealth and privilege. But whatever Valentine's compulsion to prove something, or to exorcize bitter gall in his soul, he was determined that Miranda should pick up John:

'He's mad about you, darling; don't you see? Without you we

might never've got this far. Just jolly him on a bit further, won't you? It's all for you and the kids.'

Thus she was prevailed upon to do her 'duty' once more.

She put on black tights, black skirt (short) and *eau-de-nil* top (now cleaned). Over this she draped an ersatz fox fur she had bought at Christmas. (Valentine still took such perfunctory notice of her clothes that he'd failed to spot that she'd been wearing the same hand-me-down of his mum's for ten years.) She drove the van to Prestwick, parked and looked to her face in the rearview. Making up, she turned her mind to excuses, apologies, charms – all the paraphernalia of the seductress, which made her feel frankly sick. Still, in the event, it went more easily than she might have feared.

John looked at her with love still, but he seemed relaxed. He was a rational man too (perhaps too much so), at least in a foreign way. Whereas Valentine asked much yet gave scant explanation, John appeared to demand nothing but explained all. He made no complaint about her not returning his phonecalls and writing only one hurried note on a Christmas card. He accepted without argument her excuses of 'family' and listened with interest as she described Cheveley, Oxford, Islington and now Cairngorm holiday scenes. Finally, as they came into the town of Ayr itself, she struggling to find her way, he said with diplomatic indirection:

'I talked to Tony Thomas the other day; he sends love. I think he's having trouble again being faithful. I said something to the effect that love isn't a consumer item you try on like a suit and then take back if it doesn't fit. It's ironic that at the end of a century when we're all supposed to be so self-realized we seem to need commitment even more than we used to. Maybe it's 'cause there's so little around. Once or twice I've even gotten the feeling that what's happened between you and me strikes you as just a few beddings. I guess everyone's scared of being let down, even me. But then I think, it's just trans-atlantic bad nerves; all it needs is a little time, and you'll have me trained to be exactly what you want.'

What Miranda wanted was open skies tinged with gold: the red earth, beauty, art, more permanent youth and her soulmate. What she longed for was young men to adore her, or the wealth and status to have her revenge with. John offered the latter: she saw this now more clearly than ever. She could have everything in the material world to mould as she pleased, after whatever image of perfection had moved her: on the horse with Bernardo, in the dovecote with Ollie, in the aura of Christian, even under John's hands. But all his wealth could bring her was a means of trying to preserve these. And they could not be preserved really. Life with him thus could only taper off into a process of watching them fade.

He had no fresh dreams of his own to give her, Miranda believed. From his strange, overadmiring bond with Tony Thomas, she had intuited that he was a kind of parasite finally, living off what others longed for. In her obscure way, she'd convinced herself that John was a tourist at heart; she was his education into a kind of Englishness, that was all. If she were to go away with him, he'd get bored eventually. Maybe he would leave her wealthy, as Booby had said; still, in her bones, Miranda felt it would be wrong – wrong!

Articulating this to herself, she experienced a fresh plunge of spirit. And by the time she'd located the vast, grey, corrugated-steel Eurofibre plant, she had slid into a depression so deep that it was all she could do to put on a face for Valentine and Godfrey before leaving John to them and rushing off under cover of needing a loo.

'How is he?' Valentine whispered before she'd quite escaped. (Godfrey was already directing John's attention towards a delivery-station where great stacks of shredded books, magazines and newspapers were being heaped.)

'How's who?'

'Our White Knight, of course.'

'You must ask him, Valentine. I'm done with your call-girl routine.'

With that she bolted.

She could feel her husband's eyes on her, drilling into the back of her neck as she dove into a cavernous, cold metal expanse of warehouse. Here he'd reverted to a persona quite different from his *Enfance du Christ* idealization. Dressed in a suit and avid for his White Knight, he struck her as little more than some greedy freemason from Doncaster: some ne'er-do-well, John Majorite 'entrepreneur' trying to sell a rich, naïve jet-setter on a half-baked money-making scheme.

The grubbiness and crudity of it appalled her. Here she was, a dreamchild, the Queen of the Lilacs, but this was her King's imaginative realm: a soulless, colourless throwback to the Satanic mills in which her father's forbears had laboured while his had drunk port and enclosed the green and pleasant land. Miranda still entertained no political passion, far from it; it was simply that a kind of aspiration depressed her – the puritanical streak in her husband that made him concentrate on this hell in a wasteland draining down to the sea rather than some heaven in life whose earthly representation was her.

Where was her way out then? her way up?

She seemed to swim through great lengths of rolling machines; cutting, folding and packing stations; warehoused stacks of paper and, at last, the great bowl of porridge with bits of half-chewed waste that was the pulper itself. This she paused next to. Vast and deep, it was half the height of a man and had a diameter the length of her kitchen back home. The yellow goop inside looked like the muck babies wallow in when their mums have failed to clean them up. Gazing into it made Miranda quite dizzy. She forced herself to stride on, looking for what she was not sure.

Perhaps it was Margot, who had come on the outing too, adults being required to follow up the inspection with a celebratory lunch. She, Margot, had also brought Christian, on the pretext he was too ill to go with the other children to the slopes. The real reason, Miranda surmised, was that Valentine wouldn't let him remain unsupervised in the vicinity of Lucinda, even though the eldest Cravin had her hands full babysitting the youngest Wingfields. Miranda and Margot had not spoken about it, of course. They hardly communicated with one another nowadays, only grazed eyes.

It was hardly satisfactory. But nothing was satisfactory in present arrangements, Miranda reflected as she came along a line of closed office doors. Her world seemed a chaos again; the impulse uppermost in her mind was to find that escape – that ladder to the stars or, barring it, some secret, leafy bower to hide in. What she discovered instead was Margot sitting at a grey metal desk, playing with the half-glasses on a cord round her neck and saying 'Uh-huh' to a phone:

'Speak of the devil,' she murmured, seeing Miranda at the door. 'Why not have a word with her directly?' She extended the receiver.

Thinking one of the children had had an accident, Miranda grabbed the thing and blurted, 'Hello?' But the voice on the other end was Ollie's, and she hung up. 'Why did you do that?'

Slipping on the half-glasses, Godfrey's wife studied her erstwhile friend. 'He's been phoning me all through the holidays, dearest. He has no one, you know. Not since you dumped him, without a peep.'

'What business is that of yours?' Miranda wanted to scream;

and once more she wondered if this self-righteous creature hadn't somehow arranged everything to destroy her – to pollute her relations with Ollie and Valentine; to throw her via Booby and Tony into an affair with John; to give her the world on a plate, only to whisk it back, leaving her in a muddle as thick and fetid as the sick-making porridge out in that pulping-machine.

'It's my business because it's not my business,' Margot answered succinctly. 'That was years ago, my friendship with him. But I can't have him destroying my family with his fantasies about Luke – I owe that much to Godfrey; there's no telling what he might do in this state. Why didn't you at least phone him to say you were through? He's an adult, or hadn't you noticed? He ought to be able to face the truth. So should you.'

Such monumental unfairness seemed in this that Miranda, beyond thought, merely wanted to pounce on the woman, who sat there in pomp as if still holding court in her conservatory at Ladbroke Grove. But instead of lashing out or saying another word, she turned heel and, slamming the door behind, continued on in her half-conscious, as if purposive progress through the cavernous factory.

She sped along a line of doors like the one she'd just exited, muttering, 'Yes – should have called him – my poor Ollie!' But the idea of Margot chatting to him, and of him phoning her, cut off any rise of loving memory and restored an image of him weaving kerbside with a croaking harridan; and Miranda's mutters turned more to the effect of, 'O, where is peace? Where is the still-point? Where is my lover, my twin, the one I've been searching for to be made complete?'

She saw Bernardo in her mind's eye as she opened a new door... Christian Wingfield was sitting at the grey metal desk here, his expression melancholy, distracted. On being disturbed, his pale eyes seemed to widen in fright.

'Oh Christian, dearest, I was just looking for a phone. Must just call – ' Her voice trailed off.

The space was like the one his mother had perched in: filing cabinets, a window which looked onto flatlands draining into the Firth of Clyde. On the wall was a calendar of a type found in workingmen's offices: page-three girl, eighteen-year-old corker, poking out perfect titties in a soft-porn version of what Miranda had glimpsed in her son's wank magazines – or, more embarrassing still, of what she must have looked like through the keyhole in her parents' suburban 'villa'.

It was unclear whether Christian had been gazing at this or towards the grey sea. What was certain was that, despite what Hugo had said, the boy at least thought about sex; because what he had been doing, whether out of boredom or furtive elation, was unambiguous.

The little paragon was mortal as well.

Now when Miranda realized this, the thoughts through her mind ran as follows: must pretend I haven't seen and turn away; must be kind to the poor thing, he must feel so ashamed; must tell Lucinda – no! I must tell Valentine – absurd. He's a boy still, but not so small as all that… 'I'm sorry,' she heard herself say.

Having turned crimson, he scrambled to cover up.

'Don't worry,' she added, a flare of affection rising; then, almost humourously as a further, warming wave arrived, generalized, faintly frantic, all mixed up in fear that now – in a future without Ollie or John, with only this boy's hateful father – she would have nothing she'd craved for: nothing ever again of the passion she for a minute had glimpsed – an exuberant rutting, Florio, becoming an old woman – she said: 'It's quite normal. I don't mind.'

The boy hesitated. What on earth was he thinking? His zipper seemed to have stuck.

'Don't be afraid,' she went on as if to a shying animal; then quite madly, if maternally too – 'Would you like me to help?'

Did a shade of a smile pass the angelic features? Could it be that this diminutive prince, or demon, was the solace she craved? For a second, Miranda saw herself cross the room, perch on the desk, unbutton her blouse… he was sucking her nipples like a small child; only a boy-man he was – her secret, pale lover, his alabaster erection thrusting up desperately, suffusing its warmth all through her.

Her womb spasmed. She felt weak. Footsteps sounded behind; she turned… John DuRocher's training-shoes padding away.

Abandoning Christian, she ran from the office, slamming the door on his violated privacy. John's quick form strode forwards; no about-face. Already he had passed where Valentine, Godfrey and Margot stood staring at the bowl of the pulping-machine.

'We've got the thing going,' she could hear Godfrey bray; but John's diminishing form slipped away further, almost at a run.

All heads swivelled to gaze after it. 'Where's he going,' she heard Valentine ask as she came up, slackening pace.

The machine was emitting a low, grating hum: a vague, viscous slosh as the paddles inside whirled and squashed wastepaper to muck. The hum came from below, a generator deep in the floor. As it gained momentum, the whole plant seemed to shake; and Miranda felt ill peering over the edge.

Should she throw herself in, she wondered half-frantic, anticipating in metaphor what she imagined to come.

Godfrey had set out after John. But John was gone now, she knew – the White Knight had to vanish, like the phantom he'd always been.

Valentine turned to her. 'This is the last straw,' he seemed to say, a self-righteous rictus stretching over his face.

Margot stood by him impassive. She seemed to have grown narrow all of a sudden: like some elongated, stone effigy in a church. The two looked well together, Miranda thought distractedly: as if they'd been meant to be allied all along.

'Don't you think the time's come for you to go as well?' the voice seemed to add.

'As well as what?' she thought. 'He won't take me now. Besides, I don't want him – I never have. I just did it for you.'

'Why don't you stop lying?' came with the mechanized whirr.

She felt odder and fainter, until – supporting herself on the lip of the bowl – she asked herself yet more crazedly, 'Shall I throw myself in?... Maybe push him?'

'Get out of my sight!' a voice hissed – but what she could hear now was only muffled. A lunge had been made.

Sounds behind and above her, raised voices, a keening... A hand seemed to plunge in the muck – was it pushing or pulling? meant to help her or harm?

The paddles bashed at her face, yet all she could glimpse through their whirling and squishing was what was being churned up to be spewed away... 'Dearest girl'... 'a corker'... 'the Queen of the Lilacs'... And her world, if it came back, would not find these again. For no English rose would be intact here anymore – at the least not in the imperishable form it had once so compellingly been.

III

Season of the Witch

It was eleven-thirty on a Sunday morning in mid-October of a year at the start of the last decade when John DuRocher, whose training in science sometimes made him see more than he ought to, set out for lunch on the far side of the Park. As he came over the Serpentine, geese were honking south overhead and a scud of clouds trooping its colours in from the west. The lushness yet subtle melancholy to the scene may have been what stirred him to start one of those letters which are the origin of this tale.

It was some months since he'd confided about his new life, which had been my life once too, more or less. I was one of the reasons he had come to London and got involved with the people he had. Things hadn't gone well with the first woman I'd put him on to: Miranda Cravin had turned out to be less than an unblemishable English rose. But unlike some of us 'colonials' who become consumed with contempt on discovering the decadence of the mother-country, John was not a type to flee with his tail between his legs. What held him? Was it the language, or just with what our mutual expat friend Booby Vänder called 'the pervasive London inertia'? Should he have damned Thomas Wolfe and come home again to teach writing at Yale, peppering his seminars with allusions to people he'd once known in a half-mythical *beau monde*? Was he as bored with life there as I was with my grind at Sonora State U; or following his failed pursuit of the Rose, did he just feel obliged to stick it out to prove that you can be a good guy still even if somebody's treated you badly?

Some of these questions were doubtless churning him up as he wound round an alley into Portobello Road. Remnants of market-day rubbish tumble-weeded out of his path as half-comic strides sped him towards a weakening sun over nostalgic plane trees. Branches swayed in the breeze. After such a wet September, their headdresses of leaves seemed blow-dried in contrast to when he'd first come there on his own. That had been at the dead-end of summer, to the post-funeral party of the Wingfield boy, Christian, who had died in one of his brothers' arms following a shooting mishap in Scotland. Godfrey, their father, had taken his four eldest for the Glorious Twelfth on the moors; in his hunting-and-fishing version of Englishness, he had imagined it essential that boys be educated to such things. Margot, their mother, had responded to the tragedy by at first saying nothing for weeks, then barricading herself behind the mantra that 'Christian was the most godly creature one could have ever known.'

The sidewalk peaked, flattened and began its descent into a district where magnates of a previous *fin-de-siècle* had planted their villas. A dip in the road, a heave to the foliage and John was facing a detached stucco house which seemed undetermined whether to associate with mansions to the south or West Indian district to the north. Did it seem tawdry? The eldest Wingfield boy, Augustus, apparently thought so. With spiked hair and swastika earring, he had fled to New York the day after the funeral party to market 'video art'.

'What're you really going to do there, Gus?' third son Matthew had asked. (The surviving sons were collected in a corner of the Wingfield garden to drink to their departed member.)

'Leastways it won't be tuberculosis weather like this.'

'He's just going for the birds,' fourth son Marcus put in. 'All those tweezer-bums in shorts: Gus wants to live in groupie-land.'

'Gropie-land would be more like it,' Matthew amended.

'Hookers, all hookers,' fifth son Lucius chimed up, though he didn't look old enough to know what the word meant.

'What's a hooker?' asked Johann, the youngest.

At which point, mother Margot had put in: 'I do wish you men would stop being dirty boys. Christian is not even interred.'

'O Maggo!' said Godfrey (John hadn't been sure if this were a contraction of 'Margot' or some jokey French rendition of 'maggot'). 'Boys're always on about rogering birds. That's how we avoid this beastly hysteria you women go in for.'

Was it cruel? But how could an outsider read a strange family's grief? Margot, John recalled, had simply withered her men with a look and retreated to the far side of a lily-pond, where his erstwhile Rose had been deep in chat with a tallish woman in a hat... memory of which made him step up the stones to the door with something less than his normal sang-froid.

Grey, 'tubercular' as the scene may have been to one son, it was far from dull to John. But whereas Augustus had progressed to what his father had lampooned as 'the ashtray of the world', he was going in the opposite direction; thus what must have seemed a decayed house in a waste land to the boy dressed itself up as a palazzo of a more *belle époque* to him – perhaps even a reminder of realms he had known as a child in some other country, which may have been many countries, drifting into half-imaginary realms. Raising a knocker, he tapped a brass pad. The hollow resonated; the breeze held its breath. Goose honks and traffic out on Ladbroke Grove became for the moment like cries of gulls or waves in the distance. Gazing back at the stones he'd traversed, John seemed to see a liveried black-boy at their foot, legacy from days of tethering carriages. From where he notionally stood holding the reins, more steps descended into a well, over which spilled a lush fall of clematis. Down there beyond items of paint-chipped furniture, a stone nymph or goddess stood sentinel by open French doors. Vaguely John recalled how the woman in the hat, later identified as a 'psychosynthesist', had slipped through them uninvited and Margot had said: 'I can't bear manners which smack of the contrived informality of an Eileen Moloch play – though of course nobody uses the front door nowadays, except the postman, who needs a proper mail-slot. Friends are much happier with the servants' entrance, don't you agree?'

Someone had tittered, but the synthesist had eyed Margot as if she were coming unstuck. Thus Englishness had made its half-joke for the outsider, the synthesist being continental, though of what kind John had not hung around to find out. Giving a wide berth to Miranda and Co., he had departed as soon as polite. As if an intimate, he now went down through the French doors, calling 'Hello?' and disappearing into a service corridor.

He emerged into a pantry, which led to a kitchen and on to a breakfast-room; thence by further twists around to a spiral which corkscrewed its way up to the raised-ground-floor terrace which housed Margot's office, a conservatory. This airy construction stood half-divorced from the house; it too had French doors, which led to a back garden, which led to communal gardens – those spaces of elegant refreshment for which this part of London was justly famed.

'Hello, dearest,' came her tones as he popped through the hole in the floor, as if it were perfectly natural to do so.

She was seated at a broad, blond-wooded table. The room had a faint aura of incense about it, though none was in evidence. Margot looked for all the world like the wax replica of some Tudor queen.

'I was hoping you'd come early. I'm desperate for someone to help me sort out the garret. There's a dead child still up there.'

So John was received. His options were to sit on a white wicker chair with a green pillow on it or a sofa with an Indian print bedspread. These might have struck him as bohemian or worse – where were the spaces of genteel living promised by the Wingfield pedigree or Margot's dulcet tones on the phone? – but he remembered his mother's complaints about the wet-dog smell of the 'best houses' in the American east of his youth and took what he saw as the markings of patrician insouciance. He had known it all, hadn't he – the bronchitic coughs, drink and verbal plates flying – through his years of wandering, from Philadelphia to Richmond, Tuscany to Savoy: all the exotic venues characterized by, say, a statue of the madonna in a niche of a tumble-down wall, or of St Francis feeding a goose, and the aura of calm excitement around *Maman* as she'd held forth to Alice Toklas or the pomaded Cocteau, or debated religion with her confessor (though baptized Huguenot) under the halo of an unshaded lamp. She, John's own mother, had always positioned herself in a spot which – if you had plotted the odd shapes of the floor-plan of whatever domain they'd been in – was the exact centre. Margot by contrast was out on the edge as it were, though nothing in her look suggested she was bothered by it.

She was wearing a long, loose, brown-hooded habit this morning, not the straight black jacket and matching skirt of the funeral party. Her blonde-grey hair fell in sanguine misrule down her shoulders; the lipstick was not straight on her sensuous lips. Though more than fifty, she seemed half like a blowsy schoolgirl as she rose, Nescafé in hand, and led him up the continuing spiral which drilled its way into a double reception room.

Here the scene grew grander, the faint aura of decay held in check by size of the windows, height of the ceiling and length of the vistas back to front. Despite panelled walls, there was light and depth here; also a touch of old opulence, conveyed by books – books, books, books covered in leather or original dust-jackets; a collection not to be found in most houses one entered and again reminding John of the odd country mansion of his youth: the Eagle Views and Belmonts of that vanishing breed, a WASP aristocracy so rarefied that not even his plutocratic people had belonged to it.

Early novelists passed: Fielding, Richardson, Defoe. John almost asked which she'd consulted for plot, Margot having let drop that she wanted to start a novel to 'exorcize' the dead son.

'I'm going to have to plagiarize one of these,' she mused as if reading his thought. 'Godfrey tells me it's the only solution for writer's cramp.'

'O? How's it going?'

'What going?'

'The novel.'

'Told you about that, did I? How indiscreet. I hate plots.'

'So you said. You have to read pulp to get them.'

'Did I admit to that too? Godfrey insists I should stick to the classics. But then a Fellow of All Soul's would, wouldn't he?'

Godfrey Wingfield was sometimes thought of as a philistine because he'd spent years in a bank. In fact, he'd read Greats at Balliol; and most of the titles that passed were his. History, war, genealogy of ideas... Hume and Locke were prized possessions, in first as well as subsequent editions. An Augustan predilection was carried on in a taste for the *illuminés*: bespoke cedar shelves bent low under encyclopedias, dictionaries, translations and works by *philosophes*. Also giving off an aroma of wax and old paper were first editions of Racine, Molière, Pascal, La Fontaine, Francis Bacon, Pope's *Dunciad* and an early printed edition of Ovid's *Metamorphoses*.

Up one flight further, in an antechamber next to the marital bedroom, lodged tomes of Renaissance 'science' – John Dee, Robert Fludd. Here too was pornography in various languages: an unexpurgated de Sade, for example, designated by its owner 'for men only'.

'In this day and age?' John queried and half-inadvertently wondered if his hostess had violated the rule and read, only to be able to dismiss the contents as symptoms of 'male beastliness'.

'I thumbed through *Philosophy of the Boudoir* last night,' she said.

'That's a second time in one minute you heard my exact thought.'

'Is it? Miranda says I have "powers". But I assure you I have no wish to use them.'

He ignored this second allusion to the Rose. 'You mean thinking something and having it happen in real life?'

'That sort of thing. Miranda says Gisela's quite good at it.'

'Geesella?'

'That dreadful sinthesist, or whatever she calls herself... Godfrey was flapping the duvet, and I couldn't sleep. So I came in here and pulled down poor de Sade. He's another of you men who's cross because Mummy's no longer around to change his dirty nappies.'

The phrase was too blithe to take offense at, even if she'd directed it at him. Anyhow John had already determined that, given her friendship with me and the tragic phase she'd been through, he wouldn't let any eccentricity hit him amiss. Carrying on up through a third and fourth floor, they passed a Feydeau sequence of doors, behind which lived, or had lived, her male brood. At last, her breath shortening, they arrived at the top of the house and her 'eyrie': a garret with dormer windows onto treetops outside.

'Don't foul thy own nest,' she seemed to say as they stepped down four last stairs into a pile of débris.

The room had insloping ceilings. A mélange of strange angles cast shapes over manuscripts, paperbacks, magazines with torn covers: the detritus of years of literary agentship strewn about like unswept leaves, in contrast to the volumes ordered for bibliophilic inspection below. 'The hatchery and brooding-place,' she seemed to sigh as he looked round in delight and dismay, the first for being let in on such authenticity, the second on recalling how such mess seemed essential in even well-heeled bohemia – his mother's sculpting, then painting, then ballet, then photography: her restless search for affirmation in an era after God had been declared dead, or at least in hiding, and papa had skived off to who-knew-what-or-where.

'Any good at getting heaters going?' Margot asked, uncovering two coils with a slippered toe. 'The wind comes right through bricks and mortar up here.'

Accommodating, John searched for a socket. Meanwhile, Margot slipped on the half-glasses dangling round her neck and, dashing a hand through her tresses, stared out a window as if to check on a patch of blue fluttering between denuding browns and greens.

'You fickle devil.'

What? Who? – She was not looking at him. Nor would it have made sense for her to have used such a phrase if she were. Staring dead-ahead, she gave an impression of communing with uncanny presences. So was grief making her 'a touch mad', as some said?

John buried his attention further into the detritus and shortly came up with an oil painting. 'Eureka!' he cried, forcing her to turn and confront a brave-busted madonna.

This hieratic figure was done in thick, neo-*pointilliste* slashes. It had long blondish, pre-Raphaelite hair flowing over a colourful gypsy-style cape and saucer-shaped, starry-spaced eyes. One child lay in its arms while four others clustered round its skirts: variegated tots looking starry-eyed too and done up in neo-romantic garb as if mini-Byronic dandies.

'Ah,' Margot exhaled, 'my darling babes, when they were still just lovely innocents. There's Christian and August and Matthew and Marcus in order. The one in swaddling clothes is Lucius. Darling Johann was not yet, as *on dit*, a sparkle in his daddy's eye.'

In fact, the boys were hardly recognizable to John, except for colour of hair: yellow, red, yellow, red, echoing in sequence their mother's and father's. The two blond ones had circular, angelic faces, a little too flower-like. The others were vulpine, with sharp chins and pointy ears, like elves from deep out of a forest of Arden. The whole had a fantastic, fairy-tale aura about it; and Margot seemed to go even more vague staring at them, as if about to swoon or pass into a trance.

'Who painted them?' he asked, though realizing as he did – another friend or acquaintance whose canvases I'd shown him when he'd first come to London. (John had been meant to take the canvases to New York to try out on art-collecting relatives, but the plan had been scuppered when he'd learned that the artist in question was involved with his erstwhile Rose too, a situation contributing to all our evil times.) 'It's not bad,' he went on, wondering what connection this artist might have had to Margot in dim days. 'Why isn't it hanging in a position of honour downstairs?'

'Godfrey hates it.'

That spoke volumes. Or perhaps it meant little more than it said: John had lived in England long enough to know that a certain type liked to hint at dark secrets even when there was little to hide.

'I was in art-school before I met Godfrey,' Margot added, as if that explained everything.

Whether it did or did not, it was the sum-total of what she was willing to reveal of herself at the moment, though John's appetite was whetted, which was perhaps the point. Setting the canvas aside, he took what he thought a more decorous tack:

'You pride yourself on being a mother now, don't you?'

Naïveté was not only the purview of the painting. Yet Margot seemed no more eager to take offense from him than he from her:

'People tend of me like that, yes. Just now I find it hard to see the point of bringing life into the world only for it to die.'

The future playwright's one-liner might have closed the topic had John not been forced to give up his own marriage and child shortly before exiling himself here. So he asked:

'Don't you think you're being a bit over-philosophical?'

Margot gazed at him, or through him, via the half-glasses. 'Am I? That's what The Goose says.'

'The Goose?'

She looked vexed suddenly, as if disappointed. This made him feel oddly desperate to say something of more comfort, or at least interest. But he could think of nothing. So they stood staring at one another, or through one another, until Margot stopped the silence by dropping her glasses and – as if resolving on a matter she'd been debating all along – hurried out, tossing back:

'See what you can do to make sense of this for me; there's a dear. Have to get dressed now. The lord and master won't stand for me serving lunch like what he calls Friar Tuck. Or is it Tired Fuck? With dear Godders, one is never sure.'

Godfrey Wingfield ate his pork crackling with gusto. His face was as ruddy as his glass of burgundy. His stout, balding, fifty-something body seemed to sum up generations of English roast-dinners as much as John's belied a family rule of chewing each bite thirty-two times. (This custom had allegedly enabled his great-grandfather, the original John Du, to live to the age of one-hundred-and-one and, as tradition had it, become 'the richest man in the world'.) Godfrey appeared robust. So did his attitudes. When the subject of Christian's accident came up, he wiped his lips and declaimed:

'Please don't keep making us feel guilty, Maggo. All boys love guns. Maybe Augustus and Marcus were too young to be drinking as well, but half of mankind is classified as adult by their age. Soldiers die for Islam, and black Africans are fathers three times over, what?'

This was in the dining-room, an hour later. Gentle rain had overtaken day out the windows. The foliage in the garden seemed uncertain whether to keep proliferating or retreat before winter frosts. Margot stared at it with a faraway look.

'I hate beastly autumn,' she said into a glass of the champagne which John had incongruously brought.

'Margot,' Godfrey explained, 'still thinks she could have saved Christian if she'd been on the spot.'

'Maybe I could have. Mothers have powers. You never saw inside the boy's soul. Maybe that contact was all he needed.'

'What nonsense you talk, heart. You're not some Celtic messiah. And what kind of vegetable d'you think he'd've become if you'd swept in like a fairy to give the kiss of life? He was enough of a weed as it was, poor wretch. Have you beasts left any potatoes?'

Of sons remaining, fair-haired Marcus passed a server to fire-pated Matthew, who gave it to Dad. The two youngest, punkish Lucius and baby Johann or Jon, kept clammed up.

'Godfrey gets a kick out of referring to death as if it were trivial,' Margot observed.

'See you later, Mum,' murmured Matthew, getting up.

'Maggo, please. All I was saying is, you can't have it both ways. If I show an interest in the boys like you ask and take them for a shoot, you suddenly make out that all you ever wanted was for them to stay under your skirts and wear their hair like girls. Well, I don't want my sons to grow up girls, thanks very much; and they were longing to go, and accidents do happen – that's life, and boys will be boys. When I was at their age, there was no such thing as this American habit of keeping everyone on the teat until mid-life crisis.'

He gave the last phrase a comic fillip, but John didn't have time to grin before Marcus rose too and, casting a look at the guest, said: 'Great roast 'taties, Mum.' With which he followed his brother.

'It's difficult to know how anyone's going to react to death,' John remarked against the silence that ensued. Hewas clearing his throat to add something when Godfrey excused himself too, muttering that he was going to be late for chess.

Exit, following sons.

'Does he play every Sunday?'

'Dad would escape into that game if hellfire was raging,' explained Matthew, passing back through the room. 'Bye, Mum.'

'Jolly sensible too!' chorused Godfrey from the hall.

A door shut, and then shut, and shut.

Father and eldests departed, Lucius smirked at Johann. The two last Wingfields were a perfect replica of their parents, the younger as passive and strange as his elder was rough, even yobbish.

'Lucius, stop it!' the former whined as the latter speared his last bite of pork and ran out of the room gobbling it.

'Lucius, desist,' Margot said as plates clattered to the floor. 'And both of you, behave.'

They did not. Instead they disappeared, locked in a gladiatorial combat which Lucius had won before it began. John was reminded of our expat friend Booby's remark that 'their whole island race sometimes seems to sail through existence as if propelled by an internal combustion of bullying'.

'You were saying?' – Margot poured herself another glass of Möet.

They were alone now, silence muffling remote squabbles.

'I was saying – ' But what had he been saying? Had it mattered? 'Suicide,' he tried, 'was something I thought about when I was in school. Lots of Americans did – that Hemingway thing. And then there was poor Sylvia Plath.'

'Yes, one knew her, or friends of hers. But I've always thought it odd. Virginia Woolf committed suicide too; yet one doesn't think of it as very female, or English. The only person I ever worried about in that regard is your friend Booby. She's talked about it – also odd when you think how gregarious she is, or was. Self-consciousness, I expect. Then there's that business of closeting herself away in "darkest France", as she's done recently. Why do people feel compelled to leave their own countries? Isn't expatriation a kind of suicide too?'

Booby Vänder, or Marianne as her true name was, was a midwestern heiress who'd gone to Sarah Lawrence when John had been at Yale. In the 1960s she'd migrated to Manhattan; later she'd 'fled' to London; now she was blazing an American-abroad trail across the continent, collecting bohemians and the rich as if the F. Scott Fitzgerald era had never ended. Thinking about it, it was probably as much her as me who first introduced John to these people – at a party where they'd set him up with, or at least dangled him in front of, Miranda Cravin.

'But there's you, isn't there?' Margot added as if she'd gone a bit far. 'O I can never understand what people are on about! I wouldn't dream of killing myself, ever. Only God has the right to take away.'

Just then Godfrey came back through the room, having mislaid chessmen. 'You're not going to bore him about religion now, are you?'

'Shut up, Godfrey. Go play your games.'

'Has she told you yet the Almighty's a woman?' – He chortled.

Margot turned and threw the contents of her glass at him.

The glass had been only half full and the contents colourless, still her husband's mirth sputtered to a halt. 'Honestly, Maggo! I do think you could restrain yourself in front of strangers.'

'John's not a stranger; he's family.'

'Someone's family, but not ours. You've met him what, twice?'

'Three times since Christian, to be exact. But it wouldn't matter if I'd only seen him once in the past decade. You can tell who's an ally and who's not.'

'Have it your way.' – Gazing down at shirt and tie: 'Ruddy Prozac.'

'You can't blame it on that. I haven't had any today. Besides, it's you who's wrong around here.'

'O do fuck off, my heart! Have to change now.'

Margot tried to refill her and John's glasses but the bottle was empty. 'Where's the whisky?' she asked of no one in general.

'Don't today, Maggo. You'll end in a puddle like ruddy Booby.'

'Ruddy Booby, as you so inelegantly put it, lost the love of her life to a Belsize Park housewife. What did you expect her to do?'

'I don't care what she did, or does. I only care that she doesn't influence you into becoming a drug addict. Alcoholism's enough.'

'I'm not a drug addict. And you drink more than I do.'

'But I'm not in thrall to "the Priceless Proze".'

'Where's the bottle?' she repeated.

'Maybe it's not the hard stuff Marcus jokes about, or "trendy substances"; but it's still a long day's journey into night.'

'It's bloody prescription. Anyhow, I was talking about drink.'

'Her prescription, not yours. I keep waiting for the day she overdoses on it and leaves the rest of us in peace.'

'Booby's absconded; you needn't worry. Besides, Gisela says it's good for me now. She's going to get me my own prescription.'

'Gisela, indeed! Where will the witchery end?'

Not to be bested, Margot eked out a last drop of champagne. Godfrey, who had apparently made his point, now produced a bottle of Glenlivet from behind a first edition of DeQuincey. Clacking it down in front of his wife, he swept up the sip she'd just poured, as if she'd poured it for him. Margot thereupon took the glass he'd been drinking from at lunch, swished some water around in it, poured it into a plant and wiped it dry on a serviette. This subtle marital *pas de deux* ended with her helping herself to a portion of scotch.

'Margot tells me you used to teach writing at Yale,' Godfrey said, tossing back bubbly. 'What on earth's the point of teaching people to write? just a substitute for living, what? Look at all these women novelists around London: bloody distaffs trying to get back at us men because we don't have to go through menopause!'

He chortled as if he'd told a great one. 'But we don't have to go through that anymore either,' Margot pointed out. 'Drugs have taken care of it too: HRT. Heard of it?'

Godfrey groaned; Margot winked conspiratorially at John. The marriage, it appeared, was back on keel. Then she added:

'The main difference between men and women is that no woman, whether she has a child or not, will accept negligence, or cruelty.'

Papa belched furiously. 'I suppose it's my fault that the boys begged to go with me and acted like cowboys and Indians once they got there? You might as well blame your friend here because he's American, and Americans make films full of violence: that's how logical you're being.'

Having drawn blood, she confided to the guest: 'Godfrey was surrounded by nannies when he was small. Then he went to the kind of school where they learn to say any number of rude things to make themselves feel masculine.'

At this point, impish Marcus strolled back in. 'World War III again, is it?' He winked at the guest. 'Don't mind them. It's how we have fun around here.'

'It is not fun, Marcus!' mama trilled. 'Your father is a devil. I can't think why I've put up with it all these years.'

'Because,' Godfrey said, picking up his chessmen and board, 'it's the only way you can get the world to believe that you're the one who's so jolly "nice".'

*

After that visit, John heard that Margot had closeted herself in her eyrie to attempt the novel to exorcize the dead son. At Christmas he went to the States for his daughter's eighteenth birthday; when he got back, he heard that she had turned the novel into a one-act historical play. Almost immediately this had been put on by sympathetic friends at an arts theatre in Soho, and the journeyman dramatist was being puffed by literary gossip columns. Not wanting to appear as a hanger-on in a cast of admirers, John held back congratulations until early spring. By then *Sudden Strangers* had been expanded to full length and transferred to a West End venue otherwise dark, so there seemed little chance that the authoress was about to fall back into comforting obscurity. Thus, though rather reluctant, he phoned.

Margot acted as if she'd been waiting for months to hear from him: 'Where've you been, dearest? You must come and see us. We've missed you.'

Noting the regality of the *we*, John concluded that the bereft mother was over her loss. This isn't to say that there wasn't a catch of nostalgia for him in her tone. Whom did it echo? his own mother? the lost English Rose?

'Sit down, dearest,' she purred when he arrived the next Sunday for lunch. 'Haven't been ill, have you?'

'Some days one feels as robust as Don Juan, others as pathetic as Chopin in the hands of Georges Sand.'

Her puce-shaded eyes hovered over his awkwardness. 'Perhaps one knows what you mean. It's this beastly weather. I can't bear winter, especially when it's meant to be spring. I'll make a nice cup of tea.'

She flipped on a kettle which hid in a cupboard behind her desk and stuck a spoon into a Fortnum's tin.

She was wearing a dark woollen pant-suit this forenoon: less the style of a woman in mourning than of one on the make. Her slippers were bespoke: chess queens in gold stitched into black-satin toes. Though rings circled those eyes still, they seemed to demarcate a fixed sense of loss rather than present desperation. Perhaps because of it, John began to describe what had gone on between him and his ex.

'I've never approved of adultery,' she mused once he'd finished, 'though Miranda's synthesist friend contends I do it in the head all the time. To confront it physically would make me positively squeamish. So unsanitary. Like using someone else's flannel.'

Mention of Miranda unsettled John as ever. Margot appeared not to notice a wince.

'Of course, everyone has to have something to get on with,' she went on. 'At least so my gay friends tell me.'

'Oscar Wilde believed that the only unforgivable sin is shallowness,' John offered.

'Did he indeed? Clever man.'

'My friend Tony liked quoting that. I rather liked it once too. More recently I've begun to think that, in this day and age, relationships break so quickly that, if you allow yourself to get in too deep, you'll only get hurt.'

Margot poured hot water. 'You must have been very in love… Milk?'

'I don't know. I've only been in love once. But that was in another country and, alas, the wench is dead.'

Of course his ex-wife was not dead. Nor was John sure how much he had loved her really. It was just that theatrical allusion seemed the best way to avoid the more painful topic.

Margot blew steam off her cup. 'I was talking to Miranda about this the other day. We decided that in the Middle Ages one died of plague or war by age thirty, which is as long as one's built for psychologically, according to the Goose. But nowadays one doesn't die when one should, so we end up killing each other psychologically by botching relationships. Something like that.'

This was the epigrammatic Margot whom the world was getting to know through *Sudden Strangers*. Her, John admired. The Margot who continued to bring up Miranda, by contrast, was beginning to strike him as cruel.

'She's divorced her husband now, you know.'

As a matter of fact, he did not know and almost said that the real surprise was that her husband hadn't divorced her long before, as long-suffering as he'd been. But he kept this to himself. And now his hostess seemed to take the hint:

'I don't think I can bear love anymore, not the kind you're on about. That horrible, singular passion – I fear and despise it. Matthew came in here the other night mooning about his girl; I think I found it quite disgusting. One is able to love lots of people up to a point. Beyond that, I'm not sure it's healthy.'

Once again her words had a stagy effect, putting John in mind of what one her notices had dubbed 'Ms Wingfield's female dandyism'. There was also an odd way she pulled back from a subject only to move in on it from a different angle.

'Surely that's not always been the case,' he observed.

'You mean because of Godfrey? But that was about children. O, I do get tired of all these silly birds who think all you need is Love! They don't have the faintest idea really. Love is God: that is all. One must concentrate on Him.' (John here recalled what another notice had dubbed 'Ms Wingfield's T. S. Eliotic aversions'.) 'But they don't think about Him; they think about men. And when men disappoint them, as men inevitably must, they think about themselves and become post-feminists or some such, which only makes matters worse. Then their men turn wimpish or beastly or gay – daft! What on earth is a post-feminist anyway? someone who wears make-up like war-paint and puts herself about as if her soft spot were a cock? No, I'll never become one of the weird sisters, though I half-sympathize with them. God was never a woman, despite what Godfrey says I say. I've been working up a speech about it. Perhaps I'll show you.'

John had hardly time to be intrigued before impish Marcus rattled up the spiral. 'What's for lunch, Mum?' He looked like a harlequin who had slept in his costume.

She searched for a glimmer of light in the garden.

'Not a drop to be found,' the boy grumbled, ransacking cupboards. 'Where's that whisky you were swilling last night? Didn't finish it for breakfast, did you?'

'You're sounding more like your father each day, Marcus.'

'Wha's so bad about that? He brings home the bacon.'

'Not since this débâcle at Lloyd's. Anyhow, I don't see a connection.'

'Aw Mum, you're just mad because he made you hand over that fee for your play so's he could fix the roof.'

Margot did not shift gaze. 'I happen to know that, whatever your father may pretend, he used that money to sneak in a first edition of Pepys. Keep an eye on him, child, or the house may fall down.'

'Whatever you say, Mum. Whe're you hidin' the booze?'

'For God's sake, stop it. Say hello to John.'

'Hello, John. You haven't drunk it, have you?'

The boy's pranksterish tone was indeed a replica of his father's. If he'd closed his eyes, John might have imagined Godfrey had stepped into the room.

'Marcus, don't be rude; you've met John before. Besides, you can never tell when a person might not be helpful to you.'

Whatever this meant was covered by search for her coin-purse under a pile of papers. Locating it, she slipped a banknote from between pages of a dictionary, snapped it inside and handed the purse to the boy.

'Go to the off-license, Marcus: there's a good lad. Get us some wine and some choccies – *just* some wine and some choccies – no whisky or Malibu or anything else, hear?'

'Right-o, Mum.' – Smirking at John, he exited down the spiral.

Yes, this boy was surely the image of his father, though in colouring rather more like his mother and in stature less foursquare than his immediate elder, Matthew, who now wound down through the hole from above.

'What does Marc do?' John was asking.

'Nothing. Gets in trouble with girls. None of my sons does a thing.'

'What a slander!' said Matthew, who had slipped in so softly that mama seemed not to have noticed.

'Well which one of you does?'

'Gus's is in New York; Luke and Jon are too young; and I sell – or at least try to sell – advertising for *The Hill*. I know it doesn't contribute much, but it helps you pay for food.'

Margot glowered.

'Anything to eat downstairs?' this new son inquired.

'Lunch will be served at one.'

'Served at one, eh? Sounds awfully posh. Who's coming?'

'John. You haven't said hello to John.'

'Hello, John. Who else, Mum?'

'Who else whot?'

'Who else's coming for lunch, of course.'

Though darker and sturdier than Marcus, this mild boy clearly lacked the insouciance of his brother or Dad.

'Miranda and your father and whichever of your siblings happens to be here.'

'Miranda? You don't mean Miranda Cravin?'

'What about Miranda Cravin?' Godfrey brayed, arriving on the scene. 'Hello,' he put to John as if not remembering who he was. 'That frightful creature's not coming to lunch, is she?'

'I'm s'posed to be having lunch at my girlfriend's anyway,' Matthew murmured. 'Bye, Mum.' – Exit down the spiral.

'You do that,' she said to his back.

'You haven't met Miranda yet, have you?' Godfrey put to John, whether out of ignorance or teasing was unclear. 'She's one of Margot's best friends' – he dragged the words out into genial mockery. 'One hasn't worked out yet if she's become irretrievably evil or just gone down the drain before sloshing back up. You have to feel sorry for her husband, though, shit though he was. Why is it that women start playing at being witches once they reach age thirty-nine?'

Ceremoniously, Margot rose and retreated to the cupboard Marcus had tried to loot. Godfrey plopped into the chair she'd vacated; being on casters, it tipped. 'Ruddy hell!' he grunted, righting his girth. Simultaneously the cupboard door slammed. It was *Who's Afraid of Virginia Woolf?* once again.

'I take it,' John said trying not to seem defensive, 'that Miranda Cravin's not your favourite person?'

'My favourite person!? You must be mad. The woman's demented. The only reason I let Margot invite her is because she's trying to set her up with some pouf or other.' – Guffawing to himself, Godfrey rifled his wife's papers. 'What's for lunch, heart?'

'Oleander salad and hemlock for you.'

'Ruddy hell!' – On which favoured curse, he prised himself loose and thundered away.

Margot returned to gazing out windows. 'O how I detest that horrid, conceited, little man!'

John was not prepared to gossip about her husband, who in any case was not 'little' in any sense but perhaps existential. Nor did he want to take the Miranda bait either. In fact, he might have left then; but being polite (too much so, his ex-wife said) he took up what seemed an innocuous earlier topic:

'Are you a practising Christian?'

'I do wish Marcus would get a move on! Sorry? Am I a practising... I was educated in a convent but gave up the church when I married. Only recently have I begun to toy with the idea of the C of E. Do you think they'd let me preach for them now that they've started to ordain women?'

John chuckled. 'Stick to drama – you're more adept at it.'

She glared at him. He added:

'What I mean is, the Arts are the modern religion, aren't they?'

'Ha!' she emitted, and that for a time was that. 'You should talk to Miranda about "modern religion". She's keen on something they call the Cabala.'

'The Cabala? Isn't that black magic?'

'Is it? I'm not sure. I thought it was just another way of – how does Gisela put it? – discovering your potential and maximizing it?'

She gave this phrase an odd grrr, and John was on the verge of asking about this Gisela when Marcus banged back in, carrying what he called 'the swag'.

Thumping a carrier-bag down, he fished out a half-pint: ''at's better,' he belched, upending it. 'Miranda's coming to lunch, is she? Just bumped into Matt in the street and he told me the wretched news. Bloody creature. She divorces her husband even though *she*'s unfaithful to *him*; then she lives on his dosh so she can buy drugs for those creep children of hers. They roam around the filthiest house in north London, scabby dogs all over the shop, bloody parrots shitting in your soup and a monkey who wants to sit in your lap and French-kiss you. Then she has the nerve to try to seduce Matt, who's as pure as bloody Christian and half her age and's got a girlfriend anyway!'

John looked to Margot expecting her to object to this description of her 'best friend'. Instead she covered her mouth like a naughty schoolgirl and gave way to a fit of giggles.

'Gee, Mum, didn't realize I was that funny.'

Did he likewise not realize that he was talking about someone who'd meant much to the guest? Margot covered her mirth with a shot of whisky; and John braced himself to face up to his erstwhile Rose, whether he liked it or not.

In the event, Miranda failed to appear on time; thus by male demand all sat down to lunch without her. Soon a normal routine had commenced of overfilled glasses and verbal plates flying. Another visitor might have been put off by what Booby called 'their well-heeled barbarism'; but John's interest was held, and not least by his hostess. Margot answered his questions in a way that suggested larger questions, which sent his imagination winging off. Semi-detached from her men's jokes, she voiced opinions which intimated that all here below should be viewed in the light of some abstract supertext. The mortal world was fallen – that was the message, which on the evidence at hand John could hardly dispute. Listening to her succinct arias and one-liners, he was both drawn in and wrong-footed, with the result that – by the time each reflection returned from wherever she'd led it – the subject being bashed round the other end of the table had changed.

Did she feel remorse for the Miranda canard? There was no sign of it. On the other hand, she did now seem to work at putting him at ease, as if really intent on making him 'part of the family'. On his side, John could hardly help but be impressed by the way she fielded each sally of husband and sons, which, though half-comic, and doubtless defensive, could be quite misogynistic. Margot may have disowned feminism, or post-feminism, whatever that was, but clearly she had little interest in taking guff from her men; and in the ongoing guerilla warfare with them, she made it plain that she saw herself as chief source of their power. This was not just a matter of how she parried their jibes; it had to do with material ways she buoyed them up – those cups of tea, banknotes, Sunday roasts and the rest, without which they could have only (to use her metaphor) gone to some other nanny to change their dirty nappies. Margot did nothing overt to cut off her males' receptacles of pride: when she lampooned Godfrey, she was careful to impress it on John that at some level she was devoted to her husband. Yet at some further level, it was hard for the guest not to think that she believed or half-dreamed that she could have a rosier time with someone else. Who? As afternoon wore on, lubricated by more wine than natural, he began to wonder, or fantasize, whether she were, or could be, sizing him up. He grew conscious further, to his annoyance, that he was becoming aroused. Talk had not inaptly come round to sex. Yet no sooner had the subject been broached than Margot let forth with a stream of invective so virulent that you could hardly believe it was other than dry-run for a speech in a play.

'But how can you say you hate men?' Godfrey protested. 'You have six sons!'

'I have five. And that's just like a man.'

'What's "just like a man"?'

'To see life as so plentiful and cheap that one less doesn't matter.'

'I didn't say it doesn't matter.'

'You didn't have to; you implied it. You ought to try carrying one in your womb. See how it feels.'

'But I don't have a womb, Maggo. I have a cock!'

'Exactly. How could you possibly understand?'

'Ruddy hell!' – Papa flapped a broadsheet in front of his face and buried himself in an article on Hong Kong after the Changeover.

'What do you want us to do, Mum?' Marcus chimed. 'Cut it off?'

'Of course that's what she wants! All women do. What do you think all their squeezings and moanings signify?'

Matthew passed through on his way to his girl's, at whose domicile lunch was apparently late, if not mythical. Lucius and Johann took occasion to vanish upstairs. Marcus, rubicund and loquacious with drink, retired to mum's conservatory to call his bird, off whom he was trying to cadge air-fare to Tunis. This left Margot more or less alone with the guest. 'O I do wish Miranda would phone,' she muttered.

By now John could half-forgive the reference. It was easy to see how she might long for someone of her sex as ally. But none was on offer; only Godfrey and him. And now Margot gazed over the rim of her glass as if unsure why she'd invited him in the first place.

Again he was preparing to leave when she said: 'Don't move, dearest. I was going to show you that speech I've been swotting up. You might be the one male who can see what I'm on about.'

Thus she inveigled him into her corner, a spot which our hero was only too glad to enter, if only to let her to exploit his years teaching writing at Yale. Training his eyes on a curiously erect, almost Cyrillic handwriting, he read as well as one could through a haze of claret and middle-aged presbyopia: 'Yes… Ah… Wonderful… Paradox makes for power – is that it?'

'Sorry?'

'I mean, look at how you construct this sentence. You say one thing for the philistines in the audience but appear to be reflecting to yourself that it isn't what you believe at all.'

'Do I? Sounds corrupt. Show me where.'

Godfrey grunted in his chair where he'd started to doze. Marcus schmoozed from a distance on the phone as John pointed out his little discovery.

'I see. And that's what you call paradox, is it?'

'Nonsense!' papa emitted, snorting awake. 'It's just Margot playing her usual game of trying to have it both ways!'

Raising two fingers at him, she added, 'Go on,' over her guest's shoulder. 'This is fascinating.'

So John continued tutorial style: 'You have this knack for appearing simple when you're being complex…' Her scent was billowing down over his neck. 'You do it in writing' (he lowered his voice) 'and I feel like you're doing it to me now.'

Admiration came from his words as if beyond his control. Blood coursed to his head; fortunately, his complexion was too Creole to show it. Meanwhile, withdrawing her billows, the source of these responses returned to her chair and, studying him, mused: 'You have the most lovely, almond-shaped eyes.' – Then matter-of-factly: 'Doing what exactly? I don't get you.'

Did Godfrey shift again? Was this all being played out for him in some way? Watch out, a voice said (John heard it inwardly): this is no place for some compensatory flirtation.

'Refinement of language,' he nonetheless stammered, 'always appears to find grounding in common sense.'

'O for Christ's sake!' papa blurted, throwing down his broadsheet. 'Can't a man enjoy his post-prandial kip in peace? I mean really, Maggo. Must we always turn the place into Pseud's Corner?' – Seeming to regret this outburst as soon as it had popped out, he added: 'You shouldn't try to turn her into some Mensa type, you know. That's the last thing Margot is; she just sounds high-brow. The fact is, she detests the life of the mind – all women do, like so-called religious people. They only pretend to big ideas. Emotional affectations are what rule with them.'

Having delivered this *mot*, he seemed mollified and, flourishing his papers, pootered out to the conservatory.

There Marcus continued to coo on the phone. Margot called to him to get off. A weak sun tried to glimmer through the French doors, and John was again about to depart when she said: 'Godfrey's right. My relation to his "life of the mind" is mostly to have exposed myself to it so nakedly over the years that I've come to despise it with a real knowledge of why.'

The subtext was clear: she wanted him as partisan. Nor was it just some marital wrangle which had brought this on: success was going to make her a target for the envious – you could see it already from reviews of her play. Knowing how isolating envy could be, John felt a wave of protectiveness surge (an instinct displaced from his daughter by his ex-wife?) and longed to show himself as a true friend: without agenda, sympathetic.

'So what'll you write next?' he asked conversationally.

'I'm not going to go the way of Eileen Moloch,' Margot stated, referring to the reigning empress of British drama, whose plays had made her a household name from Oban to Auckland. 'In the first place, I'll never believe you can have something new to say after you've said the same thing in different ways two dozen times. In the second, I'm always suspicious of people who compare themselves to Shakespeare… Marcus, get off the phone!'

Godfrey wandered back through the room. 'Eileen Moloch?! Margot can't bear her. Or is *she* a *he*? "Luvvies" are the most vicious people around; but Margot only dares have a go at Moloch because every hack in town's jealous at the way she's poured it out so easily for years. Play after play makes a fortune, and the one thing one writer can't stand in another is making lots of dosh.'

'Off the phone, Marcus!... Must ring Miranda.'

'What about some of the lesser greats,' John went on, seizing on this gossip as a way to hold back the more perilous topic.

'"Lesser greats"?' – Godfrey seemed to light up at the chance to pour scorn on his wife's new profession.

'Say, Martin Winter. Have I got the name right?'

'Marcus!' she repeated.

'Dreadful isn't he? Written one obscure kitchen-sink tragedy years ago and's been puffed as a genius ever since.'

'What do you mean "genius"?'

'Exactly! Being too dense for any sound chap to understand! I don't know if the man's ever had talent in this case: toilet-training's the problem, Margot contends; mother overdid it. Terminally constipated, like all so-called minimalists!'

Chortling again, papa slapped his rolled-up paper and pootered out to the 'loo. 'An indisposition dear Godfrey does not suffer from,' Margot observed.

'Whose reputation are we assassinating now?' asked Marcus, banging down the receiver. 'Nigel Anis?'

'Nigel Anis?!' Godfrey echoed from the hall, as if his son had mentioned Uriah Heep.

'In America, he's regarded as one of the greats of the new generation,' John put in. 'What an ear for the language! Tony Thomas used to say he was the literary equivalent of Mick Jagger.'

'Who?' Godfrey trilled.

'Some ancient fag popstar,' Marcus burped. 'Not your style, Dad.'

Margot went to the phone. 'I used to like his father,' she said of the *père* of the famous Anis double act.

'Smedley?!' – Marcus was as acid at this name as Godfrey had been at that of *fils*. 'He's a crotchety, opinionated, cynical old lush, Mum. You said so yourself last week. Isn't he one of Miranda's neighbours? Didn't she try to seduce him too?'

'Shut your mouth, child,' she said, dialling. 'Smedley may be doddery but he's sweet... O, where is she? I hope nothing's gone wrong.'

'That's women for you,' Godfrey summed up from his scatological echo-chamber. 'Tomorrow someone'll say he loved *The Creaking Demons* and Margot will say she finds both Anises lacking in taste.'

'That may be true too,' she murmured, hand over receiver. 'In any case, I've yet to find a male writer who can do a credible female.'

Thus drama criticism *chez eux*.

On the way out the door, Marcus accosted his father emergent: 'Lend us a few bob, Dad?' Next to the phone Margot muttered, 'O where is she?' and pressed the redial button. Amused by vicarious attachment to the famous, John failed to glean that his hostess now wished the world away – himself included.

'What do you think?' he asked as she gazed into her garden.

'What do I think about whot?'

'About your rival playwrights in this new Elizabethan era?'

'I do not think about litterachore at all if I can help it. I just want to make tuppence-ha'penny at it and get out of this wretched place.'

'Ah,' he nodded as if in on a secret. 'The deceptive change of tone again. Apparent simplicity masking common sense. Is that why you ended *Sudden Strangers* with that gnomic comment?'

'What "gnomic comment"?'

'That "nothing really matters anyway"?'

'Did I say that?'

'Did you say it?!'

Just then came a blur from behind a bay laurel, and Margot shifted eyes to a black-clad apparition swirling in through forsythia.

'"The world spins, changes come, yet it always turns out the same, no matter what new magician seems to be doing the spinning"?'

So John quoted. But his hostess was gone now. The prodigal Rose had arrived.

'That would be a fitting description of my life at the moment,' he added as footsteps tapped up the spiral.

'Stick to polite banter,' Margot tossed back; 'it's safer.'

'We've got to get him!' – A fluty voice rose, and John turned to gaze at what Margot had abandoned him to, or for.

'Get whom for what?' she demanded. 'Where've you been?'

Amber-haired, slim, almost pretty, Miranda Cravin seemed on first take to be as heart-stopping as ever. Then on second, John was obliged to reflect that she summed up what Booby had once called 'the demise of an English middle-class'. Though nearing forty, the Rose had turned spotty. Her hair, once so brilliant, now hung lank and unwashed. Her frock, loose and smock-like, looked as if it hadn't been ironed since the '60s, while her eyes, which had once launched him like a thousand ships, appeared more mad than mesmeric. What could Margot have thought of him, John concluded, if she wanted to reattach him to this baggage?

'Get whom?' she asked, noting his reaction and not liking it.

'That judge!' the newcomer breathed.

'What judge, dearest?' adopting her tone of hushed conspiracy.

'You know that common-law case Gisela brought against Lord Frome? Well the same judge's just handed down the most evil summing-up – against Ollie! for stalking me! And he's trying to blame Gisela for it as well.'

'O how I loathe the Establishment!' la Wingfield murmured as if not for a moment believing she could be part of it.

'We must get him, and I know how. You know that golf club Booby's ex-char's husband works in? Well last night he overheard another judge in the bar saying that this judge has been knocking off rent-boys for years!'

'Ah. We can call *Private Eye*.'

'No, hang about. Gisela says you ought to take the whole legal profession on in your next play.'

'Still stirring up bloody drama, I see,' chirruped Godfrey, reappearing through the dining-room. 'Hello, Meer-and-ah' – he dragged the name out in sugared distaste. 'What have you done with my chessmen today, heart?'

Margot ignored him. Keeping eyes on her hostess, Miranda said not a word. For a flash John imagined a glimmer of real hatred in them: a deep, embittered stew of resentment – against judges, against Godfrey, against all creatures of the male persuasion, even him. It burbled up in their faces, as if each had swallowed some witches' brew and fancied nothing more than to stir a pot. Absurdly it struck him that, for symmetry's sake, all they lacked was the Shakespearean third.

'Speak up, Maggo,' Godfrey chuntered. 'What the matter? Black cat got your tongue?'

'I have nothing to say to you,' she stated, impassive.

'You know the trouble with women?' he tossed at John in a well-tailored exit-line. 'Oscar Wilde said it: he's a friend of you Americans, no? They are "sphinxes without secrets".' With that, he foraged his chess things from under a stack of scripts and chortled out.

'Don't count on it,' Margot purred, looking a dagger behind him. 'Surface calm can mask terrible depths.' Then before turning to her new guest, she extended both palms John's direction – 'Dear man! It's been so nice to see you. Do come again very soon now, won't you?'

*

Summer that year came in fickle bursts: first horrendous heat, then autumnal rains, with the result that everyone left in London by August was cranky with colds – all except John. Possibly this was because of his diet of vitamin pills and habit of running five miles a day. Or maybe, having failed to find a new girlfriend after several half-attempts, he was just getting adjusted to what he did best – mooching around on his own; being what his ex-wife called 'a genial monk'. Freed from trying to please some *exigeante* female or prepare courses for students preoccupied with their own spermatogenesis, John listened to his thoughts and asked little from life but what it was willing to offer. He did not beat a path back to the Wingfields. In taking pulse of his feelings, he wasn't certain he liked them – or, to be more exact, that they could quite understand him. Anyhow, now that he was on the far side of fifty, John had grown tired of forcing his presence into places where it was not unequivocally welcome.

He was living in a flat Carine and I had lent him when we'd set out for the West Coast. Books and paintings of ours still decorated the place; sometimes he would rearrange this or that, but mostly he left things as they were. One evening while listening to Zemlinksy's *Die Seejungfrau* from the Proms, he came on a stack of old magazines in which a discarded manuscript of mine lay: *Urban Fairy Tales.* Reading the opening story, on the theme of the mermaid seduced by a prince, he identified with a character who proves unable to rid himself of memory of an earthly beloved and loses his new mate back to the waves, where she swims off to play with old familiars.

This version of the Undine legend had soothed a young man's homesickness once; now it affected John bittersweetly. Devoting another night or two to the rest of the stories, abetted by more Proms, he began to find his life so quiet that he started to wonder if anything dramatic were ever going to happen to him again. Then one tempestuous evening as the Zodiac turned from Cancer to Leo, a knock on the door brought the House of Wingfield back in the form of a dripping, half-drunken Marcus.

'It's that dreadful Cunt-burning!' the boy exclaimed almost before John had him through the door. 'Have a drink?'

He upended a half-pint of Bells.

'Cunt-burning', it turned out, was not a slang term for a new strain of VD but the tag Marcus had adopted for Gisela Cohn-Burton (the psychosynthesist's full name) once he'd 'sussed out' what she was up to: 'Mum wrote this piece in *The Guardian* defending shrinks and laying into people who try to make them out as sex-fiends, and the bloody woman's been fucking with her ever since!'

This construction was not to be taken literally, John gathered. Still, there was an undercurrent which disturbed.

'No one can stand her. Your friend Booby Vänder, who's no model of sanity, keeps telling Mum she's "not one of us". Dad calls her a female Tartuffe; Matthew says she's a succubus or something. No one can quite figure what Mum sees in her, 'cept Miranda. But then Miranda's one of those '70s casualties who's tried everything from street-walking to being a dyke.'

Having delivered himself of this slander, Marcus fell into a chair laughing. Whisky splashed over a still-life of a bowl John had propped up against a wall.

'What're these paintings doing all over the shop? Have a drink. They look like that boring Oliver Murrie Mum used to fancy when we were kids. Sip? You don't mind me barging in on you like this? What's a guy like you doing in a poxy flat anyways? I thought zillionaires lived in mansions.'

John began an explanation, or at least a correction; but his intruder hardly stopped to draw breath:

'How long're you here for? Can I move in? Mum says she's going to throw me out 'less I agree to take therapy from Gisela, but fuck that. I let the woman work me over for an hour last week, and y' know what she said? Says I want to fuck my father! Bleedin' Nazi.'

This last identification was not meant about Godfrey but had to do with the fact that Gisela was German by origin, despite a Jewish tinge to her name. 'Psychobabblers sometimes like to stir the pot,' was all John could offer by way of comfort. 'What does your father think?'

'What, about whether I want to cornhole him?' – Marcus barked another gop of laughter through cigarette-haze. 'No, I know what you mean. Dad can't stand what he calls Mum's "menagerie". As for

Cunt-burning: "Therapy, what? all for women and queers".'

This caricature of a well-known English prejudice ('Why are they so scared of finding out about themselves?' John's Manhattan friends always asked) left Margot's eighteen-year-old sucking his half-pint dry. Soon he had embarked on a search of the flat for more booze. On discovering none, he announced he was off to the pub. Since the nearest establishment of that kind was some streets away and the night blowing a monsoon, John put on a raincoat and gave up his sanctuary to escort him.

'Do you believe in possession?' Marcus asked once ensconced in the familiar surroundings of a bar.

'It depends on what you mean: in having possessions or in being what people into black magic call "possessed".'

'That sort of thing. I know it sounds daft; but Matthew, who watches everything real close, 's afraid this woman's trying to get some power over Mum. Mum's a sap for that kind of stuff.'

'What stuff? Possession?'

'Anything not quite right. It has to do with all this religion she's gone in for, Dad says. She needs to believe the're demons loose in the world; if she can't find 'em, she makes 'em. That's why she's collected such a weird circle of friends around her.'

'I never put much store in things like demons,' John observed and tried to explain about his background – its Unitarian traditions.

Marcus gazed at him with an increasingly glazed eye. 'You really are quite simple, aren't you? just like Mum says.'

It was the first direct barb he had had from the House of Wingfield, and it hurt John more than he would have liked to admit. It continued to do so for days after as he went about his business, or non-business such as it was. Marcus's tale and incipient flight from mama hung in the air, forcing thoughts willy-nilly back to their sphere. Could it be that there was actually some evil there? Had the lad's visit, even Margot's invitations, constituted a remote cry for help? No, this was just his Yankee crusader imagination. 'The complex are not like you and me,' John had read in one of my stories about characters not unlike them, the hero of which becomes a knight errant to 'save' them but only ends by damaging himself. Still, Marcus had been right about one thing: Margot's circle was surely eccentric.

Besides Gisela Cohn-Burton, whom John didn't know, or know

yet, there was Booby Vänder, whose decade-long affair with a married MP had recently collapsed. The MP had stayed with his wife, whereupon Booby had gone into a tailspin, causing a reaction against England and retreat (she declared it progression) to what Margot described as 'darkest France'. Never a raving beauty, Booby had always veered between respectable types and the artists, actors and models of bohemia. 'Too late for the swingers but not for the gays' was her summation of two decades in Thatcherite London, where she'd continued a reputation for what used to be called 'fag-hag' in Warhol's Manhattan. On the fringes of crowds where too much was drunk and people took 'substances', she had been a card-carrying member of the cult of The Sacred Sec in the '70s, The Crazy Coke in the '80s and The Priceless Proze at the start of the last decade.

Booby was the one person Margot could be counted on to speak to (or listen to, as the case was) for hours on the phone, despite the high rates from Paris or the Dordogne. And what did la Wingfield see in this *femme démodé*? Like many creative people in middle-age, Margot let communication come more and more from those who sought her; and in a world and profession where so many did, she'd developed a principle to separate wheat from chaff. In Booby's case, it had to do with the fact that Vänder was a great old Yankee name, having produced plutocrats and philanthropists for longer and with more plentitude than even DuRocher. (At the end of the last century they'd dished up a wife for an Anglo-Irish Duke). Thus the friendship was, in Booby's phrase, 'an example of the snobbery of the literary *canaille*... Margot would hardly've been interested in me if I'd been plain Mary Glutz from Dubuque.'

Booby was also, despite the lumpen demeanour, quite dramatic to look at: a kind of apogee of the horse-faced, East Coast ascendancy – a *jolie laide*, as Margot was fond of relating. That Margot aspired to some such apotheosis herself as she passed fifty was implicit from the way she applied kohl round the eyes, coiled pearls round her neck and set a faraway pout on those eminently kissable lips. Margot was a 'lookist'. So much was evident from the hours she spent studying photographs of herself next to notices about her play. And since she looked more and more like 'dearest Booby' these days, if unarguably more handsome, the attraction might also have been summed up by what one of my now-dated psychological sketches describes as 'referred narcissism'.

Similar motives may have been at base in her attraction to her next closest friend of the era. Miranda Cravin's ex-husband was heir to Lord Melot; and though she'd fallen from grace as a prospective Lady, the erstwhile Rose had hardly dimmed in interest to this member of 'the literary *canaille*'. Indeed, the more demoralized Miranda became, the more Margot seemed fascinated by her – which may be an even better illustration of Marcus's *mot* that his mother was compelled by the downright weird. Following the boy's visit, John was told by another informant that Miranda had sometimes been spotted playing at 'alternative existences' by strolling late at night through Shepherd Market. Half-tempted to go down there and catch her at it, John had a vision of becoming a knight errant and shaking the damsel out of a spell. Fortunately good sense took over and reminded him that it would more likely transfer the damsel's distress onto him again; and once bitten, twice shy.

That said, John could think of no better way to cast light on what had sent Marcus to him than by contacting this festering plant (who else did he know in London?); so he picked up the phone. The palm of his hand sweat; his breath shortened with each strident ring. At last a voice answered, uncouth, male. Having discovered through 'channelling' that she was a reincarnation of Strindberg's Miss Julie, Miranda had gone to Stockholm for the summer.

Now either the voice was having him on or a woman he'd once thought he'd been in love with had become an complete stranger to him. Whichever, John was stymied and had to turn to the others Margot described as 'part of the family':

There was the above-mentioned Oliver Murrie who, according to Marcus, wrote to her occasionally from prison or hospital or wherever they'd put him since (in the boy's phrase) he'd 'flipped his lid'. What he'd flipped over is another story having to do with Mir-anda, Gisela, Margot, John, even me; but John was interested less in this erstwhile rival for the Rose's affections now than in the others around Margot. There was a charlady inherited from Booby who'd grown up as an orphan and married a boxer from Brixton who adorned her with welts and gold chains; the epicene son of an Anglo-Irish great family who mounted minor theatricals and was in love with a vicar recently defrocked for the orthodox reason of too much fondness for boys; an octogenarian poetess, Polish Jewess turned Catholic, who went once a week to the Society for Psychical Research to contact an ancestor whom, she believed, had been burnt as a heretic in 17th century Spain. Along with these there was John. So what was he doing in this catalogue of weirdos? Clearly time had arrived for research; and since he still knew little about this 'Cunt-burning' who'd set Marcus afire, he determined to concentrate on her.

Was the new friend or acquaintance of Margot's actually applying some mesmeric force? Having laid eyes on her only at that post-funeral party, John could recall only that she'd seemed attractive, if a touch masculine. The black hat had been arguably over-the-top: certainly it made it difficult to remember her features. What Margot saw in her remained sufficiently obscure that he still needed some mutual to flesh it out. And since there were no more candidates for this in London, he had no choice but to phone Booby Vänder at her *gîte* in darkest France.

'Johnny DuRocher!' she answered, not sounding the least bit depressed. 'Long time no hear. To what do I owe the pleasure?'

John was too versed in the amour-propre of women, even ones meant to be 'just friends', not to blurt out his purpose cold turkey. Hemming and hawing, he half-hinted that he'd 'seen the light at last' and wanted to take up a 'long overdue romance'. Insisting that he come down before August had burned out, Booby invited him to spend a week at her place outside Belvès:

'Just pack a toothbrush, hon. You'll get bronchitis if you stay in that grim, polluted place. Anyway, I'm bored and pushing forty.' (She was fifty now too as she knew John well knew.) 'You can spare an ex-flame a week for old time's sake.'

'Ex-flame' was overstating it. But looking around Carine's and my ghostly space, he thought, why not? So the next morning he bought a ticket and went.

Marianne, Booby, Vänder in her latest incarnation looked like Ava Gardner in *The Night of the Iguana*; only her pumpkin-hued hair was banged and bobbed over her ears, and she'd turned gaunt in the cheek. Her voice was husky from drinking Pernod and smoking Gitanes, both of which she continued to do 'like a trooper' though 'living through these Perrier days'. A girl who had once been known for day-glo mini-skirts now wore a faded blue smock over baggy overalls and a calico bandanna beneath straw-coloured hair. Her routine, she explained, included digging in a vegetable garden rather than prancing down Park Avenue.

Booby had bought a dilapidated 17th century farmhouse; one wing was converted for holiday trade, the other reserved for herself. 'It's my Walden,' she said as they wound back from the station at Gourdon along a D road. 'You've come in the right weather – you can tell by the tourists – but at my place you won't know they're on the same planet. It's hot as baked buns there, and we have a stream. All you have to do is take off your clothes and let it flow.'

Her 2CV rasped. London passed away. Great trees and small châteaux on cliffsides sent John back to his youth and trips around Gascony, the New England mountains – wherever his parents, alone or together, had fancied to perch for a month. In this sylvan setting Booby had found her *dolce far niente,* though within a day John noted that it was not quite what the phrase meant. As if undertaking some obscure atonement, his expatriate friend had reverted to a Yankee work-ethic: resurrection of some Jeffersonian ideal perhaps hidden in all our genes. While he lolled in a hammock stretched between poplars, she threw pots in her kiln, pedalled her bike to the village, shopped, mowed the grass, cooked, cleaned, pulled weeds and left him to chew his cud as it were, watching a herd of Charolais cattle grazing in a neighbouring field. Painting the shutters or collecting wood for a fire, she seemed no less than a pioneer female transferred to the old continent. It was a transformation anyone could relate to after London, and for three days John was charmed. Then gradually, in ways too subtle to relate, he began to notice something he had when visiting his ex-wife – i.e., that whatever a hostess may say, a guest is not just there to pleasure himself. To put it bluntly, Booby wanted attention, of a particular kind:

'I'm too old not to take every chance, hon,' she confided on the fourth night as they sat by a fire drinking red Cahors and skrying shapes in the flames.

What she was getting at was that it seemed 'redundant' for an old friend like him to be bunking down in the guest-wing.

'You haven't gotten AIDS in London?' she added when he didn't immediately rise to the invitation.

'I'm not gay yet.'

'Some folks take a lifetime to discover themselves. But whatever we are or we aren't, let's have fun while we can. The Grim Reaper may be standing in the shadows over there. You never know when he's going to show.'

John liked the Whitmanesque looseness about her: it brought back sensations that had been ebbing in him. And though she'd gone to fat in early middle-age, Marianne was almost back to the taut, androgynous shape he'd lusted after circa 1969. Recalling that era and how far she'd been beyond him then, he let himself be taken down (up actually) to the bedroom she'd carved out of rafters in an as-yet unconverted side of the house. And to start with, it was a pleasure to wrestle with her there, as with memories of a bygone era. But then a soft breeze seemed to waft through the shutters, carrying apparitions of frontier loneliness. I have enough of this in me already, John thought: exposure to more is only going to stir up all the hollowness I've known through too many expatriations.

'Why did you come here?' he asked on the fifth night as they lay in the aftermath of technically faultless sex, bathed in sweat and post-coital *tristesse*. 'Margot says that living outside one's country strikes her as a form of suicide.'

Booby said: 'That's the type of thing she would say. Margot's always probing to find the weak motive. She should be made to read poetry.'

Pondering this, John listened to the stream flow. Out of a skylight, stars shone like sequins in a Queen of the Night's headdress.

'So how've you done with God's wife?' she went on, lighting a joint. 'Cuckolded the old boy yet?'

'Jesus Christ, Marianne.'

'After Miranda Cravin, you must feel like getting your own back.'

He was annoyed at the reference, though guessed he deserved it. 'Margot's hardly Miranda,' he noted.

'S'pose not. But then who am I?'

'Ah well: that's a horse of another colour.'

He threw this out it lightly, and she took it in stride. Both knew how close to sore spots they were probing. Both too were conscious of the other's fragility. A sound of inhalation absorbed the next space of minutes. Time indeed became nothing in that blessed place. At last, half-seeing how he could turn the subject to purpose, John ventured:

'I think your friend Margot's got a new problem.'

'Who doesn't? What's hers?'

He rehearsed Marcus's visit and inexplicable outburst.

'And you can't figure why a successful playwright should get herself in thrall to some "psychosynthesist"?'

'It does mystify me. And not just me, it appears.'

Booby blew a plume into velveteen darkness. 'You know, Margot's problems always struck me as a caricature of so many people's on that tight little island. Secrets – that's their trip, that and obscure melancholy. The obvious reason in her case is Christian's death; but it's almost as if she'd been waiting for something like that to hang a free-floating disillusionment on. There were other things before – her artist friend, Oliver Murrie: an open secret they'd had an affair. Then there was her relationship with her father – a real creature of the shadows so far as anyone can tell. "I had to be husband to my mother," she once told me; another time she confessed that her mother was a person she "couldn't bear". Godfrey – dear God, so harmlessly cruel – said that someone who doesn't look after his mother is someone you can never trust; but even he stayed quiet about her background. He knows better than anyone how the English obsess on the order of rank; and though no one's ever come right out and said she isn't a standard English public-schoolgirl from the Home Counties, there was no reason to let the bitches have a heyday.'

'They suspect, evidently.'

His hostess looked at him through a purpling haze. 'Johnny DuRocher, you haven't become one of them, have you? Because if you have, I'll kick your ass out of this bed right now quicker than you can say the Divel made me do it!'

That might have been more welcome than John was prepared let on, so he answered: 'If I had, d'you think I would've come down to this brokedown palace in the first place?' – And rolling on top of her, he returned to a tried-and-true method for not confronting too precise truths.

Later, while she slept in the same snoring, determined way in which she'd made love, he gazed at goddess *Nuit* through the skylight and thought fine, sad thoughts of infinitude. Past, future and present spread out before him. Figures came and went: his ex-wife, Miranda, me, Miranda's artist friend in prison or hospital or wherever he was, last but not least Margot. To his surprise, John found himself wondering what she was doing just then, where and with whom, and if she were sleepless too. Of course he had no reason to suspect she was anywhere but in bed with Godfrey, tugging at the duvet, or no further off than the antechamber sofa where she'd read poor, dirty-nappied de Sade. But then came the image of Marcus, 'Cunt-burning' and all, and he began to worry again: what had *that* been about? the black magic Miranda was said to be into? worse? Had the synthesist really been 'fucking with her ever since'? if so how, and to what end?

Stirring himself with this flow of thought, John grew increasingly wakeful. Mixed with the rumours of Miranda's street-walking had come an intuition or fear that, when some worm turns, a fall can arrive in which a congenitally slumming instinct becomes the sole comfort. To be precise, John began to fixate on an idea that there might be something actually evil around Margot, infecting her in spirit as well as taste.

Marianne drew him back to more rational grounding the next afternoon when the subject came up:

'My Daddy taught me never to speak of devils. "To name one is to make one," he said, "and there's no one on earth whose motives aren't positive to himself. Evil, if it exists, is only a kind of spiritual waste-matter squeezed out in the conflict between two goods."'

They were sitting in long grasses down by the stream. *Déjeuner sur l'herbe* completed, she was kneading a lump of clay transported from the house. In this new incarnation, Booby had become a sculptress among other things. The lump was meant to be a bust to remember John by, once he had 'fled', as she predicted he would.

'I like your Daddy,' he mused and, echoing Marcus's report – 'Real Americans can be so simple, can't they?'

'Could be, in the old days. Daddy had two favourite authors: 'Emerson – all that native Brahmanism and the Oversoul – and Poe.'

'Poe? That sounds dubious.'

'Yeah, well, nine-tenths of the time Daddy was a respected grain-broker and president of the Louisville Board of Trade. The other tenth he'd turn up on the south side in Chicago in a puddle after one of his benders... However godly we may seem on the surface, we're all in thrall to the Imp of the Perverse.'

John refrained from supporting this truth with tales of his own parents' delinquency. Gazing at the neighbour's field, he watched Charolais graze and a hot, fat bull lounge under a tree. Further down the valley a harvester chewed away at black tobacco, which was the cash-crop of the district. It was the only other sound of man to disturb a long, still, summer's afternoon.

'Take Margot,' Booby went on. (A breeze stirred the leaves.) 'Obsessing on sin's going to be her downfall. All that T. S. Eliot stuff

– Godfrey's right to mock it. As to this shrink or whatever: sounds like she's got someone to help her unearth it. Every mind-merchant's always digging up black rot; it's their profession. 's a playwright's too – look at Williams and Albee and all those guys in Manhattan when we were just nice kids. So maybe Margot's got the perfect thing going: inspiration on its own tends to flag, needs something to feed off of – a world of twisted-up ethics. "Give in to temptation", "Repeat your mistakes", "Press on the thorn", "Burn with a hard gem-like flame" – all that Oscar Wilde shit we thought so cool in the '60s? Godfrey used to toss off the same lines, only for him they were jokes. Margot would listen, playing the straight-woman; but maybe even then she was dreaming up this devil, or demon or whatever's got her. She's always needed help in turning what she pretends is just Christian virtue into a cat's paw of genuine wrongness.'

Leaning against a poplar soaking the sun, John opened his eyes.

'Am I too abstract for you?' Booby grinned, half-embarrassed.

'You're wasted down here. When're you going to come back to London and sort out the rest of us?'

'No thanks, hon. I've lived that life, as far as it goes – anyhow, for a beautiful loser like me. This is reality now. *Et in Arcadia Ego*.'

John accepted this verdict and, when the time came, left feeling refreshed, if in some part relieved. He loved this woman, he realized, though on some level both knew that there was pretence involved. 'Brother-sister incest only works for a time,' Booby remarked when he asked if she wanted him to stay. He had asked this *pro forma*, to let her know he would if she needed. In the back of his mind was Margot's comment about Booby's flirtation with suicide, though by this point she seemed more squared away than anyone else in the case. In fact, it was himself that John felt sorry for on the day he left the bright spaces of 'darkest France' to return to the chiaroscuro and grime of the September city.

He padded around aimless through Carine's and my flat. We'd been gone for so long that our paintings and books no longer evoked youthful spirits for him. Stale solitude had crept in. Why hadn't he stayed in the sun and aesthetical *dolce far niente* of the south? What was of equivalence here? The Proms were finished; programmes on Radio 3 lacked the excitement of those live evenings with their ebullient crowds; my mermaid stories had been read and read over; and now he fell into a funk. The lure of London – urban fairy tale indeed! As *Les Nuits d'Été* played on a CD, John spooned out existence to imaginative rhythms that had no relation to where he was. It was in such a mood that on the technical last day of summer he made his way over the Park:

Nature was going wild again. Wind howled in the leaves trying to dash them off, while they, in the last stages of greenness, hung tight and, twisting, fought back. So he described it to me in one of those letters unsent. Zephyr was alive, hurrying clouds across skies painted Cerulean blue. Newspapers flew out of the way of his trainers as he fought his way up Notting Hill. The same tumbleweed surrogates swirled round his legs as he descended Portobello Road and blew past a notional black-boy marking the Wingfield tethering-place.

The window-well entrance seemed more covered in green now. Daily rains through high summer had left clematis so overgrown that it seemed like some tropical creeper dragged up to an arctic latitude. Leafage overspilled so thickly that a stranger might have blown down to the French doors unseen, which is what John did. This provided him with an unexpected opportunity.

Never had he thought of himself as a *voyeur*, anymore than as one of those 'London bitches' Booby had alluded to. Now, however, in the light of his speculations, what was he to do on seeing Margot perched at the side of a butcherboard table gazing back at Gisela Cobb-Burton staring at her from an easychair? Was he to retreat up slippery, mossed stones? Should he have barged in as if not registering that neither could have welcomed a third, and certainly not one who was male? From where he stood, John observed an intimacy which seemed to confirm what Marcus had said. Part of it was conveyed by Gisela's posture: not sitting so much as sprawling, with the cuffs of pleated trousers hoiked up. She'd doffed her hat (a straw one this time) and was busy combing hair pomaded in a style John hadn't seen since teenage. The whole image was *macho*, suggesting someone cocksure, or pretending to be. Nor was Margot her usual persona in response. Shrunken, reduced, the playwright seemed to have got lost in a hard, human self-searching, reminding John of his daughter in awkward teenage trying to express feelings she could not quite comprehend and fearing that, out of timidity, she never would. Nor was that all, though it shocked him enough. The doors being open (one banged in the wind), he could hear if he wanted what was being said in the hollow the well made. One or two steps would take him as near as if he'd been standing by the Aga; only here they couldn't see him because of foliage.

Well, John stepped. If he were going to be in a Gothic drama, so be it. He was in London again for better or worse. Besides, he was enough of a believer in Fate or whatever to imagine some higher intention half-propelling him.

'But I won't let you stop there!' the woman was saying. (Her voice had a brusque clip of accent he knew now to be German.) 'You have to go back and back again. Why did the boy die? Why did he have to? It wasn't you who were at cause, no matter what you say; it's just your maternal vanity to think so. You know why he died really: you know who killed him; and it's just a ploy for attention to expect the rest of the world to admire you for wearing a hairshirt forever.'

If this sounded rough, Margot's reply was silken: 'I've got your point, thanks; it's not necessary to go on. There's something sadistic about forcing one back to the experience again and again.'

'Lady W,' breezed the other (and there was a range of upward-downward nerviness to her tone), 'forgive me for sounding what your husband might call a philistine or some other one of his deprecations; but you know as well as I do how essential it is for you to work through these Engrams until you get Clear. You know how hard it was to write that play in the first place. You know how hard it's going to be to start another – you've just been complaining to me about it. Beseeching might be a better description.'

'But I haven't asked you to obsess me.'

'I intend to press your Buttons till you've got to the point where you can't avoid full acceptance of the facts and adjust yourself to realizing that it doesn't matter after all.'

'But it does!'

'No it doesn't. He would have died anyway. You call it the Will of God; I call it medical fact. Either way it doesn't make a flea's flight worth of difference whether you'd been there or not to receive his last mortified looks.'

'You are cruel. You sound like Godfrey.'

Actually John had begun to think that, despite the accent, she sounded like some evangelical psychobabbler out of L.A..

'Your husband may be a classic Suppressive, but he isn't entirely devoid of the Reality Principle.'

Margot half-smiled. 'But I expect emotional support out of you, not the small end of the wedge.'

'Which "small end" is that?' – The synthesist seemed obscurely encouraged by this hint of levity.

'"Acceptance", "the Reality Principle" – whatever jargon you use, morality depends on making an effort. Any good vicar would tell you that. I've been right to feel guilty. I lost courage: I let Godfrey take them when I knew I shouldn't have. I deserve to be whipped.'

'Lady M, let's be clear: your son shot his brother. It isn't you fault!'

'Will you shut up? Anyone could hear! And Marcus didn't shoot him: I didn't mean that; you took it wrong. It was an accident.'

Gisela stared at her as if to confirm that she had her number. 'It's no good trying to unconfess what three sessions of Auditing have uncovered. That boy is a devil.'

'He is not!'

'All right have it your way. But don't you think it's a bit Aberrant for him to go around calling someone "Cunt-burning"?'

In a gesture John had seen once before, Margot put a hand over her mouth and began to titter like a naughty schoolgirl. All of a sudden the tension seemed to drain from her face. Air pumped into her body, her shoulders fell and before long she'd pulled herself back up into a normal, almost monarchical posture.

'You are Frau Dummkopf, dearest. Let me get you a cup of tea; then you must go. Someone's bound to come in here, and I couldn't bear them going on about us again today.' – With that she vanished into her scullery.

'You have too many people living off you, Lady W,' the synthesist said, looking elegant, chic even in her tailored tan suit as she rose, yet somehow out of place in this decadent palazzo.

'Don't be jealous,' came Margot's tones.

'I'm not jealous, damn you! If I were, I'd be mad, with the amount of attention you pay. The point is that it's pathetically Low-grade for adult sons to imagine they can live off mummy forever. It hardly helps them climb the Tone-scale. More to the point, it doesn't help *you*.'

'It is a bit of a bore sometimes. But I don't mind.'

'Yes, be blithe. Be "English"! But one day you'll see how it impedes you from becoming your Self – your true Self, which is what you must be, if you're going to write a play the world might remember.'

John hesitated no more. As the synthesist followed Margot into deeper recesses, he turned and slipped up the steps. There was no question of hanging around. He knew more than he ought to, though less than he wished; and it was both better and worse than he'd imagined. Marcus! No, the devil couldn't have been in that fair son, wastrel though he may have seemed. John couldn't think so, coming from where he did and fascinated by the kind of easy civilization that he was. The trouble here came from elsewhere: from obscure resentments and jostlings for power half-glimpsed. No mature woman was going to sell out her teenaged son because he'd called a friend 'Cunt-burning' in the ebullience of youthful sap rising.

Or was that just it?

A crack of lightning shot across plane trees and clouds dumped their contents on him as, feeling curiously unmanly, he made his way back along the Serpentine.

2.

It's one thing to write letters in your head and another to report thoughts or speeches you could never have heard. In trying to construct this narrative for me (let alone himself), John began to stumble in the gap between first and third person. Too decent to be a dramatist, he didn't seem to realize that if you concentrate on a subject hard enough you can bring his or her inner life as close to your own fantasies as if you'd never stopped hiding behind a lush fall of clematis. You can hear someone's voice as if she's never stopped speaking; or if you can't, you can at least work on someone else till you get filled in. John in short was not quite the intriguer his fascination called for. I had to go to others for details; and knowing them all as I do (or did), the *dénouement* became almost too easy for a writer-*manqué* to foresee.

It began to unfold the next time he made the pilgrimage to Ladbroke Grove – that is, the day the axe fell on Marcus.

Autumn had advanced; leaves had left the trees; the window-well was naked in comparison to when he'd been seduced into 'playing Polonius behind the arras', as he described it to Margot. And maybe it was because of this barrenness in nature that, having wound up to her conservatory, he again fell into confessional mode.

'You should've come in, dearest. I've mentioned you to the Goose.

She's prickly about rivals, but I think you'd find her quite intriguing.'

Rivals? Before John had a chance to ask what she meant, Margot had straightened her jumper over her bust and added:

'Anyhow, I'm glad you've admitted it now. It must have weighed on you, the deception. One always finds truth best in the end, no?'

She stepped to the doors giving out on her garden:

'I'm cross with the Goose, as it happens. She's been helping me over this business of Christian, but I'm not sure it's not making things worse. She says I must drop it, and we all know how dwelling on the dead can vampirize. Too much grief makes one ruddy useless for life; it *is* a form of mania. On the other hand, to carry on cheerfully to the opposite view – that there's no value in brooding over it – just obliterates any chance for what your friend Tony might call "epiphany". It trades the rich matter of sorrow for what may sound like good sense, but in the end may be sheer nihilism.'

John felt chastened, uplifted, reproved. Here was a spirit truly worthy of the attention it asked for. Why had he doubted her?

'Liberation,' she said, 'is the flag this flies under. Gisela is a throwback to the '60s, like your dear self. One can do as one pleases; she'll be there to confess to. Only *mea culpa* won't be the end of it, nor even the kind of unspoken decision to keep to the middle way, which is what one gets out of normal confession to friends. No, the Goose isn't content till she's made you into a demon. "A law unto yourself" is how she puts it, though I don't know why she doesn't just come out with the old black magical "Do What Thou Wilt Is the Whole of the Law", it amounts to the same thing. The girl's barmy, Marcus maintains. Completely over-the-top. I'd put her in a play if it weren't for the unwritten rule never to depict one's chums.' – She lifted the half-glasses dangling amid pearls and inspected her guest: 'So what've you been up to? We've missed you. Where been?'

John could think of nothing to relate but his own little aria on 'darkest France'. So he went on about the river, the stars and quality of light; he even described something of the bittersweet nights he had had with Marianne. Margot listened politely. When he had finished, she mused: 'Sounds idyllic. Only I don't like "abroad". And I'm not sure how I feel about dear Booby these days. Since going over there, she's no longer quite one of us.'

John was non-plussed. Could anyone be such a petty chauvinist as to drop an old friend for crossing the Channel?

'Gisela has a cottage in Bathshire,' she added, shifting tack. 'Lord Frome's estate. Wants me for the weekend. Think I should go?'

It seemed for a moment as if she had to prove something: that she too could go to exotic places. Or was it just that she was not so free of her 'demon' as the previous speech had implied?

'Does she really have such a hold on you?' John surprised himself by asking.

'Dear man! Aren't jealous, are you?'

'Of course not!' – He recalled a similar phrase being thrown at the synthesist. 'What I mean is, I enjoy your company, but she and I are hardly "rivals" for it. Anyhow, I'm just a country boy from Manhattan.'

'Of course you are... The Goose came on the scene when we all needed help. Miranda had one child into glue-sniffing and another into hole-in-the-corner sex, and she managed to save both. Poor Oliver meanwhile had gone off his rocker, and her auditing sessions seemed the only thing to allow him to hang onto his hat. So it seemed natural that, as Christian had just died, she might be able to keep Marcus from going into some kind of self-destruct too. Do you see?'

Marcus again. 'I should have thought that boy could take care of himself. He's a little like me at that age.'

'Ah, but strength is so often on the surface... Marc was closest to Christian in many ways, though Christian was special – can't explain. Besides, it was logical that if anyone were going to have problems, it would be him. He was right there when it happened.'

This was as close as she would get to circumstances of the son's death, and it was hard for John not to want to hear more. Whose gun had gone off? What had actually killed him? He couldn't ask; she wouldn't answer except as she saw fit, even if she excused the impertinence. Truth may have been best in the end, but it was also quite relative.

'I decided to put the whole family into therapy – all except Augustus, who'd run off like a criminal to your country. But Godfrey told me to stop being "Hebrew and Hampstead"; Matthew scrunched up his forehead and went off to his girl (that boy's too placid by half); and Lucius and Johann are mere babes.'

Which left only Marcus, John was about to fill in when Godfrey strolled into the room: 'Is Margot trying to tell you about how she tried to "save the family"?' – He dropped papers onto her writing-table; on top was a paperback of a new play, *Conversion of a Catamite* by Patrick Astroid. 'What she really means is that she was trying to save herself; the rest of us have nothing the matter.' – Plopping into her swivel chair, he teetered until nearly ejected. 'Ruddy hell!'

'That's not what Gisela says,' Margot sniffed.

'O don't be tiresome, heart! The one thing good about this person called Geesella (can you imagine an Englishwoman calling herself that?) is she got you off Booby Vänder's wretched drugs. That doesn't justify her taking over our lives like some female Rasputin.'

John was embarrassed to hear the man speak so glibly about a situation which might have made him look like a fool. Picking up the paperback, he hid in its blurb.

'What about *Sudden Strangers*?' Margot challenged.

'*Sudden Strangers* was a little miracle! a minor masterpiece of myth over misery – even this philistine said so in his review.' Godfrey indicated the book in John's hand: '"Ms Wingfield wheels on the cosmos with pity and fury. Her play is so rawly revealing that one can't help but wonder if it isn't some grand referral – one might say exorcism – of a private grief".'

'Godfrey! You've memorized my notices!'

'What do you expect, heart? Do you think I'm not proud? *Sudden Strangers* is a gem; and if Tartuffe or Rasputin helped get you unblocked, fair enough. But don't let's let cure become addiction.'

She turned from freezing November in her garden to eye her husband, who was now trying to rub down the red cowlicks on his temples. For a second, John thought he spied real affection between them. As if to disguise it, Godfrey set about fussing with papers.

John held the book out. 'Have you read this?'

'Rubbish!' papa emitted. 'Another pretentious pastiche. Reviewers should stick to what they do best: reviewing.'

'"The search for redemption,"' John quoted from the blurb, '"of the mad, bad soul who brought ruin on one of the finest writers in our language." Who's it about, Bosie and Wilde?'

'Bosie indeed!'

At that point, impish Marcus strode in. 'Who is this "Bosie" you're on about, Dad? – Hello, John DuRocher.'

Margot sighed. 'O I am tired of plays by pederasts!'

Marcus continued, 'Any cash, Dad?'

Godfrey turned out the linings of his pockets. The chair teetered.

'Empty? ruddy hell. What about you, Mum? You've always got a few bob stashed around.'

This was said innocently enough, and Godfrey's response the right one. But mama for some reason lost her sang-froid:

'Go away, Marcus,' she hissed.

'Why, what's up with you? What's a "pederast" anyway? Some form of sex-maniac, like that dreadful Cunt-burning?'

Perhaps she was suffering from a hot flush, as Godfrey would later maintain. In any case, Margot launched into a persona John would have preferred not to see and attacked her son like some vixen out of Greek tragedy or an American soap-opera:

'That "dreadful" woman whom you refer to with words that shan't pass my lips might be able to help you grow into something other than a mad, bad ruin of a family yourself! When are you going to get a job, Marcus Wingfield? I can't support you out of my paperback advance; Godfrey needs that for the dry rot. Nor will I have you stealing more of my vodka.' (The boy had opened a cupboard and discovered a bottle.) 'Give me that now!'

Ensued a battle in which mother and son threw words at each other like John hadn't heard since his own teenage. The boy chuckled lightly, so good nature seemed in it; meanwhile, Godfrey acted as if all were being played out by Swahilis on some far edge of the veldt. Even so, that was that. Incidents which lead to permanent regret can seem so minor when they happen.

The boy crashed upstairs. Margot stared after him, eyes violet, nether-lip protruding in a Churchillian pout. Godfrey chortled over a line in one of his letters as if nothing out of the ordinary had happened; and perhaps little had for that household. Then Margot stepped to the phone.

'I think... I shall call... Marianne,' she breathed, as if speaking a foreign language.

Godfrey blurted something about 'The Priceless Proze', but hardly had the phrase passed his lips before she'd slammed down the receiver and was yelling:

'Marcus Wingfield, you get off the line this instant! – He's talking to Gus, in New York... Marcus Wingfield! You get off my phone, or you can bloody well get out of this house and find a place of your own at nearly eighteen years old!'

John would have liked to offer the boy shelter. But just then his daughter had run away from her mom in New York and come to occupy the spare room in Carine's and my flat; so he had his hands full taking her to the V & A, the Natural History Museum and other places a dutiful parent could think of to amuse a teenaged girl in the great city. Mostly she holed up in a multi-coloured mélange of clothes and cosmetics, like some forest creature strewing leaves at the mouth of her cave to forewarn of predators. Before long a barrage of transatlantic phonecalls repaired whatever ructions had gone on back home, and she began to fuss about a return-ticket. By then, however, Marcus was well into his wanderings across the wintry city.

Through Godfrey, he acquired a berth in a houseboat belonging to the New Age entrepreneur, Teddy Bayer, a superficial mate from papa's days of doling out largesse at the Hong Kong and Macao Bank. Rashly, Bayer had married a third wife less than half his age; when this golddigger absconded with a currency-trader in puce braces, he was more broken up than the world knew; so Marcus's presence was a half-welcome restraint on temptation to execute a Robert Maxwell finis. All for a time was concordant. Then one midnight the lad stumbled back to the million-pound floating-palace three sheets to the wind and, mistaking the great man's cabin for a 'loo (Bayer had flown to Paris that morning in a hot-air balloon), deposited the contents of his oesophagus into a monogrammed pillow-case. When this was discovered the next afternoon by an ambitious housekeeper, the boy's days of welcome were numbered.

John heard the tale from Marcus's lips when he ran into him on the tube around Christmas. For months after, he would recall the verbal skill and hilarity with which the boy retailed his demise.

'So where're you off to now?' John asked once he'd finished.

Marcus had a bag with him. 'Yugoslavia,' he said.

'Yugoslavia?!' – This was 1991 or so.

A school-friend, he explained, had tipped him off that there was 'some good swag' to be had out there.

'In Yugoslavia?' John chided. 'Does your mother know?'

'What, about the swag? Shouldn't've thought so.'

'No, that you're going to that part of the world.'

'You mean because of the war? Don't worry, mate: Ahmed says if it really lets rip, we'll get rich. Lotsa loot to be made on guns.'

Thus son Marcus. His irises glistened amid whites already yellowed by years of 'fun' on hashish and brown ale; and John thanked his stars that he hadn't let fantasy run amok and set the boy up with his daughter. This said, he fretted to think of one so young becoming a gun-runner or something. But then Booby let drop that such activities were not unheard-of among male Wingfields; and by the time the crocuses were poking their heads up in Kensington Gardens, Margot was speculating that Marc had gone missing delivering humanitarian aid outside of Osijek. Around June, she expressed fears he might be dead – Oliver Murrie had had 'a vision', and Miranda's cousin had 'done the same thing', so there seemed a kind of wacky corroboration for it. In the air too hung an odd implication that such a finis might not be inapt: to disappear as a hero was, after all, no less than had happened to the flower of British youth in the still-nostalgic horror of the Great War.

This macabre spin gave John more pause to think. During a summer month in Connecticut trying to resurrect his marriage, he kept seeing Margot writhing in pain. He could hardly blame her for a row over the phone: such things went on in American families all the time; nor as the only one to have seen it was he keen to remember. She had regretted her words almost as they'd come, Margot claimed once he got back to London. She'd even given Gisela 'a right ticking off' for having 'pressured' her into them.

John accepted this. At the same time he was shocked to find that the woman had scarcely altered her régime. Possession can hold fast even when the gods tell against it – hadn't his time with his ex-wife underlined that? In this case Margot couldn't, or wouldn't, get rid of her other 'devil'. Indeed, to our hero's quickening bemusement the attachment seemed to be becoming exclusive.

But now it is time to leave John to his Strether-like fabulations and look at this tale from the other outsider's point of view. He himself couldn't, not knowing the 'witch'. I myself could, though for reasons having to do with my own marriage I'd never told him about my affair with her; and here is not the place to spill those beans. Suffice it to say that I had once known Gisela well enough that there was little I couldn't feel of what was going on inside her as she drove her hand-me-down Jaguar in the M4…

It was late summer by then, cold and drizzling in England, as that season there often is. But Gisela was not thinking about the weather. Her mind was churning with mild indigestion. What she'd read in the morning papers had been too rich. She'd never intended for things to go so far so quickly. A few mild, approving reviews would have been enough. Praise such as Margot's new play was getting threatened to be counterproductive.

Also disturbing was the presence of Marcus. The boy's pranksterish grace informed every scene, even the title *Jester in Flame*. The piece was hardly the clearing of old Engrams Gisela had encouraged; it was a demonstration of Godfrey's *mot* that 'artists only kill the things they love in order to glorify them'. She, Gisela, had audited her, Margot, to become her own woman. Margot for her part appeared through this new work to be reducing herself even more into an instrument to evoke spirits of departed progeny.

Sudden Strangers had been about Christian, but this one was worse. Anyhow, it was too good. The first play had had art, but this one had magic – everyone said so. Margot was theatrical London's newcomer no longer. The missing son had danced in to allow her to 'raise perception to new spheres', as one reviewer had put it:

> This is the kind of work that breaks forth only once, as if inadvertently, from an Athena's skull. It is a play in which all elements come to life, as palpable as Shakespeare's fairies. Indeed, it might be said that Ms Wingfield's new offering is a one-man Midsummer Night's Dream and at the same time a requiem masque.

Gisela unbuttoned her collar – terribly muggy, the day. She cranked down a window – danger was that extravagant praise would allow Margot to slide back down the Tone-scale to where she had been after the elder son's death. Godfrey would reclaim her. He was there already in the play's scabrous wit – Margot needed that clearly, if only to set Reactive Mind against. As to plot? Impossible for her to have come up with anything so smooth on her own. Another mind was at work there; nor was it that of her pal John DuRocher, as she'd tried to maintain. That was a Withhold if ever there was one: the American was neither so skilled nor 'a kind of male muse in some way'.

No, Godfrey was At Cause here. And skrying the astral plane for a reason, Gisela worked to envision what held the two together...

'Don't call me a snob, Maggo. That's bloody unfair. Especially given that I'm the only grandson of my grandmother not to have been awarded a gong.'

This was at lunch, an hour later. Gisela had persuaded Margot to set the event up: whether as background, cover or a therapeutic forcing of 'Engrams', it seemed the logical next step. But papa was happily subverting proceedings with genial outrageousness.

John DuRocher sat pacifically watching: he was a fixture at their table more and more since Marcus decamped. Pure-souled Matthew had gone off with his girl as per norm; the younger boys escaped as soon as mama allowed. Margot herself sat sipping and serving. Confrontation of her therapist with her husband seemed to strike her as half-amusement, half-torture.

'Anyhow,' Godfrey added, 'how could I be a snob? Look who I married!' – He laughed like a wicked child.

'Careful, dearest.'

'But it's true! My mother wanted me to marry an heiress. What good mother doesn't? That's why I can't see why you're so cross with Matthew, besotted with a Jew.'

'That's a religious distinction, not class.'

'O religion, heart! It's all pounds and pence. Jews have money, the ones who don't pretend to be mind-merchants anyway. Let Matthew marry her if she'll have him. He'll do much better than falling in love with some beautiful no one from nowhere who has no more to offer than a promise of bohemian talent.'

This was a swipe at Margot's status as art-student when they'd met. The mind-merchant slur was for Gisela, though she wasn't Jewish: Cohn-Burton was a partly marital, partly professional name, as a previous bout of conversational roughhouse had established.

'Anyhow, a Jew is preferable to an "Anglo-Catholic". Look at us: we had so many children so quickly it was impossible to educate one properly. And when there's no educated tone around the place, look what happens: you end up giving Sunday lunch to ruddy Americans and Ruritanian "synthesists", what!'

He guffawed; Margot frowned; John grinned in acknowledgement for having been let into the joke. Gisela alone seemed not to get it. In the first place, Margot was no more Catholic than she was, having taken up the C of E at about the same time that she, Gisela, had converted to New Age nostrums. In the second, as she pointed out once the men had cleared off, this was not family life; it was 'emotional blood sport'.

Margot continued to sip at the bubbly John had brought. 'Godfrey's always been cross that, as his mother put it, when the wife fails to bring further status by birth, the offspring can't be expected to do so by breeding.'

'Complacency,' Gisela said, 'may seem high on the Tone-scale to you; but it's the small end of the wedge.'

'Complacency, dearest, may be survival. Anyhow, I'm only imitating his solution. He's caught in a social limbo he wouldn't have chosen, poor man. So like a sensible chap, he pretends he chose it.'

'Well, didn't he?'

Somewhat pressed, Margot knew she could be cruel if too candid. 'Shall we go somewhere else? Anyone might come back here, and I don't want them interrupting us now...'

They passed through to the conservatory but didn't stop there. Casting an eye at grey day in the garden, Margot put a hand on the spiral and wound up.

Two shapely ankles preceded Gisela's eyes. Stockings, a full skirt and short, high-collared jacket – the playwright's costume was well above standard, she noted and took pride. Hadn't she been the one who'd advised looking smart whether one felt so or not?

'You got him through sex,' she said, trying to induce a Rock-Slam once they'd reached the bedroom antechamber.

Margot gazed to the far side of her four-poster. Wet leaves had stuck to a window pane there. 'How do you mean?'

Gisela flopped under dirty-nappied de Sade. 'You won him through sex and held him through childbirth: it's an old tale. A good marriage, on the surface: girl from obscure background obtains class, cultivation and a modicum of cash.'

Throwing a leg over the settee, she half-rued the Godfreyesque callousness in her tone; also a certain bitchery recycled from Miranda. But with someone like Margot, you had to be At Cause: find the Buttons and flatten them.

'Your husband may be eccentric, but he's too conventional not to stand by you. Which means that, whatever the vagaries of your Thetanic force, you're secure in the material dimensions of Matter-Energy-Space-and-Time. A *modus vivendi*, as he might put it, obtains. Are you going to ignore me?'

To Margot, of course, this was a rehearsal of matters she knew better than anyone else. Gathering her skirts, she sat on the hard chair which was the one other piece of furniture in that space. 'You are a devil, aren't you? I believe at this moment I hate you.'

Gisela's pulse quickened. 'No you don't. You don't care enough yet. You hate yourself, your marriage, your husband, this house maybe, but little outside of that. Opportunists only really hate whatever binds them to their opportunities.'

'Does that mean you're going to hate me one day?'

She shot this back with such smooth rapidity that the synthesist's adrenalin jumped. 'O don't play Godfrey-suppressive with me, "Maggo". You complain; you feel cheated; you run to me for help. Sure, I've seen too many dysfunctional marriages to believe every passage of whinging I hear. Still, I have a pretty good idea where the truth lies among the Withholds.'

There was something obscure here, and something ingratiating; and Gisela took pleasure on seeing how it encouraged Margot to fade inwards. Pitching her voice low, almost to a whisper, she would make her words soothe now, even stultify, to bring on a state of Uncausing:

'Does Godfrey realize?'

'Does he realize whot?'

Sometimes a subject could pretend nothing was happening at this stage – a typical Pre-Clear reaction before the Engrams were wiped.

'If you're speaking of our sessions, he's hardly bothered. Look where he is at the moment.'

'Playing chess?'

'Or bridge, or backgammon. He comes home demanding forms of household and marriage. But so long as they're kept up at least superficially, nothing would persuade him to utter a peep.'

This was annoying. The woman clung to rationality too much.

'Complacency is his weapon. He simply, at some level, just doesn't care. Your presence hasn't made a dent in his armour, for instance. His response when one would quite fancy a bit of uxorious angst is to shut himself up here and re-read Molière.'

Gisela determined to work with the eyes. Sunlight was snaking in through those wet leaves; she could feel it radiating into her face. 'You have the most mesmerizing eyes,' Margot had let slip in a previous session. So now she let them burn into the woman's features, making them come into focus, then fracture into polymorphous abstraction as if in a Cubist painting.

'Does he have any idea what goes on between us?' she repeated.

Margot lifted the half-glasses dangling in pearls.

'Doesn't he know?' she insisted, increasing the hypnotic force, as she believed, through deliberate huskiness.

'Everyone speculates; nobody knows – unless the bloody house is bugged. For Godfrey, "Tartuffe" – that is you, dearest – is simply another of my "lunatics".'

Nothing in this suggested a state of Uncausing. If she hadn't known better, Gisela might've imagined Margot to be sending her up. As it was, she decided to alter the current. Lifting the bottle they'd brought upstairs with them, she refilled both glasses:

'Doesn't it make you mad?'

'Hopping furious! I utterly resent his indifference, as he calls it. Because it's not indifference, but one-ups-manship. Power, pride: all of them have it – this beastly code: a public-school version of what John DuRocher tells me his Americans aped in Hemingway. Of course I detest it; sneer at it; use that technique you taught me – Bull-baiting, whatever. But he just laughs and tells me to stop being daft.'

She could relax now: the woman was off. All that was required was to coax her up the Tone-scale in the direction she was already headed: from Numbness to Introversion to Hysteria and (if they got lucky today) Erosion, Dispersal and Dissociation.

'You heard it down there at lunch. One way or another you tried to undercut every verbal game he played, and what was his reaction? to make a joke in French and laugh at himself till John had to laugh at the laugh; or to imply that discussion was beneath him, because you didn't go to Balliol. O, I detest the conceited little man! To stay with him, to talk to him, is masochistic – I can't think why I bother. He is a sadist. Look at yourself: you attack, he turns genial – absolutely refuses to take you any more seriously than Miranda with her Qliptoth or Diplock or whatever she calls it, or Booby when she took up trepanning after the Sacred Sec became a bore.'

Gisela wore a perfectly indulgent smile now, but there was unease beneath. Couldn't Margot be trying to build her up only to knock her down? Mightn't she be playing the classic Unliberee's trick of pretending to show interest in the Process while waiting to dismiss it as crackpot? The essential thing here was to hold one's own mask in place while encouraging the other to bore further inwards.

Margot's half-glasses were poised with one earpiece to lips. Distraction had deepened the shadows around those eyes. Actually, she looked very compelling today – so much so that Gisela might have taken alarm. Because being At Cause here was absolutely crucial. An aberrant subject could so easily Return the Current and wreak havoc on an unwary Auditor. Nor was Margot an ordinary subject – hadn't Oliver and Miranda had already warned her of that? What would she do if, for instance, she induced *her* to dive into those wells? What would she find there? Godfreyesque mockery? an existential black hole? some pandaemoniac wail in a nightmare, velvet and suffocating, like at the end of so many Engrammic spirals? One could become quite lost in this kind of psyche, Gisela knew. Still, she hadn't studied Therapeutic Psychodynamics all these years to miss when a subject was trying to Project on her. The trouble with Margot was that she came from a culture which tended to treat such processes as a joke. Well, maybe they were on some level: the level of the Godfrey Wingfields of this world. On a further plane, though, there was much more. Hadn't Gisela already located the Buttons and fingered the soft spots? Hadn't she sensed where an Auditor would have to slip in if she were going to rescue the bruised Thetan and heal the damage at core? And what injury lay there, coiled in blackness? a rancour like her own? Would Margot turn out to be her twin at long last? Were Godfrey's dismissals of her as Tartuffe or whatever not just a mirror-image of his attempts to set his wife beyond the pale, with his innuendoes about *her* origins, religion and friends? Yes, Gisela knew so, or thought she did. She knew too that if Margot were to give herself over, it would be as much out of rebellion against *him* as affirmation of her. Even so she longed for it, that halcyon moment. And how to grab it – how to grab that part of the woman she already held onto and drag the rest towards her – was the point of these efforts.

'Playwrighting,' she murmured, as if from a dream, 'takes genius, doesn't it, milady? And genius – we've discussed this enough – must be wilful, self-centred, ruthless. Don't you agree?'

For a flash, she glimpsed her own image descending. In Margot's eyes, she became some autodidactic, *mittel*-European version of the chequebook Christians John had been complaining about at lunch. 'Change, complication, tireless churning-up' – weren't these what she longed to evoke out of Margot as well? these 'stimulants to creativity and chaos' to force her out of a complacent, murkily all-accepting pose? to make her an apostle of the New Creed – *her* revolutionary approach to behaviour and forces: all things Godfrey had dismissed with learned quips from Voltaire?... Now as the look softened, she seemed to be succeeding: to be drawing her back, concentrating her enough, moving her towards the edge of that promontory from which they would leap out, to emerge on the other side as it were – those sunny uplands where the two of them could discover the miserably tramped-upon, yet indefeasible spirit at the base of their souls. Yet once there, what? be forced to fly off and wail from some crag? vilified as their kind always was and, by conspiracy, ignored? Or?

'Don't you, my lady?'

'Sorry, dearest?'

'Don't you agree?'

'Don't I agree about whot?'

So: she'd been dreaming as well; out on the plateau of Uncausing.

'About playwrighting and genius. Did you lapse again? I thought you'd mastered your Concentration Techniques.'

But Margot was gone now, the Magic Circle broken, her psyche snapping back. Rattles through the floorboards: footfalls, conversation... From the main stairwell John's reedy voice rose:

'Ah. We thought you might be here.'

'Tell 'em I'm napping,' chorused Godfrey below.

''allo, dearest,' Margot crooned as the American came in. 'Did you beat him this time? Sit down and tell Gisela about whether playwrighting takes genius – that's whot we're on about. You know something about putting words to papier, *n'est-ce pas*?'

Gisela buttoned her collar, though she'd gone from cool to hot on the spot. In fact, if her complexion hadn't been obscured by a *de rigueur* German tan, John might have noticed her blushing as she removed her leg to free him a seat.

'I'm hardly going to be drawn on that,' he grinned. 'You'll only twit me for the "Henry James act" you say may spoil my perfection.'

'I wouldn't dare say anything so intelligent-sounding.'

'Maybe it's my fate: expatriate in a frock-coat – quintessence of the civilized White European male, only not all white, nor quite with Godfrey's guile.'

'Beat you again, did he?'

Gisela felt herself tremble. The atmosphere shattered, she stood.

'Forget the frock-coat, dearest. I much prefer you in your old jeans-jacket.'

'That's only because you want to minimize me. Anyhow, I thought you were fed-up with "vestiges of the '60s".'

Gisela slipped into the spiral. 'You're not portly enough for James,' Margot wittered on, as if oblivious. 'Besides, I get so fed up with all that business of pigeons in St Mark's Square.'

'No, you don't. You know as well as I do that he's still the standard for our sort of thing.'

'What sort of thing's that?'

'By the way, d'I tell that Booby'd gone down there?'

'Down where?'

'To Venice, of course.'

And so on.

As Margot continued with this trivia, Gisela wound down to the conservatory. Pale as ectoplasm behind her tan, she went through the kitchen, indigestion returning. She could hardly fall in with the covering ruse, that she and John 'get together' ('You have such things in common, my two dearests!') She knew that Margot would giggle over this later, and duplicity was inevitable in the circumstance. Still, a sense of miscalculation nagged at her as she sped her Jaguar back to the west. The truth was that the playwright had come to dominate her psyche. Ever since she'd taken up her cause on the women's page of *The Guardian*, Margot had become the conquest the synthesist *had* to make to be regarded as serious in this foreign world she had entered. Otherwise she was liable to be marginalized forever into what a judge had once described as 'at best a fascinating fraud'.

Gisela's hideaway in the West Country was a settlement from her period as chief wifelet to Lord Frome. She'd tried to get more through a palimony suit, but this had proved still-born. Frome may have been eccentric, but he was even more a part of the Establishment than Godfrey Wingfield or Miranda's ex-husband; nor were his lawyers about to let him be deprived of part of the family entail by a German attempting an American-style legal stunt. Gisela had been reminded quite smartly just how little she mattered in her adopted country. Even her good works as a prison visitor were called into question; and if it hadn't been for that article of Margot's on her in *The Guardian*, her name in England might have been mud.

Gisela had first come to London in the 1980s with her Czech husband Oskar, who at that time was posing as a pop impresario.

London had been on her agenda since the late 1970s when she'd set aside Oskar for Oliver Murrie, an affair which had come to grief in part because of a passade with me – an episode which must remain veiled. Oliver went back to England and his friendship with Margot, who at that time was a young mother and aspiring literary agent. I came back too, my affair with Gisela like his having taken place in Munich, where she hailed from. There I married my darling Carine, who owned the flat John DuRocher was now living in.

Oliver had had his fifteen minutes of fame as an artist, partly and ironically through Godfrey's network. Gisela, feeling jilted, went back to Oskar, who had moved on to Paris and changed his name to Cohn. (Though not Jewish, Oskar believed like many of his type that, with the demise of Marxism, an L.A./New York brand of hustling was the way to get on.) Together the Cohn-Burtons had returned to London for a one-man show of Ollie's, backed by Carine's family, who were actual Jews with a disinterested penchant for culture. Many of the paintings featured Gisela's teenaged daughter as model. (Yes, she had a daughter, which is why she'd married Oskar in the first place.) But it was not images of Magdalena that Gisela had returned to London for: she had had enough of that difficult girl back in Munich. (Magdalena's flirtations to annoy *Mutti* were one cause of Gisela's affair with me, thus her break-up with Ollie.) No, the main reason she'd come was to see for herself this milieu which had produced two Anglo-Saxon males who had loved her and left her. In particular, she wanted to lay eyes on Margot Wingfield, whom Oliver had adored and I had mentioned too much. What did this English goddess, or demon, have that other women had not?

Shortly after arrival, Oskar had decamped back to Paris; then, as the Wall came down, to his native Prague. Oliver ran off with Magdalena to Italy; she became pregnant, again to spite Mum; but the baby had died – victim of a diet of green fruit, according to Margot – and Magdalena ran off with a rake of her generation. The art market collapsed, and the unstable Oliver's real troubles began. Returning to London a final time, he found Margot now fully re-ensconced in her marriage and so embarked on his adultery with Miranda Cravin, in part pushed by his faithless beloved. John DuRocher came on the scene; Carine and I left for the States; Miranda's husband took the route of Prince Charles dumping Diana; and Christian Wingfield was shot. All of which brings us nearly to date.

Gisela had met Lord Frome at that one-man show of Ollie's. Having a notion that he wanted a pan-EC harem, the hippy Bluebeard had been eager to add a Bavarian Erda to the Italians, Celts, Greeks and what-have-yous who filled his palazzo in Bathshire. To Gisela, the liaison had seemed propitious in a getting-to-know-the-English sort of way; and over the antics of Frome's unruly *ménage*, she had come to exercize a head-of-harem kind of authority. When milord had replaced her after six months with a torch-singer from Vilnius, she nonetheless stuck around to provide 'counselling' for the group out of the hodgepodge of ideas from Steiner to Scientology she'd been dabbling in since the 1960s.

Gisela's Germanic 'green' passion for things alternative fit in quite well with an indigenous culture based on vaguely 'magical', Arthurian lore. Her New Age ways of 'seeing' were complemented by its mixture of herbs and roots and visions that come from staring at open fires on hashish rather than suburban telly. To say that she became a 'witch of the west' would be slander, though Miranda grew fond of describing her thus. Miranda in fact had more interest in weird practices, some of which she'd picked up from Oliver Murrie, with whom she still consorted when he was not being arrested for breaking into her house. Gisela, by contrast, was rather bourgeois. Psychosynthesis, as she called what she practised (without certification of course), was really less occult than mainstream in the New Age mélange. But by the time she'd become friendly with Margot (introduced by Miranda, following Christian's death), she'd lived in the wilds long enough to proclaim that 'true civilization' could not be defined in terms of an Aberrant venue like London; that Higher-Tone knowledge dwelt in the Celtic places; that to get the Big World to recognize it should be part of one's mission in general.

That Gisela had a mission in general was a result of both background and history. Having lost or abandoned her family and roots, she had crystallized on an urge which seemed almost racial for a spirit the latter half of whose surname had been only superficially anglicized. To be a Truth-Sayer, a Transvaluer of Values, was what she lived for, adopting phrases from Nietzsche, whose works were cited in New Age *grimoires* she read, though without making clear what the philosopher actually meant. 'Bloody ridiculous in this day and age,' the Godfrey Wingfields might say; but they always sneered at Truth with their laws of gender and tribe – hadn't Oliver said so, and wasn't he a classic refugee from the type? Thus it was principally through the women, the Mirandas and Margots who'd married out of class and were disgruntled, that 'true progress' could be made.

Miranda had more or less explained this to Gisela when introducing her to Margot. 'Go for it!' the erstwhile Rose had added. 'She's someone who might make a difference for you. She's about to go over the top.'

What Miranda had meant (and her motives were doubtless tainted by her own fall from grace) would provide several paragraphs of rumination which we can't indulge in here. Suffice it to say that Gisela did 'go for' Godfrey's wife, who had once been Oliver's lover too. And she did succeed, up to a point – that is, captured the lady sufficiently to lead her through two plays, as she saw it, and make her rely on her 'sessions'. But then had come this plateau: Margot had too much going for her suddenly, and Gisela did not know where she stood.

'Invite her out to your cottage,' Miranda advised on the phone, pleased to play the Invisible Mover. 'Godfrey's bound to get out of his pram if you seduce her from London. Besides, you can work on her more easily there.'

Gisela had never credited Miranda with much insight. The fallen wife of a lord was a shadowy presence with indistinct aura who could only have reseduced Oliver Murrie, for instance, once that erstwhile lover of all three women had become down-and-out. Accordingly, she was not sceptical when the erstwhile Rose added:

'Who knows? you might even get something on her. Something to influence her in your direction without doing you lots of harm.'

Guilelessly, the synthesist answered: 'I have something on her already – on one of her sons, that is. But I doubt that blackmail is the way to work this.'

'I see. Well, I guess you know what you're doing. All anyone who likes you worries about is whether you're successful. Right?'

Living alone and in a foreign country, Gisela was not always attuned to native irony. 'Do you want to come too?' she asked, softening.

'Come to what?'

'To the cottage, with Margot. Make it a threesome.'

This was meant to sound jolly. There even followed some joke about the witches in *Macbeth*, to which Miranda appended something distasteful about 'cock-sisters'. But what really underlay Gisela's invitation was nervousness that she might not be able to entertain the playwright on her own.

Miranda's retort was piquant, implying its own subtext: 'Thanks awfully. But I'll let you get on with it. Two's company and all that. Know what I mean?'

Gisela did not pause to examine this. She would have time to rake through all motives later on, during her 'magical retreat'. For now she concentrated on how to make her Lady accept the invitation, which was not straightforward. Another September brought no abatement in the playwright's lionization, and by the time she was nominated for a Drama Critic's Award in October Margot could hardly be raised on the phone. Gisela mailed a card with a picture of a rustic idyll on it; no reply came, and she might've plummeted right down the Tone-Scale herself. But lionization has its frustrations, and by the week before Halloween Margot was less flattered than harassed by the new attention on her. Miranda phoned Gisela to report as much; simultaneously she urged her to 'try again'. Nothing if not persistent, the synthesist reoffered refuge. This time it was not refused.

She trimmed hedges, strimmed cow-parsley, put bowls of flowers in her deep window-wells. Squatting in a tomato-patch, she became 'nothing but a big bum in a pair of overalls', she would tell Margot in a phrase which the playwright would recycle with genuine affection. Some of these activities were new for the non-English woman, but Gisela felt inspired. Trapped in the martyrdoms of motherhood and wifedom, her Great Lady needed an ally to offer escape. Thus she knelt on the stone floor of her dark cottage kitchen and washed it clean as a pin. Meanwhile, worrying that the guest might imagine that, apart from psychodynamics, she was ignorant, she drove into Bath and bought a book on contemporary theatre to swot up on the others on the short-list. This year they included Smedley Anis for a third time, Eileen Moloch for a second, Patrick Astroid, a Fijian feminist who'd written a piece about mixed bathhouses in W2 and a Zimbabwean Jew who had discovered that 'there's no business like Shoah business'.

At the last moment, Margot phoned from London to say that Matthew wanted his girl's parents to come for Sunday lunch and she couldn't get away. 'You need this more than your son needs that,' Gisela retorted, feeling a rush of disappointment so sharp that she could hardly suppress an intimation of threat. 'You have to get out of that Suppressive city. Besides, there's almost a month of sessions you've missed – you'll slide back into all your old Engrams.'

She might've blown it then. Fortunately, it seemed that Margot needed only to be reassured she was wanted. Thus the next Friday she stepped off a train at Bath Spa, dressed entirely incongruously for the country in a trouser-suit of purple silk.

'Well, Lady W! We certainly are flattered to have such a presence arrive in our quiet corner of the world.'

'*We*?' – Momentarily the playwright was assaulted by visions of being shown to a crowd, as sometimes happened now in London.

'Don't worry: it's only me, myself and I,' Gisela awkwardly joked. 'I was just saying to Miranda the other day on the phone: it truly represents a stage in arrival – someone we know who's name is linked with the famous and influential.'

Margot smiled. Murmuring appropriate words about the abbey, she let herself be wound through a tortuous one-way system out of town. As they hit the high road, Gisela began to disgorge her new erudition about the Critics' Award. With studied insouciance, the playwright observed: 'I can't think why they nominated me. Next week I'm scheduled to be interviewed by CTV. In the Middle Ages, one was cut down by plague. Nowadays we undergo trial by meedjah.'

This was all the synthesist needed. 'Never mind that! You're here now and you've come at the right time. St Martin's summer is meant to last all week. Just change into some overalls and listen to the hay being mown.'

'Overalls?'

It did seem incongruous. But while her hostess reverted to *frau* of *haus und garten*, the 'great lady' from London lolled in a wicker chair under a Virginia Woolf hat, script in hand. This soon discarded, she let her mind wander among clouds in a daydream. The skies gave impressions out of 'Tintern Abbey'; and afternoon passed as smooth as the high, hopeful days of a young bride's first pregnancy.

Evening found Margot sitting at the kitchen table watching flickers in a fire while Gisela cooked cassoulet, poured cider and chatted about mundane things. All was so soothing that the guest had almost to be carried to bed. Figuratively tucked in, she slept like a happy child while the hostess stared through her own casement window wondering how the weekend might be made as perfect as a harvest moon shining down on her handsewn quilt.

It wasn't until Sunday morning that the first off-note sounded. Rather obscurely over breakfast Margot let drop that she felt a danger that, if they didn't watch out, they might develop a 'perverse will' between them. 'We must avoid this,' she added. 'The last thing one needs is what Miranda calls some "diabolical spirit" being evoked, whatever benefit it may have for my work.'

This mini-speech, also sounding rehearsed, jarred against the rustic mood Gisela had sought to create. Nor as she served muffins could she believe that it was Margot's true opinion. 'O let's not have any of that exhausting city-talk here. The point of a weekend in the country is surely to escape and relax.'

Margot agreed, as politeness required. By evening, however, she was beginning to show signs of being terminally bored. One of these was to ruminate on a subject she might've derided as vulgar in most other venues: 'What sort of image did you think one ought to adopt to impress the hoi-polloi on TV?' she wondered over her hostess's home-made barley-soup.

Inwardly, Gisela sighed. Still, she had done her homework, hadn't she? So after bowls were cleared, she brought out a book of photos of literary ladies to help the playwright decide on hair style: 'Is it to be on top in a soft knot like Edith Wharton; pulled back severe like Simone de Beauvoir; or cut and waved like this – Colette, my favourite. So "little cabbage", as *Mutti* used to say.'

Margot tittered. Taking this as encouragement, Gisela began to fuss with her yellow-grey hair. It was a perfectly natural gesture and entirely without subtext – hadn't she done the same with wifelets of Frome's countless times? Yet no sooner had her fingertips touched the playwright's skull than Margot recoiled. It was almost as if *Noli me tangere* were being spoken.

Gisela stepped back towards her pots. She covered mortification with more verbal play of a kind she was hardly adept at: lead-footed ironies and over-the-top panderings to her guest's vanity. Thus a superficial glee was reestablished, though one more appropriate to Godfrey's table or an Oxbridge common room.

'I wouldn't mind if Smedley won again,' Margot gossiped. 'He can't have many more chances, the dear… Patrick Astroid's a babe still: he'll have to wait. As to the foreigners – well, that means counting back to see if it's their turn again, doesn't it?'

'Leaving Moloch?' the hostess asked and listened for a view on this 'magical' writer, whose plays were the only ones she had seen.

'I'd be cross if Eileen got it.'

'O? I'm fascinated. You've said that none of the males can make a believable woman. Is it that she can't do a credible man?'

'She writes like a man, dearest! that's why they all praise her, the poufs! She's of the Sapphist persuasion: double gay marriage. Which is why, Godfrey says, everything becomes so trivialized in her work. Anyhow, I don't believe in her "good and evil".'

Vaguely, Gisela recalled that Moloch was noted for high moral postures. 'Too black and white for you?'

'Precisely!' the new lady of theatre pronounced.

The synthesist was fully caught up. 'What colour is evil then?' she asked as if her psychodynamics had never addressed this.

Lifting her half-glasses, Margot stared at her new friend: too much or too little had passed between them, it seemed. 'Shades of grey,' she concluded. 'That's what they say, isn't it? Neither one thing or the other. Confusion.'

Gisela did not make much of this at the time. The next week, however, she noted that Margot wore grey for her interview on TV. And later on the phone she made such heavy weather of it to Miranda that the erstwhile Rose had to repeat twice that Margot had only chosen the outfit because she had nothing else clean.

The synthesist hardly heard. 'Have you noticed when Pre-Clears are forced into public they take up the appearance they think is the most tough? It's Reactive Mind in attack. "I don't care if you don't like me; I'm pursuing my destiny-genius and, frankly, if you don't care for it, you can get stuffed!"'

'Your weekend was sort of the vicar's egg, was it?'

But Gisela had the bit between her teeth: 'It's a false attitude! What Margot's putting out, like so much of "success" up in that Suppressive citadel, is a mass of Overts. The more attention she gets, the more out of touch she becomes with what she really is, or wants to be.'

'That should be to your advantage then. If "flattening her Buttons" is still your thing.'

One of these days, Miranda reflected, Gisela was going to go right over-the-top. Hadn't she and Margot already agreed that the so-called therapies she peddled were just part of a middle-aged female's attempt to keep attention on her? Country life may have made her more physically fit than they were, but even that Green stuff couldn't hold off the savageries of Time. As to her 'psychodynamic techniques' – the 'bull-baiting', concentration exercizes and so on – hadn't they all dabbled in similar tricks for years? And wasn't her ultimate 'magical' secret – that the more lacking in clarity you are, the more effective – what every woman learned with her first seduction?

Subliminal suggestion was always best: that and inconsistency. The latter was perhaps why nothing wicked, deceitful or even careless was suggested to Miranda by Margot's appearance on TV on the night of the Award. This the synthesist came to the erstwhile Rose's house to watch. As images passed, her eyes turned into squares; and when her 'lady' appeared wearing charcoal flannel, a grey blouse and string of silver pearls, she intoned, 'Ah!' as if understanding all. 'The Woolf hairdo was surely the least risky option,' she added, murmuring, 'Very good... perfect!' so often that Miranda had to ask her to belt up.

Eileen Moloch won, of course. 'Of course' because, once it was announced, the nattering heads in the studio agreed that it had been a foregone conclusion. Wisdom is easy after the fact; the unpredictable, however, is what sticks in mind. This is why the most memorable event of the evening (had it been scripted? if so, by whom?) turned out to be when Margot tripped going down from the dais.

At this sight, Miranda's lentil soup almost rose out of Gisela's gorge. Her dear lady did not fall exactly, only enough to make viewers gasp. It was just for an instant; then she was back on her feet wearing a smile of gratitude so radiant that even the hacks and jades who made up the audience had to give her a second, spontaneous round of applause.

'Perfect!' Miranda nodded. 'She's got them to be protective of her.'

Eventually Matthew appeared at mama's side, looking strikingly handsome for a Wingfield in his tux. Godfrey being away on a quango, the eldest son remaining had been drafted in as escort. As he led Margot off stage, hand slipped through an arm, the world had a vision of Everyone's Mum.

'So lovely and cruel!' Miranda continued. 'Just look at Eileen.'

The award-winner, hair bobbed and face fleshly in the way of ageing androgynes, watched in silence as attention drained away from her. For even as she clutched onto her brass statuette, the reigning empress of British theatre could only reflect on how much she'd given up by producing play after play yet no children – which of course, owing to her tendencies (doubtless more neuter than gay,

Gisela had concluded in the week following Margot's outburst), she would never have done even if she could have.

The point was driven home with brutality by the image. Yet Margot did not resist underlining it when an interviewer thrust a microphone beneath her lips:

'Yes, I suppose a playwright like me does dream of proving that one doesn't have to give up being a full female to succeed.'

'You are so wicked!' Miranda breathed.

'Does that mean, Ms Wingfield, that you might be eager to win the Award at some future date?'

'Perhaps, in that sense – that one can excel at both: art and life. Be a playwright, or whatever, and mother as well.'

'Perfect!' Miranda exploded, snapping off the set.

Startled to have her images snuffed so abruptly, Gisela queried, 'What's "perfect"?'

'Can't you see what she's doing?'

'See what?' – The synthesist disliked the Rose's proprietary tone.

'The false modesty – the lies! – her position of words: *art* before *life*; "playwright or whatever" before "mother as well". Of course she longs for that – who doesn't? I'd love to be taken as a genius; but I have a difficult family to raise – three children, single-handed, with a husband who couldn't stay the course. Real people have real sacrifices to make – look at you. You should be so lucky as to have a Godfrey and Matthew et cetera; but how can you, dedicating every moment you have to Ollie in rehab, or bloody Frome's wifelets in pain? Did you remind her of *that* on your bucolic weekend? People who think they can have it all need to remember how their pretty ease depends on others who've never imagined they deserve anything without paying for it. Because no one deserves that, and Margot knows it – that's the guilty truth. That's where you'll get her, if you want to. Make her face it! What good are you as a therapist if you can't get her to concentrate her powers and realize that, if she wants the one thing so badly, she can't expect to keep everything else? Eileen Moloch knows, poor woman. Margot was too cruel. It's unforgivable!'

Gisela had never seen Miranda so exercized. From partisan, she had turned into Margot's enemy on the spot. Meanwhile, having purged herself of this stream of bile against a woman the world had believed her 'best friend', she told her guest to 'get out and get on with it!'

Her behaviour, in short, was so incoherent and odd – so full of feints, projections and Withholds – that the synthesist was frankly bemused. Was it mere jealousy? but the Rose had never shown desire for worldly attention before. Was it because Margot still maintained a respectable marriage whereas she (through no fault but her own) had thrown away one even more distinguished? Gisela was at sea. For the first time in her English existence, she had an inkling that she might be drifting towards some vortex of the native 'madness'. Perhaps it was in part to protect herself that she repeated much of what Miranda had said the next time she turned up at Ladbroke Grove.

'My friend Booby once told me that anyone can destroy anyone else's relationships if she puts her mind to it,' Margot mused.

Gisela did not quite catch the drift.

'She's trying to drive a wedge between us, dearest. You *are* Frau Dummkopf. Such an overgrown schoolgirl, as Miranda says. She's afraid you're trying to prise me away from her! But the absurd part is that I enjoy the silly creature more now than ever. I can quite see the point of her pique and forgive her most things.'

Gisela pondered. Did all of this have something to do with Oliver Murrie, with whom all three had had an affair at one time, incongruous though it now seemed? For her own part, Gisela doubted it. Oliver had not been an item for her for years; besides, that had been in another country, and the feeling was dead. But as for these Englishwomen – was some weird competition at the heart of it? some obscure undercurrent of sex?

'Actually,' Margot confided, contemplating a leaf falling outside her window, 'I'm fascinated by the girl. I don't know how anyone can let her house go so filthy and *déclassé*. I'm sure she's sticking pins into voodoo dolls and brewing up potions – the "witch of north London", as Godfrey says; good or evil, we're not sure. Perhaps dear Ollie should go back and try to sort her out again once he gets out of nick or wherever. Or no – that might make things worse. What about John DuRocher? I'd love to know what his love-life amounts to now. Perhaps I'll try him again, though the last time I did he seemed set on steering clear of her.'

Thus spake la Wingfield, and Gisela had no sense of any dart striking a soul. But the power of suggestion was more than she, with her flotsam and jetsam of psychological knowledge, had any genuine instinct for.

The fact was that something from Miranda had found its mark, via her. Meanwhile something in Margot had responded in kind. And now things began to occur:

In the first place, the playwright asked her to come to Ladbroke Grove for their 'auditing sessions' not once or twice, but three times a week. In the second, Miranda passed out of their orbit entirely, until, by the beginning of December, Margot, 'feeling guilty', phoned to ask if she'd like to come for Christmas supper, only to find that the Rose's number had been changed to ex-directory. In the third, Margot agreed in the face of whispers against her to go to Gisela's cottage on Boxing Day, as soon as familial duty was done.

To Gisela, it seemed as if her Lady were coming into focus at last. So devoted was Margot all of a sudden that she no longer seemed to care whom she cut to make time for them. Attractions between women were not a syndrome Gisela was up on, whatever her behaviour may have implied. Like most people with a mild, undetected homoerotic streak, her experience had never gone beyond the brief, unacknowledged crush; and though she'd crossed paths with one or two powerful females, she'd never been caught in a crossfire before. The effect in this case was curiously nullifying. As she had once been 'Miranda's' in a technical sense, now she became 'Margot's'. Yet in this status, she could do little but observe as her Lady began acting rashly.

Christmas was an example. It found Margot working around the clock to produce the 'civilized feast' Godfrey required. An Oxford don was invited, a financial journalist, a Treasury official and his Arts Council wife – all types to make the oaken beams of his feast-hall resound with erudite quips and laughter. From Margot's side no one was asked except those who might be expected to contribute to this: John DuRocher and the homosexual mounter of playlets, who could be counted on too to entertain mama while she cooked with laments about his defrocked beloved, recently decamped to Rome following a spat about 'cottaging'.

The day would be 'gruesome' in Margot's word. To make it less so she included Gisela. Yet despite her presence (because of it?), each hour seemed to increase an evil spell. Christmas – families – we all know the scene. Who could Margot turn to? Who could she turn *on*, more to the point. There was Godfrey, but she was already betraying him in a way. Luke and Jon were too young and the others gone – all except Matthew, that handsome presence who had looked so fine on

TV that the cameras had lingered on him almost more than on her.

Of this Wingfield, many agreed that he was too pure to seem part of the family. Matthew had never aped papa's wit; and when he'd recoiled from Gisela's therapy, Margot had contended that he'd always 'lacked spirit'. This was only true up to a point; but since Matthew was no more her partisan than Marcus had been, Gisela was content to let him be described as 'placid', 'boring' and 'not up to the rest of us really' – saintly Christian and social Marc, both deified in their absence. 'Matthew's always wanted a quiet life,' Margot summed up; nor was it false that in some ways he did seem unnaturally aged, though why father and brothers should have thought this a sin is a question an objective observer might have raised.

The opposite was the norm *chez* Wingfield that season. On entering the house, no one could have failed to notice how Margot and Godfrey behaved like squabbling siblings, he insisting that she not have a drop of brandy before dinner, she responding by getting so drunk that by nightfall she was complaining of Matt's dullness less in a tone of mother trying to improve son than of a step-sister trying to be cruel. This may have been partly a result of Gisela's counsel to 'let it all out'; nor could the synthesist see why an adult son should be exempt from the general attack on males that Margot wound herself up to. He got off lightly compared to Godfrey, whom she blamed for the 'sadism of blood-sport'; John, whom she derided for 'patronizing personæ'; even absent Gus, who came in for it for having given up hearth and home to 'wallow in sex and drugs in New York'.

This is where Matthew weighed in. 'Don't you think you're taking it a bit far, Mum? We don't actually know what he's doing.'

Compared to the others, who'd been drinking all day, the boy sounded mild and unassertive. To Margot, however, this must have come over as insufferably arch:

'That's just my point. Why isn't he here? People are meant to be with their families on Christmas, not off fornicating with strangers. Besides, Augustus was the last one to speak to Marc before he disappeared. I'm frightfully cross with him. He's a bad influence. We've all done too much to cover his tracks.'

Silence. Even Godfrey at the far end of the table drew breath; and John surmised that he might've liked to have taken his wife into a corner to reprimand her privately, a show of power which could have tipped a critical balance at that stage. But Godfrey forbore;

and Matthew shook his head and kept a low profile, as per his habit whenever parental chat reached a perilous verge.

Mama, meanwhile, descended into depths. 'Doesn't your family come together on Christmas?' she asked Matthew's girl, who was a real rose in a Jewish sort of way yet increasingly buffeted by the winds blowing through the Wingfield feast-hall.

Briefly, Margot worked at forging alliance with this new female in her sphere. Then with almost deliberate obtuseness, she added:

'I do wish Matt would get on and do something with his life. I'll never forgive myself if all my sons turn out failures.'

Here the boy was obliged to speak up again. 'They won't,' he maintained. 'Gus's already making a bundle.'

'How do you know? You've been phoning him too, have you?'

Later still, when that flurry died, Margot added:

'Why don't you two get married? Everyone should have babies; I did my bit. Now I deserve a grandchild. At least Matt could get on with that, couldn't he?'

Needless to say, Matthew's little princess was knocked off guard. And from then on winds blowing through the Wingfield feast-hall gave her such a chill that, within the hour, she'd departed, pleading a cold and leaving her boyfriend to weather the storm as he could.

'You're going to lose that girl,' Margot remarked, too gone on port to care what she said.

Her eldest remaining refused to argue.

'Women,' she added, 'expect men to take control.'

'You're drunk, Mum,' Matthew concluded and stood up to go.

'Sit down, Matthew. I'm not done with you.'

'Maggo, please!' exclaimed Godfrey, jowls rubicund. 'I don't mind what you say about me, but can't we leave off the children for once?'

This sent mama into a blue-ringed silence. And perhaps the implication was a touch unfair. At any rate, Matthew spent the rest of the wee hours talking to the homosexual mounter of playlets, who gave up trafficking in ribaldries to admire the young man's 'steady values'. John even caught him at one point suggesting that the boy had 'the makings of a religious soul'.

Gisela must have overheard this unctuous remark. In any event, it was what she latched onto the next morning when assessing for Margot why she had turned on her son.

'How do you mean?' la Wingfield demanded. (The synthesist's

Jaguar spun them down the M4.)

'It's like that high ethical pose of your American friend. You can't stand perfection in others, at least not too much.'

Margot felt cross, though perhaps less because of her hangover than out of guilt for having 'abandoned' her family to go off with the 'witch of the west'.

'It's not that,' she snapped. 'It's his dullness. Matthew makes me feel grey. I created him, after all; so it must be in me too. And if there's one thing I can't stand, it's being boring.'

'You aren't boring,' the other consoled, neglecting to say anything about grey.

'I am though, aren't I? Failed at the Critics' Award. Lost to Eileen Moloch, whom you and Miranda rate. I can't think of any more appropriate proof that I'm dull to the common punter.'

Gisela chose not to take umbrage at this. 'What have you told Godfrey?' she asked into her windscreen-wipers.

'That I couldn't think in London. That I couldn't start a new piece in that bloody house.'

'Ah. And what does he think?'

'What does he think about whot?'

'About us.'

'Godfrey can think what he pleases. Didn't you once tell him that the worst is usually the truth?'

Gisela could not recall having said such a thing. It sounded like one of Miranda's phrases, possibly recycled from Oliver Murrie. But whoever had said it, something of the kind was beginning to come true back in London for Matthew:

As mama worked on a new play in the Bathshire cottage, her eldest remaining began to experience fruition of her yuletide prophecy. At New Year his pretty girlfriend stood him up; by Twelfth Night he learned the reason. Put off at Christmas, she'd been advised by her family to avoid the house of Wingfield and go back to her childhood sweetheart and co-religionist, now a successful shampoo-salesman in Hampstead Garden Suburb.

'I told you so… told you so,' a voice in Matt's head iterated; and just before mum was due back from the country, he flew the parental nest. For some time he wandered. But winter was grim in that recessional year, and eventually he was persuaded to take what was on offer: a spare room in the house of the mounter of playlets. Some months there, under the counsel of the defrocked vicar (recently returned from Rome), persuaded him to apply for a place in an unheated commune on Iona. Thus by summer this scion of Wingfield had arrived at his place of exile or refuge, if you prefer. Like Augustus and Marcus, he became 'dead to the world' for his mother – though, as John said, the crassness of phrase may have just been one more stratagem to disguise hidden sorrow, or worse.

*

'I admire Matthew,' Margot came to admit, but only after stages of rage had been passed. ('Who does he think he is, holier than thou?' And: 'For God's sake, I hope he hasn't caught AIDS.') Gisela repeated that what she really resented was her son's usurpation of the religious pose in the family; and though she consigned him to conversational darkness, mama did gradually come to see the boy in a new light. He who had made her fear being dull was half-resurrected as having 'the makings of a saint', a phrase originating from the unfrocked vicar and passed on by the homosexual mounter of playlets. She even took on the theme in her next play, *An End to Levity*, which more than one reviewer identified as 'Ms Wingfield's T. S. Eliot exercise', though Gisela saw it mainly as a vindication of the new 'imaging techniques' she had been schooling her in.

As Margot's first piece had linked to Christian and her second to Marcus so this one bore spiritual resemblance to Matthew, though in the scene in which the heroine stood on a western promontory trying to make God materialize out of the mists Gisela glimpsed an evocation of herself as well, skrying the astral plane in her West Country redoubt. Meanwhile, what had truly happened to the most recent lost son? As with Marcus, Matthew passed into a kind of hereafter for his mother, despite Godfrey's *mot* that there was 'not much chance of holy war in Iona, if that's where the buggers have left him'. It was fanciful too to imagine that, like Margot's Leda (the new play's heroine), he might end up being inseminated, subliminally or otherwise, by a snake. That apocalyptic image, which made previewers at the Royal Court gasp, had more to do with a general impression of mishap descending and new quality of premonition in Margot's writing, for which Gisela took credit too: if the playwright could not prevent crisis from ravaging her family, at least she could succeed in raising 'life material' to mythopoeic status.

Gisela's new penchant for taking credit for all Margot accomplished was a symptom of the emboldening calm descending on her. In thrall to her Lady now completely, she was no longer shy about admitting it to herself. In her homely cottage, she padded around high on an image of Margot's success; also with a vision that she too might shortly fulfil a long-dreamt-of destiny. With muse-exemplar but a phonecall away, she set out to write up a volume meant to revolutionize a suppressed public with sharp, new behavioural metaphysics. A farrago of notes and plagiarisms she'd been working on when she had met Margot emerged from a drawer of the kitchen table. Scratching away with demonic energy, the synthesist threw herself into her most heroic effort to date. Taking up pen, putting it down again, raising it meditatively, she became so possessed that she confided to Margot, 'Writing is so difficult!' as if they were equals or the playwright a mere dauber at trivial things. Margot for her part responded with studious detachment. When asked for advice, she would murmur, 'Keep it simple' or 'I think you'd better stick to case-histories'. In fact, whatever case Gisela took up ended by sounding like hers. And privately la Wingfield began to grow alarmed.

Semiconsciously, Gisela must have foreseen that they were approaching a cataract. Sometimes she spoke now of the 'risk' she had taken in 'evoking this genius' between them. Though hardly a moralist, she had never before been so rash as to be tempted in over her head; thus a part of her must have felt something ominous, if intensely productive, in what she referred to as 'their sublime selfishness'. Nonetheless, she could not suppress her new longing to throw caution to the wind.

'If we were a man and a woman,' she remarked during one of their sessions in Ladbroke Grove, 'we might have been pregnant by now!'

Margot peered through half-glasses. Having reached a certain age, she observed, she was not sure she'd be good at child-rearing anymore – which was possibly why she'd let herself get in so deep.

Gisela, half listening, did not catch the hint. 'We can give birth to children of the mind!' she continued, inspired.

'You *are* mad, my dearest,' the other mused, shifting her gaze to the buds in her garden.

'Maybe I am! And maybe you are too – what difference does it make? You love what we're living through as much as I do. And there *is* something really good being produced here. This selfishness of ours – it's a kind of self-sacrifice really. Your neuroses, which brought us together, have vanished: I haven't heard a word about your guilt over Christian for months. And I'm certain you've come to realize that the turns you took against Marcus and Matthew were entirely justified, given what you'd been through.'

Margot peered at her sphinx-like.

'What's unique in your case is only a matter of degree,' Gisela gushed. 'You seem to feel these events, or their significance, more than other people – even if a visible part of you pretends to be indifferent. But someone who knows you as well as I do can see the pride and remorse tearing at your Thetan. It's why you've become more compelled to slip into this new coolness of yours.'

'So I'm cool now, am I?'

'Of course! It's a triumph! I say to myself: everyday she's climbing higher on the Tone-scale. Before long, she'll be as remote as a statue. A real iconness.'

This was quite accurate, if the explanation for it not exactly one the synthesist might have liked.

Margot looked grand, for instance, in her next big splash in the 'meedjah'. This was a pictorial at-home in *Chatter*, including an interview in which she explained why she wouldn't be disappointed if *An End to Levity* were not nominated for the Critics' Award:

'It's a private piece really, full of doubt and speculation. I used to be a good Christian, I think. Couldn't see the point of death if we weren't all going to meet in the hereafter, so I accepted the doctrine of Eternal Life. Now I'm not sure. Sometimes I fear the worst. Looking at the world as it is, I wonder how a sane person can hold onto the old moral values. Perhaps the law of this life boils down in the end to simple adaptability.'

Gisela took pride in this pronouncement. Hadn't she long promoted such 'realism'? What Margot had once dismissed as 'heresy', egged on by Godfrey, she now seemed to regard with less hardness, more abstraction. In fact, at this time the synthesist was able to imagine both of them throwing off old crotchets at last and approaching those sunny uplands of liberation. The real trajectory of changes in Margot was not yet apparent. So exalted was she that, if asked to describe this phase in relations, Gisela might've said that it seemed as if they were being spun round in some kind of dance, drawn down in a vortex, then flung up towards some marvellous new condition, then away from it, then back to it and off into its opposite, as Margot would depict later in another of her disingenuously 'historical' plays.

An external sign of this new volatility was the chameleon-like appearance the Great Lady took up. One day she stepped out as a woman of fashion for glossies, swathed in smart red and black. The next she wrapped her head in a scarf like a gypsy and went down to the Society for Psychical Research with her octogenarian poetess friend. A week or so later she turned up perfectly unwashed at Miranda's (a new reconciliation there) to discover 'fascinating things' by passing through the back side of the Tree of Life and going down in reverse mirror-image to the way one was meant to go up the front in order to reach the Eye of God.

About this procedure, Gisela voiced caution: 'You don't really believe you're going to contact some lost child that way?' Though having performed such rituals in the past (wasn't she the one who had introduced Miranda to the Cabala in the first place?), the synthesist was now alienated from what she called 'shabby magic', which had 'as much potential for self-deception as revelation', she claimed.

'That's what Godfrey says, dearest. Only he just sneers, whereas you've always pointed out that there's no reason to disbelieve what one can't disprove. It's one of the attitudes in you I've admired.'

With surprising good sense, the other retorted: 'But there's no justification for putting faith in them either.'

'I'm not sure I put faith in anything anymore. But as you've taught me, I attempt.'

Was Margot being more fey here than truthful?

'The pursuit of Knowledge – Miranda calls hers *gnosis* – has never been my strong suit, as Godfrey tells the world. On the other hand, as writers, we have to be open to everything, don't we?'

The formula 'we writers' settled the question. As Margot's pupil in this new alchemical process, the erstwhile synthesist could do little more than listen and learn. Thus she began to tolerate fascinations she might have tried to nip in the bud otherwise.

At about this time Oliver Murrie was released from confinement in a clinic near Bristol, and at risk of upsetting Godfrey Margot agreed to invite him to lunch. The ex-painter was by now lean and moon-faced. Dressed in black pyjamas, he looked as if he'd never quite left an era when an entire generation had fought a notional war against authority on the side of Ho Chi Minh. Out of place as well as time, he had long since stopped being a person you could converse with normally. At Margot's table he sat at first in dead silence, later expounding to the ether, blue eyes immobile under a wisp of white hair. Regaling John DuRocher with how he had 'time-travelled' while in a straight-waistcoat, he caused Godfrey to snort and depart to Oxford where he was on a committee to raise funds for All Souls. John became more or less invisible, as was his wont; Gisela, familiar with the kind of half-baked visions that grow up in prisons and rest-homes, tried to jolly Ollie back onto less fantastic ground. Margot for her part listened intently, breaking concentration only to reprimand Lucius, who had grown increasingly subtle of late in ways of tormenting his junior, Johann.

The two youngest Wingfields were teen and pre-teen now (circa 1994). Luke had grown stringy and long-necked and, of all Margot's sons, was the one the world found least attractive. John could hardly communicate with him: he worried that if any Wingfield were to take a truly wrong turn it might be this oddball who looked more like a Florentine assassin than scion of good family in a nation whose Prime Minister claimed to be 'at ease with itself'.

Luke wore the baggy jeans and reversed baseball cap of 'Generation X'. He shaved his skull and squished the floor with duckbill-flat plimsolls. 'Son number five is pretending to be rude,' Margot explained when he left the table without asking to be excused.

'Seems too cunning just to pretend,' observed Oliver.

'Yes, I'm afraid we have a devil on our hands with him.'

Gisela in her new rationality protested. 'Surely you can't believe a child just comes into the world bad?'

Margot did not answer directly; she merely alluded to the fact that this Wingfield had a history of causing disturbance. At age six he'd cracked open four-year-old Johann's skull by slamming a toy-box lid on it; at seven he'd nearly ended the hundred year life of the house by dropping a cigarette-end on his bed, then going across the road to play Dungeons and Dragons with the son of an American military attaché; at eight he'd nearly broken his father's neck by leaving a skateboard in the pantry where anyone coming in late might slip on it, especially someone coming in squiffed. Lucius was bad luck. 'I wash my hands of him,' Margot had said when, at age nine, he'd been caught shoplifting. At ten he'd been sent home from school for being stoned, at eleven interrogated for painting National Front slogans on the walls of West Indian houses. Finally, when a particularly discomforting bout of mama's hot flushes had caused him to flee her upbraiding for a week, Margot had sent the local male busy-body (ex-CID) to find him playing blackjack in a stairwell of Shepherd's Bush tube, taking hard-begged 10p's off the dossers.

Lucius was careless, moralless. 'Another antinomian in the family' is how Godfrey described him and made only perfunctory efforts at reforming the lad. Perhaps because of this, Gisela had sometimes paid him attention. Alone of Margot's brood, Lucius had never shown contempt for her. 'Let him get on with it' was the line she took when he asked mama to go somewhere out-of-bounds. The boy's eyes would shine at this sign of solidarity, though careful not to make contact with the synthesist's. Knowing how much she wished Margot free of distractions, he did what he could to rid the house of all others, except of course undetachable Johann.

Gisela might have foreseen how her rapport with Luke could affect relations with Margot in their last phase. But blinded by newfound enthralment as she was, she took little caution. On a second occasion when Oliver Murrie came for lunch, for instance, she laughed with almost the *machismo* of Godfrey as the boy returned from school to pull a rubber boa constrictor out of his bag.

'Lucius Wingfield, you are not to have such an apparatus in my house!' Margot cried as he wove the elasticated thing into her pearls.

'Can I see it?' whined Johann.

'Ecstasy!' the boy menaced and, whipping the noose loose, encircled his brother's scrawny neck instead.

Johann screamed; Margot reproved. 'Let him be!' Gisela chided, pouring wine as if host. 'A little roughhousing is good for boys. Besides, Lady W, how can you expect him to stay close to home if you don't let him do what he wants here?'

Oliver rolled eyes heavenwards.

The synthesist took this as a sign of agreement.

'Aarrggghh!' Lucius growled, yanking the noose free only once Johann was gasping. 'Get your rocks off, faggot?'

Suitably terrorized, Johann retreated behind mama's skirts.

'All right,' Margot half-conceded. 'I don't know what you want with such a thing; but if you must keep it, keep it upstairs, under lock, in your room. I do not want to see it or hear what you use it for. And if I get the faintest idea that you're frightening Johann with it, I shall turn you over to Oliver here to truss up in a straight-waistcoat! There, there, my pet' [this to her youngest] 'Mummy's not going to let them hurt you, is she?'

Gisela shook her head. 'Rich, isn't it?' she asided to Oliver, for whom all this in some obscure way seemed to be being played. 'Subconsciously, mothers always seem to believe that, because they brought the little devils into the world, they have the right to spoil them to death!'

Margot's eyes narrowed. 'Careful, dearest. I don't need a female Godfrey around here.'

'And you don't want the male one you have!' the synthesist crowed in unconscious echo of the departed host.

'You want a new guru?' Oliver inquired slyly, revolving his head as if a crystal ball.

Gisela, in her cups, fell about.

'I might,' the playwright muttered. 'One of these days, I just might.'

Gisela seemed to lose sight of the law that favourites depend on the caprice of the moment in a way family members do not. Working obsessively on her own writing, she began too to believe that she understood the 'psychological transubstantiation' by which the playwright had been able to create. Re-reading Margot's plays, she became more convinced that she had been a principal progenitor of them. *Jester in Flame* had a chemist-witch in it whom the hero consulted about magical potions – drugs, aphrodisiacs – which, in a spirit of Shakespearean romance, were taken to induce 'love madness'. *An End to Levity* had a kind of female Heathcliff who whisked Leda away from her frightful solipsism on the moors. Then came the script Margot was at work on now, a little drama of demons like Henry James's *Turn of the Screw*, a first edition of which John DuRocher had given her at Christmas. (John had reverted, like many of our tribe, to that fount of a sacred 'sensibility'.) This eerie drama, part ghost tale, part Freudian nightmare, portrayed an ambisexual Mephistopheles who led the heroine down to phantasmagorical depths which seemed all pink and purple pleasure to begin with but ended by becoming fiery pandaemonium.

Gisela accepted Margot's word that these creations were 'mostly play'. She gave little attention to how characters like her had developed; it was enough that they remained dominant. Unattractive aspects she attributed to others: Godfrey, the sons, even the shadowy father-figure Margot declined to talk about but now Miranda let drop had been a Nazi sympathizer during the War. Pressed to elaborate, the erstwhile Rose altered tattle to suggest that Margot's mother had been a white Russian *émigré* from Hull and father a minor impresario who'd spent his last years trying to turn the symphonies of Mahler into a post-Holocaust religion. Gisela discounted these whispers as revenge for the fact that Margot had consigned Miranda to oblivion again now that she'd taken Oliver in as lodger. Had she understood the Rose's disillusioned sense of humour, she might have recognized the characterizations as having satirical truth about the kind of dramatist Margot aspired to be. But what poor Gisela failed to glean at this stage was the extent to which her own attractions as inspiration, or even 'material', were beginning to ebb.

The end came, when it did, for reasons she might have predicted a few months before. But labouring over her Great Work as she was, she was neither attentive nor adept enough to recognize that – once an author has 'done' a friend or relation – what once seemed larger-than-life rapidly shrinks. Gisela, in short, was becoming a figment for Margot. As with all would-be gurus, the disciple was cutting the cord. And how did she react on waking up to this hard truth? Of all unilluminating spectacles, Godfrey would remark, the least attractive may be a magician losing his 'powers'.

First she was reduced to pathos, then to vindictive words.

'Please don't make a scene, dearest,' Margot implored as inevitable confrontation occurred. 'Godfrey says that when romanticists fall, they stop being strong and start becoming pathetic whingers. Like Napoleon at St Helena, they end up bleating about their cook and growing breasts.'

Gisela hardly noted the bizarrerie of this image. Overwhelmed by the folly of her own progress – expatriation to England, attempts to establish a profession – all she could think of was how it would all go smash in the mud. Past her sped a vision of the *magnum opus* she was at work on, and she turned bitterly cool:

'I assume there's room for negotiation here, Lady W.'

'How do you mean, dearest… I wish you'd stop calling me that.'

'I mean, I expect payment.'

'Payment? Payment for what?'

'Two years' worth of Auditing for a start. Look at the state you were in when you first came to me.' – And look at the reason, was left unsaid: the obscured circumstances of Christian's death.

'You're not going to go beastly Teutonic on me now, are you? after having made so much progress yourself?'

'Save your "compliments" for your DuRocher minion! As for "going beastly Teutonic": that's how you'll depict me whatever I do.'

'You *are* Frau Dummkopf. Why should I do that?'

'If you don't directly, Godfrey will; it amounts to the same thing. So long as you stay with him, you condone his little English prejudice: your continuation in his house is enough. Of course I'll "go beastly Teutonic" in your opinion. No doubt in his I always have been.'

Margot peered through the half-glasses. Was there a tear in a puce-shaded eye? Gisela half-hoped so.

'And what is this "payment", my dearest?'

A recently buried joy in being At Cause welled up. 'I've given you at least ten thousand pounds worth of free sessions.'

Margot looked startled. 'Surely you're not going to blackmail us?'

Us, Gisela noted. 'Godfrey must have bags of dosh.'

'What makes you think that? There's a recession on – and this beastly business with Lloyd's.'

'Don't try to hide behind that, "dearest". You have royalties, plenty.'

'We need what I bring in to fix the roof.'

We again. 'Such a shame!'

Suddenly the ex-synthesist felt wholly vengeful. She donned a mask of no mercy to cover crushed pride and real pain.

'Isn't there anything else I can do for you?' Margot inquired.

In glimpsing the future without her Great Lady, there was only one consolation she could see: 'Help me to publicize my book.'

'Your book? You mean that case-study on me you're swotting up?'

Gisela snatched at the least chance to hurt. 'What a narcissist you've become! Do you actually think these people've been going to the theatre for *you*? Don't deceive yourself, Lady Muck. It's what's behind your plays that's brought them. And what's behind them is *me*!'

'You?!' Margot exclaimed, and Gisela heard with remorseful satisfaction a first note of anger in the dulcet tones.

'Yes, *me* in the sense of what I've given you. The emotional support you've longed for but couldn't get from Godfrey. Guidance, calm, and "material" too. O don't go closed shop now and try to deny it, "dearest". I've played Holy Guardian Angel to your success, and you know it!'

In truth, she hated herself for conjuring such a diabolic persona; but what else could one do? She cajoled and contrived, pressed and gave her 'lady' as little peace as she could; soon she had even persuaded herself that all she'd ever wanted was to get her own name before the public – Gisela Cohn-Burton, genius of Insight and Technique; latest in a tradition deriving from Blavatsky and Freud via, say, L. Ron Hubbard. Into herself she summoned all the yearning and resentment she had felt during successive humiliations: from her ex-husband and daughter, Lord Frome and his wifelets, various others that had to do with her. Years of perceived slights and marginalizations mixed with congenital longing for glory and perhaps even racial instinct for vindication. Everything churned into this single obsession: to get the recognition she imagined to lie between hard covers of a book.

Margot, Godfrey and the rest could smirk. They could call her a crank and mock her by standards of their tribe; but she would not let them off – especially not now as she watched her lady reverting to type and seeming to rediscover the rationale for her marriage: that as she had once known, art-student on the make, there was no substitute in this culture for status.

As for 'payment'? Gisela might almost have predicted Margot's first tactic: to try to buy her off with a promise to dedicate work-in-progress to her: 'Godfrey says it's a risk to my career. But I wouldn't hesitate to put your name on it if you thought it might help.'

The ex-synthesist paused. For an instant she was tempted. But now her mind curved around every nuance, and she saw the playwright laughing up her sleeve, whispering to John DuRocher or some other minion: 'No one's going to notice "for Gisela" on the playbill… It might as well be "for Rosie" or "for the Man in the Moon"'.

'No thanks,' she answered. 'I'd be a fool to let you off so easily.'

Margot, a hint of alarm in her voice, added: 'I hope you don't intend to do anything more to my family, Gisela.'

It was the first time the playwright had called her anything other than 'dearest', and it seemed to drive a last nail into the coffin of hopes for reconciliation. 'I would've thought you knew me better than that,' she hissed.

'I wonder,' la Wingfield took occasion to sigh, 'if anyone knows anyone else really. I guess ther're just some types of woman one never gets the hang of.'

'Reverting to insinuation's not an answer! You're Withholding on yourself again. As to what I intend to "do": I should have it ready for you in a matter of weeks!'

Gisela enjoyed, as much as she could any of this, leaving Margot in anxiety, even fear. She might've taken care to be gentler had her ex-auditee been less well set up. But had Margot been less well set up, Gisela would never have arrived at this position with her. Because Margot was *it* for her: the only person she could have become so in thrall to, ever.

Recognizing this inwardly, Gisela could no longer quite face the fact, leading to the edge of an abyss as it did. And so she wrote. Turning her cottage in Bathshire into a shrine, she burnt imaginative incense to her demon-muse. Throwing herself into the Great Work, she erected a treatise of surreal contortion around the central pillar of Margot's case-history. Burning midnight-oil, she produced exactly the type of fringe psychobabble critics would fall over each other to dump on. Nor was she so naïve or unparanoid as to miss this. In sending the script to town for Margot to 'edit', she realized half-consciously that she was performing an act of self-laceration as well as revenge. She even took masochistic delight in envisaging reaction.

Sitting alone by her fire, she read reviews in her mind: 'Rarely has there appeared such an amalgam of the incomprehensible with the plain bad...' 'On a page, the author is finally revealed as the charlatan sound thinkers have always suspected her to be...' Phrases of the kind echoed and re-echoed. Skrying her flames, Gisela saw faces nodding around the Wingfield feast-table, minds sodden with drink, voices rehearsing the prejudices and pusillanimities of type. Conjuring us all, she saw sharp teeth chewing, lips spitting. Infernal before her rose a vision of Hell: John DuRocher as a sly Mandarin, the homosexual mounter of playlets, Miranda, Oliver, me, all with tongues as forked as our tails. And presiding over this séance in wicked mirth sat Godfrey, with Margot stately and cold as the witch in *Snow White* at his side.

In fact, the Margot who eventually phoned her shared little with this entrancing vision. There was a sweetness to her words, almost charity. Having heard the playwright purr thus to others, Gisela instantly divined a new subtext. And something different did indeed move her 'lady' now: a mix of guilt, regret, pity – even (the thought made Gisela's 'powers' drain away on the spot) Christian love.

'I'm determined to help,' Margot stated. And help she did. And Gisela would never acknowledge the folly the playwright then dared: to take what the synthesist had rightly imagined critics would brand as illiterate and rewrite it to approach common sense; then, as if in public confession of their liaison, to place her own name as co-author on the title-page.

'I hope you realize what courage she's showing,' Miranda phoned to point out. (The erstwhile Rose was now fully re-reconciled with Godfrey's wife.)

'In that hermetic world of yours up in London, I wonder if you know what "courage" truly means!'

Miranda, who'd lost all interest in 'the dreary occult', delivered this message: 'Margot can do no more for you, Gisela. And we're all hoping you're going to accept this as "payment".'

So: wagon-trains had circled.

'We'll see what the reviews say!' the foreign woman raged and slammed down her receiver.

Beside herself to think that someone else could have become intimate with a person she'd done so much for, she failed to register what she knew at some level: that given what she'd asked for, Margot was offering the most convincing proof of her debt and devotion – staking her reputation on trash.

As for reviews? She waited, and waited. Nothing. The volume was published. One or two literary editors raised an eyebrow. That was all.

Gisela rang up Miranda to complain. 'I thought Margot was such a great "star" that anything she put her hand to was copy.'

'London may not be as vicious as you think,' replied Oliver Murrie, who had picked up the receiver and sounded more sane than in years.

'What does that mean?' snapped his erstwhile physician.

'Some people have enough sense not to shit in their own sandbox.'

'O spare me Miranda's domestic metaphors!'

'They let her off,' Miranda explained from another extension. 'Because she's one of their own, the critics let it pass. It's the joke that falls flat and will be ignored, so long as it's never repeated.'

The distraught Ms Cohn-Burton gave this her own twist: 'Godfrey put the word out, did he?'

'With a comment like that,' Oliver (or was it Miranda?) concluded, 'you prove how sensible they were not to take you up.'

That was it, the last cut. And to have it delivered by the most loopy, unacceptable couple in London – a pair she had worked to help individually for years – made it seem the unkindest of all.

Margot, meanwhile, could not be reached: the Wingfield number had been made ex-directory. Thus Gisela could only lie wounded as it were: mentally frothing at the mouth; imagining her Great Lady as impervious, encircled, shoved out of her sphere.

But she was wrong again. Margot would not prove so shallow. One day a postcard arrived: a watercolour of an old woman, angular, strong-boned, with eyes like black coals – an image of strength. On back, in curiously Cyrillic handwriting, it read:

> 'I'm sorry, dearest. I can do no more. The line had to be drawn somewhere. Ever yours, Lady W.'

So: that was it. The woman was waiting. Somewhere in her soul, Margot understood that no one gets off so lightly from a contract like they'd made. She wants to be punished, the erstwhile synthesist concluded. So as skies that September keened with harsh winds, making it seem like winter with leaves; as the playwright in London completed *Firestorm* in her eyrie, trying to exorcize her lost *döppel* and evoke her at the same time, Gisela trained her inner eye on spirits inhabiting the House of Wingfield...

Lucius, that wild boy full of pranks and plots – Oliver had amused him with tales of the nick, and now a *Zeitgeist* of hooliganism swept him up. Thus it came as little surprise to 'the witch of the west' when Miranda phoned to report that this most delinquent of Margot's brood had been arrested. Caught on closed-circuit camera in a North London shopping-mall, he and two other pre-teens had been playing at strangling a younger boy separated from his mum. The 'rope' they were using was identified as an elasticated rubber snake.

3.

Godfrey Wingfield relaxed in the Café de la Mairie. It was not an ordinary venue for him. Forty years separated him from a time when he'd come down from Oxford to discover this city, which summed up the best and the worst in civilization as he saw it. The worst in those days had been all he had desired: aromatic cigarettes, Pernod, garlic on the breath, verbal political battles, girls – often ladies who did not merit the name. The best *soi-disant* had not been available to him yet. However, by virtue of an old school tie and a seat on a quango, he had enjoyed it today, in form of lunch at the Ritz and chat over an excellent *eau de vie* with a member of the French Great and Good.

Sceptical though he was about things non-British (he was a mature Englishman, after all), Godfrey was sufficiently warmed by his repast that, settling behind a cheroot in his old haunt by St Sulpice, he was prepared to see nothing but Order, Precision and Grandeur around. Across the square rose the eccentric cathedral, her great columns and arches attesting to a triumph of the classical over the medieval in even what he disparaged as a 'pagan' Catholic Church. This reassured. Something in the world would always be right, even if things here were now ruled by smooth socialist brothers of the Grand Écoles rather than radical spirits of a more enlightened epoch.

Ordo ab Chao; this massive structure rising out of decorative squalor of old Left Bank streets – it put Godfrey in mind of the Grand Lodge of the Freemasons, presiding over a Covent Garden essentially unchanged since Dr Johnson's day. Old traditions were still valid. What would the world come to if a few did not still believe in Man as the Crown of Creation? in bringing the Music of the Spheres down here to Earth? in conquest of the mysteries by Rational Thought? in the Divine Intention of the Great Architect of the Universe and realization of his programme for us mortals below through Every Good Man and True?

Dreaming in capital letters, Godfrey lost time. When he caught up with it, he stood hastily, paid his bill and – buttoning his jacket, which felt tighter than before – set off for his assignation.

The jacket was pinstriped. Godfrey wore a blue bow-tie with white polka-dots, brown brogues, flannel trousers – the uniform, as Margot would call it. Was he absurd? Was that what his French counterpart had been implying in lame attempts at English wit? that Godfrey was out of step? subtly divorced from his times? He worried about it not a jot as he strolled past fashion fops, tourists, the French looking haggard and ruthless from too much strong coffee, sex, red wine, black tobacco – haggard but vigourous, unlike so many of his kind; certainly unlike those Americans from whom the world had expected so much, but who were so often irritatingly pacific.

Was he old, Godfrey wondered, arriving at Deux Magots. Lunch receding, he began to feel flat as he bumped through the tables looking for Marianne Vänder. His eyes gazed over versions of a younger self lounging there in the '50s (or was at the Flore?) while Sartre and retinue smoked their Gitanes. Or was it Camus who had more or less made his office here? Dim days now: neither so rich nor so full of temper and hope. Every youth and his cousin had played at being a *bohème* then, a Miller or Durrell – even those who had hailed from Harrow and Balliol.

'Ah,' breathed a voice in one of many tones his wife had adopted. 'How go affairs with the Secret Élite?'

Marianne was wearing a crushed velvet beret. Still there was little hope for that face, whatever the woman attempted. Why was it that great wealth was so often at odds with fine looks? Same was true of John DuRocher, whom Booby had described as 'a Great Ant'. (Had she meant *tante*, Godfrey wondered half in alarm, having taken up chess with Margot's pal lately.) So far as looks went, it was the pot calling the kettle black.

'Hello, Marianne,' he brayed with compassion, he hoped. 'How go affairs with the *déraciné*?'

'*Tout marche bien*. Only I haven't decided.'

'Decided whot?' – He sat down heavy on a wicker seat.

'Whether to stay here or move on.'

So that's what it came down to for her kind: unending escape. 'On to where?'

'New York? Rome? Where does a Secret Élite think I'd be safest?'

In the grave, he reflected and had a fleeting thought that he might never see this dear monster again.

Booby's hair had gone greyish: why didn't she dye it? Englishwomen of a certain age did. Her fine-freckled skin, unprotected from the sun, had become a relief map of the Vosges. Was there some bogus value these old-style Yankees put on a withering authenticity? She had gone thin since he'd last seen her; hands looked like twigs bound by Egyptian rings. Then came the lipstick and powder and rouge: the patina of some ageing tart – Jean Rhys on these *trottoirs*, or *maman* on her death-bed; the ashes of a *jolie laide,* as Margot liked to say.

'Do you want tea, or something stronger?' – She waved an ungloved hand at a waiter. (Why did he imagine she should be wearing gloves?) 'I'm having whisky in a cup and saucer.'

'You would.' – Godfrey and Booby had known one other too well to put on airs. '*Encore du whisky*,' he said to the waiter, then – 'You Americans are less virtuous than you were in my youth.'

'Glad to hear we've made progress. What was it Artaud said? "When they consent to admit the existence of evil is when they'll begin to discover they have souls."'

'Artaud indeed! When will you old beatniks stop being addicted to these shabby antinomians?'

'Foreigners, like women, play at witchcraft. Like the very old or very young, we're still patronized by the Secret Élite. Look at Margot.'

'*Bon idée*. Let's look at her.'

Godfrey wondered if there were some subtler tack to take. He had reckoned on a fifty-fifty chance of getting something out of this woman if she knew there were a crisis. Marianne was a jade, perhaps useless to herself anymore: deeper exile in France was a tacit admission that she'd failed to conquer the world as she'd set out to and all that was left was this rather *manqué* existence as a mini-Duchess of Windsor. Still, he knew she loved Margot – had loved her like a sister ever since an afternoon three decades before when an ingenue from South London had appeared in a studio in Chelsea and stolen an American heiress's first English lover from her.

'So,' she intoned now. 'You're going to try to seduce my confidence by pretending she's the real reason you've come here: to see me, not to hide a few assets from Lloyd's through a fellow conspirator of the Secret Élite.'

This kind of patter softened the guilt he felt over being mercenary. 'Please don't blow my cover in this rat's nest of bourgeois communists,' he quipped.

She chuckled. The sound was like that of a Metro shuddering into a station; and Godfrey realized that, beneath it all, he liked this woman and that, if truth were told, she probably liked him too. But O how he and she had loathed one another over Margot! he warring against her in the era of drugs, she not forgiving him for stealing an artist's model from *la vie bohème* into a 'bourgeois' marriage. That, however, was history. Now they could joke over his profession – 'But I don't have a "profession"!' he would protest; 'I'm a civilized man!' To which she would retort, 'Secret élite!' And he would let her, it being both false and true, and confirming that on some level she still rated him.

'Dear God,' she purred, 'what do you expect of a broken-down Dutch-Irish-Franco-American peasant like me?'

'Quite. I've been waiting for the part of you descended from English aristocrats to turn up.'

'Not here in Paris.'

'I suppose that would be asking too much.'

Whisky came. He drank. The waiter refilled Marianne's cup from the bottle, to bemusement of tourists from Kansas nearby.

'*A ta santé,*' she toasted.

'My *santé* is fine. What about yours?'

'Desperate. Too much fresh air. And Margot's?'

He put down his glass. 'That's my worry,' he nodded, serious at last. 'Except for Johann, that sad child, there's nothing to interest her nowadays.'

Gazing at her saucer, Marianne tried to remember how she'd decided to deal with this. 'Is it her you're worried about, or yourself?'

'For Christ's sake, Booby, why be sophistic? What's difference does it make?'

'Lucius has been remanded?'

'Yes. I'm trying to get the sentence reduced, but it's political.'

Inaudibly, she sighed. Did he catch the hint of a sob? Did the entirely bad influence recognize genuine pain? Did she realize that, however remote, he was far from indifferent; it was just that he couldn't show it – couldn't let the world know it – if *Ordo ab Chao* were to continue.

'What about lezzy?'

'Who's Lizzy?'

'Thingumbob. Cause-bungled. The mind-merchant.'

'Seen off.'

Booby sipped. 'Johnny DuRocher told me a good one yesterday: "Neurotics build castles in air; psychotics live in them; and psychosynthesists collect the rent."'

'Very good, Marianne. Very Manhattan. But what does one do?'

'You said "seen off". Are you sure?'

'As sure as I am of anything now. Why else would I turn to you?'

She understood both the insult and compliment intended. 'So what do you want of me, you charming dear, since you've got me to come all the way to Paris to see you?'

Why was it that even at times like this men and women couldn't be free of flirtation? It gummed up the works, especially when you were nearing pensionable age. So Godfrey thought, unconsciously echoing a line from one of his wife's plays.

'I want to know why things are the way they are, and what one can do about them. And please, Marianne: this is important.'

She laid a bundle of twigs on his hand. 'I'm willing to do anything in my power. But all I know is lies.'

'What do you mean "lies"?'

'Margot's lies. Your lies. The ones that you've lived by and must keep on with till you're done.'

'You sound as portentously Delphic as she does.'

'Wasn't it you who said I'd taught her all evil things?'

'The ones she hadn't picked up already from the bent vicars and other sorcerers she goes in for.'

'Lie number one… no divorce, being of the Faith.'

'That hardly seems unreasonable. I've stayed married too, through worse than many husbands would have put up with.'

'Yes manny, we all know about the True Patriarch. Through thick and thin you'll protect your kind, even if they don't seem worth it – which in this case they never will. *Sanctus Familias.*'

'*Familia sancta*, surely,' he corrected, thinking: this is pointless – a recording of stock phrases that might've been amusing when we were young but hardly help at this stage.

'You want lie number two?'

If there were small point in listening, there was even less in turning her off, since he'd got her all the way to Paris to meet him.

'Her father. Having to suppress that background – it's made her ashamed, resentful and deceptive since day one.'

'I never chided her about that. God knows, I sympathized. We supported her mother till she died. Not everyone can be on the right side in a war.'

'You are generous, Goddy. And she knows that, and resents you for it. But the problem's not you: it's the rest of the class and *monde* she could never be straight with. You wouldn't let her.'

'What good would it've done her to let everyone know what her father had been?'

'It all comes out in rumour, and when it does – you know this better than most – it always sounds worse.'

Someone of Marianne's background was hardly devoid of connections, nor unaware of how the Establishment keeps track of its kind. But Godfrey had not come to Paris to discuss his wife's pre-history, which was beside the point now.

'You want lie number three? Her old lover, Oliver Murrie – having to hide that. And later, having to pimp for him. And later still the Miranda thing happened.'

'I hardly criticized her for it, though I wish she'd chosen a man instead of a mess. Didn't you once say that she was bound to get nostalgic for that art-school sort of thing? I thought I behaved rather well in the circumstance.'

'Of course you did. And she resents you for that too – what woman wouldn't? But there's still lie number four.'

'Jesus wept, Booby!'

'This Lesbos interlude.'

'I've accepted the facts there.'

'Yes, but what are they?'

'That having played Isolde to Tristan with her pathetic artist, she'd feel obliged to come into the 20th century and play Vita and Violet with her shrink. Casting me as bloody Harold Nicolson.'

'Maybe you ought to call it Vita and Virginia. But that would make you into Leonard Woolf; and whatever else you are, you're not a socialist Jew, are you?'

'Is that some kind of sin?'

For a moment, Godfrey recalled his own mother asking how he'd let himself be ensorcelled by the beautiful demon who'd become his wife. The voice then spoke again:

'You're so blind, manny.'

'How do you mean?'

'She was never in love with mind-merchant.'

'A nice circus of deception if she wasn't!'

'Lies again, lies. The real problem with lezzy began with your son.'

'Which one? I've lost several.'

'The first. Chrétien, dear lad. Accident. Margot blundered on that: she told me.'

Godfrey felt a tightening in his chest. 'Told you what?'

'About the Glorious Twelfth, when you took them to Scotland. Boys' day out to learn guns. And the angry one shot the favourite.

Cain and Abel.'

What on earth had Margot said? And how many others had she spilled to, if she had? And how on earth, he cried to the wraith in his mind, had he earned such complication in life when all he had wanted was to do the Proper Thing by Family and Class and get on?

'A's gun went off and hit C. No one else was in eyeshot, so everyone could pretend it was a tragic accident. Who was going to know otherwise, and if they suspected, who was going to be so crass as to say? Margot becomes the hysteric bereaved, a great cover; sensible family closes ranks. The culprit is sent out of the country quick as fire; and then *that* deception, no doubt your invention, tempts Margot into taking it one lie too far.'

'How fantastic your imagination is, Booby. Margot always said you were the real dramatist, not her.'

How could Margot have been so indiscreet? Did she want the full truth to come out, with all its consequences? – No, the despicable Americanne was just fishing. Needed some titbit to dine out on on her next trip to London, that was all.

'Finish the speech for me. What's your "one lie too far"?'

'She gets involved with Thingie Mind-Games; imagines she's going to get psychiatric balm. And when Thingie gets too near the truth, she panics and says that Marcus did it – the most durable one. Pretends it was his gun that went off, not the culprit's who's safe as sin in New York. From then on, putting two and two together, Causebungled has something to blackmail her with.'

Snorting, Godfrey leaned back in his chair. 'Two and twenty-eight would be more like it!' – Around them *tout* Paris in its grandeur and sang-froid gazed at its navel, comfortably obsessed.

Marianne drained her cup.

'I don't believe in your theories now anymore than I used to about the capitalist conspiracies your type went in for when I was sitting here in the '50s.'

She retracted her twigs. '*Tant pis* then, my ruddy fool. Back to the Secret Élite with you.'

Starting to rise, her form put him in mind of an elegance that might have been had she not been so punished by genes as to be born of the world's ruling-class. 'Hang about, Marianne. You've only said why, not what one can do about it.'

Was this tacit admission of her truth? 'Do I look like a person who's got the answers?' she asked, rising fully, cool as a crumbling sphinx. 'It's your problem, God. Margot jilted me too, remember? I'm the "drug addict" you warned her about, and Thingie saw off, before she'd been "seen off" herself. If she has been.'

'Don't go bitter on me now, please.'

'I'm not bitter,' she purred.

For an instant, he knew this was the last time he would see her and felt an indeterminate pang, as if he were turning his back on a relation he had once loved yet subtly betrayed. Then, as ever, his wife re-intruded, scattering rival ghosts.

'Everyone does what he can to protect his kind,' she summed up, slipping on those notional gloves. 'I can hardly resent that: it's a law of nature. But if you want someone to cry to or get advice from, why bring me all the way here when someone in London knows the situation a lot better?'

'Who's that?' he asked, helpless.

Gazing at him with something akin to sympathy, she breathed: 'Miranda Cravin? seen her once or twice, haven't you?'

With that Booby Vänder, *née* Marianne, made her way through the wicker seats. And the eyes of *tout* Paris followed her odd form and gross features, wondering what star in what heaven they might once have belonged to.

All the way back to London Godfrey brooded on what she might have known. The Miranda reference had made him more dyspeptic than ever. Was the world more complicated than he imagined? Among all the organizations that watched and recorded, was there a Secret Order of Women as well? 'Seen her once or twice...' Had the phrase been accidental, another fishing expedition, or could Booby have been making a veiled threat? Either way, it had hit home; and Godfrey arrived at Waterloo Station full of windy trepidation about who might've known what, or suspected.

He did not make straight for the house in Ladbroke Grove; he told the cabbie to go to Islington and pull up in front of a Georgian terrace, where houses varied from posh to derelict. Under a yellow streetlamp, he took some while to determine if he was in the right place. Much had altered since the last time he had come here: the garden was cleared of injured foliage; bricks and boards stood in a tidy pile to one side. The kerb sprouted a skip full of clobber, some of which he recognized as tat which had cluttered the once 'filthiest house in North London'. It hardly deserved the moniker now.

Godfrey rang at a half-sanded door. Almost on the instant a bag of bones pulled it back. Only on second take did papa recognize the moon face of Oliver Murrie. Vaguely he recalled Margot having told him that the ex-artist had become Miranda's 'tenant' again. Preoccupied with guilt and confusion, Godfrey had failed to register jealousy or any other appropriate emotion.

'Ah, it's you,' the man murmured as if papa's arrival had been foreseen in some magic mirror. Slipping through the bare hall like a servant in a '30s *film noir* (he was wearing black still, Chinese peasant style), he delivered the guest into a emptied-out drawing-room. And there Godfrey was left to experience a second or third shock. In fact, the vision before him moved him to wonder if the days of his life as he had known it were numbered. A tidied garden was one thing; Miranda Cravin transformed was quite another.

As she turned to gaze at him from where she stood atop a ladder, the erstwhile Rose appeared the picture of a perfect English young lady, fragrant and radiant as that bloom is meant to be. Her hair was washed and pulled back in a style that made it seem hardly dyed. Her skin appeared pink and milk-fed, not pock-marked or blotchy. She was wearing a loose Laura Ashley frock, not something that had fallen off the curtain rods in the '60s. 'Hello there,' she said in a voice more steady than the old Miranda's. 'I was hoping you'd turn up.'

What was this sudden wrenching in his chest? the beginning of the heart attack he knew would get him one day? Only French coffee, Godfrey assured himself, and shock. For, as Miranda climbed down three rungs, he saw. Holding her back straight, she placed a hand on her tummy in a stock, unmistakable gesture he had known in his wife too many times.

'Can I get you a cup of tea?'

Godfrey was appalled. There would be explanations, but he could see how it would unroll. She was going to tell him quite sweetly that the foetus was his. He would ask about other men: Oliver Murrie so conveniently placed, God-knew-who before. But timing would 'prove' it. And then she would have him by the 'short n' curlies', as one of his sons might have said. The 'awful daring of a moment's surrender' his mother had warned him about decades before. First Margot and then, when she'd betrayed him again, this.

'No thanks. Gives me wind.'

He remembered the scene. It had been in this room. He had come on Boxing Day bearing gifts, before the problem with Luke. Margot had gone west with 'Lezzy', and he'd wanted advice. What other oracle could he have turned to? In the event, though he'd always dismissed her as 'one of Margot's lunatics', Miranda had proved surprisingly sympathetic. 'She's spellbound,' is what she said. 'It happens sometimes between women her age. Let it run its course.'

This information, confirming the worst, had made his control slip. ('Would you like something else?' she inquired now, 'whisky?') He had wept outright. He, a fifty-eight year old *paterfamilias*, had broken down into positively Greek lamentations. And that was what had allowed things to happen. ('Another one of you men wanting mummy to change his dirty nappies...') Miranda had asked him to sit. It was the last thing he'd wanted to do in that den, painted black at the time, with geometric symbols – *tattwas*, she'd called them. (Pathetic occultism: better Margot's 'Anglo-Catholicism' than this.) But that had not stopped him from being seduced.

The room was yellow now. 'Do you like it?' she asked, following his eyes to the stripped floor.

She seemed a teenaged girl – but this was absurd! Miranda Cravin was closer to forty than he was to sixty. Still, she looked almost adolescent again, both from his sudden distance of age and the new aura of innocence around her.

'What's going on here?' was all he could stammer.

'I'm redecorating.'

'I can see that. I suppose it would be too much to ask why?'

She put a hand on the tummy again. Averting her eyes, she seemed to beg the bookcases not to be cruel. It was quite a persona, Godfrey was forced to acknowledge, quite a change from the sordid little black-magical manipulator who'd tried half the men in London since her divorce; and he felt the stab of a thought that perhaps, entirely unknowing, he had been the author of honest reformation in her.

The idea galled him the worst. It could mean his ruin.

'What are you going to do now?' he sputtered.

'We're going to do the whole house,' she explained, as if missing the point. 'Oliver's taking a self-contained flat at the top; he'll have a separate entrance. The children will be at school: their dad still pays for that. The cats and the monkey are gone – you never saw the humour in them, did you? I thought I'd let a room on the ground floor to cover council tax and bills.'

Godfrey sat, though not asked to this time. The sofa had a sheet on it which billowed as he came down. Miranda gazed at him with all the magical radiance he had known and loved in his wife through six pregnancies. And what about *her* now?

'Is it mine?' he asked weakly, knowing as he did that the question was wrong (it indicated pride) and tried to cover by adding, 'and are you going to have an abortion?'

Good lord, would tears come? Could Miranda Cravin change so entirely as to become a blushing, vulnerable maid?

'The answers are yes, and no.'

So, that was it. He knew enough not to ask more – it would just bring down the skies in female lamentation.

'Too late?' he persisted.

Miranda of course knew what he was driving at. 'By a month.'

'Ruddy hell.'

Silence. Then, before any harsh phrase could be spilt, she knelt in front of him and added: 'I'm so sorry, Godfrey: I should've rung; but please – don't torture yourself. I won't ask for a thing. And won't tell a soul. They can think it was Ollie's if they like; it'll be my child – the first that's belonged to me only. The father could've been anyone for all the world knows.'

'You mean for all Margot knows… This could kill her!' he went on, aware that what he really meant was that it could kill *them*: be the last straw for his marriage.

'I'd never breathe a word to her.'

He didn't bother to ask how he could believe this: the girl had him now – had him indeed by those 'short n' curlies' – and his frustration spilled over. 'How in Christ's name could you have done it?' he demanded, throwing her off.

'You were heartbroken. You came in here crying that you'd lost all your sons.'

'I was not heartbroken and, if I had been, I would've kept it to myself, like a sensible chap. And the idea that I've lost all my sons is Margot's puffed-up fantasy. We have Johann still; August's alive; so are Lucius and Matthew – Marcus too, for all we know. He's probably trafficking in hashish in Samarkand or some warmed-over-1960s place you'd approve of.'

Silence again. The ghosts whirling.

'I hope you're right,' she said.

'Of course I'm right!' – Striking a match, he relit his cheroot.

'It's a girl,' she stated.

'O Jesus wept, Miranda! How do you know that?'

'I just do,' she breathed with a hint of the old witchy tones and pulled herself up on the sofa.

'Fine,' he nodded. 'And what are you going to call the wretched imp – Serendipita or something preposterous?'

'What would you like?'

'I couldn't care less.'

'I was thinking about Valerie.' (This was absurd, he reflected.) 'Or should it be Valeria? You favour Roman names, don't you?'

'Vulgaria might be more appropriate.'

Suddenly the woman started to weep. Tears in a slow, quiet tap.

'Ruddy hell!' he muttered and, repeating it, got up and recrossed the room. But anger and shock were beginning to subside now. And gradually, recognizing the only honourable course, he flopped down again beside her. – 'How much do you want?'

'Fuck off, Godfrey.'

'I'll go see my bank manager in the morning.'

'Don't bother on my account.' Sniffing tears back: 'What did you come here for anyway?'

'To ask about Margot.'

'What about her?'

'What does one do now?'

'You pathetic fool!'

'What do you mean by that?'

'It hardly makes a difference. What difference does anything make in the end? we're all fools finally. Only some realize too late.'

'Very good, Miranda. Worthy of one of Margot's BBC2 dramas. Terrifically meaningful. But what does one *do*?'

Slowly she rose and started back up her ladder. 'Carries on,' she declared, ascending three rungs and, picking up her brush, resumed her painting.

Godfrey stared. 'When will men ever understand women?' he asked of the gods.

'Only when they understand themselves,' she replied, as if all-wise.

'Did you tell Booby Vänder?'

'Did I tell her what?'

That was his answer. 'About you and me?'

Miranda said: 'You can go now, Goddy boy. It doesn't signify.'

'It "signifies" to me!' he bleated, hearing another echo. 'I have responsibilities, you know.'

'Not to me you don't.'

'To Margot then. To my marriage and sons and country at large.'

'We all know that speech. What would any of us do without you?'

Her irony was too much. 'What do I do about *her*, damn you?'

Miranda gazed down at him as if from a great distance.

'Sorry,' he added, regretting the phrase.

'It's OK. Damnation, whatever that means, is something I'm used to; salvation would be the mystery for me. As for Margot, I'm not sure. When Ollie moved back in, she stopped speaking to me. And maybe she knows about us on some astral level; one can't really say. It's Gisela who's still bothering her now, I think. Passion or guilt, pity maybe; or maybe they all amount to the same thing. The last time I spoke to her she said she'd like to move to the country. That's all I can tell you. I want to be alone now. And I don't want to see you, or hear from you ever again, OK? Goodbye.'

'Godfrey is a fantasist in his way,' Margot would opine. 'One of his mates from Balliol once compared him to the type of 18th century gentleman who knelt at the altar of Reason but only applied it when it suited.'

Godfrey himself admitted to this laughingly, if only to prove his superior Reason. Meanwhile, once he was sure that Miranda meant what she'd said – i.e., that 'like some of these warmed-over 1970s feminists', she genuinely didn't want a man's presence or help – he heaved a sigh of relief and rationalized the interlude by reference to myths of gods inseminating mortal females. He sent her a cheque for a thousand quid, which is what it might have cost him to have paid for an abortion privately, as he would have done given a chance. Miranda posted the envelope back unopened. Following this, Godfrey saw little reason to burden his thoughts with the matter further.

The prospect of a bastard daughter did not in any case exercize his fancy, which focused on legitimacy. 'Godfrey adores me,' Margot commented to John in this phase. Settled postprandially in his carver, papa emitted something to the effect that overconfidence bred hubris; but it was clear he was pleased, and relieved. Both in the marital couple knew the facts about the other: he was grateful that she was inching back towards him, if only in material form; she recognized that on some unspecified level he was good – as good as a man could be in the realm of unclean situations the whole culture seemed to be living through in those dog days of the John Majorite '90s.

Whatever his sins, Godfrey had let Margot experience what she needed, and what more could a late 20th century wife ask for than that? Meanwhile, each was tied to the other by *schadenfreude* and guilt, collective and separate – though to an outsider it remained unclear how much either felt of either. When papa's attempts to free Lucius failed, the boy's name was dropped from conversation, a fact which John construed as a function of pain. On the other hand, our expat friend sometimes got the impression that the whole Wingfield operation was being ruled by invisible forces nowadays.

John watched Godfrey. Godfrey focused on Margot. Margot in turn concentrated almost exclusively on 'baby' Johann coming up. Christened Jonathan but often called Jon, this last of his generation of Wingfields was skinny and timid; yet mama doted on his every move. It had not always been so. At his birth she'd been 'thoroughly fed up', she claimed, and her chief emotion had been indifference. Then had come Christian's death and the events surrounding her others, and maternal feeling had returned with a vengeance. Now she was wrapped up in her youngest to such an extent that, as Godfrey remarked, he was in danger of being strangled.

'That's what Gisela says.'

'No one can be a complete ass.'

Margot did not rise to the bait. Neither concurrence nor ire passed her lips these days, which may be one reason her spirit seemed moribund to her husband. The couple shared the marital bed still, this out of habit, Godfrey's desire and Margot's sense of duty. Other small signs of warmth could sometimes be detected, though a cynic might say they were chiefly products of nostalgia, a condition which Godfrey viewed (perhaps rightly) as a 'disease'. Overall, John's impression was of estrangement. If papa rued this, he was in any case not so made as to rage, plead or do much to change it. Having played Harold Nicolson, Leonard Woolf or whomever, he seemed to realize that he preferred his wife on any basis than not to have her at all.

On occasion he struck John as ambivalent about his role now. Once he half-confessed that he'd be happy to stop being a man as defined by the code and behave like the rest of us mere mortals: doubting, confused, admitting our shortcomings and wondering what the sad circus is all about. But in order to do that, Godfrey would have had to have someone to pass the baton to; and now that all but one of his sons had vanished, there were only two prospects for it – wait until the last one grew and hope he grew straight, or pass it to someone outside of the family, an alternative his public-school soul revolted against, no matter how often John beat him at chess.

So papa brooded. Meanwhile Margot and Johann pottered around Ladbroke Grove almost too silently. Then one morning reading the property section of *The Times*, Godfrey recalled a few words Miranda had let drop and had an inspiration. He would procure them a bolt-hole in the country and rid his home of the atmosphere of despond creeping through it like rising damp.

'I want you to write a new play,' is how he presented this. 'I'll stay in town and try to get Lucius off; you go to the country and get your spirits back. We'll use your next theatre fee; my assets're all tied up – this horror with Lloyd's. We'll rent some daft parsonage like you women go in for. Where do you want it to be?'

'Godfrey wants to be rid of me now,' mama joked. But on balance, she seemed to be pleased.

Thus they acquired a converted barn attached to a manor on the Somerset-Bathshire borders: a long, grey-stoned structure which Godfrey found through a pal at All Souls and took on short lease with option to buy. Upon stepping through its Gothic door, which the previous owners had installed before being savaged by Lloyd's themselves, Margot intoned:

'Yes, dearest: I think I see the point. Anyhow, enough to make me suspend disbelief. One might still find a reason to carry on.'

The house was set against a low hill, which rose up into higher hills covered with beech trees; these shielded it from the manor and bijou village behind. It gazed over a field, beyond which ran a river, beyond which rose more hills and another wood crested by clouds. From here motley weather swept in up the Bristol Channel. Still freshened or maddened from flight up the Gulf Stream, Nature in this guise would blaze or rage; so that out of her deep window-wells Margot could observe the sky in all its glory and 'fickleness'. Alternatively, should solitude come to oppress her, she could go into the village and shop. There, in the rapid, invisible way news travels in such places, her fame was whispered almost before she arrived.

Godfrey saw his wife established thus. He took comfort from how it began. Fulfilling her part of the bargain, Margot started a new play, though, as she told John, she felt superstitious about 'daring God' one more time. John agreed to make regular visits (this took scant prodding); thus papa could be released from having to go down often. Meanwhile, if Folly were what Margot still yearned for (Godfrey felt she was cured now but had to admit that artists must take inspiration where they can), there was the notional presence of Gisela Cohn-Burton not too many hills off to the east.

All seemed concordant. But then there was Johann. As if in proof of some modernist notion that there can be no harmony without dissonance, the boy grew petulant:

'She's so embarrassing, that woman,' he complained to his father, imitating some decamped *frère*, when Godfrey came at Whitsun.

'How do you mean, son?'

They were sitting, incongruously *in extremis* for papa, on a stone wall at the edge of the village as mama held forth in the shop. 'Just look at her going about in that big grey cape as if she was the Almighty.'

It was a poignant perception. For to this last son Margot did simulate God, or at least a benevolent tyrant from whom there was little escape. The separation a child learns between mama and the world had not begun in his case. Maybe it would have, had brothers been around. As things stood, it was prorogued, being neither wanted nor encouraged.

In effect, the last of the Wingfields was a case-study of the single child entrapped by single parent. In his distant way, Godfrey tried to warn Margot that when mothers hug small boys until they make them into miniature husbands, disaster can occur. (Hadn't something similar almost happened to John in his youth?) At the same time Godfrey knew that, as husband, he could not treat the mother of his sons with anything but forbearance, especially given all that Margot had been through. He was no 'ruddy Christian', thank God; nor did he wish to 'be wet'. Still, the fact that his wife had no more chances for progeny (doubtless added to guilt re Miranda) robbed him of any desire to tell her off.

'What on earth does one do?' he bleated to John one afternoon in London after a vigourous chess opening.

Our expatriate friend looked up in such surprise that papa covered by adding:

'I mean, I don't want the whole ruddy thing to turn Greek.'

'Turn Greek?'

'Tragedy provokes compensation, which provokes more tragedy, until at last the gods' attention is drawn, and they intervene to sort us all out.'

John adopted a light tone. 'Ruddy hell, Godfrey! You of all people aren't becoming superstitious, what?'

'Of course not. Ridiculous.'

But a bubble of wind burst from his chest at that moment. And in secret he wondered if the models he referred to in crisis weren't just as irrational in their way as the Religion and Romance he deprecated. Couldn't veils of Order and Reason be pulled back to reveal that the House of Wingfield lay under some kind of curse? If so, who had cursed it? where was the original sin, the Oedipal lie or Agamemnonian missacrifice? The chain of cause-and-effect had too many weak links for Godfrey to follow. All he could say was that Life was turning out to be quite different from a well-made play.

As he ruminated, Margot doted on Johann. It was the one true dependency anyone could recall in her relations, except perhaps with Christian. The phone would ring, and it would be the lad wanting to come home early from school or a friend's mother saying he'd scraped his knee falling off a bike, and mama's complexion would pale. Perhaps, if in London, she might be presiding over a festive lunch (normal life had restored itself to that degree) with humour the order of the day. But once the call came, she would effectively vanish. For this son and him alone, her spirits seemed genuine; the rest was performance. It was as if every act of negligence in her past, real or imagined, were sitting in council in her soul, demanding that she treat this one well or be damned.

'Jon is my last chance,' she murmured one night to Godfrey when he tried to tackle her on the subject before bed.

'There's no such thing as last chances!' he objected, flinging his shirt on the settee beneath de Sade. 'That's just daft superstition.'

'If I'd had a daughter, I might have felt different.'

'You might turn him into a daughter the way things are going!' (Had she got wind of Miranda's pregnancy?)

'One has to love and protect something in the end,' she retorted. 'I don't know how you manage.'

'How I manage what?' papa demanded, unleashing braces.

'To live so singularly,' she concluded, pushing him out of her life. 'Without any human attachment, really.'

'What nonsense you speak, my heart!'

But in the shadows as he dropped trousers and climbed in beside her, yet as separate as if half of England still stretched between them, Godfrey knew that in time, if only out of self-defense, he was going to have to walk out on her subliminally, as she had on him years before. And the prospect grieved him as much as it had once grieved John DuRocher when something similar had happened to him.

Mama wrote. Son complained. He was a sickly child – anaemic, John decided – and at last papa dropped his guard and disliked him.

This was on another rare visit to the country. John had cajoled him into coming for the weekend and, on arrival, vanished into the hills to fill himself with what Margot satirized as 'the melancholy of poetic skies'. Ah, English autumn when the wind sweeps all before it, yellow and pale and black and hectic red! Recalling how he had taken similar walks in the aftermath of Miranda, John read from an anthology of the Lake Poets while passing over pasture and stile.

'The Lake Poets?!' Godfrey scoffed once the rambler had returned and snatched the book from his hand. 'What does that mean? Wordsworth maundering on about daffodils, or Coleridge spouting drug fantasies? My God, what the Romantics have to answer for! almost makes one embarrassed to be English. Shelley, that ignorant pontificator with his dead children – at least Byron knew how to tell a ribald joke. But then he admired Pope and was really a man of the 18th century, what!'

He followed this with the bark of a laugh – signal for a bout of verbal roughhouse. But John was tired, and Johann busy with Leggo on the floor. Margot was stuffing a marrow in the kitchen and so, sighing over a prospect of three days of such dullness, Godfrey could do little more than beat retreat to one of the guest rooms and re-read La Fontaine in the original French.

There he stayed for most of the weekend, occasionally pestering

'Maggo' for coffee but generally dozing and brooding about being trapped. Condemned to the role that his code demanded, he longed for Monday and a train to town. Did he spend the odd hour wishing he could slough his persona and grow into someone different, as his wife appeared to be doing? Gazing at the sad, far-away look in her eye and grey-blonde abstraction haloing her head, did he note a new country persona emergent, equally romantic to one he'd derided in John yet equally remote, coming out of Hardy and other middle-class spirits from George Eliot to the author of *Lark Rise*? Did Godfrey espy in this new lyric persona yet another category of malcontent Englishwoman: the kind who turns her back on the metropolis and goes to the earth for renewal? Did Margot on her side catch him staring out windows, counting the hours until he could leave?

Out there was wind, quiet, vasty space. Beauty roamed with coolness and (though Godfrey would not say so, Margot knew he knew she was thinking it) God. Out there was peace from the cheek and devilry of her world – the Gisela Cohn-Burtons, Mirandas and so on – among which she knew he knew she included him. No, Godfrey could not have missed what his wife was thinking. In the soul he hardly admitted he had, he must have lamented. Still, he appeared to accept the case as it stood, prefiguring though it did a complete break.

Out there too was BOREDOM: that cardinal sin among Wingfields. As if in parody of how it tormented his dad, Johann whined: 'When're we going back, Mum?' (The sound of the boy's voice was another reason to leave, Godfrey grumped.)

'Hush, child. Read a book, like your father.'

'I don't want to read a book. I'm bored.'

'Go outside then, like John does.'

'I hate outside. It's cold.'

'Then come and sit by the fire and give us some peace.'

'I don't want to sit by the fire. I hate you.'

'No you don't. Don't be beastly.'

'Yes I do! You're a bore.'

What was the point of life, the child seemed to be saying, if you spent all your hours brooding among endless baa-ings of sheep?

It was in its way a legitimate question: one which Margot herself might have tolerated had he not called her 'a bore'. But any such charge was still a red rag to the mother of Matt Wingfield, not least because the play she was at work on was not going as she had hoped.

Trying to capture the new, gentler spirit of life in the country, she'd come up against the problem of how to make contentment dramatic.

Possibly Godfrey intuited this. If so he forbore from pointing out the irony, knowing what illusions art and authority demand. Johann, that sad child, had no reason to be so restrained. Thus he kept harping on the greyness around, which in his case was synonymous with mum, until she lost her temper:

'Shut your mouth, wretched imp!'

'No, you shut yours!'

'I can't think why I ever brought you into the world.'

'Why did you bother? I hate this place. I don't want to be here!'

No one took this remark as serious at the time, though the boy was making such outbursts quite often.

'Don't speak to your mother like that!' Godfrey emitted, thinking the son was just trying to get mama's goat.

But Johann had long registered his parents' estrangement. And knowing who mattered to his life and who didn't, he simply acted as if papa were not there.

After this unpromising interlude, Godfrey substantially was not. Back in London he made another attempt to get Lucius released. When this failed, he began 'in good Roman fashion' (Margot's phrase) to wash his hands of the family.

'Cordial but absent,' is how she described him after one of their chance meetings in Ladbroke Grove.

The place in the country passed off his agenda. It remained to her royalties (a revival of *Sudden Strangers* was on at The Pit and Chichester inquiring about *Jester in Flame*) to continue the renaissance there. Meanwhile, assuming the House of Wingfield west to be unconcerned by what he did in the east, Godfrey chased nervousness over the haemorrhage at Lloyd's by raising more funds for All Souls, organizing an adventure cruise for teenagers under the Prince of Wales's Trust and in general looking after class and kind in a manner which had brought OBEs to all his forbears before pensionable age.

'Things seem to be getting on an even keel again,' he remarked to John after one of their weekly chess bouts. 'Maybe the problem was that ruddy Cohn-Burton witch after all. Margot doesn't seem nearly so prickly now that she's been seen off.'

Relying on these sessions for news on his wife, Godfrey appeared not to find it eccentric to be uxorious from a distance. He adopted an attitude that his true failure, if failure it had been, had been to try too hard to be a family man. Margot for her part made no sign that she minded. Gods and goddesses ever kept a distance from mortal connections, didn't they? A policy of benign neglect settled in. Thus of his querulous youngest, papa noted less and less.

The child inhabited mama's skirts now to a point of invisibility; but if that's what Margot wanted, that's what she could have. If one result was that he took out his frustration by howling curses at papa whenever they met, Godfrey could take it: a man's character was hardly going to be cracked, nor even much altered, by a ten-year-old's refusal to acknowledge his authority. Support would be there if needed: that was the male's form of martyrdom, what? Grateful or not, the family, such as it was, came first.

So Godfrey assured himself self-contradictorily as he folded his *Spectator* and, pecking his wife on the cheek, announced: 'I'm late for the ten-twenty-three.' By this group of digits he meant the train: any number of trains he rode these days – to Oxford, to Heathrow or even to Plymouth, where an antique frigate was being fitted out for the first Prince of Wales adventure cruise.

Margot didn't ask where; she merely took the peck, replying, 'Dearest man. When back then?'

'Friday. Will you be here or out west?' – The last two words were delivered with a genial sneer.

'Haven't decided. I'll leave a note. Do look after yourself, won't you? Not too much black coffee.'

'You too, my heart. Must rush now.'

So it went.

In this evolution, Godfrey tried to keep himself from missing the odd honest remark from Matthew, witticism from Marcus or even crisis over Luke. In truth, one reason he was so often elsewhere was that he couldn't bear the dead silence around. Home seemed to him more and more tomb-like, not least as the Lloyd's thing forced him to begin selling books; nor did Margot's presence when there manage to dispel gloom. She wound up her spiral, unlocked her eyrie and wrote; the new play took form, and Godfrey gave it support, not least because his wife's aspirations (and next Critic's Award) were becoming crucial to finances. John visited often, and papa voiced himself grateful. But try as he would to inspire Johann by coaching him in

French, the expatriate friend could hardly arrest the emptiness that seemed to be seeping in as if some noxious fluid.

Past emptying bookcases, the boy would loll listless, giving papa the creeps more even. Then one chill spring evening when Godfrey was at Oxford (no one would be sure whether it was an accident or some bizarre offshoot of pre-teen despair), Johann went missing, and Margot sent John to the mid-floors to find him. After a lengthy search, he pried open a door which all had thought bolted securely. Next to Luke's bed lay the last of the Wingfields, pop-eyed and blue. By his mouth havered an unpeeled orange, teeth-marks in its rind. Trousers and knickers were down around his ankles and a volume of *Les Cent-Vingt Journées de Sodom* in hand. Attached to the doorknob was a length of surgical tubing tied to the tail of a rubberized snake: its head was coiled around the boy's skinny neck.

'Horrid, rebarbative material,' Godfrey would expostulate six months later when a TV interviewer indelicately proposed that the House of Wingfield might itself be a subject if Margot were to write a contemporary play.

'Godfrey has no capacity for melodrama,' Margot observed, 'let alone terror.' – Thus she rationalized his dyspeptic attitude and general absence, which did not alter following Johann's accident. 'He'll be as attentive as proper. Otherwise, he'll stick by the code that, whatever hideousness life may offer, it's imperative for the living to carry on.'

This was exact. Mama knew her subject. Papa Wingfield (designation perhaps no longer apt) hardly broke stride. From John, he sought assurance that his wife understood him well enough not to resent his behaviour – he'd supported her through the years, hadn't he? Meanwhile, as regards the wretched fate of his youngest, his sole comment was: 'She's taken it frightfully well, don't you think? rather like a female Job, what? Still, one wishes she'd spent some of that lucre she's made to send him to a proper prep. Why is it that women have to keep children on the teat nowadays to the point of drowning them?'

If this sounds callous, the truth was that the demise of the boy shocked Godfrey such that he was left nearly speechless. What could a man do when faced with such Unreason? Instinctively, he knew he could offer no solace to Margot. So he stayed distant, leaving contact with her even more to his periodic chess-chats with John.

John's state-of-mind he did not trouble over. Like most men of his type, Godfrey assumed other men to be 'sound'. Thus when the American announced that Booby Vänder had died in a car crash outside of Pamplona, he seemed not to hear, let alone register grief. Perhaps he'd felt grief too often of late to take on more. In any case, his response simply was to pour more whisky and lay on wit.

John by contrast just let sadness flow, at the risk of sounding maudlin. 'I guess there's no escaping these crises in our lives,' was his line. (Margot, new play finished, was recuperating in the country, the London house empty except for the males.) 'When they come, you ask yourself, how am I going to deal with this? Then you start coping, but never easily – wouldn't be human if you could. Looking around, you realize that all active lives are strewn with little deaths. You've been here before; others have too; and no crisis will ever be like the first, when you realized there's no absoluteness to love.'

Was he ventriloquizing for papa? Certainly the Englishman would never have dared such sententiousness.

'You mustn't let what's happened get you down,' Godfrey puffed. (They were in the dining-room; a late summer's sun had not yet abandoned the gardens outside of Margot's conservatory.) 'She'll get through in the end; she always has. Anyhow you can't let someone else's tragedy take you over – that's how women behave with their beastly tears. Where would we be if men were like that?'

John squinted as if through the wrong end of a telescope. With light fading behind his orange clumps, Godfrey could no longer be seen well enough to tell if his words were meant as irony or just phatic communion.

'Of course you're right,' he mused. 'You'll have to forgive me. Stupid to show one's emotions. And mine aren't important compared to hers, huh? That's the point of being "a writer", isn't it? you get to feel more than the rest of us poor, blighted chumps. And then there's the fact that I'm single and haven't stuck to the hard road of marriage and children like you: it marginalizes me. That's why my responses are negligible, not that I'm male. It's what makes her life big: that she's a mother. She has a right to her "tragedy", like Steinbeck's Ma Joad. "Indomitable, though in tatters", she'll carry on regardless, excruciating though it is. The force of her will will triumph, sweeping the rest of us petty twerps before it.'

Punctuating this with an uncharacteristic smirk, John helped himself to a new glug of whisky.

'Force of her ego possibly,' Godfrey rejoined, refilling his own glass. 'You put too much importance on her, you know – especially her writing. It's all this American love-affair with success. Don't let yourself be mesmerized.'

Was the man warning him off at long last? The glow of his cheroot was all John could see. No, he assured himself. Margot was still a cross for the prodigal husband to bear, and he was still grateful for someone to help him with it.

'You may be right. We Americans, coming from the great land of matriarchy, may be overly impressed by your White Goddesses – especially ones who're such masters, or mistresses, of the language. And we probably do put too much emphasis on writing. Hell's bells, I can hardly master my prepositions!'

'Quite.'

'Only a few days ago Margot was saying, "I don't know why you make so much of me. I know what a fraud my public persona is. And if my situation has any 'larger significance', it's as a cautionary tale against *that* – being a playwright – any of it.'

Godfrey might have been forgiven for taking this as half-drunken waffle. Two weeks later, however, he might have recalled it as Margot stated something not dissimilar on TV.

This was in the run-up to the next Critics' Award, for which her new play had been nominated. Godfrey had encouraged her to do the minimum publicity, to 'bring herself back to the land of the living'. Margot had agreed to a meedjah grilling, though only because she 'felt numb to everything nowadays'.

'Writers are monsters,' is what she was saying when John and Godfrey abandoned their chess to a stalemate and switched on the set. 'All artists are. They have to be. Which is why it's a good job they have no real power.'

'Too bloody true,' papa burped, filling glasses.

'A provocative statement,' the interviewer rejoined. 'But no doubt our audience would like to know what you, being one of finest playwrights in the land, imagine is better.'

The interviewer was the raven-haired daughter of one of Godfrey's pals at All Souls. She wore magenta-rimmed glasses to match the plastic décor of the arts studio the show had been taped in.

'Truth,' Margot mused, staring into a middle distance as if about to dispense wisdom under a plasticine saint.

'Don't blow your chance!' papa muttered, thinking to himself that drinks-party gossip was what was called for.

'"Truth"?' the interviewer echoed.

'Yes. Those who can tell it: they're the ones who are "better".'

Godfrey looked shocked at this new persona of his wife's. 'Dear heart!' he emitted as a last vestige of Eleanor of Aquitaine seemed to vanish into this gaunt, ethereal mendicant who'd been fasting for months. Did he realize for the first time how she had truly suffered? At this pinnacle in the public eye, could she evoke from him a sensation she'd never been able to in person? Eerily, papa seemed driven back by the image, into some private, unrelatable grief. Margot was the best actress in one of her roles yet. Yet the role she was playing was merely herself, so the performance conveyed.

'Yes, but in this day and age,' the interviewer challenged, 'with the Church in decline and politics as it is, many believe that the Arts are the best place to look for Truth – maybe only.'

'Don't fall for that! We're liars, we artists – we literary ones at any rate. Why do you think a play's called play and fiction fiction? We're in the business of telling things that didn't happen and don't. We're actors and tricksters and no doubt charlatans.'

'Be careful, Maggo!'

'Are you saying that you, who stand a chance of winning the highest honour in your profession, are not to be trusted for your message?'

'What "message"?'

'In deep structure, between the lines, in overarching metaphors.'

'Ruddy pseud!' Godfrey burped.

'I'm not certain,' Margot mused. 'I think I'm coming to regard all art as confusion – chaos; shades of grey. Like a kind of missionary, I sometimes imagine I'm going to bring order to worlds I create; but who's to say my order isn't an illusion? a great con, as one of my sons might've teased. I don't believe in my Truth, no – surely not as I've wrought it; not even in your overarching metaphors, if I understand what that means. There is uncanny prevision, even prophecy sometimes. But in orthodox terms, that's closer to magic than virtue. It's certainly not truth in any sound Christian sense.'

'Ruddy hell, sweetheart; you've blown it there!'

'Well, I'm confused now.' – The interviewer tried to smile. 'We're not often confronted with a bankable playwright who wants to tell us her work is bogus.'

'That's a shame. Because art, being play, lies in the realm of Satan. Or at best, of man trying to play God.'

At this point papa might've snapped the set off had it not been his wife preaching on it. As it was, he poured himself another whisky (John's tumbler – indeed, presence – had for the moment slipped his mind) and braced himself to stick it out.

'That's what I'm trying to get across in *Secrets Untold*. How does life come about? Here is a lump of young woman, pretty, unthinking. She gets married; *la commedia* in the conventional sense *è finita*. So out of insecurity, or boredom, she creates. And how does she create? by sex. And what is sex to the rational mind? negation of head and law; perversity. Out of error then, birth. She brings to life shadows she's half-imagined; dreams she half-wants to wake out of; beings which by their nature grow up in part as vehicles of her own self-contempt. So she kills them, one by one, subtly. In life, she gives death. It's all a vast expression of her irritability and frustration: her permanent, ineradicable, quite human disquiet with existence, which can never be perfect and always ends up in the grave.'

'No, no, no!' papa reproved. 'They'll never accept you if they think you're morbid!'

'What about re-birth?' an androgynous voice spoke up; and the camera swung round to focus on Eileen Moloch, who'd been waiting for her turn, patient, plump and alert.

'Fuck off, you old dyke!' Godfrey exploded with no more charity than a football hooligan kicking an opponent's supporter.

The camera swung back to Margot. 'Your latest work has been compared to *The Tempest*,' the interviewer put in.

'Bosh!' she burst out, delighting her husband with this echo of his cheek. 'I'm content to leave Shakespeare comparisons to Eileen, who can boast of what I can't: the "productivity of genius".'

'*Touché*, sweetheart!'

'Your plays are on the brief side,' the interviewer quipped.

'Don't be cute!' papa muttered, asiding to John, 'Where do they come up with these infernal culture-philistines?'

'Perhaps,' his wife simultaneously shrugged, 'I have less to say. And in that sense, your *Tempest* allusion is apt. Because I doubt if there'll be another play after this one, unless something supernatural occurs.'

Godfrey nodded approval, but John doubted he caught the subtext: that to appease the strange gods of her art, Margot had no further sacrifices to make. Had he been a person to brood over the weird, pagan intimations he had sometimes felt when confronted by images like, say, the facade of St Sulpice, Godfrey might have glimpsed what she was suggesting. But as fantasist, papa was quite limited really; for while he could analogize his insemination of Miranda to ancient myth, he could not quite grasp how Margot's inspiration connected with basic life-material. Five sons gone; five plays written – that was the message, John believed. But to someone as essentially on the outside as Godfrey, the implication remained as obscure as it must have to two million other odd viewers.

'We must move on,' the interviewer concluded, 'from this astonishing revelation, which will doubtless disappoint your fans, that *Secrets* may be your last play. But before turning to our other nominee tonight, Eileen Moloch, is there anything you'd like to add – a final word, for example, on what you regard as the quality that really sets your work apart?'

'Here's your chance, Maggo!'

Did Godfrey notice, John wondered (had he registered through any of it?) how his wife had let the blonde drain out of her hair, leaving only shades of grey? how she had coiled it carefully in serpentine twists? how she had chosen to wear all white in contrast to the interviewer and studio? how she had made her eyes dark as coal and deepened the circles around them?

'Truth,' she repeated as if a mantra. (Defiance now subtly creased the slack cheeks.) 'I wish I could find it. My heart keeps trying to calm itself with the phrase, "God is One; One is All; All is Love". But then comes the irony: Love is Sex in this World. And Sex is red – sad but true. It is rage and betrayal; beauty and death. All it results in is more of the same... Too much gone. All these ghosts. If there's any message in my work, it's in the lines against sex. My critics take them as comic, or facetious. They are not.'

'Margot Wingfield, thank you,' the interviewer murmured, looking subtly vampirized; meanwhile, the camera swung a final time to la Moloch, still reigning empress of British drama, who scowled through a smile which might've struck papa as envious had he continued to watch – because, as the raven-haired girl introduced

Margot's perennial rival, she seemed to realize already that this year a factor was at work in the scheme which no other nominee could compete with: sympathy for a devastated mother.

Godfrey did not anticipate Margot's triumph. Not believing in 'irrational' sentiment, he assumed that she'd talked herself out of the prize; thus he had snapped off the telly once her part of the interview was done. When she did win, he was more surprised than anyone, and more chuffed. With a burst of exuberance worthy of a schoolboy, he became his wife's chief supporter and led the counter-attack against those who began to whisper against her.

'Don't pay attention, my heart. In that theatre world, like all professional ghettoes, backbiting is an admission of being second-rate. Thank God I've always been in a proper trade like banking or business and nothing really cut-throat like writing! Anyhow, no profession is entirely pure in its standards. You won, for whatever reason; the rest doesn't matter a damn!'

'Ta, dearest. Evidently one or two are asking, "Or does it"?'

This was true. And soon more than just one or two.

Prominent among them was Eileen Moloch. In *The Bloomsbury Review*, she penned a retrospective on the Wingfield opus and came to the conclusion that there was 'a faint smell of sulphur' about it.

Godfrey was livid. 'She's as vicious as she's impertinent,' he bellowed. 'The only reason she goes in for such libels is that somebody told her she's being sent up in one of your bit characters!'

Margot did not comment; and papa went around spreading the tale that Moloch's outburst had been prompted by jealousy, wounded vanity and megalomania, the last because she'd won the prize twice and still commanded higher fees than all other nominees combined.

This line went down well:

'Eileen may be peculiarly sensitive to the odour she complains of in Mrs Wingfield's work,' Smedley Anis sniffed on another arts' interview programme. 'All of us have heard of it, few actually whiffed it. But in Margot's case, at least it doesn't come under splashes of inexpensive perfume.'

And so on.

Godfrey cultivated friends among a set he'd always dismissed as pretentious; thus he made sure his wife had a defender on the letters page of whatever rag took her case up. This was not difficult. There are any number of has-beens, wanna-bes and also-rans among the literary *nomenklatura* in London, as I'd warned John when he'd first arrived there; and most of them could be counted on to have a go at a fellow-writer whose indefatigability they envied yet condemned through a dogma of 'Less Is Better'.

Meanwhile, as Godfrey buoyed himself with zest for battle, Margot contrived to remain above all. Unwilling to deflate his fantasy that this was his 'finest hour' in a lifetime of support for her, she merely observed: 'Beware the wee man when his blood is aroused.'

Did she realize that, with as few ways as he had to relate to her nowadays, papa genuinely needed the chance? Whether or no, as he cheered on the backbiting, a more serious furore arose:

Brooding in 'magical retreat' in Bathshire, Gisela Cohn-Burton came to the conclusion that Margot was sending her up in her most recent play, and with more reason than la Moloch. Seething from prior humiliations, the ex-synthesist chose this moment to prove that the worm had finally turned. She set out to 'tell all' to the meedjah.

The first sign of trouble seemed small enough: a reporter from the diary of an up-market London tabloid phoned Ladbroke Grove to clear a tip that Margot Wingfield had taken her ideas from a prominent therapist. Biting his tongue, Godfrey retorted that this was the fantasy of some malicious crank, a conclusion the reporter claimed he had already arrived at. 'Then why bother us with it?' papa exclaimed and slammed down the receiver so hard that it cracked.

But that wasn't the end of it.

Piqued by Godfrey's rejoinder, the diary in question ran the conversation in full. From there, the tale made its rounds to tattle columns of *The Times*, *The Independent* and arts-pages of two Sunday broadsheets. At this point, papa was obliged to go on alert. These were the 'quality' papers. People actually read them!

For a time he decided there was not much to fear. Gossip put bums on seats; besides, Gisela had been around – many would recall the ill-judged volume of psychobabble Margot had put her name on next to the woman's, so there seemed little point in trying to deny a link: it would just draw attention, an attention which among other things could hardly be flattering to Godfrey. Anyhow, the female Tartuffe may not have been entirely mistaken. She may even have had more effect on Margot's production than she supposed, if in ways she hardly would have liked. But then: 'SHE TOOK EVERYTHING FROM

ME!' raved a headline in *The Post*; 'PSYCHOLOGIST TELLS HOW TOP PLAYWRIGHT USED HER,' *The Excess* took up; 'HOW SHE LOVED ME AND LEFT ME,' rejoined *The Daily Issue*; 'THE MOTHER WHO DEVOURED HER SONS,' added *The News of the Earth*. This was sick-making, especially the lesbian intimations. And while Margot had supporters and friends as well as 'responsible' voices in the meedjah willing to defend her, all was made worse by whispers to the effect that there can be no smoke without fire.

A gauntlet had been thrown. Something had to be done. Though essentially a man of peace, as he protested, Godfrey had to put on blinders and see nothing but malice in his opponent's intentions, not the pathetic evidence of a woman scorned. Meanwhile, out in her West Country redoubt, Gisela must have realized that – as Margot had once warned her – the line had to be drawn somewhere: that, to be blunt, her cheques for exclusives from *The Daily Sun* or *The Stars* could not be allowed to be the end of it.

'The Establishment in this country can be quite forgiving,' Margot mused when John mentioned these matters to her, which she otherwise sought to ignore. 'We fancy a bit of scandal here more than boring old truth – spy scandals, sex scandals; perfidious Albion and so on. Still, when a certain mark is passed, the veil falls back in place with the precision of a guillotine. The Ancient Order depends on it.'

The erstwhile playwright knew whereof she spoke. Her great woman friend had failed once again to account for the strength of forces against her. The Bonapartist had simply pushed the *ancien régime* too far. Godfrey had contacts; Wingfield was a name. By the code, no gentleman worthy of the term could let such rumours circulate about his wife. War had to be declared.

Solicitors were called.

Perhaps the synthesist had got the message wrong, Godfrey mused. Maybe she'd thought his forbearance had meant indifference or worse: some kind of 'wetness'. But if he had once appeared to accept the value of a witch in his wife's ascent, even use of scandal in promoting her plays, he had always known that, if allowed to drone on, she could destroy not only the Wingfield reputation but also Margot's attraction for any audience in future, save a hole-in-the-corner coterie. Thus, regretfully, if with his wife's tacit consent (her place in posterity concerned Margot too, after all), he sued for libel. So began the trial (yet more beneficial for bums on seats) of what papa took to describing as 'that neo-feminist, would-be Bosie'.

This designation struck John as somewhat inapt: 'At least Bosie was a poet,' he pointed out, having recently proof-read my monograph on Wilde. 'Gisela has more in common with someone like, say, Aleister Crowley.'

Godfrey hooted at this reference to the onetime 'wickedest man in the world'. Meanwhile, he took fanatical interest in the proceedings once engaged: 'I'm going to take Margot on a tax-free second honeymoon,' he stated in anticipation of the outcome, 'if one can get blood from a stone!'

Margot remained unaware of her husband's travel plans. She consented to budge from the country only when required. Silence otherwise was her deafening comment on what went on in Mr Justice Kilkinnock's courtroom.

Had she loved the woman? That was the question on everyone's lips, conveyed *sotto voce* behind backs of hands. Whatever the answer, Margot was not prepared to throw stones at her erstwhile confidante. Perhaps this is why Godfrey encouraged his QC, Mr Stanley Stubbs-Morris, to become inexorable.

Witnesses were produced with breathtaking ease to contend that they too had paid dear for the Cohn-Burton 'therapy'. Miranda and Oliver were even rolled out and presented as if pillars of the establishment. Thus, in the end, Margot's great friend was reduced to what the judge (an old Harrovian pal of Godfrey's) summed up:

'Behold the tedious commonplace of recent decades: the phoney saviour whose concealed motives are money, power and kinky sex. An essentially mannerless, ill-bred virago who preys off credulous mothers, wives and half-broken people, trying to sell pseudo-religion. Beware of her comforts. What she really dispenses is addiction to mental masochism.'

Margot was disgusted. 'English justice!' she breathed.

Meanwhile, Eileen Moloch, still embittered, weighed in with a letter to *The Observer*: 'Ms Wingfield used to come to the defense of legitimate helpers of disturbed men and women who are constantly being accused of being sex-fiends, witches or frauds, and so are figuratively burnt at the stake. But now as she ascends towards riches and fame, she kicks down the ladder behind her.'

This stung. Nor was the jury's decision madly comforting. Comparing Wingfield theatre-takings against Cohn-Burton counselling-fees, it awarded five pounds in damages.

Godfrey was disappointed, but put a brave face on it. 'Good riddance, Tartuffe,' was his parting shot; and settling behind a victory cheroot, he wasted no time in wondering how poor 'Bosie' might feel, now that she was 'cornered and set upon'.

This phrase was Gisela's. John had heard it from Margot, who confided that – at the height of the trial – the synthesist had appeared at her door in the country and begged her to 'call off the dogs'.

'Margot's just going soft,' Godfrey grunted when John relayed this to him. 'The mind-merchant type can only be seen off by strength.'

So that was that. Papa had won. And Margot would not speak of the matter again: not to him, not to John, especially not to the Press. Somnambulistically, she put her name to a statement distributed by Godfrey through solicitors –

> I was led to believe that this woman could keep one of my sons off of drugs after another had come to a bad end. Later I found her to be an intriguing character in her own right. But I never used her ideas knowingly, nor her personæ; and I have been distressed to discover that a person who enjoyed my hearth and table could have turned on me in this way. I have withdrawn from public view as a result.

– but of course papa had drafted the statement.

'Rather good, don't you think?' he asked John, showing off. 'Sums it all up rather well, what?'

Godfrey did not mean to be cruel, or obtuse. It was just that, by the barracking code his type lived on, a man had to crow:

'Now to steal a phrase from another self-deluding "Christian" writer, maybe we can have an end to the affair!'

4.

Sleeping was the closest one could get to being dead, Margot mused. Or perhaps to being reborn. Dreaming was full of colours, terrors, unexpected renovations. It was possibly the only means by which one could penetrate that wonderful, dim landscape where no prior experience offered a map. Sleeping most of her days and half of her nights was not a way to escape so much as to transcend the otherwise untranscendable: life.

It was also a physical compulsion. She remembered a time in the days of the Sacred Sec when Booby had got drunk and she'd gone to the kitchen to fix coffee but when she'd come back the woman had disappeared, leaving the doors swinging open. Margot had discovered her out in the street, snoring away on a mattress dragged out of a skip. 'Come on!' she'd commanded, shaking her awake and frog-marching her back in. Drunken compulsion being what it is, Booby had soon disappeared again, the doors swinging open; only this time, with street-person's cunning, she'd dragged the mattress into a neighbour's front garden and was snoring away behind a latched gate, so that Margot had to pay hell to find her. When Godfrey asked the next day why she'd gone in for such daft behaviour, the miscreant replied: 'A foetus of mine has just died.' (Booby had had a miscarriage.) 'How would you propose I communicate with it?'

Margot believed she knew what the woman had meant. She'd known it then, and she knew it now, in what she referred to as 'the dog days' of her career.

'You should come back to London,' John said.

Dog days produced dogged companions. This one persisted in visiting her in the country, though she had long wearied of him.

'London's full of sharpening knives,' she observed. 'Besides, how could I possibly work in that house? Too many dead babies there.'

'You've said that before. It's a cliché. Anyhow, you're not writing here, so what's the difference? You've turned your back on your profession, like you predicted you would.'

John felt uncomfortable with his new hectoring persona. Was Henry James in a jeans jacket his fate after all?

Actually, he'd taken to wearing a Barbour and wellies to please someone, or at least reassure the villagers. But it didn't please Margot. Little did nowadays. She missed her father, she sometimes thought inaptly, murky presence though he'd been. Even a mad Celt with blood and guts in the teeth might have been better than this *nothing* she faced. For nothing it felt like. No father, no son, no reason whatever. She just wanted to sleep.

'It's not healthy,' John stated.

'Of course it is. Sleeping's restorative.'

'Sleeping? We were talking about writing, I thought.'

'You were,' Margot returned and wondered if being nasty might add some social discomfort to spice things up. 'I was thinking of sleep.'

'You can't sleep forever.'

'Why not?'

'It's depressive. You'll end up ill.'

'We all sleep in the end, dearest. The "big sleep", don't you know.'

'If you're speaking about Chandler, that was about drugs. Anyhow, what's the point?'

'I don't know. That's just my point.'

'So?' – This kind of banter was more therapeutic than silence, having at least power to irk.

'So nothing. I sleep. Perchance to dream. And if not...'

'If not?'

'I don't know. I'm waiting.'

Now he would ask 'Waiting for what?' and she would repeat, 'I'm not sure'. Then they would pause and he mention entropy, say. So it would go, like a pair of children on a hot day desultorily trying to play badminton. But she had never had time for games, Margot thought, though at the moment she had all the time in the world – which was just one more reason to sleep.

'I rather feel like being in a Shakespeare play. I know that sounds like Eileen Moloch, but I don't mean to inflate myself. One just fancies being hounded by ghosts. Like one of those rapacious kings who kill thirty-nine people to get to the throne.'

'You want to have nightmares?'

It would be something, no? One had to feel something, even if only guilt. And that was it, wasn't it? She wanted to feel guilt, hers or not didn't matter. She wanted an excuse to rush out and wail on the moors; beat her breasts, tear her hair – all that Greek sort of thing. But God or the non-God, Satan or whoever who it was that ruled the Unknown, was not yet ready to give it to her.

It was not for having failed to coax him. Margot had starved herself, fed herself cheese late at night, eaten questionable mushrooms – but nothing out of the ordinary had happened. She'd told herself she'd killed Christian, exiled August, uprooted Marcus, mocked Matthew, neglected Lucius, overmothered Jon – yet none of that had been more than self-inflation; nor had it brought one of them back, not even in gibbering spirit form, it had just made her think that life was not very fair. She'd made her mistakes surely; but her sons had had their own destinies, and what she'd done or had not had only been part of what impelled them.

She felt cold now, and grey. John was sitting on dry stone at the foot of her vegetable garden. The garden was overgrown: she'd long since tired of cultivating swedes and relied for calories on wine and bickies. He was gazing in his usual fashion towards sky to the west. Sunset was snaking in, silver and gold under black.

'Go away, dearest. I won't come to London. I just want to be alone.'

'Tosh!' he retorted. 'Ruddy hell.'

'You sound like Godfrey.'

'Maybe we all end up sounding like Godfrey with you, Margot. As much as I shuttle between the two of you nowdays, I might as well be your fan-handler, or surrogate son.'

But you're not, a look said. 'You're not even part of the family,' the words came. (Though half-prepared for this, her guest winced.) 'Luckily for you,' she added emolliently.

'So much tosh,' John persisted. 'That's what Godfrey calls these statements of yours when I repeat them: post-existentialist tosh.'

'Does he? I never knew him to go in for pseudo-academic jargon.'

'In the course of collecting articles on your plays, he's picked up one or two terms; maybe even coined a few himself.'

'Has he indeed?... So how is dear God?' she asked, less out of desire to know than to interrupt the verbal ping-pong.

'He misses you, naturally.'

'Godfrey? What nonsense. Godfrey just misses not having mummy around to change his dirty nappies.'

'He worries over your welfare.'

'I'm fine.'

John did not ping back, and Margot knew he could see she was not 'fine' in any sense Godfrey might have meant. Even she knew that she was depressed: feelingless; quite eager to pull the covers over her head, as she'd once threatened, and give up the ghost.

'I play chess with him once a week now. He's still incredibly hard to beat. The last time I brought you up, he said: "You don't think she'll do anything desperate, do you?"'

How dreary it was! How she wished she could pull those covers over her head, or that her duvet would burst into flame like some accursed garment in an ancient drama and immolate her, soul and all.

'I don't believe in suicide,' is what she said.

'So I told him. "Bloody religionists don't. Quite right too, what?"'

'Godfrey said that? It must be the first favourable comment he's made about religion since he was in short pants. Anyhow, I'm not sure I consider myself much of a "religionist" anymore, though don't alarm him by saying so. Whether I believe in it or not – suicide, that is – I doubt I could muster the strength.'

Sunset was perfect for this remark: blood-orange sliced open to reveal black rot. As a matter of fact, it was heart-stoppingly dramatic: one of those bursts of glory that make you think of God if you believe in Him, or a picture of Heaven in a children's book if you're not sure, or spring blooms in a lost garden if you're simply romantic – some garden tucked away in nostalgia, like a memory through French doors at Ladbroke Grove. Margot could see John nursing some such meditation. She avoided the almost canine look of devotion he trained on her. If she let him, he would start in about how thin she was and didn't eat properly; how she drank too much and was only standing by some miracle of metabolism; how she just stared catatonically at the sky – '"As if shades of your misbegotten brood were going to appear out of it?"'

'Whot?!'

The line from her first play was either too remote to remember or he had misquoted it. Whichever, Margot was too preoccupied with what he might say to Godfrey to parry or thrust. And what would her dear husband do on hearing of her state? gulp down more whisky and quote a line from Molière? When was the last time she'd seen true sentiment from him? not when Christian had died, or Marcus or Matthew had decamped; not when Luke had been sent up or poor Johann found. 'Someone must try to be stoic around here, what?' The last time she could recall any real emotion from her husband was when they'd taken the decision, there being no alternative, to put Gus on the plane to New York.

'You all right?' John queried.

Good Lord, what could one say to discourage this disturbance of one's inner thoughts? 'I once had religion,' she threw out, hoping that like Godfrey he might rise to this bait, attacking her faith or at least being diverted into some private sorrow – some image of his mother, say, hair wisps against pillow as she waited, indignant, for death. 'Now I sometimes wish I could get it back.'

'What's religion anyhow?' he went on Godfreyesquely.

'In this case, not faith so much as the simple strength to carry on.'

There, she thought. Repeat *that* to my husband, and he can say what he likes, addressing some other wraith in his mind. And you can come back here and insist I come up to London again, but I won't. I'm here now forever. It's where I shall die.

'You seem less "sinful" than you did once.'

'How generous of you!' – Silly, tedious man; overearnest American hanger-on, always a little patronizing… 'Yes, I suppose I'm free of envy,' she played on. 'Avarice and gluttony were never my thing. Lust? Women of our class don't admit to it, at least so Godfrey informed me when we got married – Miranda put paid to that, though. Vanity perhaps? but that's only Pride. Some might say I could use a bit more of it now. Anything I've missed?'

'Despair,' John observed, gazing at her too knowing.

'Ah yes of course. The most unforgivable, and modern, *n'est-ce pas*?' Throw in the French. Put him off into thoughts of Marianne, or his peripatetic youth, or Godfrey at Deux Magots.

Dear God – now she wished he were here – his scabrous wit to chase this sentiment doled out to a point of cruelty… Godfrey, that barking, conceited little imp of the perverse, whose caring for her was (always had been) in some sense displaced mother-love… But then all men's for women was in the end, wasn't it? All love for all people was finally. Maybe that's why she hadn't been able to love as she should have, bored and embarrassed by her own lower-middle class Irish Mum as she'd been. And was that the secret? the origin of her 'sin'? not to have felt *that* love? not to have been able to feel any love truly, except in a posturing sense?

Margot clutched her arms. She felt not only cold and grey, but soul-dead. – Yet it wasn't true, was it? She had loved, hadn't she? loved her sons… O where were they now, her darling babes, each in his own individual halo, refracted rays of some greater glory? She'd dreamt them into existence – conceived them out of fragments of herself: Christian the blessed, August the ruthless, Marcus the charming, Matthew the pious, Lucius the fearless and Johann – ? despair. O despair! that's what it all tailed into in the end, no? entropy or some such; no 'motif of redemption', as romantics might say – as this aging successor of mine might have said had she given him a chance.

'Must just go in and check on your supper, dearest. We can't have you leaving on an empty stomach, can we?'

Inside, however, she had hardly a thought. Her inner life felt as barren as wintry hills out the door; she could not even summon the passion to weep. Sunset continued out there, silhouetting John as she peered round to make sure he wouldn't follow. For a moment, relenting, she thought of him as a friend, dear, concerned, almost a lover, trying to do what he could. But she couldn't be helped now. A perverse anger had hardened the tightening core of personality inside her, though where was the *motif* of redemption, a voice seemed to cry... Her father might have used such a term, or Godfrey's mother. Still, it was a long time since anyone had believed in such cant or even yearned for it. All that *fin-de-siècle* piety, drenched in longings for some Holy Grail – couldn't be brought back here. No, her soul said, yet not without a sweet, almost sexual ache of regret.

Chaos: her kitchen. Order: Godfrey's world... But that was it, wasn't it? some ideal of perfection, and not just in "civilized" society but also the soul. That's where men and women needed to direct themselves still. Even Godfrey had thought so, back when they'd just married and read poetry in bed, quoting Keats or whomever:

> All dreams of the soul end
> In a beautiful man's or woman's body

He'd actually believed in such dreams once. But then had come rebellion: against them, against himself for not 'being a man'. Fatherhood had arrived, and in that sterilizing public-school way he had maintained that there was something suspect about feelings, at least beyond a certain age. And so the worm had turned. As his waistbands expanded, he had learned to blame all romantic 'softness' on women. ('That's just the trouble with you women! You need us to be upright, war-like, constructive but at the same time demand that we stay "sympathetic", whatever that means.') Dread God. Had he ever realized truly who he was? Even now, through this American mole, wasn't he trying to get back to an image he secretly cherished? of woman as frail, retracted from strength? Wasn't it only *that* that could refill him with the adoration he needed: some pretext to 'save' her, redeem her and thus re-erect a vision of valour for himself – Parsifal, Galahad... It was so bloody false! How had he reacted, for instance, to Gisela in her anguish? a woman struggling to be heroic but falling into petulant self-doubt? What had he done, he and his kind? rushed to tear her apart, the sad creature, misguided though she was; to shame her, attack her with all the instinctive force of a pack of little dogs when a vixen's been run to ground and put its tail between its legs.

And what had they done to Christian, her own sons, for having been too blessed? O how she hated the world for this, if no other thing – this lack of mercy! this lack of love.

Godfrey, Godfrey, Godfrey…

Revenge was too strong for that conceited little man. Weakish-strongish and wayward, he was not vicious really. Not entirely. Not enough for her to want to carve his heart out to roast on a spit. Not enough even to do more than upset him and prevent him from resting smug now or ever in his affection for her.

What were his virtues? He'd completed the launch of his adventure cruise, to considerable fanfare – smiling photos with the Prince, which John had brought out to show her. Beside this stood his efforts on behalf of what Booby used to call the 'secret élite'. What were his vices? Most current in Margot's estimation was what Gisela phoned her to spill about: Miranda's baby. Of course Margot understood on the instant how he must have sweated over that: the fear that she'd hear. But she made no sign of it. She made little sign of anything to him now. Numbness was all she felt, she pretended to John: numbness to life in general – too much to bother about what they were doing *là-bas*, which is how Gisela referred to 'despicable' London.

The ex-synthesist had started becoming an old wife or great aunt figure too. (Did all her *déracinés* have to end up as characters out of bad Henry James?) The world was a barbed place with old friends paying scores. Miranda had phoned Gisela; Gisela had phoned her; eventually thus all secrets had been told, though at each stage with the tale-bearer protesting that she was thinking only of someone else's welfare. (Who was ever thinking of anyone else's welfare in this war of deranged egos?) Meanwhile up in town, Godfrey had sent another cheque to the new mother, prompted by fear and a sense of *oblige*. Miranda had returned it as she had the two others, this time with a note scrawled by Oliver Murrie:

> Miranda sends thanks for your good wishes. Mother, daughter and family doing fine.

School-girl amusements. Suburban bitchery. Godfrey, she hoped, would mutter a curse against squalid lives and carry on as he always had: as if Order and Reason were the only permanent reality, even if his situation told against it. Godfrey, she hoped in her soul, would remain Godfrey. But that did not stop her from wanting to turn the screw on him.

Nor did the phonecalls John reported him making – to New York, to Beirut, to Iona and Feltham. These resulted in little so far as one could tell. Once he had thought he'd located Augustus through an art-dealer in Manhattan but hadn't been able to speak to the boy, only to leave the message: 'Contact your mum!' Typical Godfrey. If there were one son she wanted back less than the others, it was this errant who'd fled to 'the ashtray of the world'. Anyhow, it was doubtful the message had got through: the art-dealer was 'one of those stereotyped cigar-chompers who got a kick out of being gruff and vague at the same time', and Godfrey's announcement that he was Gus Wingfield's father had been a trigger for 'what passes for wit in your country' rather than a snap to attention.

'Some of your people are simply untalkable to,' papa had concluded to John, partly to cover humiliation, and fell back on homiletics: 'If a son wants to go off, who am I to stop him? A man has to stand on his own feet eventually, what? We all have our jobs in this world.'

John retailed this to Margot.

'But that wasn't the end of it,' he added.

'How do you mean, dearest?'

'It was for you that he did it.'

'That he did whot?'

'Made all those phonecalls. And is making them still.'

So, she thought: he imagines he can win me back, does he? Meanwhile she purred: 'So when are you going to bring the poor devil down here to see me?'

Thus, by remote control, she contrived to get her husband to swallow distaste and return to her sphere one last time.

She felt wicked about it, the manipulation. But wickedness was part of the quick of life, wasn't it? And what female, however ageing and weary, could give up manipulating and be worthy of the name? Anyhow, if Godfrey or anyone else wanted her to end up a saint, he would have to give her the space to execute a dignified death in, which she knew he wouldn't, unless she forced him to. And that was what this was all about, wasn't it? getting the space to die in, however one pleased. To achieve it, she would shove him out of her life for once and for all – by distance, politeness, subtle mockery, neglect; grey coolness like that of the November day he would arrive in;

inanimation, a landscape going cold. Thus she would pay him back for the mad, careless, bully-boy glee with which he had taken his sons on an outing as pagan as a shoot: that excursion which had come to seem original sin in their lives; an escapade which appeared now to have been fated to end in some Cain-and-Abel incident.

She had known, Margot mused in her new monody of reflection, that to have named her dearest 'Christian' had been a provocation. To have named them all, except Godfrey's cherished Gus, in that decorative, New Testament manner had been wish-fulfilment, not truth. Her sons had been pagan: *his* spawn always would be. This life, Godfrey's world, had been savage and was still, when it was not simply daft. Gisela had been right: the House of Wingfield was not a family so much as a venue for emotional blood sport. She might've called the boys Alberich or Hagen for as much mythic rightness as there was in their names. Their world had been more Nazi than anyone dared think; or Jewish – an Old Testament saga of brothers plotting against the one among them so favoured as to have received a magical coat.

Blood and death. Sometimes she wondered now if Christian hadn't gone to his grave out of some unacknowledged instinct to buy off the gods – if it all hadn't been some atavistic sacrifice set in motion by Godfrey in semi-conscious assent to obscure passions in her. To invoke success, authority, a more general notoriety for family and name, a permanent niche in that fraudulent Olympus of London – that's what it had been about, hadn't it?

If so, the spirit of sacrifice had run amok.

'Paganism,' she recalled Godfrey once remarking to Booby in a spat about New Age consciousness, 'was a thorough-going religion, not just an excuse for burning one's bra.'

Well: a pagan goddess she would be. Affecting new darkness, mystery and grace, she would not budge from her place by the fire. She would cultivate looks even more other-worldly, knowing how it would get his goat. She would make his heart reach out and then not respond. She would watch simply and, when his fussing gave way to baiting, wouldn't rise. She would close him off, force him into the shadows, a dim outer perimeter of her affections, which is where any goddess of light might exile those who displeased her. She would take up philosophical dialogue with John as if she and he had forged intimate relations at last – even (God forbid!) become 'soulmates'.

'In personal terms,' she would have him assert, 'the source of regret is that we accomplish so little of what we envision in this fallen world.'

'Artists,' she would say back, 'have an antidote to that.'

'Possibly. And the experience of art may provide some antidote for us lesser mortals – isn't that it?'

'I'm not sure. One stares at the telly and thinks: isn't it simply narcotizing us with pictures of what we aren't doing? meant to frustrate us the more?'

She would direct John to play as if entirely naïvely. 'What is your view, Godfrey, being as it were a non-artist?'

Ruddy pseuds is what he would think. 'Sorry?' he would say, looking up from La Rochefoucauld.

'Mortal limitations...' John would bore on. 'We must accept them if we're to live out our term.'

'Of course,' she would insert, 'one must wonder if sometimes, by playing God in one's art, one doesn't violate the spirit of that.'

'Yes; and the knowledge of it, even if only subconscious, must be why one goes around feeling she's made a botch of things.'

This line, unpredicted, made her wake from her daydream. What you could never be sure of was when some self-regarding actor, however admiring, was liable to subvert your subtext.

In the event, when this actually happened, Godfrey filled the gap by grunting and lighting a cheroot.

Margot did not look at him, or at John. 'I should never have had children,' she sighed, driving in a dirk. 'Eileen Moloch was right: artists should not be allowed offspring. They ought to be neutered at birth, like eunuchs in olden days, or those who share beds with them.'

Stunned by these words, papa rose irascibly. Margot watched from the corner of an eye as he stormed out to the kitchen and flicked on a kettle. John meanwhile kept to his own script:

'I wonder if the facts actually prove what you say? All one can conclude really is that artists might take more effort than the rest of us to find safe ways to connect with other lives.'

Could she peer into her husband's mind and see him registering the two of them as a pair of sickening swells out of James? As the worm turned and returned, could she tune in to his inner mutter: that if this were the best civilization had to offer under the American *pax*, they might as well search for one of Lucius's old paint-tins and spray graffiti all over it?

'Are there any safe ways?' is what she murmured, recalling with nostalgia how in the old days such chat might've led to a joke and the glug of wine in a glass. (She was in sore pain for those pranksterish scenes now, the verbal plates flying. But she kept to her lines and, with John back on cue, nudged the playlet to it climax.)

'Tony Thomas and his wife may have found one,' he mused. 'My wife and I never did. But I'm not so sure as I once was that renouncing the effort opens the way toward a better moral stance.'

'Ah,' she intoned, ear alert for a hissing of steam. 'To be good or not to be good: that is the question? Whether it's nobler to achieve that, even at the expense of having nothing of interest to offer – or jolly near nothing at all?'

To give the devil his due (or as John would say, the angel) keeping on on such levels didn't always, entirely, result in what Godfrey would call 'tosh'. 'In other words, are the old saws about Genius and License as true now as they were for the Romantics?'

'Precisely. One hopes not. One tries to believe not, in this so-called New Age, following your "moral revolution" of the '60s. But – '

'Anyone for a cup of tea?' Godfrey brayed.

' – I hated your '60s. Permissiveness never works.'

At that point, far from being unaware of the subtexts, John said something that might have jolted her into thinking that one of her sons had reappeared, had she not been training attention elsewhere: 'Hypocrisy rules OK. Is that it?'

'I say, anyone for a cup of coffee?'

Godfrey's voice bought her a moment's reflection. 'No thank you.' Then back at John: 'How do you mean?'

'Well,' he smiled, retreating into charm (how much he'd picked up in his years in their country!), 'surely that's the opposite of '60s permissiveness, as you call it – though I might prefer Openness: Truth.'

'Would you indeed,' *paterfamilias* chimed, coming in with his cup, and, planting himself mid-room, proceeded to sip, wondering whether to weigh in or just let them go on like a pair of intellectual cattle chewing the cud.

John glanced at him. Margot did not.

'Truth?' she repeated. 'Do you mean by that what we know to be right or what we actually *do*?'

'Why should the two be so different?'

'Because, my dearest, they *are*!'

'O give it up, Maggo!' (This was the moment she'd been waiting for: papa scalded his tongue.) 'Don't you realize,' to John, 'that you can never win an argument with her? Any reasonable position always ends up running into her ruddy religionism!'

Margot now turned a dead stare on him. As if on signal, John did as well. From their deep easychairs, both looked at Godfrey yet seemed to focus on him no more than the man-in-the-moon. Did his cheek twitch then? Did he realize that this was retribution for his years of authority and ideas which, in his particular kind of hubris, he'd never let on to be other than superior? Margot concentrated her stare in a way Gisela had taught her, and for an instant he seemed to feel his chest twist (gulped coffee too quick). What flashed through his mind then? some inner temple built on pillars of Reason and Passion: the classical and medieval in modernist alliance, beginning to fragment and contort into the surreal – as if a tragic misalliance after all?

'But, dearest,' she summed up with the deceptive calm of the country in tone, 'I don't believe in God anymore, really.'

'Yes,' John clarified, 'the real force in your life now is Fate, isn't it?'

Papa slammed down his mug. 'Ruddy hell!' he exploded, trying to burp. 'I don't know what to say to either of you anymore except rubbish, what is the world coming to, and ruddy hell!'

'But Godders,' Margot breathed, gazing at him fondly (revenge was sweet, and now it was done), 'that's all you ever *did* have to say!'

Cruelty to Godfrey accomplished the purpose of most petty cruelty: it persuaded the perpetrator to try to be good. Margot saw him off, back to London on the train, swearing all the way that he would rather have been in Lisbon during the historic earthquake than to have to sit through another weekend of 'country tedium'.

Such petulance was reassuring. It let her know he was all right.

'You're always welcome back, dearest,' was her parting shot. 'After all, what's mine is half yours.'

In fact, it was not. The place in the country had been secured in her name and sustained with her monies, which since the apocalypse at Lloyd's had become sole Wingfield income. But in the remorse that follows on small revenges, Margot took consolation from appearing generous. And Godfrey accepted this, albeit grumblingly, once his temper had cooled.

In other respects, his fate was not so propitious. Back in London, he was confronted with one of the worst scares of his career. In pique at a newspaper article listing a number of old Labour MPs once under the influence of the KGB, a left-wing rabble-rouser used parliamentary privilege to publish the names of two dozen establishment figures supposed to have conspired to undermine a long-forgotten government. Godfrey's name, bizarrely, was among them.

Now Margot's politics, such as they were, had long been of the *Guardian/Observer* type. But when journalists began to ring her for comment, she rallied to papa's defence: 'Godfrey a traitor? You must be joking. Patriotism is the last refuge of the scoundrel; and my dear little man, whatever else he may be, is not and never has been that!'

To John, she declared that she hated witchhunts.

'So you play with paradox and end up telling them nothing, huh?'

Margot gazed at him gimlet-eyed.

'It's a clear case of the conflict between openness and hypocrisy we've been arguing about. Truth in a platonic sense vs the facts. And just like with that trouble with your psychosynthesist, you come down on the side of concealment, or at least obfuscation.'

No one had dared mention Gisela to her in months. 'You're getting too clever by half,' she observed. 'Some days I wonder if you're not turning into some kind of witch yourself.'

Chuckling, John said he would take that as projection.

Godfrey, who would have rued this exchange, was meanwhile grateful for Margot's support. By his code, a wife was meant to stand by her man, 'fragrant and radiant as an English rose'. And though Margot observed that she considered herself 'rather more of a thistle these days, and beginning to fester', she appeared glad to be able to repay his loyalty to her during her own bout of damaging publicity. In this respect, she 'passed the test', as it were; and eventually the whole matter was hushed up, 'as establishment problems in this country always are.' That, however, was not the end of it:

The meedjah, full of unsated hunger for rumour, took occasion of the reappearance of the Wingfield name to dig into the playwright's background. Godfrey suspected Gisela again: though cornered, the erstwhile synthesist still existed uncrushed. Margot in private tended to agree, surmising that her onetime great friend had been hurt when she'd failed to renew relations following the tip-off about Miranda's pregnancy. But whatever its origins, a piece appeared in *Private Eye* about a celebrated authoress called Serena Flyover, whose father had been a IRA fundraiser and mother an Eastern European refugee posing as a Scottish heiress.

Margot was willing to let this pass with a shrug: she'd made too many fictions over the years to cause fuss. Godfrey of course was livid and wanted to sue; but he could hardly afford another libel action, to say nothing of further publicity. So, uncharacteristically, perhaps for the first time in his life, he held his tongue.

'If the world wants to think Margot's origins are that exotic,' John mused, 'I can't see what difference it makes.'

'That's where you Americans are bloody naïve,' papa barked. 'Don't you realize by now that we don't go in for that sort of *mittel*-European/Celtic angst like you do in Manhattan?'

Margot said of her American pal: 'You sound as if you've become as complacent as the rest of them up in that strange world of London.'

John conceded that by now he had lived there long enough.

Meanwhile, that 'strange world up in London' rapidly tired of rattling what skeletons Margot still had in her closet. Whether yesterday's trendy playwright had secrets untold or was a sphinx without any was of diminishing interest as her productivity lapsed. And by now Margot had ceased fully to attend to a career which the uncharitable whispered had contributed to her family's demise. When Godfrey joked on the phone about Patrick Astroid's win of the Critic's Award ('At last the turn of the pederasts, what?'), she murmured that she was no longer sure what that pejorative meant. Then when Eileen Moloch won a Pulitzer in one of our nation's periodic spasms of anglophilia, she gazed at John as if he were speaking Swahili as he relayed London witticisms about 'the clockwork mentality of a writer who lives only to write'.

She, Margot, was the obverse of this. Despite a revival of *Firestorm* at The Pit, it seemed almost an illusion that she had once been a playwright at all. She was free of 'that vain world', full of her own emptiness, apparently undisturbed by or aware of the drift in her onetime avocation – though Godfrey via John continued to pester her about it. They even cajoled her into reading Moloch's prize-winning script, about the comparative morality of one woman who gives up family to create imaginative new worlds and another who gives up exceptional gifts as an actress to wallow in nappies.

This *pièce à clef* had an obvious key for the cognoscenti, but Margot failed to see how it had to do with her. She was not even roused by Smedley Anis's summation: 'Eileen has produced her customarily hackneyed version of a theme that in Margot Wingfield's hands might have been raised to the blithely surreal.'

'It's perhaps easier,' she commented to John, 'to praise those who no are longer your rivals.' Later she added, 'I'm glad Eileen's dramatic flair hasn't left her,' and pulled a needle through her tapestry.

Godfrey was shocked when John related this *mot*. 'Only because it's been honed to a dumb science!' he replied re la Moloch's 'flair', echoing a letter in *The ILS*.

But Margot seemed content with *The Evening Review*'s reflection: 'The reigning empress of our theatre, like some latter-day Mozart, has created yet another masterpiece of technique, without apparent effort.' Nor was she amused by the riposte of town wits: 'without apparent consciousness either'.

Occupied with her sewing, tumblers of wine and numberless hours gazing out of deep window-wells, Margot sat in cloistral space in the country and tried to dream. But often she ended by listening to telly or staring at a Mills & Boon novel. She was waiting still, she contended – though for what no one could say.

Periodically, John would arrive to regale her with tales of beating Godfrey at chess. At other times, she put on the grey cape Johann had disparaged and went to the village to swan it over the natives, who still received her as if a goddess dropped off a cloud.

Godfrey took this as hopeful. 'At least she still enjoys being the object of silly people's flattery, what?'

Margot denied this when John retailed it. 'My behaviour's just one more instance of what you call "entropy"... Age, dearest. One's standards droop, along with everything else.'

Godfrey took it as a bad sign that she should speak so freely about her decay. 'You must give up this bloody quietism, heart!' he brayed over the phone. 'It's been years since anyone could mistake it for triumphal queenliness or some rot.'

Margot observed that Godfrey had never been equipped to see resignation as an option. But then he'd never been educated by nuns – which may also have been a reason he didn't mutter approval when John announced that he was going back to the States once more, to try to re-reconcile with his ex-wife:

'I'd like, the gods willing, to re-attach to some spirited life-force. At this late stage of civilization' [we were nearing the millennium], 'it might be no bad thing for one or two others to try too.'

'More power to you, dearest,' Margot observed, ignoring implications. 'As for myself, I've come to the view, why not just let sleeping dogs lie?''

'That's not what Godfrey thinks.'

'How surprising. I always assumed the male Wingfield attitude was, when in doubt, look for the next bird to roger.'

Was she thinking at last of Gus in New York?

'I've spent too much time waiting,' John persisted. 'Waiting's not moral; it's just nihilism. A landscape without weather. Nature trying to sleep, which Nature can never do, even if she wanted to, except in fits and starts... like someone who has a fever and keeps waking only to drift back into half-nightmare, half-dream.'

Margot looked twitchy, as if someone had told her half a truth for a change. She still just wanted to sleep, get lost in a dream and try to catch it again as she woke and fell back to half-slumber. But she hadn't succeeded at that very well either. Dream life had become close to mere dreariness; hardly enlivening, only grey.

'Who's description is that?' she asked crossly. 'Mine or yours?'

'I'm not sure who thinks what anymore,' the American mused, 'our ideas can be so similar. You've taught me so much. Ever since I heard the final lines of your first play: "Life is change; the wheel turns, but we must try again to do better – or not, if that's to be our fate."'

'I don't recall any play of mine ending like that. Are you sure you've got it right?'

'It doesn't matter,' he went on in tones so exalted that she could be forgiven for wondering if he were still quoting or just elegizing to 'poetic' skies. 'The alternative, if we wait, is that we're sure to be overtaken by death... or something even more weird.'

'Bosh!' she erupted, striking them both with one more echo of Godfrey; and perhaps just then, when it was too late, she realized how her husband had been the great joy of her life and making of her errant career.

The night before he dropped his head on the chessboard, scattering potentates across the floor, she caught up to him at last in a dream. Next morning, an hour before the final checkmate, she rootled out writing-paper and flourished her pen for the first time in what seemed like years:

> Godfrey cavorts like a trickster. He tells me that being a trickster is a constituent part of his soul. The trickster dials the telephone, then leaps about saying that something redemptive is about to occur. I don't believe this; the Goose says I'm complacent; John tells me to stop waiting; I say waiting for what?
>
> Godfrey's soul claps its hands. Laughing aloud, he leads me to a church, which turns out to be a Masonic temple. As he laughs more, the roof rises and columns detach and twist into a terribly blue sky, like in one of Ollie's early surreal paintings.
>
> Booby passes as Queen of the Night. She says we're all impossible frauds. Then Godfrey, who's turned into the Goose, puts on a wizard cap and laughs with bizarre self-assurance till we're forced to acknowledge that she's the one who's made the church/temple vanish.
>
> 'You are forgiven,' he says, back in his own shape. Before I can ask, 'Forgiven for what?' John and he start to play a game.
>
> 'Don't you know there's no need for forgiveness in this world?' he asks, hearing my thought. 'Ruddy absurd. You either win or you lose. There's no playing again.'
>
> John considers his move. 'Not true,' he answers. 'There's always next week. The wise player learns from his errors and comes back to do something more sensible. Anyhow, I was once Tony Thomas.'
>
> Godfrey shoves his queen forward. 'Do spare us the ersatz philosophizing, mate!'
>
> John moves his castle while I sit in my summer frock watching. 'Dear God,' I think as his eyes rove the board, 'you've never looked so wise, so at one with the anima Gisela and I were wrong to accuse you of not having. I love you, my husband.'
>
> He rises towards me, cavorting down years. He is sixteen again, not sixty: one of the boys in Ollie's painting – a mix of Marcus and August, Matthew and Johann: my lover, my son and shade of my father too.
>
> Meanwhile, John plays on. Godfrey keeps laughing and shrinks back to the board. All his moves are brilliant. We're at Oxford again, by the Thames on a glorious spring day. John has turned wizened, like a visiting Mandarin. The board is on the lawn, men as tall as the White Knight and Red Queen in Through the Looking-Glass.
>
> A cloud covers the sun; I'm filled with sadness. Christian blots out Godfrey, then fades away. I try to tug my dream back; a bird sings on a branch. It is twilight on a summer's evening and he hurrying down a city street to find me.

> We are in London, near my art-school. He is proposing unnatural things on bended knee. It happens so quickly that when he gets up, his legs buckle and face comes down purple. The pawns fly.

She hated writing this, she would tell John later. It filled her with the same nausea of self she'd once felt when working on plays, conjuring scenes half-inspired by her sons, then watching similar things happen in 'real life'. It was witchcraft, this power of consciousness. Why had she been so vain as to lift a pen? What compelled people to look into the nature of things so closely that they burned through to affect events? Not for mere mortals to prophesy or skry patterns; only God or the gods should be allowed to do that.

This would be her conclusion. Nor would it be simply orthodox – hadn't Godfrey called her plays a 'substitution for life'? and wasn't this how it had turned out? Maybe, in fact, it was worse. Maybe her work had been a provocation, a red rag to the writer or even those gods, if such outer intelligences existed. This is what happens, may happen, ought to happen, it said; I, the writer, dare events to confute what I've set down – dare them to prove me less wise than I am.

Tragically, they rarely did.

Margot gazed out of deep window-wells. Impenetrable grey. Nature, which was all you could see, was indifferent; careless. One day it dumped rain; the next it smiled sun; the next it blew like a bag-lady who couldn't keep herself still; at last it clammed up like a drunk who's passed out. But on no occasion would it stop. It might laugh and gambol, then fall down and go silent. (O dear God, she thought, a pain in her breast so sharp that she feared she was going to faint.) Then, almost tediously, certainly restless, what appeared to have gone dead drew itself up and began slowly to restart the dance.

Were these thoughts by way of premonition? Could Margot foresee what was to come? So hard and fast did it arrive that she had hardly a chance to get drunk, let alone plan suicide, which is what she would've done if she'd had the courage, she would say. John phoned from London to break the news. He would be on the next train, he promised, despite her Garbo lament ('I just want to be alone!') Grief, grief, grief reduced her to gibbering on the floor, which was no thing you could do in front of an audience. When she came to, it was dark and she sitting in a mess she recognized as the torn shreds of a duvet.

God damn the world, she proclaimed to a night sky indecently lovely with stars. Clambering for whisky, she let busy spirits weave. Where was Matthew, she asked as she tore through nettles. Where was Marcus as something stung into her thigh (she'd slipped in a bog). Where was Christian, she demanded of gods unknown, dragging herself up through furze. Where were Lucius and Johann? Where are my sons, Lord? And Godfrey, dear Godfrey – where are *you* now? Come back and console me in unspeakable grief!

So she cried, or imagined, or would claim she did. It might've been days or minutes – how could one tell? Distant in her mind, she felt something coming. John was meant to be coming. Thump, thump, thump on the door.

Thump, thump, thump on the door.

Go away, her dream said.

Thump on the door.

Grey morning. Hill under clouds. Thump thump on the door.

'Hey, lady: you in there?'

Old Margot rose, wraith-like. Creaking downstairs, she drew on her grey cape. Thump, thump on the door.

Unlatching it, she peered out. And there in the mist pacing was a strange woman, skin the colour of Guinness, hair plaited with yellow, red and green beads. She was wore skin-tight leather trousers, high-heeled boots and hundreds of pounds worth of animal fur.

'Hey!' cried a voice out of a TV drama, blotting all issues but the material. 'You brought your fuckhead son into the world, and he left me with this. And since I can't get any palimony from him, you can pay for it, white bitch! You must be rich enough.'

For an instant, Margot seemed to hear Godfrey guffawing, cavorting disembodied through impenetrable air. 'Augustus!' she muttered.

But there was no time for chat. In her arms a weight had already been lain. The woman receding in mist, a roar resounded down the lane; then silence… the just-waking baaings of a little lamb: this toffee-hued, Latin/West Indian/Third World/gypsy babe.

It was a girl-child. 'Hannibal Jane,' her mother had tossed back before flying off to her next gig (or did she say trick?) in Berlin, or wherever. That, anyhow, is what Margot told John when he arrived and they had to decide how to refer to the last, unexpected Wingfield.

Margot busied herself singing the wee thing to sleep. It was the first sound of music John had heard in her sphere; and the whole terrible sequence began to strike him as oddly blessed.

He walked into the village and bought the necessaries. Margot changed nappies, made bottles and ogled the imp till it chuckled and smiled. Then, once it was lost again in vasty dream-space, John began to ruminate over what it all might mean.

'Nothing!' she cut him off. 'It's just the happy last proof of my absolute failure.' And while he struggled to interpret that, she gazed out the window to a patch of ungrey. 'You fickle devil!'

– London, 1986 and after

Afterword

Chip Martin has always been drawn to the novella as a literary form – whether as practised by writers such as Lawrence, Maugham or Thomas Mann, or by the small band of distinguished authors whose works in this medium are the speciality of Starhaven, the publishing house based in London and California he helped to found some thirty years ago.

As a writer and a publisher – somewhat in the position of Virginia Woolf and the Hogarth Press – Martin has been able to call his own shots as to what and when he publishes. In publishing novellas he has followed an unfashionable line – most publishers and booksellers prefer longer books. But at its best, he feels, a novella has a concentration and unity that a longer narrative cannot give, and true to the maxim "less is more" he has chosen to follow this path himself

An American who has lived in London for over half his life, he has moved in many different worlds, academic, literary and artistic. Some of them are evoked in his London trilogy, *A School of London.* Set in the Thatcher/Major years, it belongs to a not so distant past that is already well removed from us in spirit. Its characters have some of the characteristics of that age – not least a privileged bohemianism no longer possible today. Martin gives us his own slant on the era in these related but distinct novellas, each narrated from a different viewpoint but with recurring characters in common.

Even if it has aspects of autobiography about it – it is hard to resist the idea that Tony Thomas, the narrator in the first novella has something of the author in him – the trilogy is never straight reportage. The atmosphere is heightened, at times almost fantastic; conversations are glancing and elliptical, suggesting more than is spoken; people change partners and their perceptions of one another like characters in *A Midsummer Night's Dream.* But the world it portrays is totally convincing within its terms of reference and one is swept up in its dramas from the first.

Perhaps because he writes as an outsider Martin takes a special interest in the social context of his characters: where they live, how they make their money, where they come from. The milieu he describes is artistic and intellectual, the men secure in their public school backgrounds, the women more uncertain in their social origins but holding their own through talent or good looks. The American characters, Tony Thomas in the first novella, the millionaire John du Rocher in the second and third, play the roles of chorus and sympathetic friend as well as being participants themselves. Less innocent than their Jamesian counterparts, they are none the less more morally grounded than the people with whom they interact. Tony, married to a member of a great Jewish dynasty, may sometimes behave deviously but at least he can recognise the consequences of his actions. The English characters are careless of what happens to others when possessed by the daemons of art or sexual passion. There are victims, above all their children, in these stories.

Each of the novellas in *A School of London* has a different central figure, the would-be writer Tony Thomas in the first, the 'English rose' Miranda Cravin in the second, the tragic and fascinating Margot Wingfield in the last. But Margot, with her brood of six sons and her abundant talents, has been with us from the beginning of the trilogy and in one way or another plays a pivotal role in each. It is round her lunch table 'near Holland Park' that the characters gather in the opening scene of *A Journeyman in Bohemia* and as her fortunes improve we follow her progress from Shepherds Bush to a large Victorian house off Ladbroke Grove. We follow the vagaries of her appearance too. She is in her forties, dressed to the nines as becomes a successful literary agent when we first meet her, switching to high bohemianism as she approaches her fifties and her career as a playwright takes off.

Beautiful, creative and mysterious, Margot exerts a magnetic pull on the clever people round her. She acts as their confidante and inspirer, but there have been sexual entanglements with some of them as well, disclosed in a kind of slow release as the story unfolds. In the end it is not her marital straying but Fate which shatters her seemingly charmed existence. Her favourite son is killed in shooting accident – or was it an accident? – on the Scottish moors. As she struggles to survive, seeking solace in the dubious nostrums of her friend Gisela (the witch in the title of the third novella), her life begins to unravel. Has she been too absorbed in her work and friends, too busy, too successful, to notice what is happening in her children's lives? Tragedy follows tragedy in biblical succession. Her husband is too detached, or perhaps too stunned by misfortune, to help her. The burden of her sorrows overwhelms her.

The last of the novellas is the darkest; fittingly, the epigraph to the first version* was a quotation from the book of Job. But not everything is black. There is hope for some of the other characters in the story, even a ray of light for Margot with the arrival of an unexpected grandchild on her doorstep. We finish the book with the feeling we have been taken on a roller coaster ride. Small in size, but big in scope it reminds us that people change, that life renews itself, that nothing ever stays the same. As a reader one is torn between gulping it all down at one go because the narrative is so exciting, or lingering over it slowly in order to savour its insights and its subtly romantic atmosphere. It is a book to read twice – and to return to.

– Linda Kelly, 31 iii 2011

* The novellas were printed as separate books in limited edition by Starhaven between 1997 and 1999.

www.ingramcontent.com/pod-product-compliance
Lightning Source LLC
Chambersburg PA
CBHW060138260626
47160CB00001B/35

* 9 7 8 0 9 3 6 3 1 5 3 2 4 *